Praise for *Nightborn: Coldfire Rising*

"What a treat this story is, both for readers unfamiliar with the Coldfire Trilogy and longtime fans like myself. It provides a view into how the world was established, the historical events come to life. For new readers, it is a fascinating colonization and first contact story. There's as much science fiction in this story as there is horror and Friedman is an absolute master at weaving those elements together perfectly. . . . Sometimes writers/storytellers will go back to the 'before times' of a story they wrote and the results can be mixed, at best. Friedman's results are anything but mixed. [*Nightborn*] is an unqualified success." —SFFWorld

"Beautiful horror sci-fi infused with ethereal nightmares: *Nightborn* will hook new fans while exciting veteran Coldfire enthusiasts. . . . Friedman is a master at interweaving perspectives so you should expect a splendid interplay between every character's personal trauma and that of Erna's hungry energy." —Black Gate

"If you enjoy science-fiction with a good dose of horror and also some fantasy elements sprinkled in, you should pick this book up immediately. But don't stop there, proceed right on to the Coldfire Trilogy and treat yourself to an amazingly written masterpiece that truly stands out from its peers. C. S. Friedman has once again solidified her place in the upper pantheon of SFF authors. . . . *Nightborn: Coldfire Rising* is a wonderful gift that will delight C.S. Friedman's already established fans and should introduce a whole new segment of readers to the multi-faceted greatness of her writing." —Out of This World SFF

"I couldn't get enough of the story. My jaw was clenching by the end, I was so invested. I was fascinated by, yet dreaded, the climax. *Nightborn: Coldfire Rising* is an engrossing and foreboding read. I highly recommend both this book and the Coldfire Trilogy. C.S. Friedman has created a masterpiece." —Witty and Sarcastic Bookclub

NIGHTBORN
COLDFIRE RISING

C. S. Friedman

DAW BOOKS
New York

Cover illustration by Jeszika Le Vye

Cover design by Adam Auerbach

Edited by Betsy Wollheim

DAW Book Collectors No. 1941

DAW Books
An imprint of Astra Publishing House
dawbooks.com
DAW Books and its logo are registered trademarks of Astra Publishing House

Printed in Canada

Library of Congress Cataloging-in-Publication Data

Names: Friedman, Celia S., 1957- author.
Title: Nightborn: coldfire rising / C.S. Friedman.
Description: First edition. | New York : DAW Books, 2023.
Identifiers: LCCN 2023012593 (print) | LCCN 2023012594 (ebook) |
ISBN 9780756410926 (hardcover) | ISBN 9780698404403 (ebook)
Subjects: LCGFT: Fantasy fiction. | Science fiction. | Novels.
Classification: LCC PS3556.R5184 N54 2023 (print) |
LCC PS3556.R5184 (ebook) | DDC 813/.54--dc23/eng/20230317
LC record available at https://lccn.loc.gov/2023012593
LC ebook record available at https://lccn.loc.gov/2023012594

ISBN 9780756412425 (PB)

First paperback edition: June 2024
10 9 8 7 6 5 4 3 2 1

For Joshua Starr,
unsung hero of DAW Books

Acknowledgments

First and foremost, thanks to my editor, Betsy Wollheim, and my copy-editor, Marylou Capes-Platt. The insights and suggestions they offered were invaluable. An author could not ask for better editors.

As always, my beta team provided valuable criticism, in addition to emotional support through some rough spells. That's David Williams, David Huffman-Walddon, Carl Cipra, Cathy Deignan, Jennifer Eastman, and Jeszika Le Vye. Thanks, guys!

Deanna Briggs set up a Discord channel for me on Patreon and hosted events so I could meet my fans. We're all grateful to you.

To Jeszika Le Vye, for Nightborn's beautiful cover painting, my heartfelt gratitude. From the day I first saw it, it has served as inspiration for me. (Do check out the rest of her art at jeszika.com—it really is breathtaking.)

Thanks to those who have supported me on Patreon, including Ben Barlow, Kai Ellis, Natarajan Krishnaswami, Zora McBride, Matt Platt, Rebekah Russell, Toni Rose, Tim Rosenberg, and David Huffman-Walddon. Your support helped keep me going during a difficult year. And also to my readers on Facebook, who provided information and helped with creative decisions along the way.

C.S. Friedman

A big thank-you to Jon Goff, who saved me from computer hell several times.

And lastly, extra special thanks to Kim Dobson, who gave me her computer when mine crashed the weekend before my manuscript was due, and Larry Friedman, who spent hours getting it set up properly so I could make my deadline. Without you guys I don't know how I would have gotten this project finished. I love you both.

NIGHTBORN

(YEAR 1)

One

Where *am I?*

She floated in a void, only semi-aware, confused.

Who am I?

Darkness parted slowly, misty images appearing that she struggled to identify. Echoes of memory in search of context. Fragments of identity gathered and coalesced in her mind, fitting together like pieces of a puzzle. She blinked hard, trying to bring her vision into focus, and details of the world around her slowly began to take shape. She was in some kind of tubular corridor with a single human figure floating in front of her. Everything was washed in a dim, icy light that made the world look frozen.

She knew who she was.

She knew where she was.

The figure floating in front of her was a man, but the chill blue light robbed his dark skin of color, making him look more like a shadow-creature than a human being. "You awake?" he asked gently.

The last thing she remembered was going into stasis. How long ago had that been? It was hard to think clearly. She managed to nod and whisper, "Yes."

The shadow-creature was coming into focus now: Leon Case, Colony

Commander of the Erna exomigration. She remembered she'd almost slept with him, back in Orientation. She couldn't remember clearly why she hadn't.

"Name, origin, assignment?" he pressed.

"Annalise Maria Perez. From Phoenix, Arizona." The final pieces of memory were falling into place now. "Chief medical officer of Erna Colony."

She could make out details of the ship's stasis chamber now, a long, tubular corridor lined with sealed pods, each with its own silent sleeper tucked inside. Two hundred men and women who headed out into the depths of space, trusting that somewhere in the darkness there would be a new world to colonize, never knowing where or when they would awaken. Now here they were. Ancient explorers on Earth had made similar voyages, setting out upon seemingly endless seas in the hopes of finding uncharted lands to claim. But those seas had been made of mere water, and those explorers had been awake to experience their journey. Her sea was comprised of darkness, frothed with starlight instead of waves, and the time required to cross it was so great that one could only do so in a sleep akin to death.

Not everyone who surrendered to that sleep survived it. Five percent of those who entered stasis never woke up. But that was a risk one accepted, to cross the sea of night.

"Are we there yet?" she asked. A child's query, fishing for reassurance.

He hesitated.

His answer should have been *yes*. An easy yes, because the ship had been programmed to wake its passengers when a planet suitable for colonization was found, and not before that. So if Leo was awake, and she was awake . . . then there must be a planet, right? But looking at his expression—mouth tight, eyes narrow—she felt a spark of panic. Stories were told about colony ships that stalled out in the depths of space, and about the crew members who had to be awakened to try to save them. Those stories never ended well.

"There's a planet," he said at last. "Help me wake up the others so I can fill everyone in at once."

It was a reasonable enough request, but the delay was frustrating.

She focused on trying to release the straps that held her in place. Her motor control was returning, but slowly; he had to help her. Finally she was free, and she pushed herself out of the pod to float in the chill air of the ship. Her hand instinctively reached out for the nearest grip to steady herself. The reaching hurt. Everything hurt.

Leo waited until she was settled, then handed her a glowing tablet. "You wake the first four on the list. I'll take care of the other five. We'll meet in Observation."

She looked at the names on the tablet and frowned. "This isn't normal protocol."

"No," he agreed. His voice sounded tired. Strained. "But these are the people I need to talk to before anyone else wakes up."

Again that spark of panic flared; this time it was harder to ignore. "Is something wrong, Leo?"

For a moment he didn't respond. "We're alive. The ship's intact. There's a habitable planet beneath us. That's good enough for now." He nodded toward the tablet. "Wake everyone up, then I'll brief you all."

He pushed off against a grip and floated down the corridor before she could ask him anything more.

Medics, engineers, data analysts: those were the people who were supposed to be awakened first. Medics to bring everyone out of stasis safely, engineers to confirm the ship was functioning as it should, analysts to review the data the ship had collected and identify any factors of concern. But there was only one engineer on Leo's wake-up list, one analyst, and no other medical personnel besides herself. Looking at the names he had given her, Lise shook her head in bewilderment. Ian Casca was a botanist. Why would one of those be needed now, while they were still in space? Ted Carver was an ecologist, so the same question applied there. And Pravida Rakhi was a xenobiologist. Unless aliens had boarded the ship, what purpose could she possibly serve? All those people should have been stage two revivals, to be awakened when it was time to descend to the planet. Not now.

The last name on the list, Danika Lin, was the most concerning.

She was the colony chaplain, a person whose job it was to offer comfort when things went wrong. Lise couldn't think of any reason why Leo would need her awake right now unless something had, in fact, gone wrong.

Stop imagining disasters, she told herself. *You'll learn what's going on soon enough.*

All four of her subjects returned to consciousness successfully, which was a relief. Ted Carver grinned as he pushed himself out of his pod, laughing as he spun head over heels, fumbling to catch hold of a grip to stop himself. Like a happy child. When he finally managed to stop spinning, he winked at her. They'd all trained for weightlessness back in their home system, and those lessons had been serious enough, but now that they were out here, light-years from Earth, answering to no one but themselves, outer space was a private playground. She tried to smile back.

When everyone on her list was fully functional, they all followed behind her, swimming through the chill air like a school of fish, to the observation chamber. The viewports there were still sealed tight, armored for the journey, but Leo had switched the room lights on and turned up the heat, so at least it was more comfortable than the frigid stasis chamber had been. Lise imagined she could hear the ship's hull groaning as its interior warmed for the first time in decades. Like them, the ship ached as it came back to life.

One by one the new arrivals found grips to anchor them. Leo smiled as he watched, but it was a strained expression that didn't reach his eyes. The others were too distracted by the excitement of the moment to notice.

Finally they fell silent, and all eyes turned to him.

"The good news," he said—and there was a hint of a genuine smile now—"is that we appear to have arrived at a habitable planet."

Ted whooped, and others laughed and clapped and cheered. Lise just waited, watching Leo. His smile had faded, and his lips were tight once more. Not good.

"Well, can we see it?" Ted demanded, and Ian said, "The suspense is killing us!"

Leo held up a hand to quiet them. "Halos III turned out to be unsuitable for human habitation. It was smaller than Colony Control had predicted, and the atmosphere turned out to be too thin to support an open-air colony. So our seedship refueled and moved on, to search for a better planet."

"Which it found," Anna Jaziri said. She was the only programmer present. "Or we wouldn't be standing here, right?"

"*Floating* here," Ted corrected her smugly.

"It did," Leo told them "but only after many tries. Each time it found a new planet it surveyed the ecosphere, sent down drones to take samples, and eventually decided it wasn't right for us. So it used that sun to refuel and headed back out. Farther from Earth each time, always farther, seeking the perfect world for us to colonize."

Joshua Indal—the one engineer present—looked at him sharply. "How much farther?"

In answer, Leo reached out to the control panel and activated the viewing ports. The heavy shielding that had protected the seed ship during its long journey slid back on one side of the ship, allowing them to see what was out there.

"Holy fuck," Ian swore. Then quickly, "I'm sorry—"

"No need to apologize," Leo told him. "I said the same thing when I first saw it."

The planet before them looked the way Earth must have in its youth, before humanity had smothered the homeworld in dust and concrete. Pristine white clouds framed the crisp blue of seas and the rich green of living continents. So much green! But much as one's eye would like to fix on that, it couldn't. The thing that was behind the planet, rising into its sky like a second sun, compelled attention.

A galaxy.

Its glowing center, almost too bright to look at directly, was like a vast eye peering directly at them. Gemstone streamers swirled outward from the core, and the ship was high enough above the galactic plane that their spiral formation was visible, albeit at a sharp angle.

"Holy shit," Joshua whispered. "Please tell me that's the Milky Way."

Lips tight, Leo nodded. "It is."

"And that we're not just dreaming." Tia Reyes was one of the colony's geologists, a striking young woman with wide-set eyes that tipped up at the outer corners, like bird wings. "It doesn't look real."

Leo smiled faintly. "There's nothing I could say in answer to that which a dream-Leo couldn't also say. So sure, for what it's worth, you're not dreaming."

"People don't dream in stasis," Lise reminded them. She couldn't take her eyes off the view. "This is real."

"How far out are we?" Johnny Kanoska asked. He was probably already mapping and measuring the new heavens in his head.

"Forty thousand light-years from Earth," Leo said. "Give or take a few." He looked back at them. "We're alone out here, folks. There'll be no updates from Earth, no supplies, no second wave of colonists. As far as we're concerned, Earth no longer exists. And this ship has been travelling for so long, who knows? Earth may not even exist anymore. Humanity may have finally destroyed itself, or its homeworld. Or both. We'll never know." He gestured toward the planet. "Beyond this system is nothing but darkness. That's where our ship would have gone searching for another planet, had this one failed to qualify. Out into the void between the galaxies, where it would have become our tomb."

"But this planet's good for us, right?" Dani gestured toward the amazing view. "I mean, the ship woke us up. That means this planet is habitable. Yes?"

Lips tight, Leo nodded. "But the ship was supposed to take five years to determine that. Observe global weather patterns from orbit, send down drones to collect data and samples . . . you all know the process. But it didn't take five years." He paused. "It took ninety."

Smiles were fading now, as the implications of that sank in.

"You think—" Lise hesitated. "That, what? It couldn't decide?"

Leo sighed heavily. "I don't know. Maybe there was data it didn't know how to interpret. This isn't an ideal planet, that's for sure. Tectonic activity is high, so there are frequent earthquakes. There's a chain of volcanos running down the center of one ocean—on the far side of the planet right now—that's like a wall of fire dividing the waters in two. That, plus frequent earthquakes, means frequent tsunamis, so the shorelines will be hazardous. And there are three moons—one orbiting opposite the other two—so tidal patterns are likely to be extreme. But all of that could have been evaluated on a normal schedule. There's got to be something more. Something the ship didn't know how to interpret." He shook his head in frustration. "I woke you all up first so you could help me figure out what it is. Then we can decide what to do next."

"Meaning what?" Joshua looked at him sharply. "Fatality rate for second stasis immersion is eighty-six percent, so it's not like we have the option of going back to sleep while the ship looks for a better planet."

"No," Lise said quietly. She'd just realized what Leo intended. "*We* don't have that option." There were exactly five men and five women in this group, she realized, and they represented a genetic diversity that was too perfect, too planned. The colony had gone out of its way to recruit people of varying heritage, but a random group of ten colonists shouldn't so perfectly mirror that plan, unless the diversity was intentional. From Ian with his blazing ginger crown to Tia with her dark honey skin, from Johnny's rugged Native American features to Leo's Nigerian darkness, the group could not have been more genetically diverse if they'd been chosen just for that. *Which is what you would do if you thought a small group might have to go it alone, with all the risk of inbreeding that entailed.* She looked at Leo. "You're thinking we ten might have to disembark and let the rest of the colony go on without us. Aren't you?"

"Let's hope it won't come to that," Leo said quietly.

"You said there were volcanos," Tia offered. "If they expelled enough ash into the atmosphere it could cool the whole planet for a while. That happened on Earth a few times. Five years wouldn't have been enough time for the ship to evaluate that kind of threat."

Leo nodded. "Check the logs, look into that possibility. And any other geological concerns you can think of. God knows, there'll be enough of them on this planet. And Johnny, look for any record of astronomical events in that time frame. Anything unusual—anything at all—I want to hear about it. The rest of you, I want you to go over the data the ship collected, each in your own field of expertise, looking for anomalies. *Any* anomalies." He looked at the engineer. "Josh, you check out the ship itself. Make sure everything is functioning properly. And triple-check the landing module and the drop pods. We've been travelling far longer than anyone anticipated; I don't want to take it for granted that everything is still in good working order."

Joshua made a checkmark with his finger. "Will do, boss."

Leo looked at Anna. "See if you can figure out why the ship's decision-making algorithms stalled out for ninety years. Was there some event it didn't know how to interpret? Or did the system perhaps degrade over time, so that data was corrupted? If you can rule anything out, at least that'll be a start."

She nodded. "On it."

Leo drew in a deep breath. *He looks so tired,* Lise thought. How long had he stayed awake while the rest of them were asleep, trying to solve this riddle on his own before involving anyone else? In their two months of Orientation she'd learned enough about him to know that he didn't admit defeat easily. He had been put in charge of the colony for its first year—the most challenging time for any exomigration—and she knew that he took the responsibility personally.

"Assuming we do wake everyone else up," he said, "you nine will be my inner circle. I want you to report to me anything you see or hear that's out of the ordinary. Even things that might seem too insignificant to bother mentioning." He paused. "I don't want to instill panic in two hundred people over a problem that may not exist. If someone raises the subject you can be honest about it, but don't go out of your way to share my concerns. People will have enough to worry about without imaginary threats looming."

"And me?" Dani asked. She cracked a weak smile. "What am I here for—to see to the spiritual health of the drop pods?"

Leo looked at her. "People will talk to you about their fears. Things they may not want to share with others." He held up a hand to silence any protest. "I realize there will be issues of confidentiality. I trust you to decide what needs to be reported, and how to do so with appropriate discretion. But remember, this is the survival of the colony we're talking about. If someone's fears might reflect a real threat, I need to know about it."

The chaplain nodded solemnly. "Understood."

Leo looked out at the starscape again. For a moment he was silent, just drinking in the amazing view. The weight of his responsibility seemed to lift from his shoulders, simple awe taking its place. "It's beautiful," he murmured at last. "Isn't it? A lush and fertile planet, unspoiled by humanity's excesses, against a backdrop any vidmaker would covet. Exactly what we were hoping for. So what's wrong with it, that made the ship uncertain about our landing here?"

He looked at the others. "Let's try to figure it out before we wake all the others up."

Two

Normally Leon Case liked to be involved in everything—an active part of the team rather than a mere observer—but in this case it was best just to wait. His anxiety was too palpable, his scrutiny too intense. It would distract people from their work.

Out of two hundred people chosen for this colony, he had been identified as the one most qualified to lead. It was only a temporary position; the job of a colony commander was to oversee the first year of settlement, then surrender authority to whatever form of government the group chose. It was a daunting responsibility by any measure, and the process by which he'd been chosen was a mystery to him. But the people in charge of organizing this colony had decided that he was the best person for the job, and despite his initial wariness, they'd convinced him to take on the burden of leadership.

The weight of that burden was just hitting home.

On the screen was a magnified view of one of the rivers on the main continent, showing where it emptied into the sea. On any other planet he would have considered the land just upriver of that an ideal settlement site, with easy access to both fresh water and transportation. But the largest moon had just passed over that spot followed by a second moon roughly the same size as Earth's, and their combined gravity had prompted a tidal wave that rushed upriver in a foaming torrent. Any settlement on those banks would need formidable levees, and transporting things by boat would be risky. Maybe that could work for them later on, once they were used to the tides of this planet, but it wasn't a good location for starting out. He needed to look farther inland, preferably near some body of water that didn't have direct outlet to the sea.

Regarding whatever issue had caused the seedship to delay their landing, all the efforts of his chosen team had told them nothing. The ship's condition was fine. The algorithms evaluating the planet were working perfectly. There had been no geological event in the last ninety years which would contraindicate colonization. Maybe Tia was right, and the ship just wanted to observe the patterns of seismic activity for a while. There was no way to know.

His eyes narrowed as he studied the planet. *What is your secret?* he thought. *Why could the ship not decide if you were a suitable home for us?* Whatever the cause, he couldn't delay a decision any longer. He'd told Lise to wake up her team first, then bring everyone else out of stasis.

But when she joined him to report on that effort, he could tell from her expression that it had not gone well. "Tell me," he said.

She drew in a deep breath. "We lost sixteen. Complete bodily degradation. I couldn't save them."

Not *WE* couldn't save them, he noted. Once she'd woken up her medical team it had been a joint effort to wake all the others, but she'd been in charge, and was clearly taking each death as her personal failure. He knew that feeling all too well. "What's the failure rate?" He did the mental math. "Eight percent?"

"Should have been five," she muttered. "Or less."

"And this should have been a twenty-year journey. We've been asleep so long, we're lucky we didn't lose more people than that." When she didn't respond he reminded her, "No one has ever been in stasis this long before."

She bit her lip, said nothing.

"Any issues with the ones who woke up?"

She shook her head. "They all seem to be mentally sound. For as much as it's possible to tell at this point."

"Well, that's a blessing, anyway." He looked out at the planet again. "We'll need everyone functioning at full capacity."

She pushed off from the rung to float to his side. "What about the drop pods? The cargo pods? The landing module?"

"I'm told everything's good to go."

"And . . ." She hesitated. "The other thing?"

He looked out at the planet again. "We're not going to be able to figure it out from up here," he muttered. "We'll just have to go down there and see what's what."

She put a hand on his arm. "We knew this wouldn't be easy, Leo. They warned us there would be problems no one could foresee."

True enough, he thought solemnly. Earth had sent out many seed-ships to colonize distant worlds, but only four of those were close enough to Earth that their reports had come in before this ship left home. That was a pitifully small sampling and couldn't possibly account for all the problems a newborn colony might face. But all four of those colonies had survived. He kept reminding himself of that. Whatever challenges those colonies had faced, they'd risen above them. His people would do the same.

What those four early reports had confirmed was that convergent evolution appeared to be a consistent phenomenon. Terran-style environments gave rise to Terran-style life-forms. Which mean that although elements of the local ecosystem might be alien to the colonists, the underlying blueprint of life should be similar enough to what they were used to that they could figure it out.

"We'll be okay." He rubbed his forehead with a weary hand.

She studied him for a moment, then asked gently, "How long were you out of stasis before you woke the rest of us, Leo?"

He said nothing.

"You look like you could use some real sleep."

A dry smile twitched his lips. "A little busy for that."

"If you don't take care of yourself, how can you care for anyone else? The people who just woke up will need time to recover their full motor function before they can even think about facing natural gravity again. So no one is going anywhere right now." She paused. "Get some sleep, Leo."

He shut his eyes. "Lise, I'm not sure I can relax—"

"So hook your arm over a rung and try. That's an order, Commander."
She smiled slightly. "I outrank you in medical matters, don't forget that."

He huffed. "Pulling rank on me. Nice."

She shrugged. "A gal's gotta do what she gotta do. So how about it?"

He sighed. "Let me find a suitable landing site first. Then I'll give it a shot."

"Promise?"

The concern in her eyes touched a part of his soul that had been closed off for too long. He longed to be able to return such feelings. Hopefully, leaving Earth would help make that possible again. He took her hand in his and squeezed it. "I promise."

☽ ☽ ☽

Black smoke rises into a murky sky, ash and smog clotting together, blotting out the sun. Leo adjusts his dust mask with a trembling hand. "Faster!" he orders. "Can't you go faster?" But the cab has chosen its pace based on the speed and position of all the other vehicles on the four-tier roadway, and he can't force it to take a riskier route. If only this were a more primitive time, when men controlled their own vehicles! He could dart in and out between the slower vehicles, then, maybe even drop beneath this tier entirely, claiming the narrow space between levels. A lot of people had crashed back then, trying such crazy things. But at least it was their choice to make.

Leo looks at his news feed again.

FIRE AT 432 MADISON NOW 92% CONTAINED. RESCUE TEAMS SEARCHING FOR SURVIVORS. 18 CONFIRMED DEAD, 11 INJURED. NO SURVIVORS YET FROM THE FIRST FLOOR REC CENTER, WHICH SUFFERED A DIRECT HIT. 35 CHILDREN WERE IN THAT PART OF THE BUILDING AT THE TIME OF THE ACCIDENT.

"Hang in there, Julian," he whispers hoarsely. "Daddy's coming."
If Leo hadn't stayed late at work, none of this would be happening.

Yes, he'd needed another hour to finish what he was doing, and yes, he'd checked with the rec center to make sure that was okay. They said it was fine—they didn't close till eight, so Julian could stay as long as he needed. But if Leo had left work when he was originally supposed to, he and Julian would be safe at home, watching the fire on the news.

It's Leo's fault they were here instead, with him rushing to get to the site where his son might be lying in pain. Or worse.

His cab is getting close enough now that when they come around a bend he can see the disaster site. Several tiers of the expressway have collapsed, and the street below is a graveyard of overturned vehicles and shattered concrete. He can see where a car from a commuter train had come loose from its mag strip and hurtled into the ground floor of a building. How many people died in that crash? How many are still trapped in the wreckage? Rescue workers in bright orange hazard suits are swarming over the smoking rubble like insects; he tries to focus on them, tries not to think about what might have happened inside that building.

The sudden voice of the cab startles him. **There is an accident ahead. The road to your chosen destination is closed. Do you wish to disembark, or should I calculate a detour?**

"Disembark," he says.

The cab pulls onto the shoulder, and its door slides open. The words HAVE A NICE DAY appear over the door as he climbs out.

There's a drop tube nearby, and its glass-walled capsule takes him down to street level. Slowly, too slowly! The air there is soup-thick and abrasive, and even with his dust mask in place it's hard to breathe. Heart pounding he races toward the accident site, fragments of glass crunching under his feet with each step. But the area immediately surrounding the building has been cordoned off, and he is brought up short. A man in uniform orders him to go back. No one is allowed on site except medics and the rescue team, Leo is told. He's not the only one who has come this far, and other people are begging for access. Mothers, fathers, and friends all frantically begging to be allowed through, so they can search for the one person who really matters.

Unable to bear the intensity of their misery on top of his own, Leo backs away a bit, then looks for another way in. There has to be one!

Suddenly the wind shifts, blowing a thick gust of smoke their way, and everyone is momentarily blinded. Opportunity! He staggers to the barrier by feel and manages to climb over it before the smoke clears. Then he is running, running desperately, coughing from the smoke that makes it past his dust mask, tears streaking the soot on his cheeks. "Julian!" he yells. It's unlikely the boy can hear him over the noise of the rescue machinery, but he has to try. He's getting close now, passing by rescue workers in bright orange uniforms. "Julian! Are you there?"

A hand falls on his shoulder, startling him. As he turns he braces himself for yet another demand that he leave, maybe even a forcible eviction. He's not leaving without his son! But the man who stopped him evidently sees something in Leo's eyes that moves him, and he points to a pair of tents at the far end of the site before disappearing into a cloud of smoke.

The tents are on the windward side of the disaster site, where the air is cleaner. As Leo approaches the larger tent he can see that it houses a temporary administrative center. They might know if his son has been found, and for a moment he is tempted to ask them, but if he just walks in and does so they will likely expel him from the site. Not worth the risk.

The second tent is quieter, and has no one guarding it. His stomach tightens in dread as he approaches it. He waits until no one is looking in his direction, then slips inside.

Bodies.

They're laid out in parallel formation, shoulder to shoulder. Bloody bodies, broken bodies, bodies charred black by fire. So many of them! He sways as he looks at them, sick to his stomach. He wants more than anything to turn away, to leave this place, but that's not an option.

He sees his son.

With a cry of anguish Leo rushes to Julian's body and falls to his knees beside it. Tears are flowing freely now as he lifts up the broken form and cradles it in his arms, pressing it against him as if he could will his own life-force into its flesh. "I'm sorry." His voice is a hoarse whisper, robbed of all strength. "I'm so sorry. I should have been here earlier. I should have protected you." He lowers his face to the boy's shoulder and sobs. "I failed you."

There are other people entering the tent now, but he hears them as if from a great distance. A woman says that he shouldn't be there. A man says that he needs to leave. But they are ghost voices, lacking the power to affect him. Nothing matters in the universe other than the small broken body in his arms. The little boy who had been, up until moments ago, the most important person in Leo's life.

Gone now.

Gone forever.

His fault.

"I'm sorry," *he whispers through his tears.* "So sorry . . . ."

◝◝◝

The drop pods fell to the planet like great white birds, gentled by parachutes that spread out above them like wings, carrying the colonists safely downward. Most of them landed in the target area, and those that went astray were not too far off; by nightfall it should be possible to get them all positioned properly. The cargo pods weren't as well guided, and some landed off target by several miles. But those could be retrieved later.

One by one hatches unsealed and people began to spill out of them, into the alien sunshine. They laughed as they did so and hugged one another, and some fell to the ground and kissed it, while a couple of people even danced. And why not? They had traveled to the edge of the galaxy in the hopes of finding a new world to inhabit. The one they had found was fresh and green and beautiful. The sky was so clean and clear that one could see miles into the distance—incredible! And the air was as fresh and sweet as it had been in Orientation, but on this world they would never have to give it up.

But there were a few people who stood apart from the giddy celebration, for they had lost loved ones coming out of stasis and were still reeling from the shock of it. Yes, they'd all known when they left Earth that some people would die en route, but people always imagined that would happen to someone else. The discovery that a loved one had lost that deadly lottery was just sinking in.

Tia's partner had been one of the casualties.

Leo and some members of his team stood on a low hill overlooking the landing site. They'd come down before all the others to verify the suitability of his chosen area, and had judged it perfect. Sprawling grasslands to the north, granite bluffs to the south, forests with mountains beyond them and a river close enough to supply the colonists with water—but not in a position where flooding would be an issue. A mile away from where the drop pods had landed was the granite plateau Leo had earmarked for the module. Solid ground with no visible fault lines. Everything looked promising, but not until all vessels were safely on the ground would Leo allow himself to relax.

Lise pointed up into the sky, raising up a hand to shield her eyes from the bright alien sun. "Is that it?"

Leo turned his attention upward, squinting as he tried to make out details of the small black dot that was slowly descending from the sky. That dot contained specialized supplies that they would need to conquer this new world: laboratories with high-tech equipment, a database with all the information a colony could possibly need, and—most important of all—10,000 DNA samples preserved in stasis. Hopefully that would provide enough genetic diversity to establish a healthy population. There were backup samples in the drop pods as well—DNA was too valuable to entrust to a single vehicle—but the bulk of the supply was inside the module.

It was dropping low enough now that details of the hull could be seen. Then its parachutes opened, and magnificent blooms of color filled the sky as thrusters labored to slow its descent even more. The landing struts began to unfold from their storage bays in the module's underbelly, preparing for touchdown. Then the ground beneath Leo's feet began to shake. For a moment he thought it was just from the force of the thrusters. But no, the ground was actually shaking. Then he realized what must be happening.

Shit.

They hadn't trained for earthquakes in Orientation, because they hadn't expected to settle on a planet where they were a major problem. So what was he supposed to do now? Lie down on the top of this hill? Run somewhere else? What about the landing? The module's thrusters had increased their output, slowing its descent even more, and for a few impossible seconds it seemed to hang motionless in the air. But such vehicles weren't designed to hover, and it wouldn't remain stable for long.

He turned to Josh and demanded, "What's happening?"

The engineer was scrolling through data on his tablet. "The ground's moving, so the sensors can't get a clean fix on it. Which means the landing sequence won't initiate." He tapped a few controls, then cursed under his breath when the module failed to respond.

They could lose it all now. If the module crashed, it would take the colony's most valuable supplies with it—along with their dreams of an easy settlement.

But the tremors were diminishing now, and Josh's fingers continued to race over his tablet as he wrestled with the module's data, trying to convince the thing to land. And after what seemed like an eternity, the streams of fire that were holding the craft aloft finally began to diminish. Leo held his breath as the module began to descend again, and not until all the landing struts were solidly on the ground and the thrusters had gone dark did he dare to release it.

There was silence for a moment. They all stood there, too stunned to speak, as the significance of the landing hit home.

"We made it." Relief echoed in Lise's voice. "We're safe."

"We're *home.*" Joshua spread his arms wide and grinned. "This is *home.*"

Lise took Leo's hand in hers. She was one of the very few people who knew why he had come here, why the sights and smells of Earth triggered such painful memories for him. Now he would never have to deal with them again. "A fresh start," she said softly, squeezing his hand. Hopefully he could leave the ghosts of Earth behind and enjoy it.

He swallowed thickly and nodded, squeezed her hand in return, then started down the hill to inspect the module. The others followed.

The ground, for now, was steady.

Three

Sunset was a vivid wound in the sky, a crimson gash flanked by bruised purple clouds. Here and there the final rays of sunlight reflected from a cloud's belly, a brief flare that quickly faded as its source dropped lower in the sky. There were sunsets like this on Earth, but they were rare enough that most of the colonists had never seen one; the display seemed alien to them, a reminder of just how far from Earth they had come.

Tia watched it all numbly, trying to feel something other than emptiness. Maybe it would be easier if people would just leave her alone with her sorrow. But she'd made the mistake of saying earlier in the day that sunset would probably be spectacular, and now that she'd been proven right, everyone was coming to her for an explanation of why. And they came in small groups, so she had to repeat the story again and again: how the ship's surveillance drones had recorded a major volcanic eruption several hundred miles west of them the week before, and how that would fill the sky with particulate matter for a while, which would make sunsets spectacular.

"Look!" someone cried, pointing east.

The heart of the galaxy was visible now, its core like a second sun rising to challenge the first. Though it lacked the power to light the sky or warm the planet the way the real sun did, it was a riveting sight none-theless. And nothing like *this* had ever happened back on Earth.

Tia felt no wonder.

She should have been standing beside Michael right now, his arm around her as they gazed at the wonderful display together, celebrating the alien moment and all it signified for them and their future. Now all that was gone. Stolen from her by the gods of random fortune, some-where in the darkness between the stars. All that was left in her heart was emptiness, a hole so black and terrible it seemed her soul would be sucked down into it. If she could, she would tear her heart from her chest and cast it away into the night. At least that would end the pain.

As the core finally cleared the horizon, Leo climbed to the top of a rocky prominence so that all could see him, and he cried out, "Your at-tention, please!" After a pause he added with a grin, "Just for a few min-utes, I promise!"

One by one the colonists turned toward him, then began to gather around his makeshift podium. Tia stayed at the periphery of the crowd, not wanting to come into physical contact with anyone. Finally, when everyone was within hearing distance, the colony commander spread his arms wide. "Obviously the workday is now over." Applause and laughter rippled through the crowd. "An auspicious start to our project. You all know what tents you're assigned to, and what teams you'll be working with tomorrow, so I won't take up any time going over that. But I do want to remind everyone of a few basics.

"First, remember: there is no such thing as *garbage* here. The mate-rials we brought with us are all we have. Someday our colony will be able to manufacture polymers and alloys and all the other trappings of a technological civilization, but we'll probably run out of Terran materials long before we get to that point. So if you break a jar, save the pieces. If you blow your nose on a scrap of cloth, rinse it out and reuse it. If a device breaks down—as all of our devices eventually will—make sure every part is saved." He gestured toward the grasslands beyond the en-campment. "Marian's team will be gathering up the grass as we clear it, to turn into hygienic supplies. Yes, they'll be scratchy but disposable. Meanwhile a latrine area will be set up to compost waste; please follow the instructions posted. And if nature calls when you can't get there . . ."

A dry smile flickered. "Please bury your offerings. For the sake of your neighbors, if not the environment."

"Second . . ." He drew in a deep breath. "Don't leave camp alone, please. We don't know what kind of venomous animals or insects may live in the area, and if you're stung or bitten, you may need someone to help you get home. So let's stick with the buddy system for now, at least until we have the local flora and fauna catalogued."

He paused. "Lastly, if you see anything unusual—anything that just doesn't seem *right*—I want to hear about it right away. No matter how trivial it seems. Tell your team leaders about it, and they'll pass the information on to me. All right?"

There was a sea of nods, thumbs-up, and OK signs.

"Good." He raised up his hands as if in benediction. "In accordance with the terms we agreed to back on Earth, I hereby name this world *Erna*, to honor the woman whose financing made this trip possible. And since we've decided to keep Earth's weekly schedule, I also officially declare this to be Monday. Today's work is done. Go. Enjoy yourselves."

There was laughter and chattering and even a bit of singing as the crowd dispersed, which left Tia feeling even more desolate. A few people were mourning stasis deaths, as she was, but they allowed themselves to be swept along with the crowd. Perhaps they hoped that if they were surrounded by the joy of others it would help ease their pain.

Soon she and Leo were the only ones left. He looked at her in silence for a few seconds, his dark eyes narrowed in concern. She forced a smile to her face to reassure him, but he didn't look like he was fooled by it.

"Promise me you'll talk to Dani Lin if you need to," he said at last. The chaplain was the closest thing they had to a professional counselor.

"I will," she said. "I promise."

He hesitated a moment longer, then nodded a reluctant leavetaking, and left to follow the others.

She was alone.

☽☽☽

The Office of Reproductive Affairs is crowded. Of course. Everything on Earth is crowded.

"Don't worry." Michael puts an arm around Tia and squeezes tightly. *"It'll be fine."*

There are a dozen other couples in the waiting room, squeezed into tight little chairs. Most of them are young, just starting out on life's journey. Too young to be approved for a family; they're probably submitting their paperwork now so that when they are ready to have children everything will be in order. But there are a few older couples too, and the look of weariness on their faces suggests they've been here many, many times, and are beginning to lose hope that things will ever go differently. God willing, she and Michael will never get to that point.

"Reyes and Cantelli?"

They rise up from their chairs and follow the greeter to a stark little room, just big enough for two chairs and a modest desk. Narrow windows in one wall look out upon a faded city, shadowy and gray. At the desk sits a nondescript agent with a desk monitor open in front of him. Probably their files are displayed on it.

Michael takes her hand in his as they sit. A lifeline.

"Good day," the man says. His tone is neither friendly nor forbidding, simply functional. A robot might sound the same. *"My name is Reginald Auger, agent number 950-74725A-5. I assume you are here to appeal your reproductive denial?"*

"Yes, sir. We have some new data." Michael hands him a small data card, which the man passes over the sensory panel on his monitor. He clears his throat as a display comes up, and reads it closely. *"Good B & L rating,"* he mutters. *"Very impressive."* He hands the card back to Michael. *"But this doesn't alter anything."*

"Our genetic profiles are both in the ninetieth percentile for health and longevity," Michael persists. *"B & L has given us a combined reproductive rating of A minus. Optimal potential in five key categories. Minimal chance of genetic disorders."*

"We've been waiting five years," Tia reminds him.

The man sighs deeply. *"Yes, I understand. And if and when you do have children, they are likely to be healthy, resilient, and intelligent. The kind of citizens that Earth could use more of."* Seeing Michael about to speak, he holds up a hand. *"Yes, such a profile does move you higher in*

*the queue than couples with less stellar potential. But it doesn't change
the underlying equation. The population on this continent has reached
its limit. No one on the wait list can be approved to reproduce until
natural death and emigration bring the numbers down. That is simple
mathematical fact."*

"On this continent?" Michael asks. "Is it different elsewhere?"

*"Not anywhere you would like to live. There are some places so
unfit for humans that few ever try to settle there. Believe me, you don't
want to go there. You certainly don't want to raise children there. Any
place you'd like to live in will be just as crowded as North America.
That's the state of the world, I'm afraid."*

"Is there any other way?" Michael asks. "Maybe a colony?"

*"In this system? Not likely. The colonies have limited resources,
and territorial expansion is complicated and costly. And they manage
their populations even more strictly than we do. You'd be more likely
to get approved eventually, but it would still be a long wait."*

*More likely to get approved eventually. The words chill Tia. Has he
really just told them that even if they wait for years, even if they jump
through all the hoops the government places before them, they may
never be approved to raise a family on Earth? Maybe she is misunderstanding him. Hopefully she is misunderstanding.*

"What about outside the solar system?" Michael asks.

*"Exomigration?" The agent leans back in his chair. "You understand
what that would mean, right? The risk involved in committing yourself
to an unknown world? The physical hardship? The fact that you would
have to leave behind everyone you love here, everything you have accomplished, your very history? Few are willing to go that far."*

"But we could have a family there," Tia persists.

*"Oh, yes." He taps the monitor. "With this kind of genetic profile,
you'd be a first pick for any colony. That's where your DNA has real
value. But there are also requirements regarding reproduction that some
find unappealing."*

*"We can have two children together," Tia says. "Isn't that right?
After that we would have to do that with other people?"*

"Yes." He nodded. "For the sake of genetic diversity, that's required."

He taps the screen in several places. "I'm sending you the contact information you'd need to pursue this. You'll have to sit down with a counselor and be evaluated before you can even join the wait list, but . . ." For the first time in their meeting, he smiles. "I have no doubt you two will pass muster."

There is no more to say after that. Michael and Tia exit the office in silence, squeezing past all the anxious couples in the waiting room, and ride down a tube in which people are packed so tightly it's hard to breathe. This is Earth, which has no room for one more inhabitant. So the people in power have decreed.

When they're finally out on the street they walk hand in hand for a while, communing in mournful silence. Then he turns to her and asks, "How badly do you want a family, Tia?" A pause. "More than anything in the world?"

She imagines what it would be like to have children—not just one, or even two, but a household full of them. Laughing and playing in the clean air, beneath the sun of an alien world, with limitless land to claim for their own, to raise their own families in peace and safety.

"More than anything on Earth," she tells him.

☽☽☽

The aftershock woke Tia up.

It was only a small tremor, really. The other five people in her tent slept right through it. Probably most of the other colonists did as well. Everyone was exhausted from the first day's work, not to mention the party afterwards. But they had accomplished their first set of goals: moving the drop pods to their permanent positions, staking out tents, and laying down a pipe to bring in water from the nearby river. Now it was a place where 184 people could live, eat, and sleep while they worked on more permanent arrangements.

Tomorrow a foraging team would start searching for edible plant life, while a band of hunters would look for game. Never mind that none of them had ever hunted a living creature before, or that their only experience with tracking had been in simulations during Orientation. They were hunter-gatherers now, and hopefully the instincts that had allowed their primitive ancestors to survive on Earth were embedded in their genes. Meanwhile, fields would be cleared, crops planted, permanent housing built. And next year, or maybe the year after that, there would be children.

But not hers and Michael's.

With a sob she turned her face toward the tent wall, so that if the others woke up they wouldn't see her tears. She would have to bear a child eventually, she knew that. The colony had too few members to waste any DNA. They had all agreed to those terms before they left Earth. But that wouldn't be the child she dreamed of, with Michael's DNA and hers combined into a new and wonderful creature, the ultimate expression of their love. That dream was gone forever.

"Hey," Lise whispered. "You all right?"

She looked back and saw Lise propped up on one elbow. She wiped her eyes and nodded. The last thing she wanted was to talk to anyone about this. "Just restless. I think I need some air."

What she needed was to be alone.

Outside the tent the night was alien, dark and yet not-dark, with a large moon overhead, a smaller half-moon on the eastern horizon, and a final scattering of stars to the west. It was all cold light. So cold. There was no comfort in this place.

She walked for a while, arms wrapped around herself. The night air was chill; she should have brought her blanket with her.

A baby cried in the distance.

Startled, she stopped walking and listened. But there was no second cry. There was no sound at all, not even of insects. Had she imagined it? Or was there some animal cry natural to this world, which her grieving mind had transformed into a baby's voice? Was she going crazy?

Then she heard it again, and this time there was no mistaking it: the cry of a distressed human infant. Why would there be a baby here, on a planet that had never known humans before today? She was shivering now, and her arms wrapped more tightly around her chest. The urge to go seek out the source of the cry was so strong she could barely resist it.

"Hey, everything okay?"

The voice startled her. She looked back and saw Steve Sheridan approaching. Wasn't he one of the cooks? The circles under his eyes suggested he was having as much trouble sleeping as she was.

"Fine," she said. She forced her arms to relax and drop down by her sides. "I thought I heard a noise."

"Yeah." He came to where she stood and gazed out at the forest in the distance. "That was pretty spooky."

"You heard it too?"

He nodded. "There's definitely something out there."

"It sounded human," she dared.

He chuckled. "I think it's safe to say all of the humans currently on Erna are accounted for. Mostly asleep, I'd imagine. And none of them would be crying like that, anyway." He gazed out into the night. "But it was odd-sounding, I'll give you that."

"Like a human baby," she whispered.

He shrugged. "There are animals back on Earth that sound human. No reason there can't be one here as well. I wouldn't read too much into it." He put a gentle hand on her shoulder. "It's all good, Tia. Arrival anxiety. They told us to expect it."

She bit her lip and nodded.

"Med's got tranks," he reminded her. "Maybe in the morning you should ask for a few."

"We're supposed to save our medicine for real emergencies."

"Yeah. I guess." He sighed. "It's going to take a while to get used to the idea that our supplies can't be replenished. No easy trip to the pharmacy here."

"Why are you up?" she asked. Hoping to turn the conversation away from herself.

"Nightmare. Dreamed I was assigned to make a hundred and eighty-four concentrated nutrient bars look and taste like breakfast. Way too real." He rubbed his eyes. "I should try to go back to sleep. So should you. Tomorrow's going to be tiring."

She smiled faintly. "Every day here is going to be tiring."

He chuckled. "Amen to that."

Lise was asleep when Tia returned, and the geologist made her way to her cot with care, trying not to wake the other five in the tent. Then she eased herself down onto it with a sigh, lay back and closed her eyes, and tried to relax.

Again the mysterious sound came. This time it was clearer. Something in the distance—some*one* in the distance—was definitely crying. Trembling, she put her hands over her ears, but she couldn't shut out the sound. So human. So very human. *It isn't real,* she told herself. *It can't be real.* The cry was morphing into words now: slow syllables, hesitant, like a baby's first attempt at speech.

Maaamaaa! it cried. *Maaamaaa!*

She shivered.

Four

Commander's Personal Log
Year One
Day Two

Slept poorly last night. So did many others. Too much excitement, too much light, stiff collapsible cots. Can't be helped. The deconstruction team will break down the pressure chairs in the pods later today, to turn the padding into comfortable pillows. Hopefully tomorrow night we'll all rest more easily.

We arranged the drop pods in a circle and stretched synth fencing between them to discourage casual visits from local wildlife. That will define our settlement for now. There's a large open area at the southern end, big enough for the entire colony to gather in, and a gate in the fencing that opens onto grasslands. In the middle of the camp there is now a city of tents, each one large enough for six people, to serve as temporary housing while we build more permanent accommodations. Since the tents were designed to be cannibalized for fabric later on, they're a motley assortment of colors; God alone knows what kind of clothing Colony Control expected us to make out of them.

To the north is a quieter area, closer to the forest, where small groups can congregate. We marked off a small area in one corner and buried the ashes of those who died in stasis, so that in their final rest they could be with us here, on this new world, not orbiting in an abandoned ship.

I have decided pod 4 will serve as my office. It's the smallest one. That's an important gesture to the rest of the colony: the person who has the most power in this place mustn't take advantage of it for personal gain. We'll assign the others as they are needed.

I will be working with the construction team when not needed for leadership matters. The show of physical labor will confirm to the colonists that I see myself as their equal, not someone above them, and the physical activity will help me work off some of my own anxious energy. That's my hope, at least.

TO DO:

Timekeeping: Ernan day is 25.12 Earth hours. Close enough that we can break it up into 24 segments, and within a few weeks no one will feel the difference. Anna is adjusting all necessary electronic components to accept the new measure of minutes, hours, days. Just like home, only we'll be a bit more tired at night.

Vehicles: The tractors need to be unloaded and assembled. We also need to create a strip of flat ground between the module and the camp that we can use to haul things back and forth. Most of the route is smooth enough, but there are a few sharp drops that will have to be filled in. One day's work at most.

*Medical: Lise wants to set up a clinic in one of the pods—which
I have approved—but the equipment she needs is in the module, so that has to wait on having vehicles to transport it. Pod 8
will be the clinic, while 9 will be outfitted for convalescence,
and 11, at the north end of the camp, will be reserved for quarantine. Hopefully the last one won't be needed.*

☽ ☽ ☾

"Hey, boss. Got a minute?"

Leo looked up to see Ian Casca standing in the doorway. "I was just finishing my log. Is it urgent?"

"You said you wanted to know if we found an anomaly."

"Indeed I did." Leo closed the log program, then shut down the computer. The solar power they had harvested was too precious to waste on idling devices. "I'm listening."

Ian offered him a slender wooden rod, as thick as his thumb and maybe a foot long. He smiled broadly as he did so, clearly pleased to be the first person to discover something significant. But if he had expected Leo to recognize the value of what he'd given him, he was due for disappointment. Leo turned the rod over in his hand and looked it over, but from every angle it just looked like a stick. "And this is . . . ?"

"Core sample from a tree." When that got no response Ian urged, "Look at the rings."

The wood was rough and it was hard to make out precise details, but the dark stripes circling the rod looked evenly spaced. "They seem normal to me. Each one is a year, right? What am I missing?"

"A tree develops wider rings during the years when conditions are optimal. Hardship reduces growth and narrows the bands. So you can learn the tree's growth history by studying its rings." He drew in a deep breath. "*Now* what do you see?"

Leo looked at the rod again, trying to distinguish some difference between the rings. "I'm sorry, these all look the same to me—"

"Yes! Yes! That's it!" Ian smacked his hand on the desk. "They're all the same. But they shouldn't be. They *can't* be. It would mean that year after year after year, weather conditions were identical. No droughts.

No floods. No seasons that were too hot or too cold for optimum growth. Just the same rhythm of growth, every single year." He paused. "You wanted to know about anomalies, Leo. Well, this is one."

Leo studied the rod again. "Do other samples confirm this pattern?"

Ian nodded vigorously. "We've cored six trees so far. All show the same pattern." He ran a hand through his ginger hair. "That counts, right?"

Leo felt the rough surface of the rod. "What could cause that kind of regularity?"

"Damned if I know. Especially on a world with so many active volcanos. You'd figure with all that ash being spewed into the atmosphere, sooner or later there would be some variation in sunlight, or rainfall, or some other element that would affect a tree's growth. But either none of those things ever happened, or they were compensated for."

Leo's eyebrow rose slightly. "Compensated for, how?"

"Not sure yet. On Earth there are trees that connect underground so they can share resources. But that kind of thing wouldn't help during a widespread weather event, as all nearby trees would also be affected. Whole different scale. I'd need more data to analyze, to know if that was the case here."

Leo was silent for a moment, digesting the new data. "If the climate here was unusually stable—*unnaturally* stable, as you seem to be implying—and the seedship detected that . . . might it have wanted to collect more data, to work out the reason for that stability?"

"Thus explaining the ninety years of surveillance." Ian's tone was nothing short of triumphant. Leo knew from their months together in Orientation that the botanist dreamed of playing a pivotal role in Erna's founding, of being the one person who could deliver solutions when others failed. Now he might actually get to play that role, by providing their first real clue to the seedship mystery.

Leo asked, "Was anything like this mentioned in the other colonies' reports?"

Ian shook his head. "I read through all four of them. If they found something like this, no one saw fit to mention it."

And the seedship might not do so either, Leo thought. *Because what is there to report? Trees here are unusually healthy?*

He was about to respond when Lise appeared in the doorway, knocking to get his attention. She looked distraught.

"Tia's missing," she told them. "We can't find her anywhere."

Leo's eyes widened. "Since when?"

She shook her head. "Don't know. She wasn't in the tent when I woke up, so I figured she probably headed out early to her work assignment. But given the state of mind she was in last night, I thought it best to check. Her crew chief said that no, she hadn't come to work today. So I searched the whole camp. Tents, pods, even the waste pit. I looked everywhere. She's not here, Leo."

He remembered how lost Tia had looked the night before. Remembered the terrible sadness in her eyes, the sense of a vast emptiness behind them. *I should have stayed with her,* he thought. *Whether or not she thought she needed me. I shouldn't have left her alone.* He handed the core sample back to Ian. "We'll talk more about this later, Ian."

"Of course," the botanist said. "I understand." He tucked the core sample into his pocket. "I'll help search."

There were several dozen people standing around in the southern field, and the somber atmosphere suggested that news of Tia's disappearance had reached them. Lise looked around, then waved for someone to come join them. Steve Sheridan. As he came over to them she told Leo, "Steve was the last one to see Tia."

"Where was that?" Leo asked him.

"Out by the fence, late last night. She was just standing there, staring into the night. There had been an odd noise earlier, like an animal crying. She asked—" Steve hesitated. "She asked me if it sounded like a human baby. She seemed obsessed with that. Asked me several times about it. I got the feeling she was pressuring me to confirm it."

Leo had seen Tia's psyche profile, so he knew that she and Michael had left their former life behind and crossed half a galaxy to start a family. Could the strain of losing that dream have unsettled her enough that she was hearing things? "Did it sound human to you?"

Steve hesitated. "If you wanted to hear it that way I suppose you could. I hadn't paid it much attention myself. But I had the feeling that if I left her alone there she might leave the camp to seek it out, and that seemed like a bad idea. So I talked her into coming back with me. I even stayed outside her tent for a while, to make sure she stayed there. That animal—whatever it was—howled a few more times, but Tia didn't come out of the tent again. Eventually I left."

"No one has seen her since then," Lise said.

Leo looked at the wire mesh gate at the entrance to the camp. It wasn't a very substantial barrier, and if someone had opened it during the night they'd have no way to know. "Lise says she's not in the camp. Which means she must be out there, somewhere." He looked out at the grasslands just beyond the fence. "So much land to search . . . ." He looked at Steve. "Did you get a sense of where the animal cry was coming from?"

"Out that way." He pointed southwest. Half a mile from the camp the grasslands ended and the forest began. "Past the tree line."

"All right." Leo looked at the people who had gathered in the field, then clapped his hands to get their attention. "I assume you've all heard by now that Tia is gone. We need to form a search party. Is Morgan here?"

A lanky young man with long hair and a black T shirt stepped forward. "Whatcha need, boss?"

"Drones. Set up a search pattern over the grasslands. Starting there." He pointed to the southwest. "Look for any sign of human passage. If she left through this gate, there's a good chance that's the way she went."

Morgan nodded. "On it." He looked around for the rest of the survey team. "Marty, Gina, Ahmed . . . c'mon, we've got work to do."

"The rest of us will search on foot," Leo announced. "Stay in groups. Tight search pattern. Look for any sign of a trail. If we can't find that out in the open, we'll go into the forest."

They would find her, Leo thought. They had to. No one was going to accept losing a colonist in their first twenty-four hours on this planet. Least of all the colony commander whose job it was to keep them all safe.

☾ ☾ ☾

Tia lay on her side in the shadow of the trees, her face half-buried in leaves. Leo knelt down next to her and put two fingers to her neck. No pulse. Cold skin. She'd been dead a while. He took her gently by the shoulder and turned her over, so that her face would be visible. Her body was stiff, and it rolled onto its back like an abandoned doll. Her torso was soaked with blood. There was a deep wound in the center of her chest, he saw, but there was too much blood-soaked fabric for him to make out details.

"Where's Lise?" he said, without looking up. A moment later she was kneeling by his side. "Can you tell what killed her?"

She pulled some of the bloodstained fabric aside carefully, revealing mangled flesh, then crouched by the side of the body, studying it. Then she took out her utility knife and cut the clothing from Tia's torso, laying bare a gaping wound in the middle of her chest. With the knife she prodded at the edge of what seemed to be a sizable gash, exploring it. She checked elsewhere, too, but except for the blood-soaked clothing, there was no other sign of damage. Finally she sat back on her heels, wiped her knife on Tia's jacket, and sheathed it.

"Whatever killed her, it likely happened fast. There's no sign of any struggle. Damage is messy, crushing and tearing, but it's all limited to a small area in the center front torso. Probably whatever killed her only had to strike once to kill." She was silent for a moment. "I can't tell if anything is missing without cleaning the wound, but the flesh surrounding it looks untouched. If that's the case . . ."

"Then she wasn't killed for food," Leo said softly.

Lise stood up and studied the surrounding area, walking around the body to view it from all sides. But except for the crushed vegetation under the corpse—and of course the blood—nothing looked disturbed. Given how large a beast would be needed to tear into a body like that, it just wasn't adding up. "There's no sign she was dragged here," she muttered, "which suggests she came here under her own power. Others can inspect the site more closely once we move the body, and confirm that." She looked at Leo. "I'll need to get her back to the lab for a proper exam."

The other members of his search team were all staring at Tia's corpse. Several looked like they were going to be sick. "So we need to carry her to the module. All right. Who'll help?"

There was a moment's hesitation, then Lee Singh took off his oversized windbreaker and placed it on the ground beside Tia. The stiffened body was rolled onto it, and four of the searchers grasped the garment by its sleeves and corners, using it as a makeshift sling to lift her from the bloody ground.

"Make sure you check for alien life forms inside her," someone said.

Startled, Leo turned back to see who had spoken. When he realized it was Wayne Reinhart, he scowled. "This isn't one of your science fiction movies," he snapped. Wayne's obsession with old Terran vids was no secret. It was even rumored he'd been watching one on his tablet while other people on the seedship were still recovering from stasis. Now he dared to treat this solemn moment like a scene from one of his vids?

But before he could respond, Lise said, "He's right." She looked at Wayne. "I'll do that first thing."

Leo's mouth tightened, but he said nothing more about it, just waved for those who were holding Tia to move off. He and Lise followed them, while the others in his search team stayed behind to search the site for clues.

Wayne did the intelligent thing and stayed with the latter group.

☽☽☽

The office of the Director of Orientation is open on two sides, allowing warm air to flow through the space. Lush plants are everywhere, cascading from pots, shelves, and a low wall separating the space from the rest of the Amazon Preserve. Leo breathes in deeply as he enters, drinking in the humid perfume of the tropics. On Earth that's a rare indulgence, but soon he will be on a planet where fresh air is the norm, where skies are never choked with smog, where the sunlight is always bright and clean.

And hopefully where grief and guilt will loosen their stranglehold on his soul.

"Come in, Leon." The director smiles at him. She's a small woman, dark-eyed and brown-skinned, pleasantly efficient. But it's easy to be pleasant in an environment like this. "Have a seat. Would you like something to drink? Fresh juice, perhaps?"

It's hard to say no to that. She goes to a sideboard and opens a decanter full of cherry-colored fluid and fills glasses for them both.

Real juice, not the synthetic stuff they served back in the city. A true luxury. He shuts his eyes as he savors it. Soon, soon, his world will be full of fresh fruit. The children born there will never know anything else.

She waits until he lowers the glass, then says, "As you know, Orientation is nearly over."

He nods. "One more week."

"Your group has been taught all the skills they'll need to establish a colony, at least in a theoretical sense. Meanwhile we've been observing personal interactions and assessing everyone's long-term potential. This week is when we decide who'll be doing what when the colony arrives, so that everything goes smoothly from day one. That includes deciding who's best suited to run the colony in its first year." She pauses. "We want you to serve as colony commander, Leon."

He hadn't expected that. For a moment he is speechless. "I don't know that I'm qualified," he finally protests.

"You have strong management experience, good social skills, and a level head." There's a flicker of a smile. "And charisma. People tend to listen when you speak. They're open to ideas when you present them. And you've dealt with psych profiles in your previous job, so you'll know how to apply the data we'll be giving you. Who else should we choose?"

"It's just . . . Jesus Christ." He draws in a deep breath. "That's one hell of a responsibility."

She chuckles. "It's not a lifetime appointment. Just for the first year. A colony needs to have one person in clear authority at the beginning, so that it can respond to unexpected events without squabbling over who's making decisions. How you run the colony is up to you. Rigid hierarchy, loosely organized commune, or anything in between. You call it. Or you can even delegate power to other people, if you want, and just sit back and watch them run things for you. But in any emergency, any disagreement, yours will be the final word. And when that first year is over, you'll hand things over to whomever the colony chooses for long-term leadership." When he doesn't respond right away she presses, "It's a process that's worked well in the other colonies. And everyone will agree to those rules before they board the seedship."

"What if someone doesn't?"

"Then they get to stay here on Earth until they change their mind. No one has a guaranteed right to exomigrate, Leon."

He shuts his eyes for a moment. They want him to be in charge of safeguarding two hundred people when he couldn't even protect one. Don't they understand how deeply Julian's death affected him?

Maybe they do, he thinks. Maybe they think this will help him.

"I understand your hesitancy," she says. "A responsibility like this is no small thing. But it's only for a year. After that, the colony will vote to institute whatever kind of government they want. Maybe that will include you, or maybe it won't. Either way, you're under no obligation to play a leading role after that point." She pauses. "I know this is a big step. I understand why you're hesitating. But our leadership algorithm says you're the best person for the job, so just think about it for a few days, all right?"

"And if after thinking I say no?"

"Then we move on to our second choice. It won't disqualify you from the colony, if that's what you're asking. But the colony would be better off if you accepted."

Duty, again. Always duty. A man could drown in duty. Or he could have his soul rent to pieces when he failed to fulfill it.

"I'll think about it," he promises.

☽ ☽ ☽

The lab was brightly lit when Leo arrived, and in the center of it, on a stark white exam table, lay Tia. So pale. So still. Lise had draped a cloth over her midsection so Leo wouldn't have to see what she'd done to her by way of autopsy. Even so, the sight stirred memories of other bloody bodies he'd seen, and it took him a minute to focus on what was before him.

Lise had called in Ted Carver and Pravida Rakhi to assist with the autopsy. The presence of an ecologist and xenobiologist made sense, given the circumstances, but the fact that she hadn't also called in other members of her medical team was an ominous sign. Ted and Pravida were both members of Leo's inner circle, and could be trusted with secrets he might not want to share with others. As for Lise herself, she looked exhausted, physically and emotionally. Little surprise, given the circumstances.

She nodded to Leo as he entered. "All right. Bearing in mind that none of us are forensic specialists—it appears we don't have one of those in the colony—this is what we've been able to deduce from Tia's body." She looked down at it. "First, there are no signs of damage outside of the central wound. No scratches or bite marks or bruises anywhere else on her body. This confirms my initial assessment, that she likely walked to that location on her own and was killed so quickly she had no chance to respond."

"Or something immobilized her," Leo said. "Then the killing wouldn't have to be as quick."

"We checked her blood for toxicity. There was none, at least that we recognized as such. We also checked her body for entry wounds like stings or bites, her breathing passages for any suggestion of foreign matter . . . every delivery method we could think of, by which she could have absorbed something that incapacitated her. Granted, our capacity is limited, since we have no data on local toxins, but I didn't see anything suggesting she'd been poisoned. Everything except the wound in the middle of her chest looks exactly like it would if she was just out for an evening's stroll. As for the wound itself . . . ."

Her words trailed off into silence. Leo waited. Finally she said, "Her heart was ripped out of her chest."

He blinked. "What do you mean, *ripped out?*"

"Literally. Something reached into her chest, shattering every bone in its path, then grabbed her heart and pulled it out, so hard that arteries and connecting tissues were torn loose. That was the only organ that was taken." She wiped her forehead with the back of her hand. "I know of no kind of animal that would do that. Or *could* do that. Not on Earth, anyway."

Ted cleared his throat. "There are predators on Earth that target the internal organs of their prey. Orcas eat the livers of sharks, for example, and sometimes even their hearts."

"Which they access through soft tissue," Lise said. "Whatever removed Tia's heart went in through the ribcage, breaking enough bones to make a neat hole. Then it grabbed hold of the heart and pulled it out. At least, that's what her remains are telling me."

"And she never fought back," Leo muttered.

Lise nodded. "Hence my suggestion that she never saw it coming."

"Or that she welcomed it." Leo was remembering the emptiness in Tia's eyes the night before. Had her grief been so great that if she crossed paths with something deadly, she might welcome an opportunity to join her beloved? The possibility couldn't be ruled out. "Jesus." He rubbed his forehead. "This is so . . . so . . ."

"Alien," Pravida supplied. "There's nothing like it in reports from the other colonies, so whatever manner of creature killed Tia, it's not like anything humans have encountered before, on any planet."

Lise looked at Leo. "Are we going to share that part with the others?"

The question startled him. He'd been so focused on the mystery of Tia's death that he hadn't even been thinking about what would come next. "People know she was killed. They saw the wound. The nature of the threat will be obvious, as will the precautions we should take to make sure nothing like this happens again. As for the odd nature of the wound, the removal of the heart?" He paused. "Maybe it would be best to save those details until we can offer some kind of explanation for them." He shook his head. "I don't know. I need time to think about it."

What little training they'd given him for this job hadn't included a situation like this. And there was no guidebook to help him choose the right course, no notes from previous colonies to offer insight. He, Leon Case, would be calling all the shots here, with no precedent to guide him. And if he screwed this up, he could well trigger a wave of panic.

"Well," he muttered, "so much for Paradise."

Five

Commander's Personal Log
Year One
Day Three

*Tia's death is hard to absorb, even harder to know how to re-
spond to.*

*I told everyone that she was killed by a wild animal, which
ate her internal organs. As far as we know, that's the truth. I've
ordered that any group going into the forest must include at
least one armed person. Some have expressed concern for the
hunting team that left yesterday, before we found Tia. I reminded them that "Team Paleo" (as they insist on being called)
is well-armed and is alert for animal activity; it's unlikely anything will surprise them. Meanwhile, since the attack was at
night and in the forest, most people seem to feel safe enough
inside the camp during the day.*

Power tools are charging. Tablets are charging. Lanterns are charging. In this season of long days, with the summer ahead of us, we can meet the colony's needs, but come wintertime, we may need to ration our energy use.

Between the light from the galactic core and three moons, it seems like it's never really dark here. It's hard to sleep when your body doesn't believe that night has fallen. Johnny says we're due for a few minutes of real darkness soon. He seems quite excited about it.

TO DO:

We're holding a vote to name the moons.

Some of the colonists arranged stones around their tiny cemetery, to delineate its border, and then prepared a grave for Tia's body. At its head was a gravestone designed by Alicia Bergen, which the sculptor had printed in polymer the color of granite. It had a simple cross on it with a dove on each side. The curve of the wings subtly suggested the sweep of Tia's eyes, and the overall design was graceful and dignified.

Some wanted to bury her in a traditional casket—or at least a shroud—but others insisted that Tia would not have wanted them to use up a share of their precious fabric stores on her. In the end the team producing disposables wove soft mats out of grass that had been culled from the meadow, and a fragrant green blanket was laid beneath her body, then folded over the top of it. She had been Catholic—albeit not overly religious—so Dani offered a traditional prayer, followed by a brief statement about how the God of Earth watched over all His children, and surely whatever angels served Him in this distant place would guide Tia's soul to heaven and reunite her with Michael. She closed with a prayer in Tagalog, to honor Tia's Filipino heritage. Then each colonist came to the graveside to say goodbye, casting a handful of soil onto the body. Leo saw Ted Carver pause as he did so, studying the soil in his hand as if looking for something in it; he seemed disturbed by the result. Finally he allowed the dirt to trickle through his fingers, like sand in an hourglass, into her grave.

This was the point at which, in a normal funeral, people would have offered condolences to the family of the deceased. But if Tia had any relatives they were twenty thousand light-years away now, and so many generations distant that any family connection was purely theoretical. So some people came to Leo as a substitute, needing to say, "I'm so sorry for your loss" to someone, to complete the ritual of mourning.

Ted stood off to one side, his posture suggesting he was waiting for a chance to address Leo privately. When the last well-wisher was gone, Leo waved him over. "Did you want to talk to me?"

"Privately. Is that possible?"

Leo glanced around, saw that no one was within hearing distance, and looked back at Ted with a question in his eyes. The ecologist said nothing. The man's right hand was twitching nervously, soil-stained thumb rubbing against adjacent fingers as if he was still sorting through dirt. Looking for what? Leo would be hard pressed to say exactly what about the man's posture or expression disturbed him so much, but something did.

"My office," Leo said.

The field between the burial site and his drop pod was strewn with tractor parts, and colonists were working assiduously to get everything removed from the packing crates and properly sorted. After that, the vehicles could be assembled, outfitted with solar-collection canopies, and allowed to charge. Tomorrow, God willing, Leo would be able to send out fully functional tractors to retrieve the supply pods that had missed the landing site, some by more than a mile. He'd feel a lot more confident once all their supplies were safely inside the camp.

As they entered the office pod, Leo reflected upon how many times in the past twenty-four hours he'd wished for a cup of coffee. Now he wished he had two of them, so that when they sat down he could give Ted something to do with his hands other than twist them nervously in his lap. During the funeral the man had looked calm enough, but now that they were alone that façade was gone, and he was nakedly nervous.

"All right," Leo said, leaning back against his makeshift desk. "What's up?"

Ted drew in a shaky breath. "Yesterday, at the autopsy, there was something that bothered me. I didn't mention it then because, well, I wasn't really sure about it. And we were focused on other things. But I checked the module's database this morning to confirm my concerns, and yes, there's something I think you would want to know about."

Lips tight, Leo nodded. "Go on."

"There were insects on Tia's body. Not insects, really. Little creatures that fill the same ecological niche as insects on Earth, but structurally they're not the same. Pravida calls them 'CCs,' short for *creepy crawlies*." He managed a weak smile. "She says it's a technical term. Anyway . . . Lise picked them out with a tweezer and bottled them up for Pravida to study later. She even found an egg sack."

Leo frowned. "Are you saying that Wayne was right, and an alien species was taking over Tia's body?"

"Oh no no no! I mean . . . well, yes, but not in a way that's significant. The same thing happens on Earth. Once a body starts to rot, all sorts of opportunist species move in. It's part of the cycle of life. But . . . there were too many of them, Leo. She'd only been out there a few hours at most, and hadn't yet . . . I'm sorry, I have no better way to say this, but her flesh hadn't rotted enough to draw that many insects to her. It's the smell of decomposition that attracts them. But with Tia, it was like they'd honed in on her the moment she died."

"This isn't Earth," Leo reminded him.

"No, but according to the theory of convergent evolution, similar environments produce similar adaptations. The first four colonies all reported that the life-forms on their planets functioned similarly to Terran ones. So I wondered if the discrepancy might be significant. I checked with our database on the progression of insect activity in a Terran corpse, to confirm my observations, then started looking at other insects—sorry, other CCs—in our environment, for comparison. And inside the camp . . ." He hesitated. "There aren't any."

Leo raised an eyebrow. "Aren't any what?"

"CCs. None at all. No pollinators, no ant-analogs, no grubs, no web-weavers—nothing to fill the ecological niches that insects fill on earth.

So I left the camp and took some more soil samples, but all those all looked normal. The land surrounding us is full of CCs, just like you'd expect. But not inside our encampment."

Leo remembered how he had studied a handful of soil at the gravesite. "You think all the insects . . . what, left when we arrived?"

"Leo, I couldn't even find worms! It's like every small-bodied species that was capable of leaving our encampment did so. I mean, I know there's supposed to be a honeymoon period with alien insects, because we don't give off the right odors to attract them, so they don't bother humans at first. But ants on Earth don't abandon their nests just because a new animal moves into the neighborhood. Least of all every single insect species in a given area, all at once. It makes no sense." He paused. "That's worthy of concern, right?"

For a moment Leo said nothing. He was remembering Ian's report. And Tia's gruesome corpse. He felt like someone had dumped a pile of puzzle pieces in front of him, but every piece was from a different puzzle so none of them fit together. Hell, he didn't even know what kind of picture they were supposed to create.

"Leo?"

"Ian found evidence of a botanical anomaly unique to this planet. Tia's death was like nothing Terrans have seen before. Now this. If there's some common thread here, damned if I know what it is." He sighed. "Let's meet tomorrow morning. The ten of us." A shadow passed over his face. "Sorry, nine of us. Maybe the others have made observations they haven't reported yet and can shed light on this one. Meanwhile . . ."

"Yes?"

A corner of Leo's mouth twitched. "You're probably going to hate me for this, but I'd like you to check out the latrine area. See how many CCs are buzzing around our shit. If there aren't any, that's important data to have."

Ted smiled wryly. "You're right. I do hate you for that." He stood up. "I'll get my team on it right away."

When the ecologist was gone, Leo stood in the doorway of the pod, looking out across the insect-free camp, wondering what the hell was going on.

☽☽☾

By the time dinner rolled around—hopefully the last meal that would consist exclusively of energy bars—the tractors were all lined up by the southern gate, drinking in the bright Ernan sunshine. Eight small ones, two large. Earth had sent enough that when the settlement finally divided the new camps would be well supplied. But until that point they might as well use all the equipment available.

When everyone had finished eating the evening's ration, Johnny called them over to the newly named Speaker's Rock, the granite perch Leo had used earlier. He waited until everyone was gathered around him before announcing, "Ladies and Gentlemen, the lunar voting has ended. Thank you all for participating. I have the results." He looked overhead, where a long, thin crescent arced like a scythe across the darkening sky, impossibly large by Terran standards. "Our largest satellite will henceforth be called 'Domina,' for reasons that seem kind of obvious." He grinned. "Our middle satellite—which first welcomed us to this planet—will be called 'Prima,' to commemorate that historic sighting. And the smallest moon, which travels in the opposite direction of the others, and so—it has been suggested, embodies the spirit of human obstinacy—is to be known as 'Loki,' after the Norse god of mischief. Their cycles will be named longmonth, midmonth and shortmonth. I trust you can figure out which is which."

There was a bit of laughter and some scattered applause, but he reached out his hands to shush the crowd. "Now, I've been analyzing the lunar orbits, and I'm pleased to announce that we're in for a surprise. Two surprises, actually." He gestured toward the sky. "You may have noticed that it never gets completely dark here. With the galaxy opposite the sun and three moons orbiting the planet, the only time the sky goes black is when all those bodies are positioned so that they aren't visible from somewhere on the surface, either due to the timing of their orbits or a well-timed eclipse. We have one such event coming up, in two more days. That's Saturday, for those of you who are calendrically challenged. 11:13 P.M. We're going to experience true darkness, for four

whole minutes. And again a week later, twelve minutes that time. This is
honest-to-God, Terran-style darkness we're talking about, like we had
back on Earth. Even darker than on Earth, because here there's no city
light bouncing off the clouds, and at that time of night there won't even
be stars visible. A true night, if you will. In other words, people . . ." his
smile broadened, "it's gonna get fucking dark." He spread his hands wide.
"Welcome to Erna, everyone."

As he stepped down from the rock and was engulfed by people with
questions, Leo watched quietly from the edge of the gathering. Suddenly he felt a warm hand slide into his own.

"You okay?" Lise asked. "You look worried."

He smiled wryly. "*Worried* is my default state these days."

She reached up and traced his hairline with a gentle finger. They'd
been attracted to each other in Orientation, and even shared a few moments of hesitant intimacy, but the trauma of Julian's death had still
weighed heavily on his soul, too much for him to let his barriers down.
He'd hoped that by leaving the planet where his son had died and embracing a new start in life, he could ease that burden. Instead, events on
Erna seemed to be adding to it.

After a moment she leaned against his side, resting her head on his
arm. And as the stars of the galaxy swept in graceful arcs across the sky,
he wondered what the world would be like when they were gone—when
all the lights in the sky were gone—and true night fell.

☾ ☾ ☾

Midnight. It was impossible to sleep. He kept thinking about Tia's autopsy, wondering what clues Lise might have missed. Intellectually he
was confident she'd covered all possible bases, but that didn't stop him
from obsessing over it.

The solar lanterns had been turned off to conserve power, and there
was only one moon overhead to see by. As he walked across the southern field he saw Heather Snow and David Saito standing guard by the
gate, fully armed. In theory he'd put them there to watch for monsters,
but they'd also see if anyone tried to leave the camp, like Tia had. Until

they understood what had compelled her to head into the woods at night, it was best to be careful.

We should build a watchtower, Leo thought. *Then we'd be able to see the whole camp, and the landscape surrounding.*

It was such a beautiful night. And such a beautiful world. CCs were buzzing in the distance, doing a convincing imitation of insects. If you didn't notice that they were all outside the perimeter fence, and that the camp itself was eerily silent, you could almost imagine you were home.

This is home now, he reminded himself sternly. *Earth is just a story we'll tell our children.*

Grass rustled behind him. He looked back and saw the chaplain, Dani Lin, approaching. He nodded for her to join him. For a moment the two of them stood side by side in companionable silence, listening to the nocturnal music of their new world.

"Wayne came to see me," Dani said at last. "When I saw you pass by the tents I figured this was as good a time as any to talk to you about it." She sighed. "I think he's a little bit afraid to talk to you directly, after the way you snapped at him when Tia's body was found."

Lips tight, Leo shook his head. "That was wrong of me. Everyone should feel free to say what they're thinking." He looked out toward the place where Tia had died. "Hell, I'm supposed to be the inspirational leader, aren't I? Tia's death shook me badly, but that's no excuse. I shouldn't have snapped at him like that. I'll apologize tomorrow." He looked at Dani "So what did he say to you?"

"He talked about an old movie in his collection. It was based on a story that he said was a classic, though I'd never heard of it. Genre stuff, I guess. It was about a world that had six suns, where the orbits were timed so that there was always at least one in the sky."

"So the world was never dark."

"Exactly."

He smiled dryly. "Like Erna, but brighter."

"Once every two thousand years, Wayne said, the suns would align with the planet so that five weren't visible, and then the sixth was eclipsed. For a brief time, the whole world went dark."

Leo raised an eyebrow. "And?"

"Wayne said all the people went mad."

"That seems a little extreme."

"It wasn't the darkness that did it—not in any physical sense—but the utter *alienness* of the experience. These people had lived in light all their life, and suddenly their whole paradigm was just . . . gone. The rules of reality could no longer be relied upon. They couldn't handle it."

"Is Wayne suggesting something like that might happen on Saturday?"

"He didn't say that specifically, but I got that impression."

Leo frowned. "It's quite a stretch. We grew up with darkness. It's not an alien concept to us. Hell, as far as our subjective awareness is concerned, it hasn't even been a week since the last time we saw night fall on Earth." He shook his head. "I'm not really worried about anyone losing their sanity over four minutes of darkness."

"Maybe not now," Dani said. "But phenomena that seemed perfectly normal on Earth may have a different effect on people here. Obviously nothing dire is going to happen two days from now, but Wayne suggested that down the road something might. He said we should watch for signs of things heading in that direction. So we're not taken by surprise if and when it does happen."

Could our own Terran heritage become alien to us? Leo mused. *That's a dark thought.* "It's an interesting suggestion. A bit out there, but aren't we supposed to be thinking outside the box? If I recall his psych profile, that was listed as one of his strengths. So I'm glad he's contributing his ideas. You can tell him I said that." He held up a hand. "No. Never mind. I'll tell him myself tomorrow, when I apologize to him."

He gazed up at the stars in silence for a moment. "He might be right, you know. We may have to let go of what we were before, in order to adapt to this world. Though it's not something the other colonies mentioned." *But they didn't have to deal with botanical impossibilities or creatures that ate human hearts. And insects didn't flee their presence. Their planets not only looked like Earth, they acted like Earth.*

"This is our home now," Dani said quietly. "Whether we embrace its differences or resist them, in the end we'll adapt." She smiled slightly. "Humans always do. He's just suggesting we embrace the change."

"And watch out for those who can't handle it."

She nodded.

He sighed. "It's not terrible advice."

She chuckled softly and patted his arm. "You can tell him that when you apologize."

Six

Commander's Personal Log
Year One
Day Four

Several loud cracks were heard today, coming from the south-east. Maybe gunfire? That could be our hunting team, though whether they have found game or encountered a monster is anyone's guess. The lush green forest that once seemed so welcoming has become a source of fear. We need to figure out what killed Tia, and how, so we can deal with it.

TO DO:

Cargo Pods: Send tractors out to bring in the ones that landed far afield. The pods themselves will be too heavy to move while loaded, so we'll bring in the contents first. Assuming nothing was damaged in stasis we should have Terran food staples in camp by this evening, as well as medical supplies and much-needed construction goods. Plus all the raw materials we'll get from disassembling the pods themselves.

Mess tent: We need a sheltered place where all of us can gather. Several large tents will be combined, stretching across the middle of the camp, to serve us for meals and meetings. The southern-facing roof will be covered with solar panels, adding considerably to our power supply. That's good, because by the time we get all our equipment up and running the need for power will be considerable.

$$\smallmoon \smallmoon \smallmoon$$

"Glad this job is almost done." Rod wiped the sweat from his face with a grimy hand and slid down from his tractor seat. He was a stocky man whose cheeks flushed bright red when he exerted himself, and a day of labor in the hot sun had made them even redder. He headed over to the water station, poured himself a drink, downed half of it in a single gulp, and poured the rest over his head. Glancing over at the other person at the water station, a lanky youth named Keith, he announced, "Jesus H. Christ, that feels good!"

They were two miles from the camp, preparing to unload the cargo pod that had come down farthest from the landing site. It had been damaged while landing, and one corner was crushed, but hopefully none of the vacuum-sealed storage bins inside had been compromised. Given how long they'd been in space there was no guarantee the contents were still good, but without proper seals there was no chance at all.

Staple foodstuffs, medical supplies, industrial-sized rolls of plastic sheeting, synthetic materials that could be used as planks or fed to the 3-D printer, and so much more: Earth had packed all the things a colony might not be able to produce locally, at least not in their first year. And the pods themselves could be broken down for steel if necessary. Even the parachutes that had brought them safely down would be cannibalized for fabric and hardware. Nothing that had come from Earth would be wasted, because none of it could be replaced.

"You're a wuss." Keith grinned broadly and waved at the work being done a hundred yards away. "This is the last unloading job today. We'll be heading back soon."

"And then tomorrow we get to come back here to fetch empty pods. Another fun task." Rod snorted. "Never ends, does it?"

"Maybe you should have volunteered for some other work team. Basket weaving, maybe? That sounds like your speed."

Rod laughed. "Bring on the raffia!"

Someone at the cargo pod whistled loudly to get their attention, then yelled between cupped hands, "Hey, you two! It's not quitting time yet. Get your butts back to work!"

Rod put his cup down. "I guess I could go gather up the parachutes."

Keith tsk-tsked. "You know what the priorities are. Bins first, pods and parachutes later."

"I know." Rod chuckled. "I was just testing you." As he climbed back up to his seat he said, "Did you ever think about how fucked we'd be without these tractors? I had a nightmare last night in which they all broke down, and we had to haul this stuff to the camp on our backs."

"They'll be fine, unless you jinx them with your bad dreams."

With a grin Rod put his tractor in gear and started to drive back toward the pod. But the vehicle only went a few yards, then the engine stalled out. "Shit," he muttered. He tried starting it again. The motor wheezed a few times, then died. The next time he tried, it made no sound at all. "Shit!"

Back at the pod, the team leader waved impatiently for the two of them to get moving. Rod pointed to his motor and then spread his hands wide: *Sorry, no can do.* Others saw the gestured conversation and looked their way, including Chrissy. She said something Rod couldn't hear and then started jogging toward them. She was the most mechanically inclined of the group, so the best qualified to help.

He slid down from his seat as she approached, giving her room to work. "Won't start," he said.

"Guessed that," she said curtly.

She climbed into the cab and checked all the controls, tested a few switches, and studied the data displays. She even stuck her head under the console, though Rod had no idea why. Finally she straightened up. "Batteries are charged, fluid levels good, circuits intact, engine temperature within normal range. Everything looks good. Let me take a look inside." She headed around to the front of the vehicle and lifted the hood. Leaning over the engine, she poked and prodded a number of things that Rod couldn't see, then cursed under her breath. "No problem that I can see."

"Meaning what?"

She stood back and let the hood drop. "Meaning that shipping heavy machinery halfway across the galaxy in DIY form may not have been such a great idea. Something to mention in our first colony report. Let's see, that'll get to Earth in, what, twenty thousand years?" She wiped a lock of sweaty hair back from her face. "This thing isn't going anywhere today. We'll have to haul it back to the camp, where I can run some tests and figure out what's wrong."

"Which'll take another tractor," Keith muttered. "That's two flatbeds that won't be hauling supplies."

She shrugged. "It is what it is."

Keith looked at Rod with narrow eyes. "You jinxed it, man."

"Hey!" The stocky man raised his hands in protest. "All I did was say I was worried about stuff breaking down!"

"And how you were having nightmares about it. That's bad psychic energy." He sighed. "I guess I know what I'm hauling home, anyway." He shook his head. "Leo won't be happy about this, that's for sure."

"It wasn't my fault," Rod insisted. "So no more crap about my jinxing it, okay? Shit happens."

Keith laughed. "Oh, I am going to tease you about that for days, my friend. Sorry, but you set yourself up."

"And I'll tell the others about it," Chrissy promised. "They'll want in on it too."

"Fuck you," Rod muttered. "Fuck you both." He kicked his tractor's tire. "And you too, you lazy motherfucker."

☽ ☽ ☽

Team Paleo returned at sunset, tired but exultant. As they proudly carried their kills into the camp, people came running to see what kind of animals they'd murdered. One that looked similar to a deer was tied hooves-up to a tree limb slung between the shoulders of two of the men. "Steak tonight!" one of them cried out, as people gathered around them.

Some people looked more repelled than jubilant. Earth had switched to vat-grown tissue long ago, and they'd never before seen meat in its original form. They were having a hard time reconciling the bloody, gutted corpse in front of them with the concept of "dinner."

Steve, the head cook, came over to inspect the corpse. They'd already gutted it, but it still had its skin, and its eyes were staring in a disturbing way. Steve's only experience with butchering had been in virtual simulations during Orientation, but those subjects hadn't looked so disconcertingly alive. Taking a deep breath, he waved the hunters toward his kitchen area, which now had several planks from the cargo pods set up as tables, and directed them to put the not-quite-a-deer on the largest one. Then, knife in hand, he discovered that practicing something in virtual reality and doing it in person were two different skills, especially when blood and gore were involved. In the end he had to play a tutorial on his tablet to guide him in real time, for which he was roundly teased by the crowd that had gathered to watch the bloody ritual. "Hey!" he snapped. "If you think you can do better, volunteer!" No one did. A few turned away to be sick, but for the rest, it was high performance art.

Leo took the hunters aside, thanked them wholeheartedly for their labor, and then told them about Tia. They should hear it from him, he said, not random comments at the dinner table. None of that would stop people from celebrating the colony's first successful hunt, but there was a shadow hanging over the camp now that was hard to ignore.

There wasn't enough meat for two hundred people to have steak dinners, Steve announced, but the foraging team had found potato-like tubers as well as some aromatics, and he was going to whip up enough stew to satisfy everyone. The alien perfume of Ernan herbs filled the new mess tent as synth planks from the cargo pods were laid out to serve as tables and benches, and when they were in place Anna proudly displayed the collection of cups, bowls, and utensils that she had 3-D printed. No more protein bars eaten as finger food for this colony!

By the time the food was ready the sun was setting, lanterns turning on automatically as dusk began. The plastic cups were filled with an herbed drink that Steve's assistants had whipped up, sweet and minty, and everyone toasted the hunters, then the team that had retrieved all their cargo. And soon everyone received portions of steaming hot stew, a gourmet meal by Ernan standards. Ian revealed he had seeds for hops and promised that soon enough they'd have beer—real beer—to wash their food down with, and so they toasted him, too.

Of course the members of Team Paleo had to describe every moment of their adventure so that their exploits could fully be appreciated. Their ancient ancestors had no doubt done the same, grouped around a communal campfire; some human rituals were eternal. Taking a seat nearby, Leo felt a spark of guarded optimism. His people clearly had the spirit of solidarity needed to make this colony work, and two major milestones had now been achieved. That still left the question of what had killed Tia, but hopefully proper precautions would prevent another event like that. And death at the hands of a local predator was a tragic but not unpredictable event, when establishing a colony in unfamiliar wilds.

"You should have seen Sky," one of the hunters was saying. "He would just point a gun at an animal and whisper where he wanted it to go. And it did! It was the most amazing fucking thing ever."

"Like it wanted to be shot," another hunter agreed.

"C'mon, guys." Sky grinned. "I was just sensing where it was about to go. Talking to myself, not to it. No magical powers, just good observation."

One of the other hunters grunted. "Fucking unnatural, if you asked me."

Sky looked at him. "You complaining?"

The hunter snorted. "Hell no!"

Was it unnatural? Or just coincidence? Keith Esper was now telling everyone how Rod had jinxed a tractor by dreaming that it would break down. More coincidence? Things like that happened all the time back on Earth, Leo told himself. If his nerves weren't so raw from dealing with Tia's death, the men's comments would have passed without notice. But right now everything out of the ordinary felt like it could be significant. So how unusual did something have to be before it was worthy of attention?

He shook his head to clear it. He needed to focus on something else for a while. Maybe this would be a good time to talk to Wayne.

He managed to extricate himself from the crowd that had assembled around the storytellers and started looking for him, but with no success. He walked the entire length of the tent, checking out every person he passed. Everyone in the colony seemed to be present except for Wayne.

As he passed Sally Chang she looked up at him. "Who are you looking for?"

"Wayne." He said it loudly enough that others could hear him. "I'm looking for Wayne Reinhart. Does anyone know where he is?"

"Off to take a piss," Lan Nguyen offered.

"That was ages ago," Jeff Hodges said. He pointed to a bowl full of stew that looked conspicuously out of place amidst all the empty ones. "Look, his food hasn't been touched."

Anna chuckled. "Probably watching one of his movies. Because, you know, the first real food we've had on a new world ISN'T EXCITING ENOUGH FOR WAYNE."

Bill grinned. "I'll eat his if he doesn't want it."

Wayne's long absence was probably nothing to worry about, Leo told himself. Maybe just an upset stomach. But his face must have betrayed his uncertainty, because when Jeff looked at him his own smile faded. "I'll check on him," Jeff said. "Gotta piss anyway." He coughed. "That stuff that isn't beer goes right through you."

Leo nodded, accepting the offer. Best to treat this as a casual concern for now. He started pacing while he waited, but then realized there were people watching him, and the look on their faces communicated a common question: *Do we need to be worried about something?* So he stopped, and he smiled at them, and acted as if he was not worried at all.

Someone screamed. It was a gut-wrenching sound, resonating with fear in a way Leo had never heard before. And it was coming from the waste disposal area. Leo started in that direction, but by the time he rounded the table others were already running downhill toward the waste tent, and some of them got there before he did. They didn't enter, or even approach the tent itself, but stood a few yards back, their attention fixed on something by the entrance. When Leo caught up to them he saw what it was.

Jeff.

The man was crouched by the door flap with his arms wrapped

around his knees and his head lowered; his whole body was shaking. As Leo approached he looked up, and the sheer horror in his eyes was chilling. "Don't go in there," Jeff whispered hoarsely. "You don't want to see."

But being colony commander left him no choice, so Leo drew in a deep breath, pushed the flap aside, and entered the tent.

Inside it was dark, with only a single dim lamp to see by. But that was enough for him to make out the form of a body lying at the edge of the compost pit. The shape of it was human, but the head seemed oddly flat, and the arms and legs were bent in ways that human limbs should not bend. It looked like a rag doll that someone had thrown to the ground.

He looked around the tent to make sure there was nothing crouching in a corner, then approached the body. Though he knew whose it must be, it was still a shock to see the face clearly. This was Wayne, all right—or rather, *had been* Wayne. Leo crouched down by his side and reached out a tentative finger to the man's neck to check for a pulse. But when he pressed on Wayne's skin it sank beneath this touch, as if the flesh beneath it was not human tissue, but jelly. He pulled his hand back, drew in a few deep breaths to steady himself, then looked more closely at Wayne's face. The head was not merely flattened, he realized, more like . . . deflated. Like a balloon that was half-full, with human features painted on it. He reached out to take Wayne's hand, then thought better of it and took hold of the sleeved forearm instead, unwilling to touch the grotesque balloon-skin. He wanted to see if the limbs were any more solid than the face and neck. But the forearm was sickeningly slack; had there not been skin and clothing to contain it, the flesh might have flowed out of Leo's hands.

Now he understood what had spooked Jeff so badly. He turned away to be sick, barely managing to lean over the edge of the compost pit first.

A flicker of light entered the tent from behind him, as someone opened and then closed the door flap.

Please God, he thought, wiping his mouth on his sleeve, *don't let anyone else come in here and see this.*

"You okay?" It was Lise.

He shook his head. *No. No. Not okay. Light-years from okay.*

She moved closer to Wayne's body, to get a better look. Her eyes widened in horror as she realized exactly what she was looking at, and she instinctively took a step backward. To her credit, she managed not to be sick.

"Holy shit," she whispered. "Holy shit. What the fuck happened?"

He forced himself to lift Wayne's arm again, so that she could see how unnaturally it moved. "No clue," he said hoarsely. When he released the arm it flopped back down to the ground like a dead fish. "You're the doctor, so you tell me. What could do this to a man?"

"God knows. I've never seen anything like it." She edged a bit closer again, to take another look. "There are venoms back on Earth that can dissolve flesh. But not as quickly as this. Jesus, he was fine an hour ago!"

"Can those venoms dissolve bone like this? Leaving the rest untouched?"

"No." She shook her head. "I don't know anything on Earth that could do something like this."

"Flesh-eating bacteria?"

"Pulping an entire body like this, in an hour? I guess theoretically it's possible, but . . ." She prodded Wayne's arm with a finger; it sank into the jellied flesh with no resistance. Testing a thigh got the same result. "All four of the first colonies said that local pathogens didn't affect them for the first few months, as alien germs need time to adapt to our biochemistry. So the likelihood of this being caused by a pathogen is very, very low."

"Which means it's unlikely to be contagious?"

She hesitated. "Unlikely, yes." She glanced back toward the tent entrance, beyond which most of the colony must be clustering nervously by now. Waiting for word. "That may not be enough to keep others from panicking. Especially after Tia's death." She leaned down to take a closer look at the body. "The ears are intact. That's odd. And I think I see a protrusion where the tip of his nose must have been, but there's no sign of the rest of it. I'd need to get him to the lab to figure out what all this means."

She stood up. "We need a body bag. And an explanation to give everyone else." She nodded toward the tent flap. "No lies, right?"

"You're the medic," he said quietly. "What do you suggest?"

She considered for a moment, then walked to the entrance and pulled its flap aside. "Wayne's dead," she announced. "We're not sure what killed him. Possibly a toxin from some animal he ran across on the way here. Nothing like what happened with Tia. I need to get him into the lab before I can tell you more. James, could you fetch me a bag from the clinic, please? Thank you."

There were some muttered protests, but evidently she'd been convincing enough—and calm enough—that they were willing to follow her lead. Wayne had been bitten by something. There was no need for people to crowd into the tent to see that for themselves.

Looking down at Wayne's body, Leo wondered how the hell he was going to carry it so that no one realized the thing in the specimen bag wasn't a human body anymore, just a bag of jelly with a face.

Seven

"Well, Ian? Is this what you expected?"

The red-headed botanist looks up at the towering trees in awe. They are old growth—ancient growth—not the product of human reforesting efforts, but nature's own work. To be surrounded by trees that could be older than human civilization itself is like standing in a sacred temple. Ian shuts his eyes for a moment to drink in the forest's perfume: the crisp scent of pine needles, the smell of early spring flowers, the pungent odor of decomposition. "It's incredible," he breathes. "Absolutely incredible. I can't thank you enough for this, Eric."

His friend shrugs. "Perks of the job. I could only get you a permit for four hours, though. It's to protect the preserve, you understand. There aren't many places like this left."

"I understand."

The breeze carries a sharp acrid scent to his nostrils: perhaps the territorial marking of some passing animal. The concept that wild beasts can do that here—living and dying and hunting and mating without human guidance or interference—is intoxicating. "I wonder if there's a way to sense it," Ian muses aloud. "Maybe smell it when it fruits aboveground. But how would you pick out a scent like that, when you've never smelled it before?"

Eric blinks. "Sorry, you lost me. Smell what?"

Ian gestures toward the trees. "There's a network binding all of these together, Eric. Fragile strands of fungus deep underground, connecting tree to tree so they can share water and nutrients with each other. Mycorrhizal symbiosis. Some even think that trees can communicate with each other—on a primitive level, of course—by sharing chemical signals through the network. A sort of arboreal internet." There is awe in his voice. "Think about it! One single being, perhaps as large as this whole forest, branching out endlessly to make new connections. Like neurons in a human brain. It's right under our feet. We can't see it. Our ancestors had no idea it was there. But the health of this forest depends upon it."

Eric chuckles. "So—just to be clear—you wanted a permit to hike through one of the few remaining forest preserves in order to commune with a brain-like network you can't see, smell, or hear?"

Ian grins. "Pretty much."

"There are trees closer to where you live."

"Reconstituted forests planted by humans after we destroyed the originals. But once we tear up the mycorrhizal network, just replacing trees won't repair it; the fungus has to start connecting all over again. But in an old growth forest like this, where humankind has never tilled the earth, it can grow for millennia, undisturbed." He looks back at Eric. "The life-form under our feet may be older than the pyramids."

His friend shakes his head. "Has anyone ever told you you're crazy?"

Ian grins. "Not this week."

"Well, sane or not, your permit's good for four hours, starting . . ." He presses a button on his chrono. "Now. You'll get a reminder at the half-hour mark, and again at fifteen minutes. You know the way back?"

Ian nods back toward the ranger station. "I think so."

"If you get lost, GPS it. If that doesn't help, call me. Unless you'd rather try spinning a magnetic needle, like they did in the days of the pyramids." He pauses. "You owe me big time for this."

"Yes," he says quietly. "I know."

"All right then." Eric pats him on the shoulder. "Enjoy the trees, my friend."

Ian shuts his eyes. As his friend departs he listens as the leaf-crunching footsteps slowly recede into the distance. Then all that is left is the forest.

He lowers himself slowly to the ground, lies back upon a bed of damp soil and leaves, and stretches his arms wide, splaying out his fingers like tree roots. Or perhaps like mycorrhizal strands? If he stays here long enough without moving, like a tree, will the fungal network eventually detect him and try to connect to him? Or is a human being too alien to attract it?

For a while he gazes up at the trees that tower overhead, allowing himself to be mesmerized by the patterns that the sunlight makes as their branches shift in the breeze. Then, with a sigh, he shuts his eyes again, focusing on the sound of leaves rustling and the smell of the soil, imagining what it would be like for a whole planet to be covered in forest like this, millions upon millions of acres of it. Earth was like that, once. Other planets still are.

Maybe this world is not where he belongs.

☽ ☽ ☽

Ian was the first to arrive for Leo's meeting, so he was able to claim the most comfortable seat, a real folding chair. Two benches had been set up for the others, using planks from the cargo pod. Not luxurious accommodations, but sufficient to accommodate the first people Leo had awakened on the seedship, now serving as his advisory council.

The others filtered in one by one. All of them looked tired, but that was to be expected. No one in the camp had been sleeping well, least of all the nine people who knew all the gory details of Tia's death. Thus far they'd chosen not to share the more bizarre details with anyone else, just nod in agreement when someone referred to her "being killed by an animal." Whether that was because they wanted to have more information to offer before they did that, or because the thought of discussing the matter awakened a visceral fear in them, Ian couldn't say. For him it was a mixture of both.

Lise and Leo arrived last. The colony commander had circles under his eyes that were dark enough to be visible even against the color of his skin. Lise had a look in her eyes that suggested she had gazed upon the kind of horror one could never unsee. This was not going to be a good meeting.

"Welcome, everyone." Leo looked at each of them in turn, meeting their eyes, offering a nod of encouragement. Even when he must feel drained inside he could be a source of strength to others; Ian admired and appreciated that. "I called you here to hear the details of Wayne's autopsy. Not pleasant stuff, I warn you. Afterward we'll need to discuss some things." He looked at Lise. "You ready to start?"

In truth, she looked like she would rather be doing anything else, but she nodded. "Wayne's body was in . . . let's say, an unusual condition. That's why we hid it from sight yesterday. Last night I did an autopsy on it, hoping to figure out what had killed him. What I found . . ." She hesitated for a moment, then said, "His bones were gone. All of them."

Pravda's eyes widened. "Gone? What do you mean, *gone*?"

"I mean, *not there*. I mean, everything else in the body was right where it should be—muscles, tendons, internal organs—but the bones were missing. Every single one of them. Even the smallest. Cartilage was untouched. I have his ears—" For a moment she couldn't continue. Leo took her hand, offering silent reassurance. Finally she nodded and continued. "I checked for any kind of wound which would suggest how the bones could have been removed. But the skin was all intact. No gaping wounds, no cuts, not even damage inside the natural entrance routes to his body to suggest the bones had been pulled out that way. And there were no bite marks to suggest a venom had been injected, that might have dissolved all his bones. They just . . . disappeared." She paused. "I have pictures. Be forewarned, they're pretty gruesome."

She turned on her tablet, cued it up to the right image, and handed it to Joshua, on her left. His face went pale as he looked at it, even more so as he scrolled through the collection of autopsy pictures. He looked slightly green as he passed the tablet on to Dani. The chaplain could only scroll through a couple before having to pass it on to the next person. Around the pod the tablet traveled, until it got to Ian. By that time he was too curious to refuse it, so he scrolled through the pictures Lise had taken, of a mass of flesh absent the structure that would have made it appear human. It was horrifying, but hard to look away from. His hand trembled slightly as he forced himself to pass it on.

Botany classes hadn't prepared him for anything like this.

Eventually the tablet got back to Lise, who turned the display off. "You see what we're dealing with," she said quietly.

For a moment there was silence. Then: "Any idea of what might have caused it?" Johnny asked.

"Well . . . maybe. But you may find that detail more disturbing than the death itself. I asked Anna to go through his tablet, see if she could figure out what he'd been doing earlier that day. Maybe he'd gone somewhere we should check out, or had some kind of wildlife encounter that might be significant. Anything that might be a clue." She looked at Anna. "I'll let her tell you what she found."

Anna reached into her bag and pulled out Wayne's tablet. It had a protective skin with a cartoon spaceship in one corner and stars painted across it. "I couldn't find the kind of information Lise was looking for, but I did find something. The last thing he was watching before he died." She turned the tablet so that everyone in the group could see the screen. "This is from one of his vintage science fiction shows. According to the log, he was watching it the night before he died."

"I fail to see how that—" Ted began. Lise raised a hand, urging him to wait.

On the screen was the image of a rustic room filled with plants. There were three figures in the scene: a deformed creature in a ghillie suit, a human in a tight leather uniform, and a woman with blue skin and clothing. The blue woman told the others: "She's a carcinovore," and the leather-clad man asked, "She eats bones?" The characters continued on with a conversation about how a bone-eating monster was hunting for food and meant to devour the bones of one of them. When that clip had concluded, Anna cued up another, in which a body was found that had been torn to pieces by the creature. Its bones had been devoured.

The screen faded to darkness.

"I don't get it," Joshua protested. "What are you telling us? That a monster from some centuries-old entertainment video showed up and

killed Wayne?" He pointed to the tablet. "That's not even what Wayne's
body looked like."

"No," Leo agreed. "It's not. And no one is suggesting that this exact
monster is what killed Wayne. But it's hard to believe this is just a coincidence."

"There's more," Anna said. She turned the tablet to her and called
up a screen full of text. "Leo asked me to see if I could find anything that
related to Tia's case. So I did a general database search for the details
we knew about. And the search engine came up with this." She started
to read.

> *The Tiyanak is a vampiric creature from Filipino folklore that
> disguises itself as a baby or child to attract victims. Typically it
> will appear in a heavily wooded area and cry like an infant until
> someone comes to rescue it. When the victim picks it up, the
> Tiyanak reverts to its true form and feeds.*

Anna turned off the tablet. "It didn't say anything about eating
human hearts, but . . ." She positioned her arms as if she were cradling a
baby; the imaginary head was positioned just over her heart.

"Jesus Christ," Ted breathed.

Dani offered, "Steve said she heard a baby crying in the forest. That
sound was probably what drew her out there."

Ian asked, "Was Tia Filipino?"

Lise nodded. "Her family was. She told me once that her grand-
mother used to tell her folk tales from back home when she was little.
It's possible she heard about such a creature in her childhood but forgot
about it later, so that she didn't make the connection."

"Or didn't forget about it," Leo said quietly. "Given her mood that
night, maybe she welcomed death."

"It's fucking crazy," Tom muttered.

"It's probably a clue," Leo said, "though a bizarre one. Let's compare it to all the others we know about. I want to hear about everything
in this colony that doesn't seem right to you. I don't care how insignificant it seems. Ian, you can start by explaining about the tree rings."

He nodded and told the group what he had told Leo. He passed around the samples he'd brought with him, now properly sanded so the rings could easily be distinguished. Then Ted told the group about how there were no CCs in the camp, and why that was significant. Dani revealed that several people had talked to her about recurrent nightmares they were having—all the same, of a blue fire emanating from the ground.

"Sally Chang described a blue light flowing along the ground that flickers like fire but gives off no heat. She tries to find its source, but she catches fire herself before she can do so, and the flames consume her. They're cold rather than hot, and they freeze her to death." She paused. "She told me she wakes up physically chilled. A tentmate of hers confirmed that her skin was like ice the last time it happened. I suppose it could be psychological. We know there are people who can control their body temperature. But . . ." She looked at Leo. "Add it to the list of weird events."

When no one else had anything to offer, Leo nodded. "I've witnessed two odd coincidences. They seem pretty minor in comparison to what you've all reported, and probably aren't significant, but we're not yet sure what is or isn't significant, so I'll share them." He told them about how Rod had "jinxed" his tractor by dreaming about how it could break down, which it promptly did, for no obvious mechanical reason. And how some of the hunters thought that Sky had demonstrated an unnatural influence over his prey. "The first example does seem to fit the pattern," he concluded. "An image in someone's mind affecting the real world."

"Fear," Ian muttered. "This is all about fear."

Johnny snorted. "I'm pretty sure Wayne wasn't afraid he'd run into a bone-eating vampire. And I'd be surprised if anyone was having nightmares about evenly spaced tree rings."

"And Sky's incident with the deer didn't involve any fear," Pravida pointed out. "If anything, it was just the opposite. It was something he wanted very badly."

"What about emotion?" Dani asked. "Each of those people had an image stuck in their mind that had strong emotional resonance. Different emotions each time, but always intense."

"And the tree rings?" Ian pointed out.

Leo shook his head. "They record events from before we got here. We don't have a context for them. So let's focus on human events for now."

"So then, what?" There was an edge to Ted's voice. "What are we suggesting? That there's some mind-reading creature out there, bringing our emotions to life? That's a little farfetched, isn't it? Or maybe the whole planet just hates us. That would explain the insects."

"Hey." Leo held up a hand. "If it's too farfetched, then let's come up with an idea that isn't. Because if this goes on much longer, people will start to panic."

"You going to share all this with the rest of the camp?" Johnny asked sharply.

Leo hesitated. "Let's come up with some workable theories first. So we have something better to offer than 'Your nightmares may come to life and try to kill you.' Especially when we could be completely wrong about that. We'd be stirring up fears over nothing."

"Well," Ian said, "whatever is going on here is good for the trees, and it was good for Sky. And maybe it's good for the insects, too—we don't know why they left. So it may not be inherently harmful. Maybe . . ." He hesitated. He was thinking of the fungal networks back home: unseen, undetected, but connected to every living thing around them. Could there be something on this planet that worked the same way, but without the same kind of physical connection? Maybe something that responded to emotional energy instead of chemical signals? It sounded like something out of one of Wayne's movies, but then, so did this whole situation. "I have some ideas," he hedged. "Let me test some of them and see if they're worth sharing."

"Fair enough," Leo said. "Meanwhile, everyone will be armed, twenty-four/seven. Any animal that's solid enough to remove chunks of a human body is solid enough to be shot. And we'll put the watchtower construction on priority, so we're better positioned to see anything approaching the camp." He shook his head. "This whole thing is so bizarre. What if it's not even real? What if there's some kind of group delusion involved, brought on by the stress of a new world?"

"Which no other colony experienced?" Joshua asked.

"The bodies I inspected were real," Lise said. "I know how to tell the difference."

"But the way they appear to us?" Leo asked. "The baby that Tia may have seen? The stranger details of her wound? It wouldn't hurt to check out the possibility. Maybe something in the air is making us all hyper-suggestible. Or hyper-paranoid. Terra had its share of mind-altering plants."

"It's spring," Ian said. "That means pollen."

"All right. So check that out. Anna, why don't you do a detailed analysis of the atmosphere, down to trace elements." He paused. "Much as it pains me to say this, I think it's wisest not to share our crazier speculations with the rest of the camp until we can rule out any mind-altering influence that might skew their reaction."

"I'll need to keep Wayne's body for further study," Lise said. "I've set up a morgue-style cooler for it, but that means we won't be able to bury him. What do we tell people about that?"

"The truth. You need to run more tests. They know we're trying to figure out what killed him, so it'll be fine."

"And what about the guns?" Johnny asked. "How do we explain the fact that we're telling everyone they need to carry twenty-four/seven?"

"They know that some large animal killed Tia. They were already worried about it getting into the camp. Now Wayne has died, and no one knows what killed him. I think most people will be happy to go armed."

"All right," Ted said. "Just remind them that bullets go through tents. I seem to recall some people forgetting that in Orientation."

Orientation. It seemed like a lifetime ago. It *was* a lifetime ago, if you counted all the years the colonists had slept. What if stasis became more unreliable over that much time? Could thousands of years in suspension have affected everyone—or almost everyone—in ways no one anticipated? Maybe compromising their ability to think clearly?

Either way, mass hysteria was real. Earth had records of many examples. But even if that was happening here, it still left many unanswered questions.

☽ ☽ ☽

The forest surrounding Ian was green. So very green. Ian just stood there for a moment, drinking in the color: emerald-brilliant, multi-layered verdure that reminded him of the Amazonian preserve where Orientation had taken place, only more intense. It was the kind of place that could only exist in a location where year after year, decade after decade, growing conditions remained stable.

Like here.

Slowly he picked his way over vines and gullies, moving farther and farther away from the camp. Leo would have his head if he knew that Ian had gone off alone like this, but that couldn't be helped. The botanist needed to get far enough from the camp that the sound of chainsaws and hammers and engines being tested faded into the distance. He needed to be alone with the planet. But Tia had died in these woods, and Wayne had died . . . well, however the hell Wayne had died. The point was, he had died when he was alone. Yet as Ian picked his way through the brush—twisting a leaf here or a branch there to mark his path for later—he told himself that his circumstances were different. If Dani was right, and the elusive monsters of Erna responded to human emotion, then all they would get from him was insatiable curiosity and perhaps a hint of awe.

Finally he found the kind of place he was looking for, a small clearing surrounded by trees just coming into flower. There was a stream nearby, and the sound of water rushing over rocks washed out the noise from the camp. If he shut his eyes, he could imagine he was the only human on this planet.

For a long time he just stood there, trying to let go of his memories of Earth so that he could embrace the essence of this mysterious new world. That was the colonists' problem, to his mind: They saw this world as alien, and deep inside felt like they didn't belong here. If something on this planet really was responding to human emotions, that was the wrong message to send. Maybe if he approached the planet from a different perspective he could gain better insight.

He took out the gun that Leo had assigned to him and turned it over in his hand, studying the way leaf-mottled shadows played across its surface. If some hostile creature should approach him, this would be his only defense. He considered that for a long moment, then laid it down gently on a bed of moss. Yes, there was a stirring of fear inside him— he'd be lying if he denied that—but he had come here for a purpose, and that couldn't be achieved if he was in a confrontational state of mind.

He walked to the center of the clearing and lowered himself to a cross-legged position, shifting in the grass until he was comfortable. All that he could see or hear now was the Ernan wilderness: branches shifting, water gurgling, and maybe—just maybe—the subtle stirrings of a fungal network deep underground, connecting it all into one vast entity. Convergent evolution suggested such a thing might exist here, though not necessarily in a form he would recognize.

"I come to you unarmed," he said aloud. Not because he thought the trees would understand English—he wasn't quite that crazy—but because the words helped give structure to his thoughts, and hopefully would channel his emotions the way he needed to. "I sit here unprotected. Not as invader, but supplicant. I bring with me no beliefs that are alien to you, no Terran expectations. Just a willingness to greet you on your own terms." He breathed in deeply, drawing Erna's air deep into his lungs. "Show yourself to me," he whispered. "Whatever your nature, I'll respect it, I promise."

But though he sat there for a long while, focusing his mind and soul upon that message, he gained no special insight. An insect landed on him, which might or might not be significant. Had he expected more? Had he hoped deep inside that there really was some kind of alien sentience that he could communicate with? What an amazing experience that would be! But though it was a pleasing fantasy, he hadn't really expected a concrete response.

Finally he rose from the grass, brushing seeds and dirt from his clothing as he stood. The long meditation had soothed his spirit, and his body felt refreshed, but he understood no more now than he had when he first arrived. With a sigh of frustration he retrieved his gun and started back the way he had come, toward the incessantly busy, incessantly noisy settlement.

The forest was not ready to speak to him.

Eight

Colony Commander's Log
Year One
Day Five

There was a quake this morning, stronger than the one on landing day. Joshua and Anna have gone to the module to make sure nothing was damaged. Meanwhile a betting pool has been established for when the first aftershock will arrive. I have – reluctantly—agreed to let the printer be used to produce plastic coins for that purpose. As they can be fed back into the printer later, no resources are being wasted. One side of the coin has an image of our new planet, the other the profile of the Terran financier for whom it was named. It seems right that she be memorialized on our first coinage, though the grandeur of the gesture seems a bit diminished when they are only plastic betting tokens. Printing any kind of coinage in this place feels a bit premature, but isn't that one of the first acts of a new nation, to signal its sovereignty? So maybe it is appropriate.

There is a sense of nervous energy in the air today, in antici-
pation of what Joshua has named "true night." I am not sure
whether that is a good thing or a bad thing.

Jeff isn't doing well, which is not surprising, given his recent
experience. I have asked Dani to watch over him, and I under-
stand she's moved him to the quarantine pod. Lise and I are
going there later to check on him, and see if there is anything we
can do to help him cope with the horror that he has witnessed.

☽ ☽ ☾

The quarantine pod was in the rear of the camp, behind the city of
tents. It was a quiet place—as much as any location in the camp was
quiet—with little traffic. Opposite the pod was the tiny cemetery where
they had buried Tia and the stasis casualties, with a few flowers on their
graves bearing witness to friends who remembered them.

After the morning work crews had set out, Leo and Lise headed
that way. As always, her presence eased his spirit. He wished he could
put aside all his other concerns and just focus on her, like he had once
dreamed of doing, but as much as he yearned for the comfort of such a
relationship, the tension of the past week would not release its death-
grip on his soul. Hopefully when things were more stable he could step
back from his position and be, for a time, just a man. That was the point
of his coming here, wasn't it? A fresh start?

Dani was waiting for them outside the pod. She smiled as Leo and
Lise approached, but the expression was forced and didn't reach her
eyes.

"How's he doing?" Leo asked.

"Not well." Dani was normally good at masking her emotions, but
there was no mistaking the concern in her voice. "He has to have the
lights on all the time. Darkness terrifies him. And the pod door has to
be shut completely, so nothing can sneak in and surprise him." She
sighed. "Lise gave me a sedative to help calm him down, but she wasn't
sure how potent it would be, given how long it had been in storage." She

hesitated. "I gather Jeff and Wayne were . . . close. No doubt that's part of why this hit him so hard."

Leo raised an eyebrow. "Close?"

"Friends, at least. Who knows?" She shrugged. "We all agreed to breed when we got here, but that doesn't mean people can't have other attachments. And I think he actually saw Wayne die. Sometimes he mutters things about how darkness rose up and devoured Wayne, and I get the impression that's not just a metaphor, that he actually *saw* something inside that tent. But when I try to get him to tell me more, he gets confused, and suddenly can't remember anything. Deep inside, I suspect he doesn't want to remember. And one can hardly blame him, given everything. But he may have actually seen what killed Wayne." She sighed. "I'm hoping with you here he can stay focused long enough to describe what he saw." She moved toward the door of the pod. "You ready?"

The visitors nodded.

She reached out and knocked, loudly enough to be heard through the pod's insulated shell. Then she opened the door, and stood aside so Leo and Lise could enter.

The interior of the pod was blazing with light. Lamps had been hung from every available protrusion, and were clustered on every shelf, table, and chair. A half-dozen cots were neatly arranged at the far end of the pod, and every one of them had a lamp set on it. Some even had lamps underneath them. The overall message was clear: *Shadows will find no refuge in this place.*

Jeff was huddled on the cot farthest from the door, his knees drawn up before him, just like on the night of Wayne's death. His skin was ashen, and he looked utterly exhausted. There was a plate of food beside him, but it looked untouched.

"Hey, Jeff." Leo tried to make his tone sound casual, but it was hard to do when so much might be riding on this conversation. "We came to see how you were doing."

Jeff looked up at him with bloodshot eyes and whispered, "Did you bury him yet?" The subtext was clear: *Did I miss Wayne's funeral?*

"Not yet," Lise said gently. "We're still trying to figure out what killed him, and I need him for that. We'll set him to rest properly when that's done, I promise you." And she added, "We'll let you know when."

"Thank you," he whispered.

Leo walked over and sat down on the cot beside him. "Dani said you might be able to help us figure out what happened to Wayne."

He shut his eyes; a faint tremor ran through his body. "Hungry," he whispered. "They were so hungry! You could feel their hunger inside you, like a thousand knives in your gut. Was that what Wayne felt, do you think? Something cutting him up from the inside? Would the same thing have happened to me, if I hadn't fled?" He opened his eyes— haunted eyes, hopeless eyes, so full of pain that it hurt just to look at them. "I should have stayed," he whispered hoarsely. "I should have saved him. Instead I ran, like a coward. *I left him alone.*" He lowered his head and sobbed.

For a moment Leo didn't trust himself to respond. He knew all too well what it was like to blame oneself for another's death, and wasn't sure how to quiet Jeff's demons when he hadn't yet conquered his own. Finally he put a hand on Jeff's shoulder and squeezed it: reassurance without words. Meanwhile Dani came to the cot, pushed the plate of food away, and sat down on Jeff's other side. "You couldn't have saved him," she said gently. She took his hand in hers. "But by warning us, you may have saved others."

Nodding dully, Jeff wiped his nose with the back of a shaking hand.

"You said they were hungry," Leo prompted. He tried to make his tone encouraging rather than demanding. "What is *they*?"

Jeff looked at him. How empty his gaze was, how haunted! "Serpents from the pit of Hell. Glowing violet hunger, bright and dark at the same time. Shit." He shook his head sharply. "I don't know what the fuck they were. Maybe just my imagination. But their presence was so cold it sucked all the heat from your body, so that you couldn't move. I tried. I tried! But I couldn't help Wayne, just watch as they ate him. They *ate* him. Then suddenly I could move again, and I ran. Like a coward." He lowered his head to his knees, trembling. "I'm sorry, Wayne. I'm sorry I left you alone with them."

Serpents from the pit of Hell. Was that a real physical threat of some kind, or a delusion? Certainly something physical had removed the bones from Wayne's body. Delusions lacked the power to do that.

For a few minutes Jeff just stayed as he was, head bowed and shoulders trembling, silent. Dani released his hand and rubbed his back gently. Finally Jeff looked up again. "True night's coming. Isn't that right? All the sunlight will be gone. All of it." He shivered. "It loves the dark. It feeds on the dark. It *is* the dark." He looked at Dani. "Promise me you'll keep all the lights on for me. And lock the pod door, so nothing can get in. Promise me!"

"You can lock it yourself, from the inside. And yes, I'll make sure all the lamps are fully charged."

They stayed with him a while longer, offering words that might have been comforting back on Earth, but here, in this alien setting, mere words lacked power. Jeff lay back onto the cot and gradually shut his eyes and relaxed into sleep. Maybe Lise's sedative had made it possible. Maybe emotional exhaustion had simply overwhelmed him.

They left as quietly as they could, and Dani shut the door behind them with care. For a moment, then, they were all silent as they digested what Jeff had told them.

"He should sleep tonight," Dani said at last.

Leo nodded. "Hopefully."

"No, I mean . . . we should make *sure* he sleeps tonight, during true night."

"He won't see it from inside the pod," Leo pointed out.

"But he'll know it's happening. And you saw his state of mind. The mere concept of darkness terrifies him."

Leo looked at her for a moment, then nodded. "All right. Make it happen."

"You do realize," Lise said, "when the story of this gets out—and it will get out, sooner or later—people will want better shelter than we've currently got. The tents were designed to fend off rain, not monsters. And regardless of whether solid walls can offer any real protection against whatever the hell killed Tia and Wayne, people will feel less helpless with solid walls around them."

Leo shook his head. "There's not enough room in the pods for everyone. We were packed in shoulder-to-shoulder for the drop, and even if they were all empty—which they're not—there still wouldn't be enough room for everyone to sleep inside them at the same time."

"The module?" Dani asked.

"Designed for efficiency," Lise said, "not comfort. Access corridors are narrow, and most large storage spaces are still packed with supplies. A couple of the labs have decent floor space, and there's the storage bay that the tractors were in, but I doubt you could fit more than a couple of dozen people inside there."

"We've got the cargo pods," Leo said. "The plan was to cannibalize them for materials, but there's no reason we can't do that later. I'll send out a team to bring them in whole. Add some ventilation, and they can provide basic shelter until we have time to build something better. That'll cover the psychological angle, at least."

"Put them end to end," Dani suggested, "and cut some doorways between them, so we'll have a longhouse-style shelter that can accommodate a lot of people. That and the empty pods should provide enough indoor space for everyone, if there are more threats."

"Hopefully there won't be." More ideas were coming to Leo now. "We can build a palisade. Whether it will keep out Erna's more bizarre threats is anyone's guess, but it'll be a solid defense against mundane beasts, and right now that's what most people think killed Tia." He looked at Lise. "Not to mention the psychological value of having a defensible stronghold. Something people know they can retreat to if anything bad happens."

Lise smiled slightly. "Now I know why they pay you the big bucks."

A corner of his mouth twitched. "Not nearly enough."

It wasn't a perfect plan, by any means. And he'd have to delay the construction of other projects to divert labor and materials to this new one. But even he would feel safer with a wall between him and the wilderness of Erna. And not just for symbolic reasons.

"You need to tell the colony what Jeff saw," Dani urged. "Don't wait for it to get out by some other means. You don't want people to think you've been hiding things from them."

But I am hiding things from them, Leo thought. *More and more with each passing day.* What was it an ancient poet had written? *Oh, what a tangled web we weave, when first we practice to deceive.* It bothered him that he couldn't remember which poet. Memories from Earth were slipping through his fingers.

Every day that he failed to fully inform the colony—to *trust* the colony—the potential complications multiplied geometrically. Dani was right. The others needed to know.

"After true night," he said at last. "Let them deal with that first. And if we can get a few of the cargo pods set up by then, we'll have solid shelter that can accommodate everyone, ready to go." *Not to mention it will give me time to review everyone's psych profiles, so that I know who is likely to take the news the worst.*

After lunch it rained.

Johnny had warned them that precipitation was coming, but hadn't warned them about how heavy it would be. With sheets of water slashing down from the sky, no outdoor work was going to take place for a while—including moving the cargo pods. And if the rain went on for long enough, the ground would become sodden, making that job twice as difficult tomorrow.

Sometimes it seemed like the planet itself was going out of its way to screw with them.

A few people took the opportunity to pair off for private activities, either in an empty pod or one of the tents. Privacy was a scarce commodity now that the forest was no longer considered safe. The rest of the colony gathered in the mess tent. Leo had brought in the parachutes from the landing, and people gathered around them, picking apart the panels stitch by stitch, like an old-fashioned sewing bee. The parachutes had been designed to provide fabric for future projects, so the panels were in colors one might use to make clothing: denim blue, khaki, camo, and a host of patterns ranging from subtle to cheery. When they ran out of the raw material their printer needed to produce cloth, they'd be glad to have a stockpile of usable fabric.

Then Malik brought out a guitar, and other instruments appeared, some in better condition than others. Enough people had brought small instruments along that soon there was music to compete with the pounding of rain on the solar panels overhead. Almost homey.

This is how it should have been, Leo thought wistfully. *No dismembered hearts, no serpents from Hell, just a small community facing the prosaic challenges of this world together.*

He sought out the other members of his inner circle and filled them in on what Jeff had said, then headed back to his office to start going over everyone's profiles. The nine of them would meet in the morning to discuss everything, and after that . . . After that they would need a game plan.

He left his door open so he could hear the music.

The dinner bell woke Ian up.

For a moment he just lay there, not sure what was going on. He didn't feel hungry, and there was no sunlight brightening the tent cloth, so no meal was being served. Yet all around him people were rising from their cots. One of them turned on a lamp; the sudden light hurt Ian's eyes and he turned away.

"Hey, sleeping beauty!" Someone kicked his cot, jarring him fully awake. "You wanted to see this more than anyone."

True night! That was what they were talking about, he realized suddenly: true night. Had the rain stopped? When he'd gone to sleep it had seemed like the sky wouldn't clear in time. But he could no longer hear the patter of rain on the tent's roof, so maybe people would have a clear view.

Or lack of view, more accurately.

He disentangled himself from his blanket, grabbed a lantern of his own from the hook near the door flap, and followed the others out. Those who were carrying lights were using the dimmest setting, just enough light to keep them from stumbling over unseen obstacles without compromising night's darkness. As people gathered in the southern field it was as if a swarm of fireflies had arrived. There were lights from atop a few of the pods as well, where armed sentries with night goggles would stand watch during the event, alert for the approach of anything that didn't belong inside the camp.

Loki was setting in the east now, distant mountains silhouetted black against its final glowing sliver. There was so little light coming from the heavens that the night already seemed pitch-black, and it was hard to imagine that when that sliver was swallowed by the horizon it would make any substantive difference. Dark was dark, right? The mere setting of a moon shouldn't have been exciting enough to draw half the colony out of their beds. But the fact that this was an alien event—a uniquely Ernan event—made it feel like a rite of passage.

Purple snakes rising from the darkness. That was what Leo said Jeff had described. Ian wondered if these people would be embracing total darkness quite as enthusiastically if they knew about that. More likely they'd be huddling in their tents with solar lamps blazing, like in Jeff's pod.

"One minute and counting!" Joshua announced.

All that was visible of Loki now were points of light between the distant mountains: jewels sparkling at the edge of the world. Joshua began to count loudly down to totality, and people joined in. Ian had a flashback to a New Year's Eve party he had once attended, with fireworks ready to be launched the moment a glowing ball hit the ground. *Nine! Eight! Seven!* People were turning off their lamps so that they could experience true night in all its glory, firefly after firefly snuffed out. Some joined hands, creating a human chain of expectation. That was a little much for Ian, and he moved away from the gathering, not wanting to be distracted by someone grabbing hold of him. *Three! Two!* He wound up near the boundary fence, between two of the pods, and gazed out at the grasslands. Or rather, at the lightless expanse that had once been grass. The ground was as black as the sky overhead, even more so as he turned off his lantern to greet the true night. An expectant shiver ran through him.

Then Joshua's counting concluded—*One!*—and the black monster at the edge of the world swallowed the last few jewels, casting Erna into total darkness. Intellectually Ian knew that it was no different than the darkness of a few seconds before, but it *felt* different, in a way that was hard to define. And it awakened a visceral fear inside him that no mere darkness should have, all the more unnerving because he didn't know why he felt that way. Domina would rise in a mere four minutes, he knew that. Yet deep within his soul, in the shadowy recesses where mankind's most primitive instincts lay coiled like serpents, it felt as if the light was gone forever. He wanted to run away—he *needed* to run away—but there was nowhere to run to. Blackness had swallowed the universe.

This is Erna, he told himself. He had to force himself not to turn on the lantern again. *Not an alien world, but our home. This darkness is part of it. We can't run from it any more than we can run from the air or the sky.* He hesitated for a moment, then opened his arms wide. "Come," he whispered to Erna. "Make me yours." And for a moment he imagined that all his senses were sharper, so that he could smell the grass beneath his feet, hear the sound of leaves shifting in the distance, and even see subtle variations in the darkness surrounding him.

And more.

Light was rising now, as if flowing forth from the earth: a strange blue glow, dim in illumination but intense in color. He could see currents in it, and as the light intensified waves became visible; they seemed to pulse across the ground in time to the pounding of Ian's heart. It was as if the entire field was a vast luminescent lake, and he was part of it. The sight of it was mesmerizing enough, but the sensation—the sensation!— was like nothing he had ever felt before. Fear and awe in such perfect balance that he was frozen in place, as if any human movement might banish the alien display. Was this experience even real, or was it a bizarre hallucination brought on by Erna's unnerving darkness? Was his mind perhaps so hungry for light that he was creating the illusion of it, drawing upon his memories of bioluminescent seas back home?

He forced himself to look away from the hypnotic display and back toward the camp, to see if the strange light was visible there as well. And it was, but in a very different form. Whereas the light outside the camp flowed smoothly over the ground, rhythmic waves rippling across the grasslands with mesmeric calm, inside the camp the waves were shattering, frothing into the air as they came in contact with the colonists, sending cascades of tiny sparks into the air that hung there for a second before sinking down once more into the tide. It was wild, like the whitewater of a raging river.

And not a single person was looking down. He could see that by the dim light that the tide afforded: not one single colonist was staring at the ground, wondering at the azure light that surged around their feet. Everyone was looking upward, their attention fixed on the black horizon as they waited for Domina to appear. Clearly none of them were seeing what he was. The implications of that were chilling.

I'm going mad.

He turned away from the camp and shut his eyes for a moment, telling himself that there was nothing really there. His mind was just playing tricks on him. Once he accepted that, maybe he could banish the delusion. But when he dared to open his eyes again the currents were still present, brighter than ever. Had he really expected them to disappear? Or did he know in his gut that this was something real, even if he couldn't assign a Terran name to it?

Pull yourself together, he told himself sternly. *You're a scientist. Act like one.* He hooked the dark lantern onto his belt to free his hands, then reached into his back pocket and pulled out a few of the small specimen bags he always carried with him. Crouching down (close to the light, so very close!) he lowered one into the strange blue tide, holding it so that a current of light flowed directly into it. He shivered as he did so, anticipating . . . what? That he would feel liquid flowing over his hands, or fire, or some alien, unfathomable substance? But the light had no physical presence at all, and though goosebumps rose along his arms when he submerged his hands in it, he felt nothing. After a moment he sealed the bag, then repeated the process with a second one. If there was some kind of organism causing this display—as there was when the oceans of Earth produced similar light—hopefully he'd just captured a sample.

Suddenly a new movement caught his eye. From a place near one of the pods, deep violet light was rising up from the ground. It didn't appear in a shapeless tide like the blue light had, but took on a distinct shape, long and slender. Like a tentacle. Another followed, and then another. Snakes rising from a nest, alight with purple fire. Their color was so dark he could barely see them, yet so intense that it burned his eyes to look at them directly.

Purple serpents.

With a sinking in the pit of his stomach he stepped back quickly, stumbling on the uneven ground. Were these the same serpents that Jeff had described, that had killed Wayne? They were coming toward him now, slithering across the ground as if drawn by the heat of his life, the power of his scrutiny. *What the hell are you?* he wanted to scream. Every instinct in his soul was crying out for him to run away, but he dared not turn his back on them for a moment. And weren't some predators triggered by the flight of their prey? He backed away as quickly as he could, watching in horror as violet tendrils slithered across the ground, mirroring his every step.

And then there was light. Domina's leading edge had finally breached the horizon, and he could feel its light spreading across the land, not yet bright enough for a human to see by, but natural, blessedly natural. The purple mist-serpents felt it as well. They flinched and began to withdraw, to return to whatever Hell had spawned them. Back, back they drew, and as they sank into the earth the last bits of foul violet light were swallowed by the blue tide, and vanished.

But the blue light was fading as well now, as the moonlight gradually intensified. Unlike the violet serpents it didn't sink into the earth but faded slowly. Or perhaps it was still there in all its strength, but he was losing the ability to see it. He tried with all his might to hold onto his vision, but even as he watched, the blue currents faded to thin veils, then disappeared entirely.

Ian took up his lantern and turned it on, to see what was left. All he saw was dirt and grass, the normal elements of a mundane landscape. Nowhere was there even a hint that it had ever been anything else. He looked back toward the camp, where people were starting to relax. A few were even laughing nervously. True night was over, for them.

But not for him.

He looked at the specimen bags he had tried to fill. They were empty. "I'm not insane," he whispered. Trying to convince himself. "I'm really not." But the words sounded hollow, even to him.

Nine

Ian was the last to arrive for the meeting. He had planned it that way. The last thing he wanted after a long night of frustrating experiments was to have to sit there while everyone made small talk around him, trying to look normal. He didn't have the energy or interest to engage in superficial chat right now, much less field nine different versions of "Are you all right?" or "You look tired."

He wasn't sure he was sane, and he didn't want to talk about it.

The only seat available was at the rear end of the office pod, directly facing Leo. The colony commander didn't look like he'd gotten much sleep himself, but as usual he was making an effort to look strong and confident. It worked better on some occasions than others, but Ian always appreciated the effort. Someone needed to look strong while things were going to hell around them. When Leo looked his way Ian tried his best to look equally steady, but subterfuge had never been his strong point, and he felt strangely naked before that piercing gaze.

What did it mean, that Ian had found no evidence to prove the blue light was real? *Lack of evidence isn't proof of anything*, he reminded himself. *I didn't even know what kind of proof to look for.* But the thought offered little comfort.

"All right," Leo said. "We're all here now. Let's begin with a round of observations." He looked at Ian, a slightly raised eyebrow suggesting that he had seen past the botanist's façade and wanted to know the reason for his mood. "You want to start us off?"

Lips tight, Ian shook his head. "The others can go first."

So around the circle they went. Lise went first, describing the crowd of colonists that had greeted her at sunrise, seeking medication for one thing or another. Headaches, anxiety, nausea—symptoms of a stressful night, she said. Nothing significant or mysterious. The medications from Earth were still potent enough to handle such mundane issues, which was good, but although the colony now had bins full of analgesics and sedatives, the supply was nonetheless finite. The colonists would have to learn to deal with minor discomforts on their own, if the supply was to last until they could produce local substitutes.

"I've set up fermentation tanks in the module to breed Penicillium mold," she told them. "As soon as the first batch is mature we can start to make our own antibiotics."

How her eyes gleamed as she reported that! What a milestone it would be, for the colony to be able to produce its own medicines! One more step toward true independence. How rewarding it must be, Ian thought, to achieve something measurable, rather than chase after the intangible!

Then it was Dani's turn.

She had done her share of counseling that morning, mostly guiding people in calming meditation after a night of strange dreams. The nightmares themselves were no surprise—the true night seemed to have opened the floodgate for bad dreams—but the similarities of some of the dreams was disconcerting. The more details she described, the more Ian leaned forward to listen, drawn to her words with an almost physical force. More than one person had dreamed of a strange blue light, she reported, that either emanated from the ground or flowed along it, like water. Some had seen sparks of blue fire, like in Sally Chang's recurring nightmare.

If he was going mad, then others shared his madness.

Finally the others were done, and Leo turned to him. Ian inhaled slowly, taking a moment to steady his nerves. He didn't want his voice to betray how uncertain he felt about his own observations. Then he said,

"I saw it. Not in dreams. For real." When he saw that some seemed confused about what he was describing, he clarified, "The blue light. What others saw in their dreams. I saw it while I was awake." *Which still doesn't rule out the possibility of delusion*, he reminded himself. God knows there were times in Earth history when a group of people had shared the same delusion. Sometimes a whole community. But surely if he was having visions of the same thing that others were dreaming about, that meant that something real must have caused it, right?

"I was looking out at the land beyond the camp, when a strange light seemed to rise up from the ground. A blue glow that rippled in waves over the grass, like water. There were visible currents, and in a few places it looked like they were flowing around invisible obstacles. It was . . ." He drew in a deep breath. *Beautiful. Terrifying.* "Otherworldly." Then he smiled faintly. "For whatever that word means on an alien planet. Sometimes parts of the current would go dark, and be nearly invisible, and then they would brighten again, to almost neon intensity. It looked like they were reacting to something on the ground. I honestly wasn't sure if the whole vision was real or not, or if my mind was just playing tricks on me. But then I heard your report." He looked pointedly at Dani. "Clearly it wasn't my imagination. Or at least, not *only* my imagination." The last statement was a question.

"When did it start?" Leo asked. "Before or after the true darkness began?"

At least Leo was taking him seriously; that was reassuring. The knot in his chest eased a bit. "I'm not sure. That's when it became visible, but it could have been there before that, and I just became able to see it. I don't know." He paused for a moment, struggling to find the right words to communicate what he had felt last night. "Have you ever seen those pictures that are made to trick the eye? They seem like normal art at first glance, but when you start to look away, or your eyes go slightly out of focus, suddenly you realize there's another picture hidden within the first, that you couldn't see when you were looking directly at it. You have to *not look* for it, in order to see it."

"Magic Eye," Anna supplied.

Ian nodded. "Exactly. This felt like one of those pictures. There was a moment when my eyes suddenly focused properly—or perhaps, *unfocused* properly—and then the light was visible. Maybe it had been there all along, like in those pictures. Or maybe the true night generated it somehow." He shook his head. "I've replayed it in my mind a thousand times, but I'm still not sure."

"Sally Chang has been dreaming about her blue fire for a while," Dani offered. "So that wasn't dependent on the true night."

"Did the stuff you saw look like fire?" Johnny asked Ian.

"There were parts of it could be mistaken for that," Ian said. "If you didn't see all the rest."

"That argues for it having been here all along," Pravida mused. "But maybe the true night is what made it visible in something other than dreams."

"To humans," Joshua reminded her. "We have no idea what the local wildlife is seeing. Maybe that kind of landscape is normal in their eyes."

The concept that all the animals on Erna might be seeing something that humans couldn't was unnerving; what if Terran life forms weren't equipped to perceive this world properly? That would be one hell of a handicap to have to deal with. "I tried taking samples," Ian said. "Not that I had the best equipment for it." He pulled two small plastic bags out of his pocket to show them. "I figured whatever was causing the light show, maybe I could capture a bit of it to study." *To prove it was real*, he thought.

Leo's eyes narrowed. "That is assuming there was anything to capture. Light itself has no substance."

"No, but the things that create it do. Back on Earth there are numerous species that can do that."

"Bioluminescence," Ted mused. "Is that what it looked like?"

Ian nodded. "I've seen a glow like that on the shores of New Zealand—waves of blue light breaking against the beach. *The Aurora of the Sea*, they call it. In that case it's caused by plankton, but many other species on Earth can conjure light: Insects, fish, algae, even bacteria."

"And worm spit," Ted reminded him. "Don't forget worm spit."

Despite his mood, Ian smiled slightly. "And worm spit. The salient point is, light like that doesn't just appear out of nowhere; it almost always has a biological source. So I figured whatever was causing this light show, maybe I could scoop up a bit of it to study later. But I got nothing." He shook his head in frustration. "A few grains of pollen, dust, insect detritus, just like you'd expect to be floating around in the air over a grassy field. Nothing that showed any sign of luminescent potential."

"Don't forget about the Northern Lights back home," Johnny said. "Nothing there could be captured in a specimen bag."

"But those don't cling to the ground like this did. And . . ." He hesitated. "There's more." Now he would have to depart from Dani's narrative, and with it the precious anchor of common experience that had been keeping his spirit steady. *Jeff saw the same thing I did,* he reminded himself. But seeing the same thing as someone who was mentally unstable wasn't exactly comforting.

"There was violet light as well. The deep shade of purple that bleeds from an ultraviolet lamp, at the very limits of human perception. It was mist-like, as if it had physical substance. Tendrils of fog, rising up from the ground like living creatures. . . ." He shuddered.

"Jeff's purple snakes?" Lise asked.

Ian hesitated. "Could be. I didn't see what Jeff did, so it's hard for me to compare. But these seemed to be coming toward me, almost like they were sniffing me out. I backed away as fast as I could." He was looking down at the floor now, so that their reactions wouldn't distract him from the memory. "As soon as Domina appeared they began to pull back, and then just disappeared into the ground again." He drew in a deep breath. "I returned to that spot after the sun came up. I wanted to see if anything there might explain what I'd seen. I found . . ."

For a moment he couldn't continue. He was remembering the sharp bite of fear he'd felt during that exploration.

Lise said gently, "Ian?"

"I found an animal burrow," he told them. "Probably the opening to some kind of underground warren. It was exactly where the purple light had appeared. As if the light had been deep inside those burrows, waiting for darkness to fall." *Or waiting for a human to come near enough for it to touch.* He shuddered.

"Purple snakes rising out of darkness," Dani said quietly. "That's what Jeff described."

Ian nodded.

"But Wayne wasn't killed during a completely dark night," Pravida said. "At least one moon was out, as I recall."

"But the waste pit was enclosed," Lise reminded her. "Maybe that blocked out enough light to accommodate these . . . things."

No doubt everyone was remembering what the misty 'snakes' had done to Wayne. It was something Ian had been trying hard not to think about, given that he might have come close to suffering the same fate. But the fact that this group had taken his report seriously, and was trying to come up with theories to explain where the things came from, eased his spirit a bit. At least they believed that his vision was real. "There's more," he warned.

"Jesus," Joshua muttered. "Worse than that?"

His lips tightened. "That depends on how you interpret it."

He told them about the blue light inside the camp, how the serene force that flowed across the grasslands became turbulent and chaotic inside human territory. And not only where humans were standing, but anywhere within the camp's border.

"Shit." Ted whistled softly. "I just . . . holy shit."

Ian drew in a deep breath. "Whatever this stuff is, it doesn't like humans."

There was silence for a moment as the implications of that sank in. Finally Anna said, "You're thinking—what? That it's somehow sentient?"

Ian hesitated. "The snakes seemed to have conscious intent. The blue stuff? I don't know. But it's clear that our presence here disturbs it."

"What if it was some kind of network?" Ted offered. "Some kind of force, or life form, that connects all the local species? That would explain what happened to the insects. The network identified us as bad, so the local life fled."

Ian nodded. "Like a mycorrhizal network."

"Yes."

"But what's providing the connection? It would have to be something humans lack."

"Or don't know how to use."

Joshua scowled. "In English, please."

Ian's mind was racing now. So many possibilities! It was hard to slow his thoughts down to focus on any one of them. "Back on earth, there are fungi that live underground, that can connect to trees. They can pass water and nutrients from one tree to another, and if one is attacked by insects, others are chemically 'warned' so they can take defensive action. All without thought or intention. Just biochemical signals."

Ted's eyes were bright with excitement now. "There are whole forests that are networked, so that all the trees there are extensions of the same living entity. A sort of vegetative hive mind. Why couldn't that happen here? Only not just with trees, this time. With all living creatures."

"That would not only explain the insects," Pravida allowed, "but the attacks as well. If the network sees us as an alien invader—disconnected from the whole—it might respond to us as a body responds to an infection . . . ." Her voice trailed off into silence.

"What you're suggesting," Johnny said, very quietly, "is that the planet hates us."

Lise shook her head. "That would imply sentience. A global consciousness. Nothing like that exists on the other colony worlds."

"That we know of," Anna reminded her. "Maybe the other planets are just more . . . friendly."

"Again," Johnny observed, "the language of sentience."

"Any sufficiently complex system can appear sentient," Ted told them. "Look at how we talk about evolution—as if nature had conscious intent and planned the best adaptations. We know intellectually that's not how it works, but it can appear that way if we only look at the end results. The point is . . ." He drew in a deep breath. "This ecosystem appears to be rejecting us. That may be what cost two people their lives. Obviously not a viable situation. But what the fuck are we supposed to do about it?"

For a moment there was silence. *How do you address an infection when you are the infecting agent?* Ian wondered.

"Okay," Pravida said at last. "If we're going to start talking strategy, we need a name for this phenomenon. We can't keep calling it 'the mysterious network that appears as blue light in people's dreams.'"

Lise was about to respond, but suddenly there was a loud boom from outside the pod; the floor shook. An explosion?

Leo was first to the door. As he opened it, a wave of acrid smoke greeted them. They all covered their mouths as they exited, with whatever fold of clothing they could. But then the cloud blew past, giving them a clear view of the place where the palisade was being erected.

A tractor was burning.

It was the largest one they had, and with the help of a backhoe attachment it had been digging a narrow trench for trimmed tree trunks to be set into. Now the tractor was consumed by fire, waves of smoke belching forth into an otherwise pristine sky. A woman was being dragged away from it—the operator?—while others gathered around her. Yet others were shoveling dirt onto the flames, from the mounds of loose soil the backhoe had just gathered.

Lise hurried to where the operator was being tended to, and knelt down by the woman's side to check her out. Her face was streaked with soot, making it hard to identify her at first, but after a moment Ian saw that it was Melisande Seely, a member of the construction team. It didn't appear she'd been badly burned, thank God. She was coughing, but after Lise examined her for a moment she seemed satisfied. "She'll be all right," she announced. "But I'll give her a full checkup at the clinic to make sure."

Leo crouched down by Melisande's side. "What happened here?"

The woman wiped sweat-soaked soot from her eyes with the back of a sleeve. "Damned if I know." Her voice was shaking. "It was digging just fine for a while. Then I smelled oil smoking, and I got down from the cab to check the engine, and then—it just blew." She shook her head. "Thank God I'd climbed down to check it."

The flames were dying down now, leaving behind a charred metal armature splattered with dirt. The vehicle looked beyond saving, but hopefully at least the backhoe attachment was salvageable; the colony couldn't afford to lose that.

Looking at the ruined cab, Ian thought, *The same technology that makes it possible for us to tame this new world makes us vulnerable. What would happen to us if it all disappeared tomorrow? Would our book-learned skills be enough to save us?*

"That's the second tractor to fail," Ted said from behind him. "Unlikely to be a coincidence, don't you think? The tractors in all the other colonies worked fine, so the problem isn't our equipment."

Ian turned to look at him. "What are you suggesting?"

"Well, if there is something here that hates humans . . ." He nodded toward the tractor. "Maybe it would attack the things we need to survive."

Ian's eyes narrowed. "You know that sounds fucking crazy, right?"

"This whole place is fucking crazy."

"You're suggesting that a biological network—assuming that's what we're dealing with—could not only manipulate living things, but destroy machines. That seems a bit fantastic, even for an alien world."

"Is it? A single bird can bring down a jet plane. Mold can foul an electrical connection." Ted gestured back toward the camp. "There's nothing we brought with us that biological entities couldn't destroy. Assuming they were directed properly."

"None of which would explain the attacks on people. Tia appears to have been killed by something straight out of a Filipino horror vid. Wayne died in the same way as someone in a science fiction movie. How would a biological network know what we were thinking? What we *feared*?"

For a long moment Ted said nothing. The two of them just stood there, watching as the smoldering ruins of the tractor slowly cooled, the last tendrils of smoke dispersed by the breeze.

"Just because we don't understand something," Ted said at last, "doesn't mean it's not possible."

Ten

Commander's Personal Log
Year One
Day Seven

We have given a name to the strange blue force: fae. It was Ian's suggestion, unanimously approved. It harkens back to Terran legends of mysterious lights that lured men to other worlds—or perhaps to their deaths—and of shadowy creatures that might be either good or evil, who took pleasure in toying with mankind. Whatever is causing the phenomenon here, there is no denying that it appears magical, so the name suits it.

That said, if it is a natural force, woven into the fabric of this world, such forces have no emotions, no intentions, and no guiding intelligence. They are as likely to favor you as to harm you. We must keep reminding ourselves of that, as we seek to analyze the events of recent days. "The planet hates humans" is a tempting metaphor, but ultimately misleading.

Tonight I will tell the colony about the fae. It's not right to keep the truth from them any longer. But I can't share all the details. Telling people that an unseen force has been killing our people and attacking our equipment, and we have no clue how to defend ourselves, would be the equivalent of locking a man in a box and pumping in toxic gas. He can't flee and he can't fight, so what happens when his most primitive instincts demand he do one or the other? Our world may be larger than a box, but given the circumstances, such distinctions are moot. We are trapped as surely as that man is, unable to flee from this planet but lacking the knowledge we need to protect ourselves. Some may realize how bad the situation is once I tell them about the fae, but for most it will take a while, and I will not hasten the moment when two hundred people must be told how existentially fucked we are.

☽ ☽ ☽

Angie Carmelo was working outside the mess tent when Ian found her. She had one of the battery units disassembled and was so focused on the tangle of wires in front of her that she didn't even see him at first.

He waited a few seconds to see if she would notice him standing there—she didn't—then said, "Hey."

She looked up and smiled. "Hey, Ian. What's up?"

"Nothing urgent. Can you spare a few minutes?"

"I'm almost done. Give me a bit."

He nodded. As she turned back to the unit she explained, "Two of the batteries in the main array gave out this morning." She was twisting the wires one by one back into their proper position. "Losing one would have been a bad enough piece of luck, but two at the same time . . . shitty coincidence, huh?"

Given the discussion in the pod, it was hard for Ian to view it as only that. Every coincidence seemed suspect to him now. But she didn't share his knowledge and hence didn't share his misgivings, so he kept a casual smile on his face and just said, "Good thing you can fix them."

"One of them." She picked up the cover of the unit and snapped it back into place. "The other one, I don't know what the fuck is wrong with it." She wiped her hands on the front of her jeans as she stood. "I have nightmares about our solar collectors failing, you know. Pretty much every night. No power, no tech—not a pretty picture." She looked at him. "So what's the question?"

He hesitated. She had nightmares about the collectors failing, then they started to fail. Just like with Rod. How often was this kind of thing happening in the camp? The destruction of a tractor was public and dramatic, but smaller, more trivial malfunctions might not even be reported. No one outside Leo's inner circle was watching for them.

If he could find a way to change that pattern, to keep peoples' own fears from jinxing them, he would go down in history as the man who had saved the colony. The savior who had led them out of darkness. The thought was a rush; it was all he could do to stay focused on the moment's business.

"Ian?"

He forced himself back to the present. "You showed me a medallion you were wearing, back in Orientation. I was wondering if you still had it."

She raised an eyebrow in curiosity, then reached inside her shirt and pulled out a small silver medallion on a black cord. "This?"

He nodded.

She took it off and handed it to him. It was the same as he remembered: a flat silver disk with geometric designs etched into each side. Circles and crosses and bits of ancient script were arranged inside and around those circles. The design had an ancient feel to it. "You said this was for protection?"

"I told you it was originally designed for that purpose, yes." She smiled slightly. "It was a gift from someone back on Earth, who thought my work might stir up demons."

"I doubt there are Terran demons in this place."

She chuckled. "No, they all died in stasis." She took the necklace from him and slipped it back over her head. "Seriously, Ian, what's this about?"

He drew in a deep breath. "You said you wrote a paper once on the application of traditional symbology in neurological research."

"In a previous life, yes. But I don't imagine anyone on Erna will be worrying about neural interfaces for a while. Probably not in my lifetime."

"You believe that primitive symbology can be used to control electromagnetic output from the brain?"

With a sigh she leaned back on the battery housing, balancing herself on its edge. "If you want to render twelve thousand words and several years of research into a single sentence, yeah, that's pretty much the gist of it. Why?"

"I'm doing some experiments with local plant species," he said. "Trying to see if human brainwaves can affect their growth." Hopefully that would sound reasonable enough to avoid any probing questions.

She considered for a moment, then nodded. "If brainwaves are strong enough to be detected outside the body, I suppose it might be possible that plants would sense them. Not sure how that would affect them. Never worked with plants myself. Certainly an interesting question. What do you need from me?"

"I'm trying to figure out how to fine-tune neural output so I can control what the plants are receiving."

"Okay." She nodded. "Well, I proposed that since spiritual symbols ultimately become embedded in human culture, we absorb their meaning unconsciously from our earliest days, and they can be used to influence neural responses. Triggers for emotion, if you will."

"So your medallion . . ."

"The symbols on it are associated with protection. By wearing it, I stimulate pathways in my brain that make me feel safe, and perhaps will cause me to exercise more caution, thus making me safer in fact. That's the theory, anyway." She looked down at it. "Like I said, it was a gift."

"And the neural interface part of your research?"

"Normally it takes time for a person to learn how to stimulate different parts of his brain, to control a computer, voice replicator, prosthetic, whatever. My goal was to shorten the learning curve. If we use culturally embedded symbols for stimuli, I reasoned, there are neural pathways already in place. Tapping into them can shorten the training period considerably." She paused. "That was confirmed in a double-blind study, validating my work. But evidently that wasn't enough for the scientific establishment to take me seriously. The traditional mind rebels at the thought that the Pentagram of Solomon might help control a technological device." She shrugged. "I thought I would improve the world, but all I did was provide fodder for tabloids."

"Is that why you left?"

She bit her lip for a moment. "One of the many reasons." She waved a hand to dismiss the subject. "Anyway, what do you need? Training in applied symbology?"

"If you've got the time. Just for a few key emotions." He smiled slightly. "I doubt plants care much about subtlety."

"Shit. I've got all the time in the world." With a grin she spread her arms wide. "Isn't that what this place is all about?"

ꙧ ꙧ ꙧ

With a flutter of brightly colored wings the bird launches itself from its perch and takes to the sky, flying directly over Lise and Leo as it does so. Its scarlet feathers trail behind it like streamers of fire as it cuts across a field of clean blue, pristine and perfect. There is no choking smog here. No industrial fumes. No sense of a planet that is gasping for breath as it dies, or towering cities that are graveyards of hope. At this moment, in this place, the rest of the world called Earth does not exist.

Lying on the damp grass beside Leo, Lise shuts her eyes for a moment, drinking in the scents and sounds of her native planet, trying to fix it all in her memory. Once not so long ago, a day like this would not have seemed noteworthy. The skies had been clean back then, nature abundant. Thank God the Preserves were established before all that was gone, so that a few oases remained. And thank God the Colonial Orientation Project had been given a corner of the Amazon Preserve so they could teach the colonists how to deal with nature.

Soon we'll have a whole planet like this, she tells herself. Endless expanses of clean air and sunshine. Less than a week now. Soon the great ship would load, its passengers would surrender to stasis, and

Earth's newest colony would head out in search of an unpolluted planet to claim. The thought of it sends a shiver of delight down her spine.

"We probably shouldn't have skipped the meeting," Leo murmurs.

She chuckles. "What are they going to do, strike us from the roster? You're the colony commander now, remember? And I'm chief medical officer. We'd have to do far worse than sneak off for a picnic before they cancelled our tickets." She reaches out and strokes his cheek gently; In the tropical sunshine her pale fingers glow like alabaster against the polished mahogany of his skin. Sharing affection with him is a symphony of contrast, as pleasing to the eye as to more primitive senses. The thought stirs hunger inside her, but also wariness.

She leans down and kisses him, gently at first, and when that is well received, more deeply. He draws her to him, wrapping his arms around her until her entire body is pressed against his. She can feel the heat of his body enveloping her, the pounding of his heart against her own chest. Then he reaches one hand up to slide his fingers through her long hair, and the other down to grasp her thigh, while she runs her fingers down the side of his chest, to where his heat is centered. Could it be that they will finally consummate this new relationship, out here in the open, surrendering to nature like wild animals do? The thought is intoxicating.

But the shadows are still strong in him, and after a moment she can sense them coming to the fore, as always. Her heart sinks as she senses his spirit drawing away from her, and she knows that nothing she might say or do will bring him back. Though he continues to embrace her, he is operating on automatic now; his mind is elsewhere. With a sigh she disentangles herself from his arms and lies down by his side again, laying her head on his chest.

"I'm sorry," he whispers.

"I understand," she says softly.

She doesn't know all the details of what happened with his son, but she does know that he blames himself for the boy's death, and that guilt has erected barriers around his soul. Deep inside, he doesn't believe he is worthy of love. That will change when he leaves Earth, the psyche evaluator assured them. It's a pattern so common that it even has a name: Colonial Mnemonic Syndrome. Many people leave Earth to es-

cape painful memories, and heading out to a distant planet seems to achieve that better than travelling within the home system. Maybe it is a side effect of prolonged stasis, altering the pathways of memory. Or maybe it is the knowledge that no one from the Colonies ever comes home—that one's life is being severed cleanly in two, the Terran part being left behind forever. Whatever the cause, the psych team seems confident that this trip will give Leo a fresh start. And when the shadows of grief and guilt finally loosen their death-grip on his soul, maybe he will be able to let another person into his heart.

It may take a while. But some men are worth waiting for.

By the time Leo returned to his office, the workday had nearly ended. The afternoon shift had been long but productive, and even with their largest tractor gone the colonists had managed to get a good stretch of palisade erected. At the eastern end of the wall a metal shelter now served as part of the barrier, made from three cargo pods attached end-to-end. Vents and doorways had been cut into the steel shells, turning the pods into one long facility, and some of the precious synthetic material from Earth had been used to create double-decker platforms running down the length of one wall, that could be used for seating during the day and sleeping at night. It would take a lot more work to make the space truly livable, especially when summer's heat warmed the giant box like an oven, but at least this was a start.

The resulting longhouse was narrow and stark, but strangely comforting. Most of the colonists had grown up in similar spaces, cargo units stacked high to create featureless apartment buildings, each one identical to the next. Less than two weeks ago in subjective time, these people had wanted nothing more than to escape that kind of surrounding forever; now they longed for the kind of safety—and sanity—they had once taken for granted. A dozen people had already marked out their bunk spaces on the upper platform, and Leo expected that more would soon follow, especially if there were any more surprise attacks or explosions.

But thus far today no one had died, and nothing had blown up. That shouldn't be the kind of thing one was grateful for, but this was Erna, where nothing could be taken for granted, and the fact that night was falling with no catastrophe to record was somewhat comforting. But he'd been hearing reports of small technological failures throughout the camp, so minor they hardly seemed significant on their own, but chilling in aggregate. Power tools glitched, solar batteries failed to charge, diagnostic tools gave inconsistent results: he understood now how all those events might be connected, and dreaded each new report. If it turned out that some unseen entity was indeed sabotaging their technology—not to mention killing people—it could stress the colony in ways they couldn't address.

We don't know for a fact that's what's happening, he told himself. But as each new incident was reported to him, it became harder and harder to deny the connection. And he was the one who must decide when and how that connection would be explained to the population at large.

On the seventh day God rested, he thought. Was it right to be jealous of a deity? He ached for a good night's sleep.

Tonight he was going to decide who would be his second-in-command, ready to take over his job should he be incapacitated or killed. It was a disturbing task, but one he couldn't avoid. That he had to choose one of his inner circle went without saying, but those people already had duties of their own, and asking them to do this as well meant they would be distracted from their work. So on whose head should he place the thorned wreath of authority in this terrible place?

Lise was going to meet with him later to go over everyone's personnel files and help him decide. She was one person he clearly couldn't choose for the job, because her service as head of the medical team was too vital to compromise. But he trusted her more than any other to give him sound advice.

"Leo!"

He turned and saw Dani jogging toward him. "What's up? Everything okay?"

She nodded to reassure him as she joined him. "I'd like permission to set up a chapel. A space that wouldn't be used for anything else."

He glanced at the half-finished palisade. "Dani, it's going to be a while before we can think about new building projects." She of all people should understand that.

But she waved off the objection. "It doesn't have to be a building. A meeting tent is fine. But something earmarked specifically for religious services." She smiled slightly. "Not that holding a prayer meeting next to someone cooking breakfast isn't a deeply meaningful experience."

"This isn't a very religious group," he reminded her. The fact that colonists had been chosen from so many different backgrounds for the sake of genetic diversity meant there were almost as many varieties of faith on Erna as there were people, so Colony Control had sought candidates who could handle that kind of situation. Most of the people here had little or no interest in religion.

"Men turn to faith when their world is most uncertain," she told him. "And given what may be on the horizon for us, I think we may need such a space. Not only for formal services, but to serve as spiritual refuge. Somewhere that people can retreat to for a sense of safety. And we should have it in place before we need it, so that it is ready and waiting."

He considered the suggestion. "Where would you put it?"

"North end of the camp. That's really the only option, given the new palisade. The southern field gets too much traffic."

"Between the memorial garden and the quarantine pod."

"It was traditional on Earth to build churches next to cemeteries. It sanctified the ground there and comforted mourners."

He nodded. "All right. See what we have left in stock and take what you need. But you'll have to recruit volunteers to set it up; I can't spare anyone from the regular construction teams right now."

"Understood. Thank you."

She could run the colony, he thought as she walked away. *People trust her. They seek her guidance. Weren't those the qualities Colony Control saw in me, that made them think I was right for this job?*

He sighed heavily. *Damn that day!*

When he got to his office he turned on his tablet and called up the profiles of the other seven counselors. Ian, Ted, and Pravida weren't options, because their expertise in analyzing alien life-forms was crucial right now, and they needed to stay focused on that. There were a few notes in Ian's file that concerned him, regarding the botanist's desire for public acclaim. A colony commander must focus on the welfare of the whole community, and not worry about who got credit for what. Johnny's astronomical studies were no longer a full time project, but he was a bit of a hothead. That left three possibilities. Leo scrolled through their files, looking for any detail that might cause him to favor one or the other.

"Daddy . . ."

The sound was a whisper, barely audible, but it sent a chill down his spine. The voice of a ghost—a memory. He twisted around and saw the figure of a young boy standing in the shadows at the far end of the pod.

His son.

The boy looked just like he had when Leo had dropped him off at the Center that ill-fated day, his dark skin neither lacerated nor burned yet, but gleaming with ebony health. He was even wearing the same clothing he'd had on that day. For one dizzying moment it was as if past and present merged: Leo was back on Earth preparing to go to work, and he was inside a drop pod on a distant planet, and both worlds were equally real. It was a terrifying sensation.

"Daddy?" The boy stepped out of the shadows. Or stepped *from* shadow. It was as if the figure was gaining substance even as Leo watched. "I'm here now."

It isn't Julian, he told himself. *It can't be Julian*. But rational thought was drowned out by a tide of emotion so powerful that it left him trembling. "I'm sorry," he whispered. "I tried to get to you in time."

The boy was walking toward him. Leo knew in his gut that this was wrong—all wrong!—and that he should back away from this vision that was definitely not his son, but the sight of the boy had him mesmerized and he couldn't move. *It's just an illusion*, he told himself. *I haven't slept in so long that my mind is conjuring dreams while I'm wake. Nothing to be afraid of.*

"I forgive you," Julian said, and tears came to Leo's eyes. How many times had he dreamed of hearing those very words from his son? How easy it would be to sink down into them now, to give himself over to this dream of absolution. Deep inside, a voice was screaming for him to be afraid, to run away from this thing which was not his son, and not let it touch him under any circumstances. But the voice was drowned out by his need. He reached out a trembling hand toward the boy, and Julian reached out as well, and their fingertips touched. Leo gasped as he felt solid flesh, and there was no·ill effect, none at all. Nothing to justify fear. *This is just a waking dream,* he told himself. *I created this image in my own mind.* He gripped the boy's hands tightly, then stepped forward and embraced him, casting aside the last vestiges of reserve. *Just a dream*: the words repeated over in his head as the scent and feel of his child's living body filled his senses. He pressed his face into Julian's hair, sobbing softly. That inner voice was screaming its warnings, but it had no volume or power. What danger was there in being comforted by a dream?

But slowly the smell of Julian faded from his nostrils, and the flesh Leo had embraced dissolved into smoke, and the warmth of memory became a clammy chill that reached deep, deep down into his bones. And he understood in that moment just what he had embraced, and what the cost of that would be. But it was too late to change anything. All he held in his arms now was a cold, hungry wind, and he was dissolving into it.

I'm sorry, he thought, as his mind sank down into a terrifying darkness. Not addressing his son, this time, but his colony. *I failed you.*

Eleven

"Come on in, Angela."

Dean Silton is sitting behind his desk, as always: the king on his throne, awaiting petitioners. He motions for her to take the seat opposite him. "What can I do for you?"

Be calm, Angie tells herself. A display of anger will accomplish nothing. "I came to ask you about this." She put the letter from him on his desk.

To Dr. Angela Marie Carmelo:

    I regret to inform you that your application for tenure has been denied.

"Ah." He nods solemnly. "That."

"The Rank and Tenure Committee approved my application unanimously. Their letter of recommendation praised my service to this university in glowing terms. My research has been published in leading journals. I've delivered papers at numerous professional conventions. I even have five stars on rateyourteacher.com." A smile flashed briefly, then was gone. "So I'd like to know why you chose to disregard their *recommendation and deny my application." She pauses. "Which effectively ends my contract here."*

"That's my prerogative as dean," he reminds her.

"I understand that." Despite her best intentions, irritation is creeping into her voice. This arrogant asshole always brings it out in her. "I'm asking why you made that choice. Where did I fall short of department expectations?"

He sighs. As with all his other expressions, it's hard to tell whether this one is spontaneous or staged. "You do have impressive credentials, Angie. But a university looks for more than that, at this level. Tenure is a mark of approval that says to the world, this is the kind of person we want to represent us. The kind of person our students should aspire to become."

"And I'm not that?"

In answer he opens a drawer and takes out a newsfeed. Turning it on, he scrolls through several pages until he finds the article he wants. Then he turns it toward her and pushes it across the table so she can read it.

MAGIC OR MEDICINE? the headline reads, and beneath it, LOCAL PROF SAYS ANCIENT RITUALS HEAL BETTER THAN DRUGS. She can feel the color drain from her face as she reads. She shuts her eyes for a moment, trying to compose herself. At last she says, "This is nonsense. You know what my hospital study was about."

"I do," he acknowledges.

"I'm exploring the effect of targeted meditation on psychosomatic illnesses. If a patient who made himself sick can be convinced that he has the power to banish that sickness, will he? The potential benefits—"

"I understand your work, Angie. So do your colleagues. No one here has ever questioned its legitimacy."

"This is just a tabloid," she points out. "They make up all kinds of bullshit. Gossip sells subscriptions—the more lurid, the better."

He takes the newsfeed back from her. "Would you like to see some of the others? I have articles from several journals which picked up the story. Not the most reputable sources, in many cases, but popular ones. You're the news story of the week, Angie. And that's not even figuring in

social media, where hordes of ignorati are spreading tales of your oc-
cult experiments to every corner of the globe." He shakes his head. "The
prestige of this university is rooted in centuries of dignity and academic
excellence. When we find teachers who enhance that reputation, we
give them our full support. But when we find teachers who compromise it, and who would harm this university by remaining here . . ." He
pauses meaningfully. "I'm sure you understand."

Oh, she does. She and the dean have butted heads over so many of
her projects that she is sure he'd been waiting for an opportunity just
like this, a way to get rid of her without it seeming personal. "You know
this is bullshit."

"What I know is that my opinion on the matter means very little.
You've been judged in the court of public opinion, and it has found you
worthy of mockery. All the jokes people are making at your expense
right now, all the cleverly deprecating memes, all the lies people will
add to the story later as they embroider upon it to make a name for
themselves—it will be out there in cybersphere, forever. And that is
what potential students will see when they search for information
about this university. If they find out you're a full professor here, with a
lifetime appointment—someone we obviously value and support—
how do you think that will reflect upon this institution? And impact
our application numbers?"

She doesn't trust herself to respond politely, so she says nothing at
all. Carl Jung didn't have to deal with this kind of bullshit. But Jung
hadn't lived in the internet age, when public mockery was a viral phenomenon that could destroy institutions.

"You can finish out the year and complete your current study. We
simply won't be renewing your contract after that. You can give whatever reason you like for your departure; if it's reasonable, we'll back it.
And you'll get recommendations that reflect your excellent teaching record. It is, as you point out, quite impressive."

That's all great, she wants to say. But any other school that would
hire me will have heard the same stories. How many will be willing to
hire a professor with that kind of baggage? She feels like a mouse in a
maze that has no exit.

But what's done is done. Authority has spoken. "Thank you for the explanation," she says.

Fuck you, she thinks.

ↄↄↄ

The thing that disturbed Lise most about Erna (other than the fact that an invisible force was killing colonists and disabling the equipment they needed to survive) was that she didn't know what to worry about.

Take Bill Guan's sore throat. On Earth it would have been a trivial matter, hardly meriting medical oversight. But before they entered stasis the colonists had been cleansed of the pathogens that commonly hitchhiked on human flesh, so it wasn't a Terran germ that was causing him discomfort. Earth had learned from its first four colonies that it took time for alien pathogens to adapt to human biology, so each colony had a grace period of several months before people had to worry about local germs. Theoretically, it should have been the same on Erna. Yet here was Bill in her clinic, suffering from what looked like early stage strep throat. Had he brought the bug with him from Earth? Or were Ernan germs adapting to humanity's presence with unnatural speed? If the latter, did the strange blue fire have anything to do with it?

At least they had antibiotics now. And soon enough they would have their first batch of home-made penicillin, a major milestone as far as Lise was concerned. She gave Bill a shot and some pills and assigned him to an empty pod for the next three days. Jeff was still using the main quarantine pod as a refuge, and the last thing he needed was to add strep throat to his list of miseries.

With a sigh she put her supplies away, making sure that everything was secured well enough to withstand an earthquake. There had been minor tremors since the big one on landing day, most of them so small that the colony only knew they occurred because the seismic detectors said so. But sooner or later a bigger tremor would hit, and everything of value in the camp and the module had to be stored with that in mind.

She closed the clinic and locked it behind her, a habit from Earth. No one here had any history of medicinal abuse, but why take chances?

Her stock of anxiety meds could become the most valuable commodity in this camp if current trends continued.

She checked the time and sighed; she was going to be late for her meeting with Leo. She started to jog across the camp, trying to save a bit of time. Not that a few minutes mattered so much—on Earth they would hardly have noticed that much lateness—but he was so wound up these days that she didn't want to add even a tiny bit more stress to his plate. Everyone she passed was armed. Given how little experience some of them had with firearms, she hoped there would be no need to use them.

The door to the office pod was slightly ajar. She knocked lightly to let Leo know she'd arrived, and then, when he failed to answer, pulled it open.

And gasped.

He was lying on his back on the floor, eyes shut, motionless. His dark skin was tinged with gray, an ominous color. And on his chest . . . She drew in a deep breath, struggling to process what she was see-ing. On his chest was a young boy, also dark-skinned, lying full length on Leo, arms and legs wrapped around the colony commander like a spider's.

There were no children on Erna.

The moment of shock passed, and she could move again. She yelled for help as she grabbed the child by his shoulders and tried to pull him off Leo. Its skin was strangely cold, and had the texture of slime. She managed to get a good grip on him despite that, but couldn't move him an inch. He turned his head and looked at her with cold, expressionless eyes, more like those of a dead fish than a human. Then he lowered his face back to Leo's chest, and his flesh began to ripple rhythmically, pulsing like a human heartbeat.

Cursing under her breath, she looked desperately around the room for anything she could use as a weapon that wouldn't put Leo at risk. Anything. At last she grabbed a chair and swung it around with both hands, careful to aim at the boy's head and not at Leo, putting as much force behind the blow as she could. When it struck, the boy flinched, but it failed to dislodge him. She tried again, and this time his body moved a bit. The alien eyes fixed on her again, and this time they were gleaming with an eerie light, as if a blue flame was burning inside his head. Was that the fae? She screamed in outrage and swung at the non-human thing again, with a force that would have shattered the skull of anything made of skin and bone. Apparently this thing wasn't, but her attack was enough to drive it back from Leo, and a second blow drove it against the wall, away from his inert body. If she had done it any damage, it wasn't visible. It crouched there for a moment and stared at her with its glowing fish eyes, no doubt taking the measure of this human who had dared to attack it, and deciding how to defeat her. But it was on the west side of the pod, she realized suddenly—the side facing away from the camp.

She pulled out her gun, flipped off the safety, and fired. The sound of the shot was so loud in the small space that pain shot through her ears. But the bullet slammed the thing back against the wall, which was more than the chair had done. So she fired again and again, until her head rang from the shots echoing back at her from every direction. And little by little, the barrage was having effect. The bullets entered the foul thing and lodged within it, and though she saw no blood, it was moving as if it was hurt. Again she fired. The thing cried out like a wounded animal, and then began to collapse in on itself: arms and legs dissolving, head sinking into the shapeless mass of what had been its body. For a brief second she could see it being sucked down into a pool of bright blue fire—and then it was gone.

Someone grabbed her by the shoulder from behind. She spun around, ready to fight her new attacker, but a hand grabbed her wrist and forced the gun down, long enough for her to see that other colonists had entered the pod. They must have heard the shots. They were talking to her, but she couldn't hear a thing. She jerked away from them and dropped to Leo's side, feeling for the pulse in his neck. It was still there, thank God, weak but steady. "Get him to the clinic," she gasped. She couldn't even hear her own words, but shaped them with her mouth and prayed they would come out right.

Several men reached down to pick Leo up. She glanced back at the place where the thing had been, but saw nothing other than a few holes in the wall. She tried to get to her feet, but she was shaking so badly that she stumbled, and two people had to grab her by the arms and hold her upright. "Get me to the clinic," she gasped. Words cast out into a sea of silence. They must have been heard, because now she was being helped in that direction, stumbling behind Leo's inert body as they carried it to safety.

If there was such a thing as safety in this place.

◗◗◗

Leo opened his eyes slowly. Every muscle in his body ached, every organ hurt, and for a moment even his brain wouldn't function. Then memory suddenly returned: the creature that had pretended to be his son was on top of him again, sucking out his very life-force. He began to beat at the air in front of him, trying to push it off. He hit something, hard. Other things grabbed his arms and held him down, trying to restrain him. He fought harder.

"Leo!" Lise's voice somehow broke through the madness. "You're safe! It's all right. That thing is dead."

Her words banished the terrible presence and eased the pressure on his chest so he could breathe again. Shuddering, he lowered his arms and forced his encrusted eyes to open, though the lids felt like they each weighed ten pounds. He was in a lab, he saw. Lise's lab. The same lab where Tia had been autopsied. He blinked hard, bringing details in focus. He was on a table that had been outfitted like a bed, shirt gone, a sheet laid over him. On one side of him was Lise, her pale face lined with concern. On the other were Ian, Ted, and Pravida. The exobiology team.

He was alive. He had died, and now he was alive. The knowledge was overwhelming. A shivering began that was rooted deep in his flesh, spreading outward until every cell in his body was trembling in relief—and in horror. He struggled to find his voice, but for a few seconds could not get control of his body. Then, finally, he managed to rasp out a weak, "What the fuck?"

Ian grinned. "He's back."

Lise stroked his forehead gently with a cool, damp cloth, working around the leads that had been attached there. "You tell us," she said.

"When I showed up there was a young boy on top of you. Or at least something that looked like a boy."

"My son," he gasped. "It pretended to be my son."

"Do you know what it really was?" Pravida asked.

He shook his head. "No clue. It looked just like my son. It . . ." He choked on the words. "It *smelled* like my son."

The memory was too painful to bear. He closed his eyes, wishing he could wipe the whole encounter from existence.

"I beat at it with a chair," Lise told him. "I managed to move it a bit, but it didn't look hurt at all. Then I shot it. The bullets definitely struck, but again, there was no visible wound, no bleeding. It just . . . dissolved. There was a pool of blue light on the floor, and it seemed to melt into that."

"Fae," Ian whispered.

"By the time we got you to the clinic," Lise continued, "your flesh was completely dehydrated. Every organ in your body was in the process of shutting down. We fought for hours to save you, my team and I. When you were finally stable we brought you to the module so I could run some proper tests."

"How long was I out?" he whispered hoarsely.

She glanced up at the time display. "Thirteen hours, give or take. We watched you all night."

His head hurt to do the math. "So it's morning."

She nodded. "A few of the work shifts went out, but mostly people are waiting on news of your condition. No one but me saw the . . . the thing. They just know you collapsed."

His mouth tightened. "They should be working. They shouldn't wait. We need the wall built."

She put a hand on his shoulder and said softly, "Would it have made a difference last night, if the palisade had been complete?"

He sighed. "No. Probably not with Wayne, either."

"Okay, then. We'll finish it as fast as we can. Maybe it will protect us from some threats, maybe not. It's there mostly to make people feel safer, to give them the illusion of doing something to protect themselves." A shadow passed over her face. "Which may turn out to be no more than an illusion."

"They'll need to know what happened to you," Pravida said. "Otherwise they could be fooled like you were. They need to be prepared for that."

Leo winced, but nodded.

Ian folded his arms across his chest. "Whatever is behind this is learning how to read us. And it's turning our own fears against us. Attacking us with images conjured from the darkest recesses of our minds, that embody our worst fears."

"Very poetic," Leo said sharply. "But not true in my case."

Slowly, carefully, he sat up. For a moment he was dizzy and had to fight the urge to be sick, but it passed quickly. Lise shut off the machines that had been monitoring him. "What I saw wasn't something I feared," he told Ian. "It was something I wanted—something I hungered desperately for. To see my boy again. To have a chance to tell him what was in my heart, and . . ." Sorrow welled up inside him as he remembered what the fake Julian had said, and it was a moment before he could continue. "Whatever force created that thing wasn't responding to my fear but giving me what I wanted most. So I'm sorry, Ian, but fear isn't the only pattern here."

"A hostile force that turns our own desires against us." Pravida's expression was grim. "One might argue that's even more frightening."

"And a damn lot harder to explain to the colonists," Leo muttered. If their fear did affect the fae, how the hell was he going to tell the others about this without triggering enough fear to spawn an army of monsters?

Twelve

The sky was gray at the edges when Leo called the colony together, so he held the meeting in the mess tent, in anticipation of rain.

He'd already spent the morning answering superficial questions about his condition, and sharing mundane details of the attack. Thus far he hadn't told anyone but his inner circle about the more disturbing facets of the incident. But he was going to have to. There was no way around that. Some kind of creature was stalking and killing colonists, and his people couldn't begin to protect themselves without knowing what they were facing.

But where was the line to be drawn, between encouraging caution and inspiring fear? He remembered what Lise had said about the faux-Julian dissolving into fae, and he shuddered. Given that the fae appeared to be a constant presence in the camp, effectively inescapable, the suggestion that it might generate monsters at any moment was terrifying on levels that the human mind could barely fathom.

At least Jeff Hodges had come to the meeting. He was still an emotional mess, and spent his days cocooned in his light-drenched pod, terrified by the very thought of darkness, but evidently Dani had talked him into emerging for this. He walked by her side with reasonable steadiness, and only someone paying close attention would note that his eyes kept darting from side to side, as if expecting something fearsome to jump out from the shadows at any moment. Would it reassure him to know that what he had seen in the latrine tent was real, that someone else had also seen it? Or would that just terrify him more?

Never have I walked such a tightrope as I must now, Leo thought.

Stepping up onto a small stage the construction team had rigged for him, he was able to look out over all of his colonists at once. The faces that looked back at him were tired and stress-worn. But in their eyes he could see the spark that had driven them to this world in the first place, the hunger for a kind of life that Earth could never offer them. He needed to keep that spark alive, if they were to survive the coming days together.

He held up his hands, and a hush fell over his audience.

"We came here expecting to find a world like Earth," he announced, "and in many ways, we did. A beautiful planet that could become anything we wanted it to, as long as we were willing to put in the time and effort needed to transform it. You all have met that challenge, and more. We've made great headway this first week and will soon be planting our first Terran crops, a crucial milestone in the settlement project. But we've also encountered problems that our training on Earth didn't prepare us for, and phenomena which we don't fully understand yet. I've called you here today so I can share the information we've gathered thus far, so you can all know what we are dealing with.

"First, the infamous 'blue light' that many of you have seen in your dreams, which we are calling *the fae*: It appears to be quite real, though few people can see it while awake. We haven't yet figured out why that is. It's probably a form of bioluminescence, similar to the kind that exists on Earth, and we're trying to identify the species that produces it. For that, we need data. So if any of you see such a light again, awake or asleep, please report the details to Anna." He nodded toward her. "She's offered to collate all our information into a single report."

He paused for a moment, watching for people's reactions. Thus far they looked more curious than uneasy, but he hadn't shared the truly unnerving part yet. "Next item of interest: we seem to be having more mechanical problems than we should. The first tractor that broke down turned out to be irreparable. No one can identify the cause of the malfunction, so no one can fix it. The tractor that exploded yesterday is obviously beyond repair, and is being disassembled for parts and materials. Meanwhile, some other electronic devices also have failed, including several of our larger batteries. There is no consistent cause that we can identify. It may be that some event in deep space damaged our equipment during our journey here, or maybe such an unprecedented time in storage was simply more than Terran components could endure. Alternatively, there may be some element unique to Erna that affects our equipment. Biological, electromagnetic, whatever; we're just guessing at this point. But we need to identify it before more things break down. So I'll ask you to report any incidents of equipment failure, no matter how trivial they may seem, so that we can look for patterns. Joshua has volunteered to collect that data." He nodded toward the engineer.

A few people were looking concerned now, no doubt imagining how the colony would function—or not function—if their high-tech devices failed. *If our fear really does affect how this planet functions,* Leo thought, *I just handed Erna an invitation to screw with us.* But there was nothing he could do other than keep his expression as unemotional as possible, trying to project a confidence that he wished he really felt. Jeff was gripping Dani's arm with an intensity that must surely have been painful, he noticed, but the man was still here, which was something.

He carefully reviewed what he meant to say next, before speaking again. "As most of you probably know by now, I was attacked the other night. Earlier, Tia and Wayne were both killed by local beasts. Those three attacks shared some disturbing features. That's the main reason I called you here today: to tell you what we've learned about them." A pang of regret caused his chest to tighten, and for a moment he couldn't remember what he had intended to say. *This is your last hour of innocence,* he thought sadly. *After today, we can never again tell ourselves that things on Erna are going to be normal. That dream has died.*

"Four colonial expeditions reported back before we left Earth," he said at last. "They told us that the worlds they had settled were so like Earth, being there was like stepping into our motherworld's past."

He sighed. "That's not going to be the case here. There's at least one species on Erna that has no Terran equivalent. It's taken two lives already, and tried to take mine. And it has a rather frightening ability, which we'll all have to guard against."

He drew in a deep breath. "We believe that in all three cases, the targets saw their attacker not as a local predator, but as something from their own past. I experienced this myself. When I was attacked, what I saw wasn't an alien beast, but my own son, looking just like he had back on Earth." The words stirred such painful memories that he had to fight to keep his voice steady. "We believe Tia saw the baby she yearned to bear. And Wayne . . . it's possible he saw something from a vid he'd been watching. So now we must ask, how is such a thing possible? Is there a species on Erna that has power to make us hallucinate, as part of its hunting strategy? Or is there something in this location that makes us prone to delusion in general—something in the air, perhaps, or the water—which these attacks took advantage of? Or is there some other explanation? We don't know yet. But what we do know is that if this thing strikes again, it may appear to be something—or someone—other than what it truly is. And so that is what we must defend ourselves against."

Now there was fear in their eyes. Thank God everyone had been vetted for mental stability before signing on for this trip. He couldn't even imagine what it would be like to tell a group of average Terrans something like this.

"All three attacks took place while the targets were alone, so if we stay in groups, this predator will probably keep its distance. Try not to be alone, even inside the camp. We should all trade private information with each other—either personal details or agreed-upon codes—so that we can confirm each other's identity. Hopefully this thing will never disguise itself as one of us, but given what it did with my son, it's best to be prepared for that possibility. And any ideas you may have about how such mimicry might be possible—any ideas at all—please bring them to me. Nothing will be dismissed out of hand, no matter how crazy it sounds. We're dealing with a species that defies Terran understanding, and we're going to have to think outside the box in order to protect ourselves.

"Lise beat the creature off me, then shot it. No wounds were visible—probably as a result of the same illusion that made it look human—but it was clearly hurt, and her quick response saved my life. You're all armed, as per my previous order, so at least we have that for defense. But remember, there's nothing at the center of this camp that's going to stop a bullet, other than human bodies. Please be careful where you aim."

He paused. "That's all that we know, right now. I'd offer to answer questions, but I'm not sure that I'd have any answers for you. So let me invite those who want to know more to seek me out after this meeting, and we'll talk in a less formal setting. Meanwhile, all of you . . ." He paused. "Be careful."

Had he given them enough information to protect themselves? The way they were looking at one another, and whispering nervously, suggested they didn't think so. And truth be told, neither did he. But what if he had told them more? The concept of a predator who could trigger hallucinations was frightening enough, but at least it was a concrete, comprehensible threat. The suggestion that there might be an invisible force hostile to human life—that the planet itself was hostile to human life— and that this force was present all around them, all the time, could well push some people over the edge. He owed it to them not to risk that until he had better information on what they were facing.

Not for the first time, he wished Colony Control had never chosen him for this job. Maybe someday he would wake up and find it had all been a bad dream, engendered by an unusually long stasis. No one really knew what happened to a human brain when it was suspended for that long. Even the thought of potential madness was strangely comforting. At least it would explain the anomalies on this world in terms that the human mind could grasp. But Lise had seen the same creature he had, in the same form. so that was off the table. He was, regrettably, quite sane.

Erna may be responding to us as a body would to an infection. Was that what Pravida had said in the meeting? If so, and if she was right, then they were all fucked. Beyond fucked. Twenty thousand light-years beyond fucked.

◡ ◡ ◡

It wasn't until late in the afternoon that Ian could finally sneak away from the camp. A couple of days ago it wouldn't have been so damned complicated. He and his team would have been wandering through the woods collecting samples of local flora, and he could just point them in one direction while he went off in another. No one would think twice about his absence. But now that everyone had been told to stay in groups, and enough of the palisade had been built that traffic in and out of the camp was being channeled through two narrow openings, it was harder to leave unnoticed.

He volunteered to work with the people who were erecting the final portion of the wall, at the north end of the camp, where the tree line was closest. It seemed like it took forever before he got a chance to sneak away, but when he did he was able to move quickly into the depths of the forest, until a screen of foliage stood between him and the camp. Yes, it was dangerous to go off alone—he knew that—but earlier the fae had shown signs of accepting him, and hopefully that would translate into some degree of safety.

Hopefully.

Deeper into the woods he went, until the sounds of the camp were left far behind. Here all was quiet and damp, and eerily still. Now and then he passed a trap that Team Paleo had set up, marked by a bright orange ribbon, but thus far all were empty. Evidently local animals didn't like coming this close to the camp. Perhaps the team's more distant snares would be more productive. There was no sign of alien light flowing along the ground, but that was to be expected. He probably wouldn't see it again until he learned how to focus his vision properly.

Finally he reached the clearing he had visited before. This time he kept his gun at his side. Disarming himself had been a valuable gesture during his first visit to this place, but now he had other, more meaningful gestures to offer.

He took out a drawing that Angie had made for him, a complex geometric pattern sketched on a strip of flattened bark, and he studied it. The design had no meaning to him, but Angie had said it was inspired by ancient symbols that he would recognize unconsciously, and by concentrating on it he would strengthen the spiritual qualities he needed to draw upon. That was her theory, anyway. It sounded fantastical, but it wasn't like he had any better strategies to try. He'd give it a shot.

Tucking the drawing back in his pocket, he picked up a branch and began to sketch a large circle in the dirt. That was the most ancient symbol of all, Angie had explained, traditionally used by sorcerers and shamans to guard against hostile spirits. He tried to focus on the more scientific aspects of her theory, and not on the parts that made him feel like he was role-playing a sorcerer's apprentice. When his circle was complete, he cleared a small patch of ground in its center and sat cross-legged in front of it. For a moment he just breathed in the scents of the forest—growth and decay so perfectly balanced—trying to settle his spirit. Then he took out Angie's drawing again and focused on it. Tracing the pattern visually, fixing it in his mind, he repeated the entreaty he had made during the true night. "Come to me," he pleaded—to the forest, to the fae, to Erna itself. "Make me yours." He envisioned his Terran spirit leaving him, carried away on the breeze until only the seed of a newborn Ernan soul remained. "All that I was before, I surrender to you. Show me how to belong here, like native creatures belong. Make me part of your world."

But that alone brought no enlightenment. Not that he'd expected it to. Revelations rarely came so easily.

He had brought some discarded tree cores with him to serve as kindling, and he arranged them in a small pyramid on the patch of ground he'd cleared. Then he took out a lighter and set fire to the pile. It was slow to catch, but he breathed on the first sparks gently, and soon tiny golden flames were dancing in front of him.

Sacrifice is one of the most powerful symbols in the human repertoire, Angie had told him. *It destroys that which existed before, and therefore represents total commitment to transformation. By sacrificing something of value we become the phoenix, accepting the loss of what we previously were in order to become something new. The design I gave you has symbolic value, therefore it can serve as an offering.*

He fed the piece of bark slowly into the fire as she had instructed, tracing the pattern with his eyes until the blackening of the bark made it impossible to see. Then he continued to trace the pattern in his mind, visualizing it drawn in lines of glowing blue fire. The exercise was mesmeric, and slowly the rest of the world faded from his awareness, until only the pattern remained. The glowing lines expanded, flowing outward farther and farther, until it seemed the entire planet was glowing with alien power. The design was absorbed into it, and it faded from his sight. But the light remained.

He saw the fae.

It was brighter than it had been back at camp—so much brighter!—and its color was the rich blue of a twilight sky, impossibly intense. Rivulets of glowing cobalt flowed past him as smoothly and as naturally as they flowed past the trees surrounding him, with no hint of the disruption they had previously displayed around humans. *It accepts me,* he thought in wonder. He put his hand down into the light and watched streamers of azure play across his fingers, a hundred different shades of blue in shimmering fractal eddies. It seemed so real that he closed his hand around it, expecting to feel something, but it had no more substance than a dream.

For a long time he just sat there, mesmerized by the alien display, overwhelmed by the concept that he, and he alone, had found a way to commune with the planet. Deep in his heart, he realized, he hadn't expected this experiment to succeed. Yet here he was, trembling as fae flowed around him and then outward, expanding beyond the limits of his vision. He felt as if his senses were expanding as well, following the inexorable blue tide, and he could sense the presence of other living things in its current. Trees, brush, grass, insects, worms . . . all the living things that surrounded him were part of a network of interconnected life, he understood now, bound together in a delicate codependence. The revelation was exhilarating, but also humbling. Was this how trees felt back on Earth, when they first made contact with a mycorrhizal network? Were plants capable of feeling wonder? Or was this kind of connection just second nature to them, as natural as blossoms opening in the spring and leaves changing color in the autumn?

The real question was: could he control it? The idea was insanely hubristic, but that didn't mean it was impossible. The previous attacks had made it clear that the fae responded to human thoughts. Perhaps properly focused thoughts could be used to influence it.

Drawing in a deep breath, he focused on the fae that was closest to him, imagining its flow shifting slightly, trying to alter its course by sheer force of will. But there was no hint of response. He tried for a while longer, focusing his attention on different parts of the flow, but still nothing changed.

Emotion, he thought. *That's what it responds to. It's been reflecting our own fears and desires back at us. That's the common thread.*

Closing his eyes, he tried to focus on the yearning for knowledge that had always driven him, but that had no effect. Maybe it was too general an emotion, and he needed a specific image to focus on. So he reached back into his childhood, searching for a suitable memory. Something so intensely emotional that it had burned itself into his brain forever. God knows, that was an emotional time for him. In a world almost bereft of natural greenery, a child obsessed with plants was asking to be mocked, and local bullies were happy to comply. Cruelty was an intoxicant to them.

What have you done? There are tears in Ian's eyes. What have you done!

He falls to his knees amidst the ruins of his botany project, gathering up mounds of soil in his hands. Roots are jutting out in all directions, reaching for nutrients they can no longer harvest. Can plants feel pain? There are so many tears in his eyes that he is half-blinded. They aren't dead, he tells himself. I can save them. He turns to put them back in . . . what? The pots are all gone, smashed to shards all around him. The growth lights lie on the floor in fragments. And blood is dripping down his forehead from the gash made when one of the bullies struck him with a rock, when he tried to defend his precious work.

Rage burns so hot within him he can barely contain it, but he knows he must suppress it at any cost. These bullies will only beat him more if tries to fight back. Cradling the injured plants to his chest, he swallows back on his misery, letting them mock him and his project until his lack of response eventually bores them. But his hands are shaking, and he knows that as soon as he gets his experiment set up again, another bully will come along to destroy it. Only by keeping his work a secret from everyone can he hope to bring it to completion . . .

He opened his eyes. At first the fae looked the same as before, but no, the azure current had shifted ever so slightly. It seemed to be drawing back from him now, coalescing into a pool of light a few yards away. Breathless, he watched as some of the fae began to rise from its center, creating a vertical protrusion: a stalagmite of power. He was so fascinated by the transformation that his fears were temporarily forgotten. Dimly he understood how much danger he was in, but the knowledge was a distant thing and no longer had power to move him. Now he could see features forming, sculpted in light and shadow. Eyes. Mouth. A face—

With a gasp he rose to his feet, backing quickly away from the ghostly image. The face of one of his childhood tormenters was taking shape before him, and as each new feature manifested, a new wave of memory rushed over him, stoking ancient fears anew. Desperately he kicked at the remains of his sacrificial fire, scattering its embers, and tried to focus his mind on the real world, the *solid* world, once more. And indeed, as soon as his concentration shifted, the fae became invisible again. Now all he could see was the forest that surrounded him, veiled in the early shadows of dusk. Did that mean the misty creation was gone now? Did shifting his mental focus rob it of the energy it needed to manifest, so that it collapsed back into the pool of its creation? Or could he just not see it? The thought that it might still be out there, but beyond his detection, was terrifying.

If the fae could conjure his personal demons like that, could it do that to anyone? They already knew it could take on the form of lost loved ones, so it stood to reason it would be able to imitate one's enemies and tormentors. And in theory it could do so in any location, at any time.

We need to figure out how to control it, he thought. Then he corrected himself: *I need to control it.* He was uniquely attuned to the fae, that much was clear. No one else had been able to shift their vision to see the blue currents, or consciously alter their flow. If there was going to be any breakthrough in understanding the fae—in *controlling* it—it would have to come from him.

Savior of the colony. Was that how future generations would remember him? The concept sent a thrill up his spine.

In the distance the dinner bell rang, breaking him out of his reverie. Suddenly the sense of being immersed in an unseen alien force vanished, and he was surrounded by nothing but grass and trees: normal, everyday vegetation. But the fae was still out there, he knew, and at any moment some fragment of repressed memory could be brought to life, for anyone. If he couldn't figure out how to prevent that—or at least control how it manifested—none of the people here were going to survive very long.

ᴐ ᴐ ᴐ

Ian dreams they are all watching him: Leo at the far end of the group and the others arranged in a circle around the pod, as always. Misty dream-figures, waiting.

"I saw the fae again," Ian says. The words are so significant they seem to hang in the air for a moment, as if waiting to be admired.

But their expressions are maddeningly impassive. Damn it, don't they understand what he's telling them? He's offering them the key to Erna! Their eyes should be filled with admiration—nay, envy—while he, flushed with pride, exults in the existential satisfaction of knowing he is the one who is going to save this colony from ruin. History will surely remember him for that.

"I conjured the sight I needed," he persists. "Angie designed the symbols I needed, and I meditated on them until the fae appeared." Still no response from them. How he wishes Angie were here, so that she could explain the process involved! She could explain it far better than he can.

But does he really want them to understand that process? Right now he's the only person in the colony who can discover how to control the fae. If others learn how to alter their sight like he did, that will no longer be the case. Someone else could make the breakthrough discovery, and vault a name other than Ian's to history's honor roll.

A flush of shame comes to his cheeks that he is even thinking like that. All for one and one for all, right? That's supposed to be the motto of the colony. Back on Earth they had all signed contracts agreeing to honor it. The welfare of the colony matters more than the pride of any one man.

But the pride is there, and the temptation cannot be denied.

Now Joshua is asking how Ian knows that his vision was real. Is it possible his intense meditation could have served as a kind of self-hypnosis, conjuring images of the fae from his own mind and nothing really happened? It takes all the botanist's self-control to respond calmly, but inside he is fuming. How dare they question his insight? Ungrateful bastards! He has risked exposing himself to the fae in order to save them—reliving one of his darkest memories to do so—and this is how they reward him?

They are not worthy of the truth.

Thirteen

Commander's Personal Log
Year One
Day Nine

No one was attacked yesterday, at least that we know of. The mere fact that I consider it worthy of mention speaks to how tenuous our situation has become. It will take many more days of peace before I dare risk optimism. Deep inside I feel as if the planet is waiting, metaphorically holding its breath while it figures out how to get around our various precautions.

Yes, I am guilty of personifying Erna. We're all doing it. The language of sentience is too convenient a metaphor to avoid. But will talking about the planet as if it were a living entity, capable of conscious intent, affect how it functions? The creatures we have dealt with thus far have reflected our own thoughts back at us. If language affects how we think about the planet, will that affect the planet itself?

At least the palisade is finished. Joshua is printing a lock mechanism for the northern gate, which will allow colonists to come and go as needed while leaving it locked between uses. The larger southern gate will be watched 24/7. Once we have a watchtower, sentries will be able to see the entirety of the camp. If anything gets past our wall—or manifests in the open space inside it—we'll at least have some warning.

Ian has asked permission to add Angela Carmelo to our advisory circle. I've reviewed her file, and though I'm hesitant to add someone at this point, given the chemistry of the group, the request has merit. Her background includes study in many relevant fields, and her reputation for maverick thinking suggests she might be able to come up with out-of-the-box solutions. I've told him he can fill her in and bring her to the next meeting, if and only if she understands that some of our speculations need to be kept private, lest the others panic over things that turn out not to be true. We need the freedom to discuss things without worrying about what others will think.

TO DO:

Finish the watchtower. The logs for it have already been harvested, and I expect the basic structure to be completed by nightfall. All joints are being reinforced with rope bindings designed to make the structure flexible enough to withstand earthquakes. At least that's the hope. According to the seedship analysis, we're due for another one soon.

Work on the chapel. Now that the palisade is finished, we can spare the labor to set up Dani's prayer tent. It was a good suggestion. Those who were badly shaken by my news yesterday may find comfort in prayer, and even atheists can use it as a meditational space, a respite from the tensions of the camp. Dani says she will design some services that even non-religious folk can relate to, focusing on the essence of hope and inner strength rather than worship of a divine being. She wants this tent to become a sanctuary for all.

☽ ☽ ☽

Lise spent the morning handing out drugs to people. In most cases they were simple anxiety treatments, just enough to help ease them past the initial shock of Leo's announcement. But every pill she dispensed hastened the day when they would have to find native substitutes or go without, so she hoped the need ended soon. That said, if ever there were a legitimate reason for the colonists to need mood stabilizers, learning that alien predators could show up looking like their loved ones definitely qualified.

She was trying to lose herself in her work, but her mind kept going back to the creature whose attack she had interrupted. Of all the creatures that had attacked thus far, this was the first whose appearance could not be explained away as a simple delusion. Tia could have transformed some animal sound into a baby's cry in her head; Ian's light-serpents could have reflected nothing more than the power of suggestion, after he'd heard Jeff's description of them. But she had seen Leo's son herself, and since she didn't know what the boy looked like before that, her mind could not have created such an image. Whatever that creature was, it had really looked like Julian Case.

Which begged the question: how the hell was the fae doing that?

As she entered Leo's office pod she tried to set such thoughts aside, to concentrate on the meeting at hand. Everyone else was already seated and waiting, and she took her customary place beside Leo. There was a newcomer to the group, she noted: Angie Carmelo. She was sitting beside Ian and the two were murmuring softly to one another in a vaguely conspiratorial manner. Interesting. She couldn't remember enough about the woman's resume to guess why Leo had added her to the group, but there had to be a good reason. Did she and Ian have a relationship?

"Welcome," Leo said, when they all were settled. "As you can see, our circle has a new member, Dr. Angela Carmelo." He nodded toward her. "Back on Earth, she studied methods used to manipulate neural function. Given that we're dealing with a species that appears to be reading our minds, I thought her input might have value." He looked at Ian. "You've gotten her up to speed?"

Ian nodded. "I have."

"All right, then. Let the brainstorming session begin." He turned to Anna. "Any news on the dream front?"

"Sally Chang is still dreaming about blue fire, and waking up chilled to the bone. As far as I know she's the only one experiencing physical effects after waking. Others have reported fae-dreams to me, but most of those were from the previous night. Whatever caused so many people to see the fae in their dreams after the true night, the effect seems to have passed. A few more nights and I expect all dreams will be normal." She paused. "Except for Sally's. Hers preceded the true night, so there's no reason to think they'll stop."

"Thank you." Leo looked at Joshua. "Tech update?"

"Five more equipment failures." The engineer tapped his tablet to bring up his notes. "All small items, nothing of great importance, but the pattern is becoming ominous. Whatever is affecting our tech appears to be escalating in its activity."

"No idea what's causing any of the failures?"

"No. I'm sorry. Sometimes we find a malfunction we can blame, but most of the time there's no cause we can identify."

Leo looked to Dani. "You brought Jeff to the colony meeting. How is he doing?"

She hesitated. "Better than expected. I was afraid that when you started talking about the fae that it would trigger a flashback, but he actually seemed reassured by your words. I think when you suggested that people were seeing illusions not because they were crazy, but because something external was affecting their minds, it made it easier for him to deal with his own encounter. Now he can tell himself that what he saw wasn't real, without having to question his own mental health. It seems to be helping." Her expression grew solemn. "He's still terrified of the dark, though. I don't see that getting better while our situation is . . . what it is."

Leo looked at Lise. "Medical update?"

She sighed. "I've been giving out sedatives for nerves, bandages for injuries, and quite a few sleeping pills. Nothing significant. We'll be decanting the penicillium soon, after which we'll be able to produce our own antibiotics. I'll breathe a lot easier once that's accomplished." A dry smile flickered briefly. "No fae involved there."

Leo looked around the room. "Anyone else?"

Ted raised a hand. "I've been bringing CCs into the camp to see how they behave. As soon as insects are released they head straight for the exit. So whatever drove them away in the first place is still active."

Leo looked at Ian. "News from our seer?"

Ian drew in a deep breath. "I saw the fae again. It was in my dreams this time, but it seemed very real. At first it looked the same as the first time I saw it, but then it began to change shape. Part of it rose up, and then . . . then it began to take on the shape of someone from my past. Someone I hated and feared. I felt as if those emotions had summoned it."

"Holy shit," Anna muttered.

"The image was ghost-like—insubstantial—and was only visible for a moment before I woke up. So I can't tell you anything more, I'm sorry. It shook me pretty badly." He hesitated. "I felt like it was showing me something real. Not just a dream."

"Like with Sally Chang," Anna suggested. "Connecting physical reality and illusion."

"Maybe."

What was so odd about his tone, that drew Lise's attention? Why did she sense that Ian was holding something back? He had never been the secretive kind, preferring to be admired for his insights, but there was an odd evasiveness to his manner today. It sounded like things were being left unsaid, and that worried her. She started watching him more closely, noting subtle changes in his body language. What was he hiding?

"Well," Leo said, "we discussed the possibility that the creature which attacked me came from the fae, so your dreaming about another such incident might just have been inspired by those talks. Did you see anything unusual when you woke up, that would suggest it was more than a dream?"

For a moment Ian was silent. Angie looked at him. "Not that I noticed," he said at last.

He's lying, Lise thought. *But why would he not share the whole
story with us?* The group had been so close-knit since their arrival that
it was hard to imagine why he would distance himself from the rest of
them, but she sensed he was doing just that. *What kind of secret are
you guarding, Ian Casca?*

Leo looked around the room. "Any other reports?" When no one
else responded he turned to Angie. "Very well, you were invited here to
share your thoughts. Now's your chance." He smiled. "Go for it."

"Thanks." She smoothed her clothing and said, "Ian told me the fae
seems to respond to our thoughts, and may be able to read our memories. He asked if I had any ideas on how that might work." She smiled
faintly. "Something a bit more scientific than 'it reads our minds.' The
first part of that is easy. The brain uses electrochemical signals to trans-
mit information. Every thought leaves a trail of voltage spikes in its wake.
There are species on Earth that can detect such activity with remark-
able accuracy, so it's not beyond the realm of possibility that an alien
species could do so also. How that species would be able to interpret
those signals is another question." She looked at Leo. "The night you
saw your son. Were you thinking about him right before that?"

His eyes narrowed slightly. "No, I wasn't."

"So at the time, there was no mental activity connected with your
son's image. No electrical signal for your attacker to read. It must have
been getting information through some other channel."

"Such as what?" Pravida asked, and Ted said, "What are you pro-
posing?"

"Long-term memory is episodic: we tend to remember events, not
isolated facts. Stimulate a memory, and it triggers a cascading network
of associations—a pattern of interconnections, if you will. That set of
responses is what we experience as memory."

"You're thinking those pathways might exist even when they aren't
in active use?" Pravida asked. "A biological road map recording the path
to one particular memory?"

"Exactly." Angie nodded. "A mnemonic fingerprint, if you will."

"But how could that be detected from the outside? Much less interpreted?"

"Well . . ." she smiled slightly. "I can't claim to have all the answers yet. But we know there are wavelengths of light we humans can't see, sounds we can't hear, vibrations too subtle for us to be consciously aware of, any of which could be used to gather information from inside the human body. It's not impossible that some alien sense, incomprehensible to us, might be able to detect the pattern of a neural network. Perhaps well enough to mimic its form."

"And thus the conceptual barrier between magic and science is breached," Ian said quietly.

"All right." Leo rubbed his hands together. "So let's say for the moment that your theory is correct, and that's the mechanism we're dealing with. How do we keep the fae from reading us?" A corner of his mouth twitched. "Tin foil hats for everyone?"

Lise chuckled. "I don't think we brought any of those with us."

"But *why* is it doing this?" Johnny asked. "I mean, that's the real question, isn't it? What species would have a vested interest in replicating our memories?"

"A predator that saw us as food," Pravida said. "The mimicry could be instinctive. Like a chameleon who takes on the appearance of its environment to get close to its prey. On Earth there are species that evolve to resemble their prey. This could be an Ernan version of that."

"Not a comforting thought," Dani muttered, and Johnny said, "How the fuck do we fight something like that?"

"We don't," Lise responded. "The thing that attacked Leo was withdrawn into the fae when I injured it. Once that happened, there was no further way to attack it." She sighed. "We're going to have to focus on keeping it out of our minds. Somehow."

Dani leaned back in her chair. "That would require controlling our thoughts. And not just the ones we're consciously aware of, but every neural pattern embedded in our brains." She shook her head. "I don't see how that would be possible."

"It probably isn't," Ian said, "But maybe we could learn how to choose which patterns it reads."

Leo raised an eyebrow. "You're suggesting we try to control it rather than kill it."

"Do we have any other choice?"

In the distance, the lunch bell sounded. After a moment of silence, Leo stood. "I think we all need some time to digest this. And I, at least, need some food." He looked at Angie. "Thank you for sharing your perspective with us. It was . . . enlightening."

"Thank you for inviting me." Her eyes were sparkling. "A puzzle like this comes along once in a lifetime. I'll do my best to help solve it."

Leo watched as the others filed out of the pod. The exobiology team gathered right outside the doorway: Pravida, Ted, and Ian. They invited Angie to join them.

Four creative minds, Leo thought, *trained to analyze unfamiliar life-forms. If they can't figure out how to deal with this shit, no one can.*

Soon only he and Lise remained in the pod.

"And then there's Ian," he said.

She sighed. "Yeah."

"Something is up with him."

"Definitely."

"I'm not imagining it."

She shook her head. "I don't think so."

"I'd ask you to keep an eye on him—because you're the one I'd trust most with that kind of job. But I know how busy you are."

"I can ask one of my assistants to keep an eye on where he goes. If there are any red flags, I'll look into them myself."

"Thank you." He hesitated. "Discretion—"

"—Comes first, Leo. I know that. Especially when we're talking about investigating one of our own."

He looked toward the mess tent, where people were gathering up bowls and utensils, preparing for their next meal. "Is this when we're supposed to feel optimistic?" he asked softly. "Or is it premature to invest any hope in these crazy theories?"

"They're just theories right now. But they may lead to something constructive." She smoothed his forehead with gentle fingers and smiled slightly. "I think a bit of hope is permitted."

☽☽☽

The framework for the chapel tent was already in place when Lise stopped by to see how Dani was doing. Some people were assembling benches while others hung up colorful pieces of parachute cloth to brighten the space, and still others worked at unfolding the thick canvas roof with its built-in solar panels. Dani was conducting the workers like an orchestra, with an authority that seemed to come naturally to her. Leo had talked about leaving her in charge if anything happened to him, and Lise could see why.

But nothing is going to happen to Leo, she told herself stubbornly.

Dani saw her standing there, grinned, and waved her over. "Come to pray?"

"Doesn't look like you're quite ready for that."

"Soon enough," she promised. "And people need it. That's why so many came out to help. I've never seen a group of people so hungry for spiritual comfort."

"Maybe it will cut down on your private counseling sessions."

She chuckled. "One can only hope."

"Has Jeff been helping you? I don't see him here."

"He may still be asleep." She glanced over at the quarantine pod. "Though how he managed to do that with the place so noisy, I haven't a clue."

A man came jogging toward them, half a dozen religious pendants swinging from his hand. "Where do you want these?" he asked Dani.

The chaplain looked apologetically at Lise, who nodded. "Go. Do what you need to. I mostly came to see Jeff."

"Tell him the dedicatory service will be at four," she said as she walked away. "And that I'll make sure the chapel tent is brightly lit."

"Will do," Lise promised.

It was a short walk to the quarantine pod. Lise knocked on the door, but there was no response. After a couple of tries she gently pushed it open a bit.

"Jeff?"

He was lying on the cot, probably asleep—though how anyone

could sleep in a space so brightly lit was beyond her. Half the solar lamps in the camp must be here. She looked at him for a moment, then decided to let him be. He needed sleep too badly. But as she started away she caught a glint of reflection from his eyes, and she turned back to take a second look.

His eyes were open.

She felt a sinking in the pit of her stomach. "Jeff?"

No response.

Warily, she approached the cot. His body looked peaceful, utterly relaxed, and except for his eyes staring emptily in the distance and the eerie pallor of his skin, one would think him merely asleep. But he was clearly not asleep. There wasn't a mark on his body, nor any sign of struggle, but there was also no sign of life.

She reached out with a shaking hand to feel for a pulse in his neck. Nothing. Then his wrist. Still nothing. His flesh was cool to the touch, but pliable, so he'd died a short while ago. Maybe right after the big meeting.

She drew in a deep breath and then began to search the body for some hint of what had killed him. Anything.

She found it, but not on his body. It was on the wall. The small locked cabinet in which she'd stored restricted pharmaceuticals had been pried open. On the bottom shelf a small plastic jar lay on its side, its lid beside it. She'd been giving him pills to help with anxiety, Lise remembered. One a day's worth, maybe two at a time. Enough to blunt the edge of his fear, though not enough to banish it.

All gone now.

Frustration welled up inside her, and with it anger—at this world, and at herself. Jeff had been doing so well up till now, and Leo's speech seemed to have calmed him. From what Dani said, it sounded like he had finally started coming to terms with the nightmare he'd witnessed, and was ready to move beyond it. So what had driven him to suicide today, just when things were looking more positive? He'd managed to survive in a much worse state.

Then she noticed the lamps.

There were more than a dozen of them in the room, all solar powered. He'd hung them at regular intervals, creating a palisade of light that no creature of darkness could possibly breach. But one of them was out now. Its didn't make the room any darker; there were so many lamps that the loss of one was barely noticeable. But she remembered what Leo had said earlier, and realized with a sinking heart what conclusion Jeff must have drawn.

There may be some element unique to Erna that affects our equipment.

Devices were failing, in large enough numbers that Leo had warned the colony about it. Jeff likely hadn't thought about the consequences of that at the time. Neither had Dani. But when he returned to the pod and saw that one of the lamps had failed, and he must have realized that soon another would follow, and then another, without end. Darkness would close in on the colony lamp by broken lamp, until only primitive fires were left to hold it at bay. And that would not be enough to fend off the monsters that had killed Wayne.

"I'm sorry," she whispered hoarsely. "We should have foreseen this. We should have protected you. I'm so sorry." Her sense of frustration was as powerful as her grief. After all the time they had spent trying to save him, the loss of a single lamp had undone all their work. *At least he looks peaceful now*, she told herself. The monsters that had stalked his spirit for so long no longer had the power to torture him.

Whoever was in charge of the afterlife, she prayed they would be kinder to Jeff than Erna had been.

Fourteen

Commander's Personal Log
Year One
Day Ten

We buried Jeff this morning, right beside Wayne. Anna printed a new headstone to serve for both of them, with clasped hands under the names, and Dani offered prayers that praised the power of love. As far as anyone outside my inner circle knows, Jeff killed himself because he could not bear the loss of his lover. And of course, that is part of the truth; Jeff's grief over losing Wayne played a clear part in his mental disintegration. But it was fear of Erna that eventually pushed him over the edge.

There was an undercurrent of relief among the mourners that no one would admit to, but one could feel it. The story of a man unhinged by grief, who had chosen to follow his lover into the lands beyond death, was something within the bounds of human comprehension. Tragic as Jeff's death was, it involved no alien horrors. Even as people mourned for him, I suspect many were secretly grateful for that.

If only they knew.

Lise and Dani insisted that I move my office, as my current pod might stir memories of the attack there. I told them it was important for me to show the colony that I was strong enough to move past such things. They reminded me that the fae responded to strong emotions, and if being in that pod triggered memories of my son's doppelganger, that might invoke another attack. Fair point. Dani said her office has very little in the way of contents, being mostly a meeting space, so a move would be easy for her. She'll trade pods with me this afternoon.

Team Paleo has been setting traps in the forest, with decent success. Steve is accumulating small animals in his freezer, saving them up for when he will have enough meat to serve the whole colony.

Another true night is coming up. People are clearly nervous about it. Given that the fae seems to respond to human emotion, I am more concerned about their state of mind than mere darkness.

TO DO:

Trade pods with Dani.

Finish the observation tower.

Prioritize technology. Reports have come in of more equipment failures. If this pattern is going to continue, we need to priori-

*tize use of the tools we can least afford to lose. Accordingly, I
have assigned extra teams to farming, logging, and construction, in the hopes of tilling enough land and collecting enough
lumber to see us through if our power tools all fail. I do not look
forward to cutting down trees with a hand axe.*

ꙨꙨꙨ

"Got a minute, boss?"

Leo looked up from his current project—cleaning the smaller
branches from tree limbs to prepare them for use in construction—to
see Sky, the head of Team Paleo, waiting respectfully for his attention.
"Sure. What's up?"

"Actually, it's more like something I'd like you to come see. Is now a
good time?"

Leo took a closer look at him, noting the tense posture, the hint
of nervousness in his gaze: not Sky's usual demeanor. Whatever the
man wanted Leo to see, it wasn't good. "All right." He saved his work
and turned off the tablet. "Do I need to bring anything with me? Or
anyone?"

"It's outside the camp, so if you're fine with just two of us, no."

Outside the camp. The words had a different flavor now than they
had a mere week ago. Then, it had seemed like the whole planet be-
longed to the Terrans; now their dreams were constrained by a rough
wooden wall. It was a hard thing to adjust to.

Wordlessly Sky led him to the north gate, opened it, and waved Leo
through. He didn't seem to want to talk about his business yet, and Leo
didn't press him. Clearly there was something Sky felt he needed to
show Leo first. "This way," the hunter said, gesturing toward a narrow
trail marked by flattened grass and crushed branches. Humans were
leaving their mark here.

The path led them into the deep woods; Leo followed Sky in silence. Now and then they passed a bright orange ribbon tied to a bush.
"Snare markers," Sky explained. "So we can find them easily, and so
others don't trip over them." Finally they came to a place where two

ribbons were hanging side by side, and he led Leo away from the trail, into the deep brush.

"There," he said, finally stopping. "See for yourself."

They were standing in front of a large tree with wide-spreading branches, in appearance somewhat like a Terran oak. Hanging from one of the branches was a large snare net made from salvaged parachute cords, intricately knotted. Its corners were gathered up at the top so that whatever was caught inside couldn't climb out, each point held in place by a steel clip also salvaged from the parachutes. Something appeared to have triggered it, but there was nothing inside.

"We figured the colony would need domesticated species eventually, so we set this up to trap live specimens, to see what was available to work with." Sky looked at the netting expectantly, as if waiting for Leo to comment on . . . what?

"Something triggered it without getting caught," Leo said.

"Look more closely. The top edge."

He did so. It all looked perfectly normal to him, except for a place where one of the steel clips was no longer attached. That part of the netting, robbed of support, sagged a bit. "You meant that?"

Nodding, Sky pulled down on that loose part of the net, showing him that with the clip gone there was a gap big enough for a man to reach into. "It caught something, all right. There are bits of fur inside, where an animal obviously fought to get out."

"And eventually did, it seems."

"Not on its own. The net is still intact." He shook the net slightly, making the steel clasps rattle. "That clip was opened neatly, not mauled by an animal. A person did this."

It took Leo a moment to process the implications of that; the process spawned more questions than it answered. "If you didn't do that . . . or one of your team . . . then who?"

Sky snorted. "That's the question, isn't it?"

Who would want to rob a trap? And why? "Maybe someone wanted more meat than Steve was currently serving and decided to take matters into his own hands."

"In which case the most logical target would have been one of our kill traps. No need to deal with an angry animal just to get food. Whoever did this wanted a live one. And I can't think of a benign reason for that. Hell, I can't even think of a malign one that makes sense. It's just fucking weird."

Like so much of this planet, Leo thought grimly. He walked up to the netting, pulled down the open section, and looked inside. Short orange hairs were visible in a few places, and the rope was frayed where a trapped animal had gnawed at it. Clearly whatever had been trapped in there hadn't gotten out on its own. Which meant either one of the colonists had released it—for God alone knows what purpose—or something even more disturbing had taken place.

It was Sky who put a name to that. "What if there's someone here other than us?"

"You mean, another sentient species?" To say that the concept was unnerving would be an understatement. *Sentient natives, competing with us for food. That's all this colony needs now.* "If that was true, the seedship would have detected it. That's what the survey period is for. And ours was ten times longer than usual." But would the seedship know how to recognize that kind of intelligence? Humans had reshaped their planet and left monuments behind: every square mile of Earth bore witness to humanity's reign. But what if an animal species were on the cusp of higher intelligence, but not yet at the human level? Reshaping no forests, building no monuments, but fully self-aware and capable of manipulating a simple mechanical trap like this one? What clues would there be for a seedship to interpret? Enough to extend the survey period, but not enough to record concerns about?

The thought that they might be sharing this planet without even knowing it, and trespassing upon territory a higher intelligence had already claimed, was truly chilling. But the last thing Leo needed to do was inject a new fear into the colony, when there was no evidence to support it. "We need to talk to Pravida about that. It's her specialty. But honestly, I think a human agent is more likely."

He helped Sky reset the snare, scattering leaves over the net so that animals wouldn't see it. As they left the area he turned back briefly and looked at the land where an unknown beast had wandered, and another

unknown beast had set it loose. Would he rather the latter be an indige-
nous alien or a member of his own colony? It bothered him that he
couldn't decide.

)))

The girls wouldn't let him help move his stuff. They said the colony
commander had better things to do than carry boxes from one pod
to another, and by the way, if he ever referred to them as "girls" again
they'd stick his head on a spike to scare off the fae-monsters. Fair
enough.

They said they were worried that if he returned to the place where
"Julian" had appeared, his memory of that event might be traumatic
enough to conjure a new visitation. But he didn't think that would happen. Something about that confrontation had *emptied* him, not of sorrow but of obsession. He had seen his son. He had been able to say to
his son all the things he had ached to say, and in return had heard the
words he most hungered to hear: I *forgive* you. Yes, intellectually he
knew it was just an illusion created by an alien predator, but knowing
that didn't diminish the power of the moment or its effect on him. As
Angie would say, the doppelganger served as a symbol of absolution
for him, and as such it had served a purpose independent of its lethal
intent.

But the trade would get him a bigger office, so what the hell.

He did an inspection tour of the various workshops instead. Most
seemed to be doing well enough—the team leaders were clearly on top
of things—but the mood in the tech shop was gloomy. Little wonder,
given that three more devices had failed that morning. They'd set up a
canopy so they could work outside, but even the crisp spring breeze
couldn't dispel the lingering miasma of despair. The guts of numerous
lamps, batteries, and solar panels were laid out for techs to peruse as
they struggled to find a damaged cord or corroded contact or some other
specific component to blame, but most devices had simply stopped working. Like the difference between a living body and a corpse, it was not a
structural issue but a functional one, and humans lacked the power to
return the spark of life once it had fled.

Angie was in a group disassembling batteries. She looked up as Leo entered, nodded a greeting, and watched in silence as he looked over the various projects and listened to reports. When he turned to leave, she got up from her work and followed him out of the work area.

When he saw her he raised an eyebrow. "Is there a problem I missed? Or something else?"

"I have a request."

"All right." He stopped walking and folded his arms across his chest. "Let's hear it."

"I'd like permission to hang some warding sigils inside the palisade."

He frowned. "Which in English means . . . ?"

"Symbols of protection inscribed on a plaque. We hang them inside the palisade to foster a sense of safety. Not on a conscious level, of course. But I believe I can design something that will help."

He knew her background, so he didn't dismiss the request as quickly as he might have otherwise. To her this kind of thing was science, though not necessarily to everyone else. "I don't think that would be a good idea, Angie. I'm sorry."

Frustration flashed in her eyes. "Who can it hurt? If it doesn't accomplish anything, we're no worse off than before."

He sighed. "We're facing an enemy with abilities some might see as supernatural. Already I'm hearing people talking about 'unseen powers' in ways that disturb me. I need to keep everyone grounded in scientific reality, so we can deal with these threats appropriately. Displaying symbols that remind people of ancient magical practices can do as much damage to the zeitgeist as good. Isn't that consistent with your own theories? That such images might impact their perception, hence their behavior? I'm sorry," he said. "I appreciate why you're making the offer. But for right now, I think it would be the wrong message."

There was a pause. "I understand," she said finally, in a tone that made it clear she didn't. But he was in charge and she accepted that; that was also clear. "The offer stands if you change your mind."

"I'll remember that," he promised her.

As she returned to the tent he sighed again and thought, *God help us if we ever get to the point where magical symbols are necessary.*

))C

It was late afternoon when Dani informed him that he could enter his new office. By then he was tired, worn down by the constant need to act like nothing was wrong, when all he could think about was Paleo's plundered net. Which of the people in this camp would have reason to do something like that?

The non-human possibility was too unnerving to think about.

Dani's pod was past the mess tent, farther back in the camp than his had been. The door was slightly ajar when he arrived, inviting him to enter. With a sigh he opened it and stepped inside.

What he saw left him speechless.

His desk and meeting chairs and a box of personal items had been moved here, and were neatly stacked near the door waiting for him to unpack them. Beyond that, the interior of the pod had been draped with panels of parachute silk attached to the ceiling from a central point, like an Arabian tent. A small table beneath that was likewise draped in fabric—sky blue with stars—and on it were two clear wine glasses and a bottle. Striations from the 3-D printer refracted the lamplight, tinting the glass with spectral colors that shimmered as he moved. At the far end of the pod was a low couch made up of cushions and blankets, covered over with yet another piece of parachute silk.

In the middle of that impossible scene stood Lise. She was wearing a silken shift the color of a twilight sky—real silk, not parachute fabric. The fabric flowed softly over the curves of her body, accenting it in just the right places. Her hair was dressed up for the first time since the landing, with flowers tucked into a thin crown of braids that held thick waves back from her face. Damn. He'd forgotten what she looked like when she wasn't in work mode.

As he looked at her, speechless, a smile slowly spread across her face. "Welcome home, commander."

"Jesus. I mean . . . this is . . ." He looked around the pod again and breathed deeply. "Wow."

"But first we have to see if you're worthy of it. Protocol and all." She put her hands on her hips. "Demonstrate your humanity to me, Leon Case."

He chuckled. "I remember when you made snow angels in Orientation. It was very cold out." The sheer impossibility of such an event in
the tropics made it the perfect identifier for them, as it stirred no pas-
sions for the fae to detect. A bit of shared humor that no Ernan monster
would understand.

"And I remember how your snowmen stood guard over me, so that I
felt safe." Her smile broadened into a grin as she stepped back and gestured around the space. "So, do you like your new pod?"

"It is," he laughed softly, "not exactly what I expected."

"It's only temporary," she assured him. "All will be back to your normal spartan mode tomorrow."

She picked up the bottle and poured its contents into the glasses.
The liquid was deep red with just a hint of violet. "This isn't exactly Dom
Perignon, I warn you. Laboratory booze has its limits." She handed him
one of the glasses, her fingers brushing his as she did so: just a delicate
touch, but it left tingling warmth in its wake. "To sweeter days ahead."

"To sweeter days," he agreed. The plastic glasses didn't clink properly when they touched, but the wine turned out to be . . . interesting.
An odd mix of local berry juice and purified alcohol from her lab, but
she'd managed to mix them in just the right proportion, and the result
was not unpleasant. It wasn't very potent, but he hadn't had a drink in a
very long time, so it went straight to his head. A relaxing warmth began
to spread through his body, cell by cell, soothing his physical tension.

"Are you trying to seduce me?" he murmured.

Her eyes sparkled mischievously. "Is it working?"

Maybe it was the wine that made the difference. Maybe the exotic
atmosphere she'd created. Or maybe it was sheer emotional exhaustion
that urged him to embrace this moment body and soul, if only to escape
the suffocating stress of the last ten days. Here, in this moment, in this
crazy multicolored faux-tent she had painstakingly prepared, there was
no sense of Erna anymore. No sense of anything outside these walls. He
shut his eyes for a moment, drinking in the blissful illusion. The stress
of leadership fell from him like a discarded chrysalis.

"Done with waiting?" she asked. He could hear the smile in her
voice.

He opened his eyes again and drank it all in, everything, from the shimmering draperies to the warm topaz glow of her eyes, to the soft ivory skin which seemed doubly pale as his dark fingers stroked her cheek. He took her in his arms and let his hands drink her in as well: loose flowing hair and crumpled silk and a sweetly perfumed warmth that comforted, healed, and enticed.

The rest of Erna did not exist now. Nothing existed but her.

"Screw waiting," he whispered.

Fifteen

Commander's Personal Log
Year One
Day Eleven

I have decided to assign sentries to the module. I don't know why anyone would want to steal things from it, but then, I can't come up with a reason why anyone would steal animals, either. Best to err on the side of caution.

I can't stop thinking about that theft. If an animal disappeared on Earth there'd be no lack of theories about why, because there would be no lack of mentally unstable people who could be blamed for it. But everyone here was vetted thoroughly before we left, and if anyone had a past history of mental instability they would not have been cleared for departure.

That said, one of the risks of prolonged stasis is brain damage. Lise said no one in our colony had suffered that, but what if someone was damaged in a way that wasn't immediately apparent? There are no cases like that in the database; brains

*damaged in stasis are always noticeably deficient after awak-
ening. But this group was suspended so much longer than anyone back home had anticipated—longer than our equipment
was designed to function—who is to say whether that data is
relevant to us? It's possible that someone who was mentally
stable back on Earth might not be so any more.*

*And then there's the possibility that the fae is behind this. If it
can sense and respond to human emotions, can it influence
them as well? Altering the way a man views the world, or how
he responds to it? Of the two, I'd rather deal with a simple
madman. If that's the case, then Ian is the one most likely to be
affected. He's clearly more sensitive to the fae than anyone else.
And he has been acting very strange lately. But none of that is
proof of guilt, and it still begs the question: Why steal an animal?*

TO DO:

*Arrange with the security team for a constant presence at the
module, of no fewer than two people at any time.*

*Confer with Dani about how best to ease people's fear of the
true night, so that they don't exude the kind of emotion that
could make it worse. If that is even possible.*

The clanging of the large triangle that served as a dinner bell rang out
across the camp, stirring the chill air of what was hopefully winter's last
gasp. Already half the colonists were gathered in the mess tent, shivering slightly as they waited for others to arrive. Steve had promised them
something special for this evening's meal, and people were as curious as
they were hungry. They pressed in close beneath the long tent, craning
their necks to try to catch a glimpse of the nearby cook's tent, searching
for clues of what was coming.

Leo and Lise claimed seats near Joshua and Anna. The way those two were acting suggested they were developing more than a professional interest in each other. That was a good thing. In a year's time, those who hadn't come to Erna with a bonded mate would need to choose their first birthing partners. Joshua and Anna seemed well on their way toward making that choice.

Leo took Lise's pale hand in his and squeezed it. *Mocha babies*, she'd said in Orientation, when they talked about combining their genes in the first wave of newborns. *We'll make beautiful mocha babies together.*

Steve stepped up to the podium. "Ladies and gentlemen, tonight we will have a special treat. I won't say a feast, because we don't yet have enough local food to pull that off, but definitely a dish I think you will all enjoy. Something that I suspect many of you have secretly been longing for." He flashed a broad grin. "As I'm sure you've guessed from the smells coming out of my kitchen today, we borrowed enough ingredients from our Terran supplies to bake fresh bread for all. So that is treat number one. Meanwhile, our peerless hunters in Team Paleo have been gathering meat, as a result of which we have finally accumulated enough—"

"Show us!" someone yelled, and another, laughing, yelled, "We're starving!"

"Very well." He bowed his head. "Without further ado." He signaled for one of his assistants to bring forward a tray with a towel laid over it, which he took and held up in front of him. "I bring you tonight's main course, a dish I fondly call *Ode to Earth*." He nodded toward his assistant, who reached up and pulled the towel off with a flourish.

There was a moment of silence as a hundred and eighty humans took in what he was showing them. Then there was laughter. Then a sprinkling of applause. Then more applause, until the tent was full of it.

On the platter was a hamburger.

"My people will be bringing around platters of shaved and sliced vegetables," Steve said, "which you can try as toppings. Do let me know which ones work out! There are also bowls of a red paste which, regretfully, tastes nothing like ketchup, but may serve the same culinary purpose. Again, I value your feedback. Oh, and lest I forget," he turned back again and was handed a covered bowl, "we don't have enough oil yet for deep frying, so I had to do the best I could with the oven, but I think for a first try they came out pretty good." He whipped off the cover and tipped the bowl toward the crowd so everyone could see what was inside it. "Ernan tuber strips!"

This time the applause was loud, and people started standing up, until the bowl of faux-French fries was receiving the kind of acclaim normally reserved for visiting royalty and hit stage shows.

"Thank you, thank you. And thanks also to my team." He waved at the two cooks standing by his side, who waved to the crowd. "Without their stalwart efforts grinding meat and slicing tubers we would not be standing here today. Give them a round of applause also!"

Laughing, everyone did. And then the food was brought out, so they all sat down to enjoy it. When Joshua got his, he gazed at his plate in rapture and said, "Never in my life did I think a burger could look this beautiful."

Lise chuckled. "Maybe we should add that to our list of colony milestones."

The flavor of the meat was unfamiliar—gamier than beef or lamb—but the texture was right, and the way juices ran out when one bit into it brought back many memories. Cups were brought around and filled with Steve's version of iced mint tea, refreshingly chilled in the meat storage locker.

"We should hold a bonfire Sunday night." The speaker was a member of the construction team who was sitting nearby; Leo had been working with Jake and his crew earlier in the day. "Say *fuck you* to the true night," Jake said and took a swig of his tea.

Leo looked at him. "We've got plenty of lights, you know."

"Yeah, and I also know they've been breaking down. You want to wait until then to find out we don't have enough left to fend off the darkness?" Jake shook his head. "People are getting pretty anxious about darkness. Those strange dreams they had after the first true night were damn unnerving. And it'll be worse now that we know more about this blue stuff."

"The fae," Joshua supplied.

Jake nodded. "So I say, let's light a big fire, gather around it, and sing . . . well, something." He paused. "I think you're supposed to sing around a bonfire. Never actually been to one myself."

"You stick little balls of sweet gelatin on sticks and hold them in the fire until they burn," Anna said.

Jake made a face. "Sounds dreadful."

"We can't afford to waste fuel," Leo pointed out.

Jake nodded toward the palisade. "We've got plenty of small branches we stripped off those trees. Pile them together they'll burn well enough. Probably only for a short time, but we only need light for a short time." He paused. "Hell, I'll organize it if you want."

Leo was silent for a moment, considering. The fire might indeed prove comforting to many, and setting up the pyre would allow the colonists to be proactive in challenging the darkness, which would be good for their spirits. "All right," he said at last. "Clear enough ground for it in the center of the south field, plus six feet of grassless border. Have buckets of water ready and extras by the watchtower and mess tent."

Jake's eyebrow rose slightly. "You expect it to get out of control?"

Leo snorted. "Probably not. But I don't trust this damn planet." He looked at Anna. "Tell Steve about the gelatin balls. Maybe he knows what they are and can whip some up."

Lise stiffened suddenly. "What's that?"

There was a low rumble, as if from a truck driving in the distance. The ground began to vibrate. Items on the tables rattled, and the tent poles started to sway.

"Earthquake!" someone shouted. Some people fled from the tent, while others scrambled under the tables for cover. The shaking of the ground became more and more intense, and Leo could feel the bench beneath him vibrate. Should he be running somewhere? He looked up and saw nothing overhead that was particularly dangerous—at most the solar panels attached to the roof might bruise him if they fell on his head—but he felt like he should be doing something more than just sitting there. Then he glanced across the table and saw Jake doing exactly that, sipping from his cup with one hand while steadying his plate with the other. When he saw Leo looking at him he chuckled. "Grew up in West Montana. You get used to it." He pointed to Leo's cup. "You'll want to pick that up so it doesn't spill."

He did so, but by then the vibrations were already starting to diminish. Another few seconds and the ground was still again. The rumbling had faded, and people were starting to creep out from under the tables. Many looked ashamed for having responded so dramatically to so little. Some discovered that their plates had shimmied off the table, their precious nostalgia-feast dumped unceremoniously on the ground. Leo saw one man stare at his for a few seconds, look to see if anyone was watching, and then pick up his burger, brush it off, and put it back on the table. Probably others were doing the same. Why not? There were no bugs inside the camp. Local bacteria hadn't had time to adapt to them yet.

"I suppose someday we'll get used to this," Lise muttered.

"Not like we have a choice," Leo agreed.

Suddenly a scream sounded from the far end of the tent, followed by others. Leo rose quickly to his feet, knocking over his chair in the process, and turned toward the source of the sound. A large beast was atop the table—twice the size of a man, at least—and it was unlike any creature Leo had ever seen. Its head was rat-like but its torso reptilian, and black spider legs jutted out on both sides. Its tail had the diamond patterning of a snake, with a long stinger at the end. A dark and viscous fluid dripped from that stinger, and when the tail whipped toward a nearby colonist—who quickly jumped out of the way—drops of it splattered across the table.

All this Leo saw in an instant, and then he was running toward it, Lise following close behind. What he was going to do when he reached it, he had no clue.

People were screaming and running in the other direction, and one of them almost knocked him over. A few people were simply frozen, and they stared at the beast in horrified helplessness as it grabbed Tom Bennet by the neck and shook him from side to side like a dishrag. Several others had pulled out their guns, and Leo did so as well. One shot rang out from across the table, then another; the first one missed the beast and whizzed by Leo's head, dangerously close. The beast twitched as the second bullet struck it, but otherwise seemed unharmed. It turned to focus on the shooter.

And that was when Lise charged it. She was carrying a chair, which she swung full force into the thing's head. It rose up with a roar, and she jumped quickly back. Now it was possible to get a clean line of fire angling up at its head, and as Leo aimed and fired, shots rang out from all sides. The creature wasn't bleeding—visibly at least—but from the way its head jerked back and forth as bullets struck, it was clear the barrage was having some effect. Waves of bullets slammed into the creature. One of them pierced its right eye, and now there was only a black hole on that side. One of the shooters barely jumped out of the way in time as the glistening stinger whipped past his face.

Steve broke through the circle of shooters with a long iron spit in his hand, wielding it like a spear. *"Get the fuck out of my mess hall, you motherfucker!"* As the creature turned toward him he thrust the black rod into its chest—deep, deep into the hellish flesh. Whether he hit a vital organ was anyone's guess, but he must have stabbed something important, because the creature howled in pain and rage, and stopped trying to attack people. It began to draw in on itself, legs curling up against its chest like those of a dying insect, neck and tail pulling back into its body, a grotesque contortion. It began to shrink—no, *dissolve*—features running down its face in rivulets, legs melting like wax, all of it sinking into a pool of undefined flesh that was taking on a strange blue light. It was exactly what Lise had described from the fight in Leo's pod, and he watched in horrified fascination as the blue light grew stronger, the flesh lost all definition—and then suddenly it was all gone. Only Tom's body remained, so mangled that it hardly looked human.

From the other side of the table there was the sound of someone weeping, and a voice saying "Help him! Please!" Someone had gotten hit during that first careless volley, and the bullet that had passed through his shoulder had probably shattered bone. Lise called for her assistants to fetch a stretcher, and tried to staunch the flow of blood while she waited for it. But each time she applied pressure on the wound her patient cried out; even Leo could guess that there were shards of bone inside that wound. At last Lise's team returned, and with her help they got him onto the stretcher, then carried him off to the clinic to be diagnosed and treated.

His throat tight, Leo looked around the mess tent. Those who had fled were returning now, and he heard a few asking what had happened. But those who had witnessed the creature's demise didn't answer. Some of them looked like they were in shock. One stood with his arms wrapped around himself, visibly shaking. A third was vomiting.

They now know what we have known for days, Leo thought. *That the mysterious force which permeates this planet is connected to the monsters which have been attacking us. Which means the wall won't stop them; anywhere there is fae, there is danger.* That creature might not have killed many people, but for the survivors, it had wounded their capacity to hope.

He saw Angie standing by a tent pole. There was no horror or fear in her expression, more like a dark fascination. After a moment he walked over to her.

"Spider and rat," she said quietly as he approached. "Lizard and snake. That thing wasn't shaped by the fears of a single target, but by the common fears of our species." She gestured around the tent. "And it had nearly two hundred specimens to harvest fear from."

It will have even more fear now, Leo mused darkly. *Since everyone now understands just how vulnerable they are. The fae is everywhere—invisible, malevolent. How can we fight such a force?* The key battle from now on would not be against alien monsters, but human terror and despair.

"Put up your wards," he told her. And before she could respond he headed back to the place where the monster had been, to comfort those who were still too shaken to move away.

Sixteen

A pounding on the door woke Leo up.

Disentangling himself from Lise's left arm and the blanket, he had to step carefully over two other people to get to the door. Now that all the colonists wanted to sleep indoors, every square foot of available space had been commandeered for that purpose, including his new office. Thank God Lise had foreseen the need for this, so they already had the longhouse ready and waiting. If she hadn't . . . well, people would have had to be very, *very* friendly.

The knocking sounded again, this time louder. "Coming!" Leo yelled. Force of habit. It woke up Pravida and Ted, whom he'd invited to bunk with him so the exo team could stay together. Well, most of the team, anyway. Dani was in her own office, and until he knew what was going on with Ian, Leo was loath to trust him with anything sensitive.

Finally he got to the door and pushed it open. Rod from the construction team was waiting, alone. Behind him was an empty camp awash in dawn's cool light. Leo looked at the visitor for a moment, then said, "Do you remember the night we got wasted together at Orientation?"

Rod looked surprised for a moment, then realized what Leo was doing. "Pina coladas. How could I forget?" Now that he had proven himself a genuine human being and not a doppelganger, he nodded back across the camp. "Dani needs you. She said to bring the exo team. Whatever that is."

It was the term they'd coined for the members of his advisory council who had skills related to the analysis of alien life, or—in Dani's case—its effects on humans. "Give us a few," he said. He looked at his podmates. "Grab your clothes, we've got work to do." The fact that Dani had asked for the whole group suggested something significant had occurred. Not exactly the kind of thing one wanted to deal with first thing in the morning, but time and the fae waited for no man.

Stepping outside, Leo saw a camp as still as death, utterly devoid of any human presence save their own. The only sound they heard as they crossed the south field was the stirring of tent flaps and something rattling in the distance. Maybe the cook's tent? Was Steve awake, trying to do his breakfast prep before everyone else appeared? Other than that, the place was a ghost town.

As soon as they entered Dani's pod, they saw why they had been called. A body lay in the middle of it, still as death. Where skin was visible, there was an odd sheen to it.

"Sally Chang," Dani told them. She was leaning against the desk with her arms wrapped tightly around herself. Normally she was good at staying composed in the face of tragedy, but the discovery that a dead body had been lying beside her while she slept had clearly shaken her badly. "It happened while we were asleep. Nothing else in the pod was disturbed. The door was still closed when I got up, though that doesn't necessarily mean anything in this place." She looked down at Sally. "Maybe it took her in her dreams."

Whatever had attacked Sally, she hadn't seen it coming. She was in the same position she probably had been while sleeping, curled up on her right side with one arm beneath her head and the other resting on her hip. Her skin seemed unnaturally smooth, giving her the aspect of a polished statue rather than human flesh.

"Touch her," Dani urged. "Go ahead. But gently."

Leo reached down and gingerly touched Sally's hand where it rested on her hip. It was as cold as ice—colder than ice—and hard as stone.

Frozen? He looked up at Dani, perplexed. Then Lise knelt down beside him and felt the body as well, less tentatively than he had. Hand, cheek, leg. All of it as hard as stone, and so frigid to the touch that when she was done she rubbed her hands together to warm them. "Can we turn her over?" she asked.

"We can try," Dani said.

She and Leo took hold of Sally and tried to ease the icy corpse onto its back. But as soon as they started to move her there was a sharp cracking sound, and the hand that lay on Sally's hip shattered like glass into a thousand small pieces. Leo pulled his hand away quickly. "Hell," Lise muttered. "You didn't even touch her there."

"We were wrong," Pravida whispered. Lise looked at her sharply, but the xenobiologist didn't elaborate, just stared down at the frozen corpse in horrified silence.

Lips tight, Lise looked at Rod. "I'll need to take some samples before we try to move her again. Would you mind fetching my tools from the clinic?"

"Sure thing." He looked grateful to have a job to do, other than stare at Sally's corpse.

"There should be a black bag under my desk labeled 'specimens,'" Lise told him. "That's got everything I need."

He nodded. "I'll get it for you."

"And some salt," she added quickly. "Ask Steve to give you some from the kitchen. I won't need much, just a tablespoon or so." She turned her attention back to the frozen body, cutting off any opportunity for questions.

When he was gone Ted shut the door behind him. "What was that about? Salt?"

"Time." Her expression was grim. "The bag isn't where I told him to look, so he'll have to search for it, and Steve won't give up any of his precious salt without a fight. That'll buy us a few minutes for exo talk, without having to fill in someone who hasn't been updated on everything." Her eyes narrowed as she looked at Pravida. "What do you mean, *we were wrong?*"

Pravida looked down at the frozen body and shuddered. "The heat was drained from her flesh. Tia's heart was removed. Wayne's bones were gone. You told us that Leo was mysteriously dehydrated." Her mouth tightened. "Each time these things attack us they remove something. It's a different thing each time, but there's always something. So do they really want to kill us? Or is that just a side effect of them taking whatever element they hunger for?" She ran a hand through her hair. "The fae isn't creating those creatures, but *we* are. We reach out unconsciously to an alien force that connects all the living things here, and we shape it with our thoughts and our memories, giving it a form we recognize. We've been assuming the resulting creature wants to kill us. But what if it doesn't? Maybe it's just an illusion when it first appears, without volition or desire. But once it exists—once it is an independent being—it responds as if it were truly alive. It needs to feed. And because it comes from us, and in a way is still part of us, we are its natural food source. Maybe its *only* food source."

She looked at Leo, a terrible tenderness in her eyes. "It's just a theory, you understand . . . but if I'm right, maybe when your son's doppelganger appeared it just wanted to talk to you, to offer the comfort you needed. That was the Julian that your own mind created. But once it gained substance it had needs of its own, that you couldn't control." She was silent for a moment. "That's my current working model."

"If you're right," Dani said slowly, "this planet doesn't see humans as pathogens, invaders, or anything else. The antibody response is an illusion."

"But how does that change anything?" Ted asked. "We still have to defend ourselves against assault."

Pravida nodded. "But if we understand why those attacks are happening, maybe that can point to a way to prevent them." She sighed. "Look, natural forces don't care about us. They just exist. Fire, wind, and water are neither benign nor malign; they simply are. Controlled, they can serve us; uncontrolled, they can kill us. I'm suggesting that's how the fae works. It doesn't care if we are alive or dead. This whole planet doesn't care. We have to let go of that whole model, and focus on the part we are playing in this."

Leo nodded slowly. "It's a new perspective. Perhaps a more credible one."

"Something to brainstorm with the rest of the council," Dani suggested.

Leo hesitated. "I've got something I need to take care of before our next meeting. After that, we can discuss this as a group." The last thing he wanted to do was to tell them he was coming to distrust Ian, and didn't want the group to meet until he was more sure of the man's mental stability.

Lise understood. She looked back down at the body and said, "We'll need to get this to my lab so I can really study it." She paused. "Might have to wait for it to thaw a bit first."

"You think it will be less brittle then?" Dani asked.

Lise shrugged. "Who the fuck knows?" She looked tired—not physically, so much as spiritually. Leo's heart ached in sympathy.

She looked up at him. "We need to talk. After the work crews have gone out for the day."

He nodded. "All right."

She started to gather up the shattered pieces of Sally's hand. Dani knelt by the other side of the body to help. By the time Rob returned with the tools, the bits of frozen flesh were all stowed in a specimen bag. Waiting for whatever kind of test might tell them what the hell had happened.

God willing, some test would be able to.

☽ ☽ ☽

There was no announcement about Angie's project, but word-of-mouth travelled quickly through the camp, and many were at the south gate when she got there. Good, she thought. The more people present, the better.

She'd already nailed hooks into the palisade at the four cardinal points—north, east, south, and west—so she was all ready to go. She took out the plaques which she'd spent the morning designing and printing and held one of them up high for all to see. The background was colored like natural wood and the black lines on it looked like they'd been burned in with a hot iron: very rustic-looking.

"These are the signs and symbols that our ancestors used to

safeguard their homes and temples," she announced. She was used to addressing college classes larger than this, so her voice carried easily through the crisp air. "Tradition says they can help protect those within their circle. If you offer up prayers to any god, spirit, or ancestor in front of it, or even just give voice to your hopes, it will connect you to it, and serve as a ward against the negative energies of this place."

Lise walked to where Leo was standing near the back of the crowd, arms folded across his chest. That he didn't approve of Angie's choice of words was clear from his posture, but he'd given permission for this performance, so he was voicing no protest.

"You free for a while?" she asked quietly.

"I can be." He looked at her. "You going to tell me what this is about?"

"Not here."

In silence she led him to the north gate. There were crude spears leaning against the wall next to the door, available to anyone whose business required them to leave the camp. Steve had proven that such weapons were more effective than bullets in dealing with fae-monsters, so the construction team had spent the morning printing spearheads and attaching them to the straightest branches they could find. Few were straight enough to be thrown with any accuracy, but the heads were viciously sharp, and they'd work for both bludgeoning and stabbing anything that came too close. Ugly but effective.

When they got to the gate Lise reached into her pocket, took out a small item, and handed it to him. "Here, put this on."

It was a small silver-colored medallion on a long cord. Turning it over, he saw the same symbols that were on Angie's plaques. "Oh, no. No way." He offered it back to her.

"Leo, this isn't about superstition. We know that the fae responds to our emotions. If this can trigger the right mental associations, then it's worth trying." She took it from him and slipped the cord over his head. He didn't bend down to make it easier, but he didn't pull away from her either.

When the medallion finally lay on his chest he frowned at it, then said, "Wait, you're right. I can feel new emotions rising inside me. What is that one? I feel . . ." He glowered. ". . . annoyance."

She smacked him on the shoulder. "Smartass."

He tucked the medallion into his shirt where no one would see it as she chose the two straightest spears for them. Then they passed through the gate, locked it behind them, and started down the same path that Sky had used earlier.

"I'm curious what you think of Pravida's theory," she said.

He exhaled in a soft hiss. "On the positive side, it's a much more rational model for the fae. More scientific, if you will. We're still missing a few crucial pieces of the puzzle, but it's easy to believe that when we find them they'll be consistent with her hypothesis. Not to mention, it frees us from the concept of a planet-wide force determined to eradicate all human life, which has considerable psychological value. On the negative side—how the hell do we fight something like that? Must we spend all our time here exchanging passwords like spies in a grade-B vid, sharing stories of pina coladas and snow angels and God knows what else to prove we're human, with no end in sight? When something is your enemy at least you can figure out its motive and try to address that. But when it's just a force of nature, as inexorable as fire or wind, with neither desire nor agenda—or even hate—what would you be fighting?" He paused. "Neither offers a clear path to follow, but I think Pravida's has more potential." He looked at her. "You?"

She sighed. "I dreamed of coming to a place where the practice of medicine was straightforward. No bureaucratic red tape, no budget restrictions, no supervisors to be sucked up to—just doctors tending to patients who were sick or injured, in the most effective way possible. And now here we are, in a world where I can't even give a name to what's killing people, much less do anything to help keep them alive. Pravida's model at least gives it a name. That's more than we had yesterday. But the thought that we might be generating the very creatures that are trying to kill us . . . I don't know, Leo. That seems more daunting than dealing with an outside power."

The thickly woven canopy eventually began to thin out, with more and more sunlight filtering through as they walked. A gully was now visible beside them, running parallel to the path; Leo could hear water trickling in the bottom. The trees gave way to brush, and then to a wide, grassy clearing awash in sunlight. She led him to the center of it and spread out her arms. "Here we are."

A small area in the center of the clearing had been stripped of grass, with a circle of stones demarcating its border. Not unlike what he had ordered for the bonfire back in camp. That there had been fire here was evidenced by a small mound of ash and blackened wood chips in the center of the circle. Off to one side of that was a wide, flat stone with dark markings on its surface. Leo moved closer so he could get a good look at it, and saw that some kind of geometric pattern had been painted on it, but dark brown stains obscured most of the details. "What the hell is this?"

"Your guess is as good as mine. But wait, we're not done yet. This way."

She led him to a thick cluster of bushes at the edge of the clearing, then crouched down and began to dig into the loose soil beneath them. A few inches below the surface she unearthed what she was looking for, and stepped back so he could see.

Bones, charred black from fire. Several were broken. "What am I looking at?"

"Sky's missing quarry, I'm guessing." She picked up a bone—a tiny vertebra—and showed it to him. "These marks on the bones weren't made by an animal, but by a knife. And this was all buried very carefully. Whoever killed this animal didn't want anyone to stumble across it. But he didn't anticipate someone would come here specifically to search this clearing, as I did." She looked into his eyes. "You know what this is. You don't want to give a name to it any more than I did when I first saw it, but it's the only possible explanation."

He drew in a deep breath. "You think someone is sacrificing animals."

"Don't you?"

His jaw tightened. "Ian?"

"He's the one I followed to find this place. He didn't kill anything while I was watching, but seems a logical suspect."

He looked back at the clearing—at the severed vertebra—at her. "Shit," he said finally. "Goddamn it." He wished that he were a religious man so that he could rage at God, *Why the fuck are you doing this to us? Why can't you just leave us alone?* The last thing they needed right now was for a member of the colony to go off the deep end. But it certainly looked like Ian was doing that.

They had no way to handle a mentally unhinged colonist. No place to keep him if he became a danger to others.

Gently she reached up and stroked his cheek, and after a moment of resistance he closed his eyes and turned his face into her palm, accepting the comfort.

Quietly he asked, "You didn't actually see him sacrifice anything, right?"

"No. I didn't."

"All right. So we're guessing. Our first order of business now is to confirm that's what's he's doing. Because it's not like we don't know someone else with a penchant for ancient rituals, right? We've got to be sure he's not partnered with someone who did this."

"Angie?"

His mouth tightened. He said nothing.

"You do know that killing animals is a mark of sociopathy."

He shook his head. "A sociopath would never have made it past psych screening—"

"Back on Earth," she interrupted. "But if something happened to him in stasis? We've been talking about that possibility."

"Then all bets are off," he muttered. *And what the hell do we do with Ian if it did?* He looked back at the ritual circle. "We need to figure out when he's planning his next ritual exercise so we can witness it."

"True night's tomorrow," she said. "That's what triggered his faesight last time. It's also when he started acting strangely. If this ritual has anything to do with the fae, I'm willing to bet he'll want to take advantage of that."

"I'll see if I can't find a way to confirm that without giving the game away." He paused. "That's why you didn't want to discuss this inside the camp, isn't it? You were afraid I might react in a way that would make others suspicious, and he would realize we were on to him."

She smiled slightly. "You know me too well."

He rubbed his forehead wearily. "God willing, this will all come to nothing."

"God willing," she agreed. She probably didn't believe that would happen any more than he did, but the words were comforting.

They held hands on the walk back, to remind each other they were not alone. It helped. A little.

Seventeen

Commander's Personal Log
Year One
Day Thirteen

The fear within the camp is palpable today. Now that people understand there's a connection between the fae and the creatures that are attacking them, they are like swimmers in a shark-infested sea: at any moment, from any angle, death might come. But a swimmer has hopes of reaching the shore eventually; we have no such hope.

True night will fall again tonight. Malik is overseeing the effort to collect fuel for a bonfire. Nearly all the wood is green, which means it will be hard to get it burning, but there's no avoiding that. He found some tutorials on the subject, and he and his team of volunteers have gathered bags of fallen leaves, mostly dry, which they are binding into bundles to serve as kindling. Hopefully that will work. I've given him some accelerant to help get the fire started, but we don't have enough to douse the whole wood pile, like we would have done back home.

I asked Ian if he would help me oversee some matters during the true night, but he made excuses about an experiment he needs to run then, which would explain his absence. There's no question in my mind now about where he will be when the true night falls. But if Lise and I do confirm that he's sacrificing animals in an ancient blood ritual, what then? Killing animals like that is supposed to be a warning sign of deeper disturbance, but we have no facilities to hold a madman. Am I capable of killing a man if he becomes a threat to the colony? I don't know.

☽ ☽ ☽

The gully was cold and damp, and though the tarp Leo and Lise had laid down to protect them from the soggy ground had served its purpose well enough, the chill of evening nonetheless invaded their bones. The dying trickle of light from Prima was barely visible through the trees, and soon even that would be gone. Lise had made a wall of leaves and brush to channel their lantern's light, which was on its lowest setting; hopefully no one outside the gully would see its light. It offered no real illumination, but might ease the suffocating weight of Erna's eerie total darkness when it finally came.

Leo tried not to think of all the things that might be in that darkness, things that human eyes couldn't see. Was the fae reading their fears, preparing to manifest them? Were serpents of deep violet fae rising up from their havens within the soil and heading toward Lise and him? Unlike Ian they couldn't see such things, and would have no warning before a fae creature attacked.

Maybe Angie's amulet will help, he thought. Though he'd mocked its superstitious nature before, its presence on his chest was strangely comforting. If the fae responded to their state of mind, then anything which calmed his spirit might offer real protection. Damn it. He would hate to have to admit that Angie was right.

"He should be here soon," Lise whispered.

The camp must have kindled its bonfire by now, and probably turned on all the solar lamps as well, to fend off Erna's primal darkness. Leo looked up at the sky over the camp and thought he saw a faint glow reflecting on the belly of a low-hanging cloud, reflecting the light from the camp. Would that compromise the true night? Or was it only sunlight that mattered? There was so much they didn't yet know about this world.

A low rumbling could be heard in the distance now, and two beams of light became visible, blinding to their night-adjusted eyes. Apparently Ian had decided to drive to the clearing. Lise turned off their lamp, then they both peered carefully over the edge of the gully, their bodies masked by shadows that the headlights were casting. They watched as a small tractor approached, pulling a flatbed behind it. As it came closer, Leo could make out the shapes of two large amorphous sacks and a duffel bag. Was Ian bringing more animals to sacrifice? Or was this something more ominous? Leo's stomach tightened as he took note of the size and shape of the sacks, and considered what they might contain. *Please God,* he prayed. *Let them just be animals.* His hand trembled as he lowered it to his gun and released the safety. Just in case.

The tractor pulled up to the edge of the clearing and then stopped. As the driver descended, his hair was briefly visible in the spill from the headlights: bright red. So there was no longer any question about who was responsible for those sacks.

They watched in silence as Ian prepared himself, like a pagan priest at the dawn of human civilization. First he took out a long strip of scarlet cloth and hung it around his neck, like the stole of a priest. There were symbols painted on it that glittered in the tractor's headlights, from all different Terran traditions: Hebrew letters, astrological signs, Norse runes, Egyptian hieroglyphs, and some designs that Leo had never seen before. They reminded Leo of Angie's wards, but the symbols were more chaotic. Here there was no sense of order, of cohesion, only a random scattering of shapes. Leo wondered if Ian even understood what all of them meant.

One of the sacks on the flatbed was beginning to squirm, and a moan was audible. There was no mistaking that sound: Ian had brought humans with him. Leo's hand tightened on his gun. If his botanist had reached the point where he was planning to sacrifice human beings, he had passed beyond the boundary of what the colony could or should tolerate.

Now Ian was taking a small cloth bag out of his duffel, which he carried to the edge of the clearing. He drew handfuls of white powder from it as he began to pace out a perfect circle, dribbling a thin line onto the ground to mark its boundary. Salt? If so, he was wasting a precious resource. The last item he took from the duffel was a lamp—not the solar kind, but a small bowl with a wick lying in it, like one might expect to find in an ancient tomb. He filled it from a flask, draped the wick over the edge, and lit the tip. Then he placed it on the flat rock, as one might dress an altar, and returned to the tractor and shut the headlights off.

Darkness fell upon the clearing, compromised only by that one tiny flame. Ian stood by the tractor for a short while, no doubt waiting for his eyes to fully adjust. Then returned to the circle and stood before the altar rock. Raising his arms wide as if seeking to embrace the forest, he stood there in silence for a moment, then began to chant. His words were as jumbled as the signs on his stole, a random string of prayers and entreaties in at least a dozen languages. Leo recognized bits of Hebrew, Latin, and Greek, but the rest were unknown to him. They might even have been imaginary for all he knew, the product of Ian's skewed imagination.

The chanting ended. Ian looked out into the night, drew a deep slow breath, and called out, "Erna! I come to you not as invader but as petitioner. Not to reject your nature, but to embrace it. We have resisted you for too long, clinging to our Terran inheritance instead of seeking transformation and rebirth. Tonight, we do not resist. Tonight I ask you for the gift of communion for all my people, as you have granted it to me. In return, I offer you sacrifice: the heartsblood of Earth. Cleanse us of our Terran past and make us part of you, like the species here are part of you. Let us be reborn in your image."

One of the bodies on the flatbed was struggling now. Startled out of his religious reverie, Ian pulled out a knife and headed toward it. Leo and Lise moved simultaneously. She sprinted to put herself between Ian and the tractor, blocking his access to the bodies, while Leo pointed his gun at the botanist and yelled, "Stop!"

Ian froze. "How did you get here—"

"Quiet. Just stand there. Hands where I can see them!" Leo looked at Lise and nodded toward the flatbed. She climbed onto it and started unknotting the closure of one of the sacks.

"Leo," Ian pleaded. There was fear in his voice now, and rightfully so. It would take very little right now to convince Leo to fire, and end this dark game—this insane game—forever. "I can explain—"

"Quiet," he ordered. He looked at Lise, who had opened the second sack.

"It's Eric Fielder," she said as she started to untie the second sack. "He looks drugged. And Liz Breslav. She's out cold. There's bruising on her head. I need to get them both back to the clinic ASAP."

Eric and Liz . . . it took him a minute to realize where he'd last heard those names. They'd been part of the security detail that was guarding the module, and had been assigned watch during the true night. No one would realize they had been taken until the next shift came on duty, at which point it would be too late to interfere.

Leo's jaw tightened as he looked back at Ian. "You're a threat to the colony." Rage was a fire inside him. He raised the gun up.

"Leo. Please. Just listen." Ian drew in a deep breath. "We need a way to communicate with this planet. A common language that the fae can understand."

"And these rituals of yours are going to accomplish that?" he asked harshly. "Assaulting your fellow colonists is going to help? Beheading animals?"

"Sacrifice is the most powerful ritual there is, Leo. Ancient man understood that. Primitive humans offered up their own blood to placate the gods. Abraham was asked by God to sacrifice his own son to prove his faith, Christ gave his own life to cleanse mankind of sin. Humans understood the power of sacrifice to create a bridge between humanity and the Divine. Modern humans simply deny it." He drew in a deep breath. "I believe we can use it to connect to the fae. Teach Erna the spiritual language of our species, as it were. Once it understands that this is how we communicate with unseen forces, we'll be able to connect to it—"

"This sacrifice is over," Leo said sharply. He gestured with the gun. "Move away from the tractor."

Ian blinked. "You thought . . . I was going to kill them?"

"You brought them here as prisoners. You came at them with a knife. What the hell was I supposed to think?"

"I brought them here to *protect* them," Ian said. "The knife was to cut them loose once we got here." His hand opened, dropping the knife to the ground.

"We were here, Ian. We heard you. *I give you the heartsblood of Erna—*"

And then he stopped. He looked deep into the man's eyes, and for the first time, he saw clearly the spark of madness that burned within their depths. And he understood, in that one terrible moment, what Ian had done . . . and what he planned.

It was too late to stop him.

Light flared in the distance, brilliant enough to turn the sky bright as day for a few seconds. As it faded, the sound of an explosion roared across the land, followed by a hot wind so dry it stung Leo's eyes. He didn't have to look back at the landing module to know that it was burning furiously; the look in Ian's eyes said it all. *What have you done!* he screamed inside. Hot grit began to rain down on them, smoking fragments of what had once been data storage, lab equipment . . . And DNA. Not all their Terran DNA, thank God, but enough of it that the loss made him sick.

"Now you'll see," Ian said. His eyes were gleaming with religious fervor. "Now we can start over. We can be part of this world."

"You idiot!" Lise cried. "What have you done?" If the module was gone, then so was the lab. Ian might as well have killed her child.

Ian's eyes remained fixed on Leo. "We needed to let go of Earth. There was no other way." He spread his hands wide, pleading. "Don't you understand? We identified ourselves as Terrans, so that's how Erna saw us, and how the fae sees us. We had to let go of all that. But we couldn't while our lives still revolved around Terran artifacts. Now there's no barrier. We can embrace this planet without reserve. We can be part of it."

He was proud of what he had done, Leo realized. The colonists' heritage had been destroyed, their genetic survival compromised, and everything they had worked for and dreamed of had been reduced to a cloud of hot ash, now spreading on the wind. And the man responsible for all that was standing in front of him, describing his actions as if they were something to be admired—nay, celebrated!—waiting for Leo to praise him.

Next he'll go after the tech gear in the camp, Leo thought. *And the data in our tablets, and the backup stores of DNA . . . all of that would have to be destroyed for us to be cut off from Earth completely.* Had Ian planned that out already? Or was it something that would occur to him after he returned to the scene of his crime and took stock of what was left? Looking into the man's eyes, sensing the depth of insanity behind his elation, Leo knew he could not risk waiting to find out.

He fired. Again and again, each bullet an expression of his rage and his despair, each splatter of Ian's blood a monument to justice. The botanist cried out and fell to the ground, but still Leo kept firing, until his gun was out of bullets and his soul was rent, and still he kept shooting until Lise came to him and took the gun away from him.

"He's dead," she said gently. "It's over."

"Not over," he whispered hoarsely. Then words failed him, and he took her into his arms and held her, his whole body shaking. And he wept, and she wept, while the ashes of their Terran heritage rained down around them.

Eighteen

Shaken, silent, they drove back to the camp, each cocooned in private thoughts, private fears. Eric was beginning to wake from his drugged stupor and seemed unharmed, but Liz was in bad shape, and from the way Lise was cradling the woman's head in her lap, protecting it from the jostling of the flatbed, it was clear she was worried about her. As for Ian, his bullet-ridden body was double-sacked to contain the blood, and as of yet none of it had seeped through the canvas. Leo would rather have left him in the forest to rot, but given that most of the colony's DNA stores had just been destroyed, genetic material was not to be wasted.

Domina was rising now, ending the true night at last, but little light made it through the forest's thick canopy. Leo's hands shook with impatience as he urged the tractor through the shadowy woods, but he dared not drive any faster, lest he fail to see some pit or obstacle that could stop them cold. The fact that the drive required so much concentration was good, though; Leo needed the distraction. He was still shaking from the shock of killing another human being, and as for what was happening back at the camp in the wake of the explosion, he was trying not to think about that. Hopefully Dani had been able to keep everyone calm. In a world where one's negative emotions could give birth to monsters, the panic of two hundred people could have terrible consequences.

By the time they broke free of the forest there was enough moon-light that he could see that the palisade in the distance was still intact. Thank God. There was debris in the field surrounding it. Some of it was still smoldering, bright red embers glowing like devil-eyes deep within the grass, but fortunately the land was damp enough from recent rains that the grass hadn't ignited. Metal fragments glittered briefly in the headlights and fell into darkness again. Most of the fragments were small enough for him to drive over, but he winced every time he heard the remains of Terran components being crushed beneath his tires.

"Wait!" Lise cried suddenly. Startled, he turned back and saw her staring at a spot off to the side of their route, where she had spotted a large round shape glinting in the spill from his headlights. He slowed the tractor as quickly as he could without jarring Liz too badly, but Lise didn't even wait for it to stop, just jumped off as soon as she could. Whatever she had seen must have been damned important, because he knew she wouldn't have delayed Liz's return to the camp by so much as a minute if it wasn't, so he watched with curiosity as she dug down into the grass for the item she'd spotted, then came running back to the tractor with it clutched to her chest. It was about the size of a basket-ball, with ragged edges, and the part of its shiny metal surface that was not charred black was no doubt what had caught the light. "Go!" she ordered, as soon as she was on the flatbed again.

He did so.

They were coming close enough to the camp to see light seeping through the gaps in the palisade. Hopefully that was from the remnants of the bonfire and not anything worse. Who could say what might have happened here once panic set in? He remembered Wayne's story, in which humans driven mad by darkness had burned everything in sight.

We've lost everything, he thought. It was a concept so vast, so dark, that the human mind could barely contain it. Yes, his people might sur-vive this loss, but the bulk of their heritage was gone. Was he, Leon Case, responsible for that? Could he have handled Ian in a manner that kept the man from going off the deep end? The guilt inherent in the question was suffocating.

Someone in the watchtower must have seen them coming, for the great wooden doors began to open as the tractor approached. Bright light poured out from the doorway as if from a demon's mouth, turning the tips of the grass a blazing gold, and Leo braced himself to face whatever terrible surprises the camp might hold. But as they entered the south field they saw that it was eerily empty. Except for the sentry who had opened the gate for them, there were no humans in sight. Even the bonfire in the center of the field was little more than a bed of glowing embers half-buried in ash. So many solar lamps had been hung around the periphery of the field, all turned on high, that the space blazed with light almost as bright as that of the sun. People must have gathered every lantern in the camp and brought them all here. He tried not to think about how much power such a display required, just prayed that all the chargers would still be working when the batteries expired.

Where the hell was everyone?

He drove to the door of the clinic pod, where Eric helped ease Liz down from the flatbed. The woman was barely conscious, and Leo saw her sway as she tried to stand on her own. As Lise reached out to support her the medic glanced at Leo, her expression apologetic. *I'm sorry for leaving you*, her eyes seemed to say.

"Do what you have to," he said. She nodded gratefully, and Eric put Liz's arm over his shoulder so they both could help her, while Lise reached out and grabbed the metal item she had retrieved from the field, tucking it under her free arm. Then the two of them started walking Liz to the door of the clinic pod, step by painful step.

The sentry had followed them, and by the time Leo slid down from his perch he offered a hand to assist. Leo accepted it gratefully. His legs felt strangely weak; the shock of killing a man had robbed him of strength. "Where is everyone?" he asked, trying to sound more steady than he felt.

The sentry pointed. "North field."

"All of them?" he demanded. "All alive?"

"As far as I know."

Fear eased its pressure on his chest just a bit. "Anyone hurt?"

"Cuts and bruises. Nothing more serious that I know of."

"All right. All right. Thank you." *Thank God.* He shut his eyes for a moment and breathed in deeply, trying to will strength back into his flesh.

"What happened to the module?" the sentry asked.

"Gone," Leo muttered. It wasn't the answer the man was asking for, and he knew that, but he didn't feel like getting trapped in a lengthier explanation. There'd be time enough for that later, when he knew what had happened in the camp.

Everyone is alive, he told himself. *That's what matters.* But in what sort of mental state?

He had to cross a strip of empty tents to get to the north field. Canvas walls twitched in the breeze as he passed, like ghostly vestments, and they blocked the light from the field, causing him to stumble several times. Not until he got to the last row of tents did the light of the north field become visible, as bright as that in the south. He could hear voices as he approached: a low, indistinct murmur, at first, then a clear, strong voice that filled the night, offering what was almost—but not quite—an ancient prayer.

> *I will lift up my eyes unto the heavens*
> *From whence shall my help come?*
> *My help comes from the Lord, creator of Erna and Earth.*
> *Behold, the one who protects us does not slumber.*
> *He shall not suffer your foot to be moved.*
> *The sun shall not smite you by day, nor the darkness by night,*
> *Nor shall nightborn terrors feed upon your soul.*
> *The Lord God of Earth and Erna will protect you from evil.*
> *He will preserve your spirit*
> *Now and forever.*

Now the north field was fully visible, immersed in a sea of light. Directly ahead of him was Dani's chapel tent. She was standing behind a narrow podium, atop a platform that raised her up a few inches so she could see the faces of all the people before her. There must have been a hundred of them at least, and the walls of the tent had been rolled up to make room for them. Some people seemed enraptured by her words, almost hypnotized, while others appeared lost in their own worlds, whispering to themselves (or to unseen forces?) as Dani prayed. A few were crying, or perhaps struggling not to cry; Leo could see their shoulders trembling. But they all were alive; that was what mattered most right now. No fae-disaster had swallowed the whole colony, as he'd feared might happen.

Dani herself was dressed in vestments that Leo had never seen before: a brilliant white robe with a deep red stole over it, the latter embroidered with a collection of religious symbols. It reminded him of the ritual stole Ian had been wearing (now spattered with blood and torn to bits by gunfire), but this one was benign in aspect, and the symbols were all ones that he recognized, representing various Terran faiths. Dressed in this way she served as a symbol of unity, a spiritual anchor that colonists of any faith might turn to for guidance. And it was clear that her audience was doing so.

There is power in faith, he observed. *And the more people need comfort, the more power she'll have.* He had been chosen to oversee Erna's first year precisely because he had no hunger for power, and the colonists had trusted him for that reason, confident that he would give orders only when necessary and surrender his authority at the end of his term. What would happen with a leader where those things were less certain?

Those colonists who weren't attending Dani's service were some distance away, gathered in small informal circles on the grass. Atheists, perhaps, or maybe just those who wanted a more intimate spiritual experience. But the fact that they had chosen to gather here, within sight of Dani's service, suggested that her chapel had become more than a simple house of worship. It was, as Dani had intended, a spiritual refuge that transcended the trappings of religion. He gave thanks that Dani had foreseen the need for such a place, so that it had been ready and waiting for them tonight.

She saw him.

Relief came into her eyes, but also exhaustion; he could only imagine how much it was draining her to maintain the mask of confidence that her role required. Meanwhile, some of the congregants (it was hard to think of them as anything other than that) turned around to see what had caught her attention. Several gasped when they saw Leo. Had they not expected him to return? People were packed so closely together that there was no aisle, but as he started to walk toward the podium they managed to clear a path just wide enough for him to pass. Like waters of the Red Sea parting. Some looked at him with fear in their eyes, which seemed odd, given that they didn't know what had happened with Casca. A few people at the edge of the crowd got up and ran toward the open part of the field, probably to alert the various groups there to his return.

"Welcome back," Dani said. There was a strange expression in her eyes as she looked him up and down, and he followed her gaze to see what was drawing her attention.

Fuck.

Ian's blood was on his clothing. Probably on his face as well. In the turmoil of their return no one had thought to mention it to him. Then again, no one had expected he'd be addressing the entire colony under lights that intensified the scarlet of every stain. He wiped his face clean with the back of a sleeve, but there wasn't much he could do about his clothing. Damn.

As he approached the podium, Dani stepped back to let him take her place. From here he could see the faces of all of the people at once. His people. The ones he was responsible for leading—for protecting. Whether they lived or died was in his hands. The concept was so unnerving that for a moment he just stood there, his hands gripping the sides of the podium, watching while people who had been sitting out in the field came to join the assemblage, to hear what he had to say.

He breathed in deeply to steady himself, then said, very simply, "Ian Casca is dead." He gave that a moment to sink in, then continued, "He convinced himself that in order for us to be accepted by the fae we would have to abandon our Terran heritage. That required the destruction of all the things we brought from home. Equipment, data, DNA, all of it. He's the one who blew up the landing module. He would have gone on to target the equipment and the data stored inside the camp next; his delusion required that all of it be destroyed." It took effort to force the next words out. "I killed him. He was a threat to this colony, and I saw no other option. I'm sorry. I will bear the weight of that killing on my soul forever, but it had to be done." His mask of confidence slipped from place for a moment, and his voice cracked. "I ask for your forgiveness."

He hardly dared look at them now. If he saw half the condemnation in their eyes that he was feeling himself, he might not be able to go on. "Whether his actions will change anything about the fae or the dangers we're facing, I don't know. No one knows." *Because I killed the only man who could tell us that.* "Tomorrow after breakfast I'd like everyone to gather in the south field. I'll share what information I have, and any of you who want to ask questions, or contribute ideas, can do so. Then, together, we'll figure out what the colony needs to do next."

Dani touched his arm gently. "I've been asked to keep services going until dawn."

Because no one wants to be alone until the sun is up. That makes sense. He nodded. "So we'll meet after lunch. One PM. Try to get some sleep before that. God knows we all need it." He nodded respectfully to Dani. "I'll leave you to your prayers now."

He left the way he'd come, down the narrow path they had cleared for him. As he neared the back of the crowd he saw Angie standing off to one side. In his mind's eye he could see the symbols that Ian had painted on his rock, probably in blood, and fresh anger stirred. He needed time to think. He needed sleep. He needed to let go of the rage that had driven him to kill a man, before he confronted the woman who might have contributed to his madness.

"We need to talk," he said as he passed her, just loud enough for her to hear. "Find me tomorrow morning."

She nodded.

No one else tried to talk to him as he left. Or maybe they did, and he ignored them. There was only so much shit a man could deal with, and he'd met his quota for the day.

Nineteen

Leo was busy at the watchtower when Angie found him, checking the earthquake reinforcements. It was early morning and most of the colony was still asleep, but after a restless night he'd decided that physical activity might be healthier for him than running the events of the night before on an endless loop in his head. And indeed, for as long as he stayed busy, visions of Ian's bullet-riddled corpse didn't haunt him.

Evidently Angie hadn't been able to sleep either. He put down his tools as he saw her approaching, but offered no greeting. Until he knew what part she had played in yesterday's events, social niceties seemed inappropriate.

As she came up to him he asked curtly, "Did you know?" After last night he lacked any desire to beat around the bush.

"About what? That Ian was going to blow up the module?" She exhaled sharply. "How can you ask that? I'm as screwed by what he did as everyone else is. Don't you think I'd have stopped him if I knew?"

"Yeah. Well. He was in the midst of performing some kind of ritual when the module exploded. And he was wearing this." He pulled Ian's stole out of his pocket and gave it to her. She unfolded the bloodstained cloth—now dry and stiff—and her mouth tightened as she looked at the symbols painted on it.

"Those look like the ones you hung on the palisade," he challenged her. "Or am I misreading them?"

"He asked me about my work. He wanted to learn how to use symbols to trigger specific emotions, so that he could control the emanations of his brain. He was trying to connect with the fae by conscious effort, in the hope of being able to restore his ability to see it. Since we think the fae responds to human thought patterns, I considered it a valid experiment, so I gave him the sigils he was asking for, and I taught him how to use meditation to focus on them." She paused. "Nothing more."

"Did it work? Was he able to alter his vision?"

For a moment she was silent. Deciding how much to reveal? The thought that she might be keeping secrets from him didn't exactly soothe his anger. "He told me that he did," she said finally. "At least for a short while. He said he wasn't able to affect the fae in any way, just to observe it."

Leo glared. "And neither of you felt this was something you should be telling me about?"

Her eyes narrowed. "He told me that he wanted to make sure that he could repeat the results before he told anyone about it." There was an undercurrent of defiance in her voice. "I made him promise that he would share all the information he gathered. How he did so was his business."

Frustrated, Leo turned away from her. He hungered to vent his anger by striking out at something—smash a breakable item, perhaps, or bloody his knuckles against the supporting poles of the guard tower— but that would accomplish nothing. When he thought he could keep his voice steady he turned back to her. "Tell me all you know."

"He told me he meditated on the designs I prepared for him and prayed to the spirit of Erna, asking it to accept him. Apparently that's what he did during our first true night, and he thinks that may be what invoked his fae-sight that night. If he performed any rituals, or added any props or costumes, he didn't tell me about that. He just said that the fae did indeed become visible, but he was unable to affect it with his thoughts in any way, only observe it. He saw that as the first step in learning how to control it." She paused. "I advised him to share that with you, and he said that he would, but he needed to know more first. Like I said, it was his choice to make."

In a voice as chill as ice he said, "How did animal sacrifice fit into that picture?"

"What?" The look of shock on her face seemed genuine. "Are you saying he did that? Or just talked about it?"

He said nothing.

"That didn't come from me, Leo. Moral issues aside, it would have been a wasted effort."

Leo's eyes narrowed. "Explain."

She sighed. "Sacrifice is a powerful tool because it invokes subconscious emotions. In theory, those might affect the fae. But that effect is derived from the dynamics of loss: first one's natural reluctance to destroy something valuable, then sorrow over its absence. The effect is proportionate to the nature of the loss: the more valuable an item one sacrifices, the stronger its effect. But that loss has to be personal for it to matter. The death of a random animal would mean nothing to Ian, because it cost him nothing. Shedding its blood would be meaningless."

"And thus without power."

She nodded. "Correct. Look . . ." She held up one pinky finger. "There is more potential in a single drop of blood from this finger than there would be in the death of a thousand deer. Because those animals mean nothing to me, while this—this is the very essence of my life. No sacrifice could possibly be more personal. But the blood of a random animal, on the other hand—that would only be meaningful to someone of such high moral standing that the act of killing shook him to his core. And then the real sacrifice wouldn't be of the animal itself, but of his morality."

"Early humans sacrificed animals," he challenged her.

"Yes, but what did those animals represent to them? Food. Security. Survival of one's bloodline. Diminish the supply of food in a primitive society, and you put all those things at risk. Perhaps that's not an issue for the modern ritualist, whose refrigerator is stocked with frozen dinners, but for a herdsman, the loss of breeding stock could impact the food supply for generations to come. That kind of sacrifice has power. It's what Abel offered to God. And what Cain failed to offer. Hence God's response."

He exhaled sharply "So I guess the big question is, did this damn bloody ritual accomplish anything? Has the fae changed at all?? Is our relationship with it any different than before?"

She shook her head slowly. "Without the ability to see the fae, we have no way to answer that question."

"You haven't tried to see it yourself? That surprises me."

"Oh, I did. Several times. Thus far with nothing to show for it." She shook her head. "Maybe there's some kind of innate talent a person has to possess, that makes them sensitive to the fae. Ian had it. Sally Chang might have had it. I appear not to."

"But you're not sure."

She bit her lip for a moment. "No. I'm not sure."

"So you can keep trying. And if that doesn't work, find someone else in the camp who shows signs of having that gift, and teach them what to do. Out of a hundred and seventy-eight people here, there must be someone else who has the potential."

A faint, dry smile twitched the corners of her mouth. "Is that an order, Commander?"

"Let's call it your new work assignment." He took the stole back from her and began to fold it up again. "Our long-term survival may depend upon our ability to manipulate the fae, and that's not going to be possible if we can't even see the damn stuff." *And I killed the only person who could do that. But what other choice was there?*

As he started to slide the stole back into his pocket, something brushed against his neck. He slapped at it reflexively.

Angie's eyes widened. "Leo . . ."

Slowly he held out his hand, palm up. In its center was a tiny back spot, waving its tiny legs as it struggled to right itself. An insect. Leo's breath caught in his throat as he watched it, his hand trembling slightly as full implications of what he was looking at hit home.

"I do believe," Angie said quietly, "that your big question has been answered."

☽☽☽

"I don't know how long I can continue to look confident," Leo confided.

"Then don't worry about it," Lise said. "There's no shame in admitting to vulnerability, so long as you make sound decisions. People will have more faith in your leadership if you're honest with them." After a moment she added, "Everyone's afraid, Leo."

The sun was shining brightly when Leo took his place at Speaker's Rock, a reassuring contrast to the fear-filled darkness of the night before. He chose to sit on the granite mound rather than stand, which gave him enough elevation to see everyone but felt less formal. Like he was meeting with the colonists to discuss common problems, rather than to give them orders.

They gathered around his perch in silence, which said much about their mood. Lunch had also been more somber than usual, voices pitched low in private conversations rather than merging in a noisy social ruckus. He wasn't sure how to read that. Had Dani's pre-dawn prayer service calmed their nerves, or were they simply so overwhelmed by recent events that they had no excess energy for social interaction? Their expressions offered no clue which it was.

He'd brought the last of his lunch with him, as had many others. The combination of greens, fungi, and slender strips of meat sautéed in local spices and wrapped in a large mano leaf—so named for being the size and shape of a human hand—tasted of this world, not of Earth. The very blood in his veins, generated back on Earth, was slowly being replaced by blood cells generated on this world, using nutrients from food like this. Cell by cell, all the colonists were being transformed. The same would occur mentally as their memories from Earth faded in favor of more recent Ernan experiences. That was the irony of Ian's madness: the transformation that he had tried to force upon them would have occurred naturally over time. All he'd done was advance the schedule.

Whether that would impact the colony's chance of survival was anyone's guess.

When people had arranged themselves as close to Speaker's Rock as they could, so that all one hundred and seventy-eight of them could hear him, he put down the last piece of his wrap and looked out at them. Their bloodshot eyes bore witness to a sleepless night, but food and drink had clearly refreshed their spirits, and they waited attentively for him to speak.

He cleared his throat, took one last look at Lise (who nodded her encouragement), and then said, "I told you all last night what Ian did. We're facing a dark time now—a frightening time—but we have the tools we need to survive it. The most important of those tools is knowledge. So I'm going to share with you what we've learned about the fae, and the threat it poses.

"Most of you have no doubt heard that during the first true night Ian actually saw it. Not as we did in the mess tent when that monster attacked—a momentary glimpse at best—but as naturally as you and I would look at the grass or the stars. He said that it appeared to connect to all living things, but . . ." He hesitated for a moment. "That it was disturbed by human presence. It didn't connect to us."

He paused for a moment to see how that news was received. It wasn't wholly surprising to them—Ian had talked about that night in general terms, and some might have guessed at the details—but for the colony commander to state outright, in plain words, that the planet had rejected them, was an order of magnitude beyond that. "Whether Ian's recent actions changed that," he continued, "I don't know. How well will Angie's sigils protect us? I don't know. We're going to have to discover that together.

"Meanwhile, I was informed this morning that two more tech items have ceased to function: a solar battery and a tablet. The pace of equipment failure seems to be accelerating, and the inclusion of a tablet in the list of casualties is very concerning. I hope we can figure out why this is happening, and find a solution, but meanwhile we have to face the very real possibility that we may lose our powered tech. All of it. So we need to prioritize the work that depends on it the most. That is: agriculture, lumber acquisition, and the transformation of our longhouse into an all-season facility. Those who have been working in those areas should continue to do so. As for the rest of us . . ." He paused. "We've lost our main database. The only data we have left is what you all downloaded onto your tablets. If the others fail, or we lose the ability to charge them . . ." He shook his head. "We'll lose everything. All the information we brought with us from Earth, all the data from the seed-ship survey, all our tutorials on survival skills, even the data we've collected about this world . . . all gone.

"We need to start preparing for that. Since our printers were all in the module, we'll have to write things down by hand. So that's what I'm asking you to do. Every free minute you have from now on should be spent transcribing the data on your tablets. I'll put up a board in the mess tent where you can note what subjects you've saved, so we don't waste time on redundancy." He paused. "The most important thing to preserve is the seedship survey. If you have data from that—any at all— it's the first thing you should save. The seedship mapped this whole world. It located deposits of salt and iron and other important resources so we'd know where to seek them out. It identified tectonic boundaries, weather patterns, the stability of waterways. . . . Every detail of this world that could possibly be measured, the seedship recorded. *We must have that information.* So when we're done here, please, start that task right away.

"Lastly . . ." He sighed wearily. "I was given this job to help provide stability and direction in time of turmoil. In that five people have died here already—nearly including myself—I must consider what would happen if I were suddenly removed from the picture. Accordingly, I've asked Dani to take over leadership of the colony for three days if that happens. Last night she proved her ability to rise above a crisis and serve as a stabilizing force. If some catastrophe takes me from this world, I have faith in her ability to handle things.

"That will give the colony three days to choose a new leader. I've considered various ways that might be done, and I'd like to propose that the people who have been serving me as advisors thus far choose my replacement. They've been privy to the fine details of all our investigations, have been testing various theories regarding the fae for as long as we've known it existed, and I believe are best suited to evaluate the needs of the colony following my death. Three days of lead time will give people a chance to express their concerns and offer nominations to someone in my advisory council. I'll post their names on the data board.

"Whoever is chosen will inherit my contract, which means running the colony as he or she sees fit until one year from the day we landed, at which point you all will decide what form of permanent government you want to establish."

He paused for a moment, studying the crowd. A few looked skeptical, but no one seemed particularly resistant to his ideas. They'd all agreed to accept his authority as a condition of coming here, and most seem to feel it extended to his choosing his replacement. Good enough.

"We need to collect as much data on the fae as possible, so I'd like to ask anyone who feels they may have observed it to report that to Angie." He gestured toward where she was standing; she raised her hand and waved. "Sally Chang apparently saw it in her dreams, so if you think the same is happening to you, please tell her that also. We have got to figure out what the hell this force is, and how to control it, if we're to survive here." A faint smile flickered. "You're all on Team Fae, now."

Slowly he stood. "I'm going to open the floor for questions and concerns now. Anything you want to ask, please feel free, and if I know the answer I'll share it. If I don't, I'll try to find it for you. And don't worry about saying something that might sound crazy; we're dealing with crazy shit here, and who can say where the next insight will come from?"

As hands began to shoot up, seeking permission to speak, he glanced over at Lise. *Good?* he mouthed. She smiled and gave him a thumbs-up. *Good!*

He felt oddly lighter in spirit, as if a burden had been lifted from his shoulders. Was that because now he could be confident that if he died the colony wouldn't falter? Or because for the first time in days he was a true partner to these people, not an enigmatic overseer whose days were spent worrying about who knew what part of the truth?

Such is the power of surrendering secrets, he mused, as he chose his first questioner.

☽ ☽ ☽

If Ian can do it, Angie thought stubbornly, *I can fucking do it.*

Her brain ached from hours of intense concentration, but still she had nothing to show for it. And no clue why she was failing.

Damn.

She got up to stretch her legs and started pacing around the inside of the tent she'd commandeered for this project. At this point what she really needed most was a stiff drink to calm her nerves and maybe get her creative juices flowing, but since the nearest bottle of Scotch was twenty-thousand-plus light-years away, she'd have to make do with pacing.

What the hell was she doing wrong? She'd given Leo a nice little speech about how seeing the fae might require an innate talent that she lacked, but there were other things in her life she didn't have natural talent for, that she had ultimately mastered. Determination and persistence could often compensate for a lack of natural aptitude, and God knows, she was determined.

She'd tried meditating on the mandala she'd designed for Ian. No luck. She'd tried other symbols with similar meaning, from numerous other Terran traditions. Still no luck. She'd even entertained, *very* briefly, the idea that Ian's animal sacrifice was the key to his success. If he genuinely believed that killing an animal would help him connect to the fae, wouldn't that belief affect his mind, and thus the fae? But since there was no greater resonance to the act it should not have had a stronger effect than her designs. And since she knew such a sacrifice was meaningless—hell, she'd written her master's thesis on the subject—it would have no effect at all on her.

Which left her . . . where, exactly?

I should start looking for someone who can do better. Leo had asked her to do that if her own efforts failed, and while it would take time to teach anyone all the symbolic theory they needed to attempt that, it was the next logical step. But pride wouldn't allow her to admit defeat until she knew without a shadow of doubt that she was completely and irrevocably incapable of doing this herself. And she wasn't there yet.

With a sigh she sat down in front of her workbook and began to review her designs. Each page held a symbol capable of stimulating a specific response in the human subconscious. Combining them into a single image should produce a mandala which merged those elements, like combining different musical notes to create a chord. But if one of those notes was off? Maybe she'd been going about this all wrong. Maybe the problem wasn't that something was wrong with Ian's mandala, but that the same notes which worked for him wouldn't work for her.

She spread out the designs before her on the ground and considered each one in turn. Most were related to Harmony and Communication, patterns designed to foster compatibility between Ian's mind and the fae. One signified Family, to nudge the other influences in a more intimate direction. Those should work for her as well. Confidence and Optimism, ditto. Submission . . .

She stopped.

He'd asked for that specifically. Said he was petitioning the fae to accept him, so it was important he acknowledge its sovereignty on this world. Terrans were outsiders here, and he was begging Erna to adopt them.

But what if he really had changed things? What if the destruction of the module meant that the fae no longer perceived humans as an infection, but as part of this world? This design would be irrelevant now, a discordant note in the harmony she was trying to create.

Feverishly she began to sketch, drawing elements from many of the designs before her, but excluding any that referenced a power imbalance. As she did so she could not help but imagine the fae in human terms, responding to her previous attempts: *Stop nagging me about the domination bullshit, and focus on the issue at hand!* If humans were connected to the fae now, they needed to shut up and act like it.

At last she had what she needed, a mandala that incorporated all the other elements she'd provided for Ian. The relevant elements. With shaking hands she put the drawing down before her, drew in a deep breath, and began to trace the pattern with her mind. Line by line, turn by turn, etching the meaning of each element deep into her brain. Ian hadn't known what these shapes signified, but she did, and that should increase their effect many times over.

When she had absorbed the entire design, and could visualize it drawn in glowing lines in front of her, she gave herself over to the rhythm of it—to the *music* of it—and let that fill her, willing her heart to adopt the same beat, so that the flow of blood through her veins pulsed in harmony with every sweeping line. She was not viewing the mandala now; she *was* the mandala.

And the world shifted. She could feel it happen, though she couldn't say how. Like a receiver tuning into a different wavelength.

She saw the fae.

It was only a faint blue wisp on the ground, and the ambient light inside the tent made it difficult to see. But it was there. It was there! As real as Ian had described it, and just as wondrous. She put her hand down to touch it, and while her regular human senses detected nothing, she felt strangely *aware* of it, as if new senses were stirring within her.

Entranced, she rose to her feet without taking her eyes off the ground. It was flowing just like Ian had described it doing outside the camp: smoothly, fluidly, elegantly. She left the tent and the bright sunlight nearly erased the vision, but not entirely. She could see the flow as she walked, and even perhaps a faint rippling as she moved, as if it was responding to her motion. Or to her scrutiny?

Slowly she made her way to the southern gate. She was afraid to turn her eyes away from the fae even for a moment, lest the magic of her vision fade and leave her trapped in the empty, cold world of normal human senses again. As a result she bumped into a few people who hadn't seen her coming, and stumbled into a dip in the ground that she hadn't been paying attention to. The fae had her mesmerized, and all that mattered was not losing sight of it.

When she reached the gate she started to lift the heavy bar that held the great door shut. A sentry shouted down from the tower, "Hey! What are you doing?" and she shouted back without raising her eyes. "Just need to look!" Maybe that wouldn't be enough for him, and he would climb down and try to stop her. Too late now. The gate was unlocked, and she began to pull the heavy wooden door open, revealing the landscape beyond. When the opening was wide enough to stand in she stopped, just staring at the land ahead of her, trying to focus her new fae-sight on features farther away than her own feet.

Thick grass obscured the ground in most places, but nearest the camp, where tires and feet had worn away the grass, she could see the faint blue light flowing along the earth. It wasn't only the same pattern as the fae inside the camp, it seemed to be the same current. Back and forth she looked, several times, to confirm it. And yes, the same fae that was flowing southward within the camp appeared to be flowing under the palisade—or more accurately, *through* it—to continue on the outside. One smooth, unbroken current, binding the human territory to the rest of the planet. All her theories and her experiments and a whole lifetime of speculation were manifesting in a single vision—a single symbol—and the power of that discovery brought tears to her eyes.

"You shouldn't leave it open like that." The sudden voice from behind startled her out of her reverie, but her fae-sight remained. She turned her head toward the voice and lifted her eyes as much as she could without losing sight of the ground. It was the sentry from the tower, come to see that the protective circle of the palisade remained unbroken.

As she stepped back into the camp, allowing him to shut the door, her peripheral vision caught sight of something right next to the opening, that she had forgotten about. Her ward. She walked closer to it, but couldn't see it clearly without looking at it directly, so she finally dared to raise her eyes up from the ground to do that. For a moment the plaque looked like it always had, a piece of faux-wood with her design engraved in faux-woodburning. Then she thought she saw a flicker of blue in one spot, just for an instant, and her heart nearly stopped. She stared at the design intently, studying every inch of it, and here and there she thought she saw another flicker of blue. There was no doubt about it; whatever substance or force the fae was made of, a bit of it was clinging to her creation, reinforcing the pattern she'd drawn. Would that affect the ward's protective influence? She put out a trembling hand to the ward and ran her fingers along the ridged pattern. "Not enough," she whispered. "Not enough."

It seemed like she spent an eternity staring at her creation, watching the dance of tiny blue sparks along its surface. At one point someone behind her asked, "Are you okay?" and she managed to nod. But it wasn't enough. She could see that. She'd managed to create something that the fae responded to—which, in and of itself, was a miracle—but so faint a connection couldn't possibly affect the entire camp. But if enough fae were bound to each of her four wards, maybe the fence would serve as a ritual circle, connecting them, surrounding the colonists with protection.

Which would require something more powerful than mere meditation.

Slowly she reached into her jacket pocket and took out the utility knife she carried with her, which she opened. *I should have alcohol to sterilize this. Or fire.* Staring at the ward again, she focused on the pattern she'd created. *But I didn't create the ward itself,* she thought. *I designed it, but a machine produced it. Would it have had more power if I'd burned the pattern into it by hand—felt the heat, smelled the smoke, struggled to draw each line perfectly? Maybe that's why it's weak.* She looked down at her left hand, then quickly drew her knife across the back of it. Blood welled up in the wound, and she focused on its spiritual significance as she dipped a finger into it, then applied it to the ward. Line by line she painted over her pattern, intersection by intersection, her mind focused on the meaning of every twist and turn. And it seemed to her that as she did so the blue glow increased a little, echoing the movement of her finger. Were her ritual actions really controlling the fae? The concept was too much to absorb. Tears came to her eyes as she worked, but she blinked them away and forced herself to complete the sacrifice. Then, when she was finally done—when the whole of the design had been outlined in her blood—she let her hand drop to her side. Her mind felt drained, her body weak; she could barely stand upright. *You have to do this three more times*, she reminded herself. *The circle must be properly balanced.* She pressed her right hand against the wound to quell the bleeding. The skin felt sticky beneath her palm.

She turned around—and saw that a small crowd had gathered to watch her. Leo was front and center; someone must have fetched him as soon as she began. He didn't look pleased by her performance, but it was clear from his expression that he understood what she was trying to do.

"Can you see it now?" he asked.

Could she? She focused on the ground again, but this time saw only grass. The magical vision was gone. The sudden loss brought tears to her eyes. "I did. For a while. It was . . ." For a moment she was at a loss for words. "Beautiful," she whispered.

"Could you tell if it had changed?"

"It looks the same inside and outside the camp now. No different around humans. So yes, Ian changed it." *He altered the course of our future. Will our children say that it was worth the price?* "The wards seem to work, at least in theory. Not enough to make a difference when I first saw them, but maybe now." She glanced back at the plaque. Already her blood on it was starting to dry, its slick gloss disappearing. She turned back to say something more, but a wave of weakness came over her; she put a hand out to the palisade to steady herself. The blood began to flow again.

He was by her side in an instant, holding her shoulders for support so that she could free up her hands to press the wound closed again. "You need to get that closed up. Let's get you to the clinic—"

"No. No." She tried to pull free, but lacked the strength to break his grip. "I have to do the other three."

"It doesn't look like you have the strength for that."

"I have to finish it," she insisted. "The pattern has to be balanced."

He sighed. "All right. But we stop and pick up some bandages along the way, okay? So at least you don't have to bleed your way around the camp."

But that would be in a circle, she thought. *Circles are good.* "Okay," she whispered. She tried to take another step and almost fell.

"Angie . . . ?" he asked, in a tone that her father might have used.

"Just a little rest," she breathed. "Only a short while. Promise me."

"I promise."

Did she walk the rest of the way? Did he carry her? It was all a haze. A dizzying, triumphant, glorious haze.

Ian, you changed the world. Now it's up to me to explore it.

Twenty

Leo sits in his office, staring at emptiness. He doesn't remember how he got there, or know why he is there, but he senses with dread certainty that the time and date matter. There is something he has to do now, right now, or he will never forgive himself. But what? The memory slips through his fingers like a ghost.

Then a form begins to take shape in front of him. At first it is nearly transparent, visible only when he squints the right way, but slowly it gains in solidity until it is substantial enough for him to see clearly. He gasps and rises from his seat as he recognizes his son. Julian is wearing the same shirt he was wearing the day he died, and when he sees it Leo suddenly knows what day it is. He glances up at the clock and sees that the hour is too late for him to wrestle with fate. Only minutes remain before his beloved son will die, and he is still far across town, incapable of getting to him in time.

A silent scream wells up in his soul: No!

He longs to reach out to Julian, to embrace him, but he remembers all too well what happened last time he did that, so he reigns in the instinct. But this visitation doesn't feel like the last one. This time there is no outside force drawing him forward, reflecting the power of a fae-creature *that wants to feed on him, only the terrible yearning of a father who is about to lose his son a second time.*

I am dreaming, he thinks. I must be dreaming. Please God, let me be dreaming.

"*Daddy,*" *his dream-son whispers.* "*Help me. Please.*"

A knot rises in his throat. He must struggle to find his voice. "*I can't,*" *he whispers hoarsely.* "*It's too late.*"

Tears are in the boy's eyes now—not of sorrow, but of terror. "*I don't want to die!*"

"*Then run!*" *he says.* "*There are still a few minutes left. Maybe you can get out of the building before—*"

"*Too late,*" *the boy gasps, interrupting him. He glances upward and flinches, as if some fearsome thing is bearing down on him. God in heaven, is he going to have to watch his son die? Surely not even a dream could be so cruel.* "*Help me, Daddy!*"

Tears are filling Leo's eyes. "*How? How can I save you? I'll do anything! Tell me!*"

The boy's eyes fix on him, pleading. "*Really anything?*"

"*Anything,*" *he swears fervently.*

"*At any price?*"

His heart is pounding. "*Yes. At any cost. Tell me, before it's too late!*" *He can imagine the train car outside the rec center plunging down from its track, hurtling toward his little boy.* "*Tell me what to do!*"

"*Even if it costs you your own life?*"

For a moment he can't speak. "*What?*"

"*Take my place,*" *the boy says. His eyes are pleading.* "*Be here when the building falls, instead of me. Take on my death, to give me life. Will you do that, Daddy? Will you die for me?*"

For a moment he can't speak. All the emotions of the past few years are flooding back into his soul, a tsunami of pain, loss, regret, and the terrible, terrible guilt of having failed someone he loved. A guilt so intense that he had fled Earth to try to escape its suffocating grip. Yet even that didn't work.

He is being given a second chance.

"*Yes,*" *he says.* "*Yes.*" *There is strength in his voice. Resolution.* "*Let me die for you, Julian.*"

—*And suddenly the office is there, the ghost of Julian is there, but he is also standing in the middle of the rec center at 432 Madison. All around him are children playing games, blind to the disaster that's about to befall them. He tries to yell out a warning, but the words catch in his throat, and he finds he can't make a sound. He can only bear terrible witness to the fate that his son was destined to suffer.*

He can hear it now. A screeching sound so loud it hurts his ears. Crashing sounds from outside the building. He remembers the concrete blocks that had littered the ground when he ran through the smoky ruins in search of his son. His precious son. That boy would live now, thanks to his sacrifice. Tears flow freely down his cheeks as the children look up, startled by the noise. Once, Julian had been among them. This time, he would be spared.

Because of Leo's love.

The train hits with enough force to make the whole building shake. He hears rebar snapping and glass shattering, and pieces of brick are flying in every direction as the walls and ceiling split into a thousand pieces. But Leo is not afraid. Standing at the edge of chaos, he is strangely calm. His body is about to be crushed, but for the first time since Julian's death, his soul feels complete. The emptiness inside him is gone. He is giving his life to save someone he loves, and there is a terrible and terrifying ecstasy in such sacrifice.

He spreads his arms wide in welcome as the wall collapses upon him.

Commander's Personal Log
Year One
Day Fifteen

Bad dream last night, unable to sleep after that. Up at dawn to transcribe all my existing logs with pen and paper, then a solemn breakfast with frightened people. This is my first attempt to compose a document without electronic aid. How strange it feels, to shape each word with my hand, conscious of every letter! It is a much more intimate experience than typing on a virtual keyboard or using voice transcription. Once, this was the only option humans had available. We have come so far as a species since then, but now, in this fearsome place, we are forced to surrender that progress. My heart aches as I shape each letter.

Ted confirmed that the CCs are back, though we hardly needed him to do that. At breakfast people were showing off their bug bites. Thus far none of them look particularly threatening— or so Lise announced after inspecting them—but one person said he had squashed a gnat-like creature while it was trying to draw blood from his arm. Great. The last thing we need now is a swarm of pseudo-mosquitos. On Earth such species were known for carrying diseases, and the mere fact that they are here today, just two weeks after our landing, suggests that we are not going to get the "honeymoon period" other colonies enjoyed regarding insects and pathogens. Is that the fae's doing? Now that it recognizes us as part of the ecosystem here, is it helping species adapt to us? Yet another unnerving possibility.

New equipment failures have been noted, including one tablet. I will admit that in my heart I was hoping that particular branch of technology would prove immune to Erna's corrupting power, but why should it? We also lost two more solar panels. We're going through the motions of trying to repair everything, but I don't think anyone here believes we'll be able to. Whatever is destroying our tech is beyond our ken or correction, and the day is coming soon when we will just have to accept that.

The list of transcriptions on the board I set up is steadily growing. I am relieved to see a number of survey maps have already been preserved. People have devoted themselves to this task with enthusiasm; I think they are glad to have a task they can focus on, to keep from thinking about darker things. Some peo-

ple's handwriting is so execrable I question whether we'll be able to read their notes, but that's something we can work out later.

I see people going over to Angie's wards, touching them like one would a holy relic, sometimes offering prayers in front of them. I'm not thrilled with that development, but if Angie is correct, and her wards are channeling emotional energy, perhaps it will help. Whether they will protect us or not is something we have no way to know until a fae-creature tests them. But every hour that passes without incident makes it seem more likely that we're safe, and a guarded optimism seems to be seeping into the camp. I am glad to see that, but also saddened. Never did I imagine I would live in a place where having a day pass without someone dying would seem like a major accomplishment.

"Knock knock."

He looked up to see Lise standing in the open doorway. "Hey."

"Busy?" she asked.

He smiled. "Never too busy for you." He turned off the tablet and put it aside.

She looked genuinely happy, which was rare for anyone these days. For a moment he just basked in the warmth of it. "Is there good news? I could use some."

She didn't answer him with anything but a broader smile. Eyes sparkling, she reached out a hand to him. "Come."

He let her lead him out of the office and across the southern field. At one point they passed some people sitting in a circle, fashioning spears from tree branches. He would rather they be working on transcriptions, but until the wards have kept them safe long enough for people to be sure of them, defensive weapons would be good to have.

"Where are we going?" he asked, but she just put a finger to her lips and said nothing. Clearly she was enjoying being mysterious, and truth be told, he was enjoying it as well. The playfulness of her manner reminded him of Orientation, and all the memories associated with that were good ones.

Apparently she was bringing him to her clinic, where she held the door open and ushered him inside. The place looked more or less as he remembered it, save for a few items on top of her desk. One was the strange metal object she had picked up the night of the explosion. It was the size of a human head, the end of a cylinder which had been torn from a greater whole. The outside was smeared with soot in a few spots—or perhaps charred—but the inside looked clean.

"What is it?" he asked.

"The inner sleeve of my fermentation tank. I thought that maybe the contents had been protected enough that something survived. A single spore caught in a seam, perhaps, dry but still viable. It's pretty tenacious stuff." She directed his attention to the glass petri dish on the desk. "Look," she said, as proudly as a parent might when showing off her child's art-work. So he looked. It took him a moment to see anything on the surface of the agar, save for a few thin circles of blue-green growth. He held the dish up to the light so he could see it better, then looked at her, a question in his eyes.

Grinning, she nodded. "Penicillium mold. I got it." She exhaled dramatically. "Do you know what that means? By the time we run out of antibiotics from Earth we'll be producing our own. Antibiotics, Leo. It's one of the two things we would need to practice modern medicine when the Terran supplies run out. This is a milestone, Leo."

"What's the other one?"

"Anesthetics. We lost the Terran botanicals we brought with us, but new ones shouldn't be hard to find. On Earth both natural numbing agents and mind-altering plants were common enough; we should be able to find some here, before our supplies from home are used up."

"And you may not have to replace all of them."

She raised an eyebrow.

He looked at the petri dish. "If your mold survived the blast, isn't it possible some of our Terran seed stock did also? Scattered across the grasslands maybe, or blown by the wind to distant places? If any of those seeds were viable, we might someday find those plants growing on Erna."

"Priceless Terran plants popping up as weeds—that's a great image! But you're right, we'll have to check every plant that starts growing in this vicinity before we pull it up." She chuckled. "Ag team will hate you for that."

He shrugged. "There are worse things to be hated for."

"I'll need to transcribe drawings and data for the most important species. Make sure that's not lost."

Hope. Was this what it felt like? To know that the future might hold something better for the colonists than being picked off one by one until the planet was cleansed of Terrans? Part of him wanted to embrace the feeling—explore it—drown in it. Part of him was afraid that the moment he did so he would lose sight of it—or else discover it was nothing but a thin mask of self-deception, hiding darker emotions.

"Two women came to see me," Lise said. "They wanted to know if I thought you would give them permission to impregnate now, using some of our Terran DNA. Five hundred samples came down with the drop pods as backup, but if the storage unit loses power they won't last long. A hundred and seventy-eight people aren't enough to establish a healthy gene pool. We really need to use those samples while we've got them."

"There are tribes on Earth that survived with less," he said.

"You don't like the idea?"

"Of numerous women getting pregnant right now, with all that's going on? All of them due to give birth at the same time, in mid-winter? No, I don't like the idea." He paused. "But you're right, of course. Any day now, we could lose all that DNA. Do you think others will want to join them?"

"I suspect as many as you'll allow. We can stagger them a bit, but if we wait too long, the opportunity may pass."

He sighed. "Yeah. I'll have to do some math, weigh all the different factors, come up with a viable plan." He blinked. "But why did they come to you instead of me? I'm the person who would have to give that permission."

"I'm a woman, Leo." She smiled gently. "Not to mention, I'm the one who would have to deactivate their contraceptive implants."

Her eyes widened, as she realized what she'd said. There was a moment of silence.

"Shit," Leo said.

"Ditto that." She wiped a stray lock of hair back from her face. "I'll get to work on some kind of backup contraception, in case that tech fails too. Which we should make available as soon as possible. We sure as hell don't want everyone getting pregnant at the same time."

"That would be something to see in December, wouldn't it?"

"Knock wood, we never will." She started to reach out to fulfill the traditional ritual, then realized there wasn't any wood in the pod. Chuckling, she had to settle for tapping her knuckles on the top of her desk. "Knock polymer?"

He tapped the cabinet beside him in agreement. "Knock polymer."

Twenty-one

The body was discovered just after dawn.

Ted and Pravida had already left to work on some joint project—
or perhaps to claim a few moments of privacy before the day's work
began?—so Leo and Lise were alone in the pod when the knock came.
It was earlier than visitors would be expected, so Lise watched with curiosity as Leo got up and opened the door. Outside were Chao and
Asahi, part of the group staying in the quarantine pod. The expressions
on their faces were grim enough that there was little doubt about what
kind of news they had come to deliver.

"Faren Whitehawk went missing this morning," Chao said without
preamble. "He must have left while the rest of us were asleep. Once we
realized he was missing, and not just off taking a piss, we went to look
for him." His jaw tensed. "We found him."

For a moment Leo was silent. Then: "Still alive?"

Mouth tight, Chao shook his head: *No.*

"Where is he?"

"In one of the tents in the last row. We left the flap down so passers-
by wouldn't see. We thought we should report it to you first."

"That was a good thought. Thank you." He glanced back at Lise,
then told the two men, "Give us a minute, will you?"

"Of course." Asahi closed the door to wait.

Leo looked at Lise. For a moment neither of them said anything. Then he sighed deeply. "So much for 'the worst is over,' huh?"

"No shit," she muttered.

They pulled on fresh clothes and joined the two men outside. This early in the day there were few people around; most of the colonists were still sleeping, blissfully unaware that Erna had claimed yet another life. The emptiness of the camp reminded Leo of when he had returned from Casca's ritual. Not exactly a comforting image.

The body was in a tent in the northeastern corner of the camp, close to the pod Faren had been sleeping in. Chao pulled aside the door flap for the others to enter. There was enough light coming through the canvas walls to make the interior visible, albeit dimly, and Lise could see Faren's body lying in the center of the tent. With his limbs askew and his eyes staring into nothingness, he looked more like a broken doll than a person. Lise's stomach tightened in dread as she remembered the state they had found Wayne in—so similar!—and she reached for a lantern hanging by the door, buying a moment to gather herself. By its light she could see the body more clearly now. Faren's normally ruddy skin was a ghastly bleached color that made it look like he had been dead for days, and the expression frozen on his face was one of horror. She crouched down warily by the side of the body so she could inspect it more closely. A touch to his neck confirmed the lack of pulse, but his skin was slightly warm and still pliable.

"Whatever happened to him," she told the others, "it was recent."

"What killed him?" Asahi asked. "Can you tell?"

"Not yet." She looked up at Leo. "Give me a hand turning him on his side, will you?"

Leo helped her roll the body on its side so she could pull up Faren's shirt and inspect his back. "No lividity," she mused. "So this was *very* recent." She brought the lantern close to the man's face so she could inspect his neck. She thought she'd felt a small bump there while checking for his pulse, and wanted to see what it was.

There were two bumps, she discovered, about an inch apart. Both had black holes in their center, with ragged white edges and flakes of dried blood around the rim. An insect wouldn't make holes that large, and an animal's bite would have left the impression of more teeth than that. A snake, perhaps? God, she hoped so. The only other possible explanation seemed crazy. But wasn't that par for the course on Erna?

"What is it?" Leo asked. He was on the other side of the body and couldn't see what she had found. Nor could the two men standing respectfully near the doorway, because she was blocking their view. For one terrible endless minute, she was the only one who knew the truth. Then she forced herself to turn Faren's neck to one side so that the twin wounds caught the light, and she moved back far enough that everyone could see them.

"What the *fuck*?" There was fear in Asahi's voice now. "I mean . . . what the _fuck_?"

"Please tell me those aren't what they look like," Chao begged.

She took out her utility knife and made a deep cut into Faren's neck; her hand was trembling. The flesh she revealed was bloodless. So much for snakes. "I'm afraid they probably are."

"*Vampires?*" Asahi sputtered. "Are you telling me there are vampires on Erna? Jesus! What's next? Werewolves? Zombie hordes?" An edge of hysteria was creeping into his voice. "What the fuck are we supposed to do now?"

"Shush," Chao warned. "Keep your voice down."

"Why?" he demanded. "Shouldn't everyone know about this?"

"Not right now," Lise said sternly. "Not until I can confirm this is what it looks like. Unless you want everyone to panic over a monster that may not even exist, in which case, go ahead and shout it from the rooftops."

"Monsters do exist here," Chao reminded her. "Everyone knows that."

They exist because we create them, she thought. *And then they feed on us. Whatever killed Faren came from his own mind.* The bizarre alien intimacy of such a relationship was almost as disturbing as the death itself. "Come on," she said, "help me get him back to the clinic so I can do a proper autopsy. We can all decide what to do then." She doubted an autopsy would tell them anything new, but at least that plan would keep Asahi calm and buy her and Leo some time before these two started talking to everyone in the camp about vampire killings.

As for Leo, he looked like he had aged ten years in the last ten minutes. Little wonder. This was about more than a single killing. It was proof Angie's wards weren't working. Lines of stress aged his face in a way they hadn't the day before, and the spark of life that had been so bright in him yesterday had been swallowed by shadows once more. Her heart ached to see the change in him.

Chao hoisted the corpse onto his shoulder while Asahi pulled the door flap out of his way, and the four of them headed back toward the clinic. The camp was marginally brighter now; soon the sun would rise above the horizon and bathe Erna in its cleansing light. Nearly all the fae-creatures had appeared during the hours of darkness. *Night-born*, Dani called them. The colonists would think themselves safe while the sun was shining; not until nightfall would they have to deal with the wave of panic this new assault would conjure.

When they had laid Faren's body on Lise's exam table, Leo asked Chao and Asahi to please tell Angie and Dani and to come to the clinic, after which they should go get some breakfast and try to relax. Leo would share with them whatever the autopsy revealed, he promised.

He closed the door behind them so that he and Lise were alone.

"It came from inside the camp," he said in a strained voice. "Otherwise the sentries would have seen it. It probably manifested inside that tent. And damn quickly, or Faren might have been able to run from it or at least yell for help. Which means there's no safety anywhere, not within the camp, not even in enclosed spaces. No safety and no defense. Jesus." He rubbed his forehead. "How can I protect people from something like that?"

"You're not alone in this," she reminded him. "We're all here with you." But she could see in his eyes that her words had no power. In his mind he had taken personal responsibility for the welfare of this colony, and every new assault was further proof of his failure. She didn't know what to say that would help.

"We can't escape this thing," he muttered. "Or fight it."

"We'll find a way." She wasn't sure she believed that anymore, but she had to at least pretend that she did, so she could reassure others.

We all banked our hopes on Angie's wards, Lise thought. We convinced ourselves they worked because believing in them helped us

maintain our sanity. What will happen when that illusion is shattered?
When primitive instincts cry out for people to fight or flee—-only there
is no way to fight, and nowhere to flee to?

With a sigh she turned her attention to examining Faren's body, but
the process revealed exactly what she had expected: the body was completely bloodless, with no sign of damage other than the two holes she'd
already observed. There weren't even defensive wounds, which either
meant that the creature had attacked too quickly for a human to react,
or that some kind of mesmerism had rendered Faren incapable of self-
defense. Similar to what had happened with Leo, perhaps? The creature might even have lured Faren from his pod, convincing him to go
off alone against his better judgment, like Tia's attacker had done with
her. Why else would he have taken a risk like that? If all fae-creatures
had such power, what hope was there for humans?

Evidently Angie and Dani had been briefed on the situation, because when they showed up they didn't ask any questions, just came to
the exam table and stared down at the body in a combination of fascination and horror. Angie took Faren's head and turned it to the side so that
the marks were more visible; she inhaled sharply when she saw them.
"Words can't prepare you for something like this," she murmured.

"Or wards," Leo said quietly. "Apparently yours don't provide the
protection we were hoping for."

She looked up at him sharply. "My theory was sound. And now that
I know how to alter my vision properly, I can see with my own eyes how
they affect the fae. There's no question that they're having an effect."

Lise said, "You see it all the time now?"

"No. It still takes effort. But not nearly as much. It's like the Magic
Eye pictures we keep talking about; once you know how to look at them
so the hidden picture appears, it's not hard to make that happen."

"Yet your designs failed in their purpose," Leo challenged her.

"They weren't strong enough," she said. "I tried to reinforce them
with blood sacrifice—as you saw—but apparently even that wasn't
enough." She shook her head in frustration. "These creatures we're
fighting, they're reflections of the human mind. And there are more
than a hundred human minds in this camp, all broadcasting their hopes
and fears and dreams into the ether, day and night, offering the fae

hundreds of guises to adopt. One small personal sacrifice clearly can't supply enough energy to suppress all that."

"But a bigger one could?" he asked. The words were voiced casually enough, but there was an intensity in his tone that suggested he was trying to mask his emotions. That worried Lise.

"Maybe," Angie said. "It worked for Ian's final sacrifice, so we know the planet responds to such things. But that entailed a terrible price."

"Loss," Leo muttered. "The emotional pain of nearly two hundred people."

"Well," Dani said, "unless you're planning to build a bonfire and throw all our tablets into it, Ian's precedent isn't really applicable, is it?" She looked at Angie. "If human minds influence the fae, can't we use religion to do that? A hundred minds praying in unity must have some kind of power."

"It didn't the night the module blew up," Angie reminded her. "Or if it did, the effect didn't last. Who knows? Maybe we were really safe during your service. Maybe a hundred human minds focused on divine protection was enough to hold the fae creatures at bay. But once the service was over they resumed killing us, so that clearly wasn't a long-term solution."

"You talk about the power of sacrifice," Dani countered. "Christianity is all about sacrifice: a divine figure suffered and died to save mankind. Isn't that exactly the kind of symbolism you're looking for? I usually prefer a more syncretic approach to my services so everyone will feel welcome, but if a traditional Christian service will help protect this camp, I can certainly offer that. You can't get a more powerful symbol of sacrifice than Christ on the cross, Angie. If we focus on that—"

"It's not the same, Dani."

The chaplain's eyes narrowed. "Why?"

"Because it's someone else's sacrifice, performed half a galaxy away. Your congregants aren't participants in that, just observers. The people here, on Erna, wouldn't be sacrificing anything. In fact, according to Christian mythos, they benefit from that sacrifice, don't they? That may have value in a theological debate, but it's not going to conjure the intensity of emotion that we need."

Leo looked at Angie. "Maybe that's why your wards failed to protect us. It was a token gesture, nothing more."

When did you learn so much about ritual sacrifice? Lise wondered. She wasn't sure what disturbed her more, the fact that he had learned the details of ritual sacrifice or the strange intensity of his tone. *Angie did make a big public show of smearing her blood on the palisade,* she reminded herself. *He might have wanted to understand why she did that.* But the words rang hollow. Something about him was off; she felt it in her gut.

"Perhaps," Angie said. "I should pay more attention to my own teachings."

"So, what then?" There was an edge to Lise's voice now. "Someone needs to injure themselves to empower your wards? Is that what you're saying?"

Angie sighed. "All I know is that my wards have the potential to protect us. That wouldn't solve our problem with the fae outside the palisade but could turn our camp into a haven of safety while we seek a more permanent solution. But the wards aren't strong enough for that yet." She looked down at Faren's body. "And we're running out of time to come up with new ideas. I'm sorry. I don't have an answer for you."

You didn't even try to answer me.

"I'll hold a prayer service at sunset," Dani said. "Maybe that will help people deal with this tonight. But we need a better long-term solution than praying for the problem to go away." She looked down at Faren's body and shook her head sadly. "Assuming there is one."

The breakfast bell suddenly rang in the distance, startling everyone. Dani and Angie looked at each other. "Go," Leo told them. "Get some food. Try to relax. We can talk more about this once Lise has had time to study the body."

"You sure?" Dani asked.

She seemed hesitant to leave. Had she sensed the same change in Leo that Lise had? They were the two people who knew him best, so the most likely to notice if something about him was off.

"I'm sure," he said, and if the smile that followed wasn't genuine, it was a convincing enough mimicry to satisfy her.

Leo closed the door behind Dani and Angie and for a moment just stood there, his hand on the latch, his eyes half-closed as if in thought.

"You okay?" Lise asked.

Her words seemed to startle him. "Yeah." He released the latch and turned back to her. "Just a lot to process, that's all."

"I'm worried about you, Leo."

He came to her and took her hands in his own. Strong, warm hands. "I'm fine, Lise. Really."

"All the talk about sacrifice . . .".

"Angie can be a bit obsessive."

"You really think her wards might work?"

He sighed heavily. "If they don't, then we'll need to come up with some new ideas."

Again there was a subtle change in his tone, and she sensed that something about him was not quite right. Normally, if that were true, he would confide in her. The thought that he might not want to was deeply disturbing.

She placed her hands on his cheeks. "I'm here for you, Leo. You know that, right? Whatever you're worried about, whatever you need, you can talk to me about it."

He whispered it: "I know."

"I would never judge you."

"I know."

She gave him a minute to say something more, hoping that he would share something—anything!—that would give her insight. But he was silent, and after a moment she reached up and kissed him, gently: communication without words. For a moment he didn't respond, but then he put his arms around her and pulled her close. So very close. She sensed a need in him that was born of fear as much as desire, an almost desperate hunger for human intimacy whose cause she could not fathom. When he kissed her, it was like he wanted to lose himself in her.

After a few minutes more he took her by the hand and led her to the storage space in the rear of the pod, where they could put a door between them and Faren. And for a brief time there were no words between them, and no need for any.

Twenty-two

Commander's Personal Log
Year One
Day Seventeen

News of Faren's death has spread, bringing with it a new kind of despair. We are like rats in a maze now, who have finally realized there is no way out. What damage will it do to the human psyche to exist in such a state, day after day and night after night, with no end in sight?

No fae creatures appeared yesterday, but there was no need for them, for our inner monsters assailed us instead. Fights are breaking out over nothing, simply because nerves are at the breaking point; for some, violence relieves the pressure of constant fear. Some people have reported visions that sound more like the leading edge of human madness than fae-born delusions—but who knows? Sky was accidentally speared by a podmate who mistook him for a fae-creature.

We can't go on like this.

There may be a way for us to escape the maze. It's a path I con-template now in solitude, without advisors to counsel me and without Lise to comfort me. If they knew what I was thinking they would surely try to change my mind, or else get too in-volved. This is the kind of path a man must walk alone.

Will it work? I don't know. But there are no options left, other than to watch this colony devolve into madness and death.

Lise, I know that in deciding not to confide in you I will be wounding you deeply. It breaks my heart to do that. But you of all people have the most power to shake my resolve, and I know that if I tell you what I'm thinking of doing you'll try to stop me. I can only beg forgiveness for the pain I'm about to cause you. Whether my plan will help our people escape the trap we're in I don't know for sure, but without it there is probably no hope at all. I'm sorry.

Fate is like a tree, branching out into a thousand different di-rections. One by one we prune its branches, reducing our op-tions until only one path is left: a single limb laid bare by choices we made and events that were out of our control. This is what is left for us now—for the colony—the only branch strong enough to hold us. We can nurture it and keep our tree strong and whole, or deny its truth and watch the greater whole wither and die. That is the choice I must make today, my friends, my love. And it is the reason I cannot seek your coun-sel. Some things a man must decide for himself.

Forgive me.

☽ ☽ ☽

It's time, Leo thought.

He stood in front of the southern gate, next to Angie's protective talisman. The blood she'd painted on it had long since dried up and blown away, but supposedly there was still fae clinging to the pattern, doing . . . something. Beneath his feet was a tarp that he had laid down to demarcate a stage. No rock or platform would raise him up higher than everyone else, as that would compromise his purpose. The slope of the stage mattered, as did the location. Everything was arranged perfectly.

A few people had been watching as he set up his space, more out of curiosity than concern. But now that he was standing in the middle of it as if something were about to happen, they began to gather around him. Good. Soon everyone else would join them. He needed as many witnesses as possible, if this was to work.

Sweat was beading on his brow. He shut his eyes for a moment and breathed in deeply, willing the freshness of the Ernan air to banish his anxiety. Such a beautiful world.

When he finally felt ready, he picked up the meeting bell and rang it, calling for the rest of the colony to join him. One by one, his people did. How tired they looked, how threadbare of spirit! It made him feel sick to see them like that. He had never wanted to be responsible for so many, but Colony Control had put them in his care, and now here he was, Leon Case, figurehead of an extrastellar colony, representative of one hundred and seventy-six human beings. The embodiment of their colonial project and the focus of one hundred and seventy-six minds, capable of impacting their thoughts, shaping their imagination. Would that be enough to give him influence over the fae? Or were all their theories about how that force functioned just sloppy guesswork?

Ian got it right, he told himself. *We may rage at the path he chose and curse what it cost us, but if what Angie saw is true, he succeeded in altering the flow of the fae. That means our relationship with the fae can be changed, if the catalyst is strong enough.*

Will mine be?

Lise pushed her way to the front of the crowd and stopped at the edge of the staging area. In her eyes was a look of such confusion and hurt that he couldn't bear to meet her gaze. *What is happening?* her expression said. *Why didn't you tell me about this?* He had no way to answer her now, but soon enough she would understand. Soon everyone would understand. He wished he could believe it would hurt her less when she did.

When it seemed that at last the whole camp was present, he held up his hands to silence the murmurs of the crowd. Angie and Dani had slipped into the front row next to Lise, he saw. Dani looked worried, but Angie was clearly fascinated—excited, even. *Taking notes for your next doctoral thesis?* he thought dryly.

"By now all of you know what happened to Faren," he announced. "The palisade we'd hoped would protect us from outside threats didn't save him. That's because fae creatures don't come from the outside world; they come from inside us. And we have to do battle with them not in the field, but inside our own souls."

A few people looked like they understood what he was trying to say, but not enough. He needed their minds to be focused properly, so that the proper emotions were channeled. All of them at once, a hundred and seventy-six minds with a single message.

"Angie designed wards to protect us. I'm not going to pretend I understand the theory behind them, but they're meant to channel the power of the mind in a way the fae will respond to. But apparently they're not strong enough to give us the protection we need. She tried empowering them with her blood, but even that wasn't enough to provide protection for everyone. No simple offering will be."

His hand closed tightly about the item in his pocket; he could feel his pulse beating in his fingertips. A wave of doubt suddenly came over him. Angie's theories were just that, academic hypotheses, and in any other time and place they would simply have been dismissed as crazy. Hadn't she lost a teaching job for failing to distinguish between science and fantasy? Now here he was, about to offer up his life in the name of those theories, without any certain knowledge that she was right. Hell, he didn't have any proof she'd really seen the fae! Only her word. Might a discredited scholar lie about her accomplishments to claim the limelight again, to bask in the admiration and envy of others? Or might she talk herself into believing she saw something that wasn't really there? His hand in his pocket was shaking, and sweat from his palms was making it hard to hold the item as tightly as he should. What did he really know about her, anyway? Hell, what did he know about the fae, other than what two people of questionable sanity had told him?

He was getting ready to speak again when he saw Julian.

The boy was standing in the front row of onlookers, as real to his eyes as the colonists standing next to him. When Julian saw Leo looking at him he smiled. *You saved me, Daddy.* Leo could hear the words as if they had been spoken out loud. *Now save them.* He reached out a hand to Leo. *Don't be afraid.*

Fixing his eyes on the boy, trying to shut out everything else, Leo drew in a long shaky breath. Maybe Angie was a madwoman, or a charlatan, or worse. Or maybe her theories were valid, but this still wouldn't be enough to change things. He had no way to know. The one thing he did know was that his colony was going to descend into violence and madness if he didn't do something to save it.

He took one last look at Julian, drawing strength from his presence, and then back out at the crowd. "I offer myself on behalf of this colony," he said. "Let my blood represent us all. May it be the last blood this colony needs to shed for this purpose."

"No!" Lise cried. She must have realized what he intended. "Don't—"

But it was too late for anyone to stop him. He withdrew the spearhead from his pocket and stabbed upward into the side of his neck, targeting his artery. The movement was so swift that by the time anyone was able to react the damage had already been done. People gasped as he twisted the spearhead and then pulled it out, and maybe it should have been painful, but all he felt was a surreal elation. Blood was pouring from his neck, bright red, arterial. He shut his eyes as he fell and let the pulse of it envelop him. People were running to his side, anxious to save him, but they wouldn't be able to. He'd used the spearhead instead of a regular blade because the wound it left would be harder to close. Hands pressed against his neck as people desperately tried to staunch the flow of blood. *Get my emergency kit!* he heard Lise yell. He wanted to reach up and take her hand, to tell her that it was all right, everything was going to be all right, this was what the colony needed. But she wouldn't understand. None of them would understand, until they saw what followed. Hopefully that would be what he had predicted, and his final efforts would not be wasted.

Angie's voice was audible now, eerily steady, directing others to gather up his blood from the tarp. She understood what he'd done, even if no one else did. She would make sure the proper actions were taken. *Use my blood for your wards,* he thought. *Paint the palisade with my sacrifice. Write a thesis about this even for posterity's sake. Just save them all, please. If you fail—if we fail—there is no hope left.* The other voices were fading now, merging into a warm red sea. The pulse of blood from his neck was slowing, and as the last drops left him he could feel his soul's tether to his body weakening. *Let me go,* he thought. *Just let me go.*

"Daddy?"

Startled, he opened his eyes. Julian was standing before him, clean and whole, just like he had been the last time Leo had seen him alive. The sun was setting behind him, turning the edges of his hair into a halo. An angel's crown. "It's okay, Daddy. You're free now. Come with me." As the boy reached out a hand to him he felt strength coming back to him and he grasped it tightly. Tears came to his eyes as Julian helped him to his feet, while the shadows of living people moved about his body. He searched for Lise among them, but they had become faceless ghosts to him. He no longer was part of their world.

"Come on," his son said, and they walked hand in hand away from the field, away from the fae, and into the cleansing, all-forgiving light.

☽☽☽

Lise surfaced slowly from sleep, swimming upward through layers of blood-tainted darkness. She had to wipe a layer of crust from her eyes before she could open them, and as she did so the memory of Leo's death—and the fact that he was lost to her forever—hit her like a sledgehammer.

"You okay?" Dani asked gently.

She saw that she was lying on a cot in the quarantine pod, with Dani sitting by her side. Her head was pounding and her eyes stung from tears she'd shed while sleeping, and the man she had loved and wanted to make babies with was gone forever. "Yeah," she managed to whisper. "Physically." Her throat was so dry it was hard to force words out. "What happened? I don't remember anything after the . . . after the . . ." She couldn't make herself say it.

"You fainted," Dani told her. "We thought it best to let you sleep for as long as you needed."

No children for us to raise together. The lost dream was an ache in her heart. *I'm so sorry.* "Did it . . ." She hesitated. "Did it work? His sacrifice?"

"It hasn't even been a whole day yet, so there's no way to answer that question. But there haven't been any new manifestations." She sighed. "One can only hope it lasts."

Please let it last, Lise prayed desperately, to any god that would listen. *Please. Don't let him have died for nothing.* "Where is he?" she whispered.

"He asked to be cremated. But we didn't want to do that while you were still asleep. He's in the clinic pod for now."

Lise blinked. "He asked for that when? Before he died?" Her eyes widened. "He *told* you what he was going to do?"

Dani shook her head quickly. "He left notes for a few people. We found them after he was gone. Here's the one that was addressed to me." She handed Lise a folded piece of paper. With trembling hands Lise opened it.

Burn my body and crush what remains. Scatter the ashes on the wind so that no one can ever retrieve or reassemble them. Erect no marker or monument that bears my name, that future generations might make a ritual out of cursing or venerating. It's human nature to focus on the people who make sacrifices rather than what they sacrificed themselves for. I would rather be remembered as a man than as a symbol.

For all you have done for me I thank you, and leave Erna's colony in your capable hands.

When Lise looked up Dani offered her another letter. "This one's for you," she said softly.

Thank you, my love, for waiting so patiently, and then—when the time was right—for not waiting. Thank you for replacing the memories of Earth with a love so joyful that my soul could

*begin to heal at last. I lived in self-imposed darkness for so
long, I forgot what it was like to bask in the sunlight. Thank
you for reminding me.*

*There is nothing I regret right now more than leaving you.
For that I can only beg your forgiveness. But if what I do today
helps protect you, it will have been worth it.*

My eternal love,
Leo

She lowered her head and wept. All the feelings she'd been struggling to repress since they'd arrived on this godforsaken planet came
pouring out, a tsunami of pain, fear, frustration, insecurity—these were
the emotions she'd choked back on so she could look strong when others
needed her, but the dam was breaking now, and they poured out of her
with a force that left her shaking. Dani held her as she wept, anchoring
her to the world of the living, preventing the whitewater pain from washing her away entirely.

Finally, after what seemed like eternity, the flood subsided. She
drew back from Dani and wiped her face with the back of a sleeve. Dani
handed her a waste cloth to use instead. It was a coarse thing, woven
from local grasses, but it did a better job than her sleeve.

"Do you want to see him off now?" Dani asked gently. "Or wait a
while? It's your choice."

The chaplain was in charge now, Lise realized. Had Leo known this
day was coming when he'd announced that Dani was his successor? Or
had that just been a general precaution? Damn, she was going to spend
the rest of her life wondering when he had first thought of killing himself. "Please. I'd like to see him."

Dani nodded and helped her to her feet.

His body lay on her exam table, draped in a broad swathe of parachute
silk. His face had been cleansed of blood and fabric had been positioned
to hide the wound on his neck. But the beautiful chocolate color of his
skin was gone, tinged by the somber gray of death.

"I was going to put him in the chapel tent so people could pay their respects," Dani told her. "But that would have gone against what he wanted. So he's been here, waiting for you."

Lise reached out and touched Leo's cheek, stroking it gently. He looked so peaceful it was hard to believe that his soul was absent, that this was just an empty shell. She wanted to take his hand one last time, to warm it in her own, but she knew the body would be stiff by now, and she didn't want to feel that. She settled for leaning down over him and touching her lips gently to his cheek, banishing the chill of death in that one tiny spot. *Goodbye, my love. May you find the peace in death that eluded you in life.*

Finally she drew back from him, sighed, and said quietly, "We need to collect his sperm." It pained her to be so clinical at a moment like this, but they couldn't afford to waste any genetic material.

"One of your med techs has already done that. We collected Casca's, too . . . though the colony will need to discuss whether we want to use that. If the seeds of his madness are inheritable, we may not want to risk replicating them."

"Inbreeding brings its own kind of madness," Lise pointed out. "That risk we know about."

Dani nodded.

Lise looked down at her lover. *I'll tell our children how you died to save them,* she thought to him. Then she lowered her head and let Dani lead her out of the pod.

☽ ☽ ☽

In the center of the southern field, over the remains of the previous night's bonfire, a bier of interwoven branches had been constructed. Leo's body lay atop it, wrapped from head to toe in a length of white parachute silk. Given that the colonists might soon have to spin and weave all the cloth they needed themselves, it was the highest honor they could offer him, burning a portion of the precious resource in his name. Sacrifice to honor a sacrifice.

Slowly, numbly, Lise walked to the bier. In the back of her mind she was aware that some of the people now gathering around Leo's body were carrying burning torches, but the fire, like the people who carried it, seemed distant. Unreal. The whole world was unreal right now, save for the man whose layers of shrouding proclaimed the esteem in which his fellow colonists held him. The head was wrapped so snugly in the thin cloth that one could almost make out his features, and she leaned down and gently kissed his head one last time. Then she stepped back, wiped tears from her eyes, and nodded. Two men moved forward to light the fire, inserting their torches deep into the kindling beneath the bier. They had to make several attempts to get it to catch. When it finally did, she was standing close enough that the flames threatened to singe her, but she refused to move away so much as an inch. This was the closest she could come to holding his hand as he departed for the afterlife, and she would stay there to the end.

In the background, Dani prayed.

Lord, keep the lamps of Heaven burning;
Turn the darkness into light with Your Grace
That this precious spirit may find his way to You,
And in Your presence, enjoy eternal peace.

As the fire burned, ash that had once been Leo Case's body was caught up by the wind and carried away from the pyre, away from the camp, and far beyond the sight of any human.

"Rest in peace, my love," she whispered. "You belong to Erna now."

Twenty-three

Commander's Personal Log
Year One
Day Twenty

It has been three days since Leo sacrificed himself in the south-
ern field. He was wise in giving us that long to decide who
would succeed him; everyone here needed time to process what
they'd seen and to mourn the death of a man who sacrificed his
own future so that this colony might have one, before they
could make such an important decision.

The Council will honor Leo's final orders, and the new Colony
Commander will serve until the end of Leo's original term of
office. Assuming the colony survives that long, we'll then hold
a popular vote to decide what kind of government we want to
establish here. Already some people are debating what that
should be, which tells you just how much the atmosphere here
has changed. People are confident enough in our future now to
argue about it.

There have been no new attacks in the last few days, so Leo's sacrifice appears to have succeeded: the blood-wards are now protecting us, at least within the palisade. A few people have reported seeing the ghost of Leo, but whether that comes from the fae or just human imagination, no one can say. None of the sightings have manifested solid form or attempted to harm anyone, so the latter seems likely. On the negative side, we continue to lose equipment. More tablets fail each day, and we race to complete the project Leo started, transcribing our most important data before all screens grow dark. There have been enough failures now that a pattern is slowly emerging: the devices we most fear to lose are first to go, along with devices owned and operated by the most fearful colonists. Alas, there is no easy solution for that. Telling a man that bad things will happen if he is afraid bad things will happen is not exactly helpful advice. Hopefully we can figure out a way to limit the effect of human emotion on the fae, so that over time we can legitimately have less reason to fear it.

The Council has chosen Leo's replacement. The vote was not unanimous, but a strong majority, and all will support it. It has also been decided that that there will be no more blood sacrifice of any kind, ever. The danger is too great that in restoring practices we associate with barbaric cultures we will influence the fae to favor them, and thus encourage our own return to such a state.

We have a long road ahead of us, and I am sure there will be many setbacks, but I believe that we can fulfill Leo's vision and develop a working relationship with this ecosystem. All we needed for that was a safe refuge to operate from, and Leo's sacrifice has given us that. Hopefully, as we adapt to this planet, it will adapt to us.

We are true Ernans now. And I think Erna knows that.

Dr. Angela Carmelo
Second Colony Commander of Erna

Epilogue

(Year 2)

"Angie?"

She looked up from the stack of papers she'd been sorting, to discover Pravida standing in the doorway with two wooden cups in her hands. The xenobiologist grinned.

"I thought a bit of celebration was in order." She handed Angie one of the cups.

"For what, the end of packing?" She chuckled. "If so, yeah, that's done. Finally. Or do you mean the end of my tenure as grand pooh-bah of Erna? That's not *quite* over yet. But I'm happy to celebrate my coming freedom." She looked around the room. "I'd invite you to sit down, but . . ." She gestured helplessly with her free hand, toward the piles of camping gear and colony records strewn across every surface in the tiny room. Space inside the palisade was at a premium, so even the colony commander's room was small.

Tomorrow, God willing, all that would change.

She breathed in the bouquet of the wine—delicately sweet, with a barely there hint of native florals—and drank. Alcohol spread outward in her veins, warming her body and her spirit. "Damn, that's good."

Pravida grinned. "Don't tell Paulo. His ego has been insufferable since his first batch of beer was served."

221

Angie chuckled. "You'd think it was manna from heaven, the way people received it."

"Hey. Beer withdrawal is a pretty serious condition."

At midnight tonight someone else would take over leadership of the colony, meaning Angie would be free at last. Tomorrow at dawn she and her hand-picked team of explorers would head out into the wilderness, entrusting their lives to the talismans she'd created. Would her creations be able to tap into the earth-fae as planned, providing more power than the minds of the explorers could have supplied? If so, then humans would no longer have to huddle inside the safety of the palisade at night, but could spread out across the surface of the planet freely. The camp that Leo's sacrifice had secured for them had been as much a prison as a refuge up to now, but hopefully that was about to change.

Through the log cabin walls the dinner bell sounded faintly. Chas must have finished tallying the votes, and was ready to announce the results. Angie started to rise to her feet, but as her weight shifted the bench beneath her creaked ominously. Concerned, she handed her cup back to Pravida and leaned down to inspect it. The backless chair was an old piece, made from some of the synthetic building material they'd brought with them from Earth, and while it had the color and grain of wood it would never pass for anything natural.

The top of the bench looked fine, so she picked it up and turned it over, then swore under her breath.

"What is it?"

Angie angled the bench so Pravida could see the underside, where a patch of yellow-green fungus was visible.

The smile on Pravida's face faded. "Shit."

Angie sighed. "I realize something like this was bound to happen eventually, but I'd hoped for a little more time before it did." She reached for the bottle of fungicide on her desk. "Here's to wasted effort," she muttered, as she poured some onto a disposable grass pad and wiped the chair clean with it. "Maybe we should just accept the inevitable."

Back on Earth the fungus would have been deemed a miracle of nature, and scientists would have devoted endless time and energy to figuring out how a species could develop the ability to digest plastic a mere year after first encountering it. Evolution clearly functioned at a different pace on Erna than it had back home. And while the colonists might be able to slow the spread of the new fungus with homemade fungicides, no one expected they would win the larger battle. A hundred years from now there would be nothing left of their synthetic goods, or of the culture that had depended on them. The last physical vestiges of Terra would have been erased from the planet.

Perhaps that was as it should be.

The dinner bell rang again, and the two women hurried outside, joining the other colonists in the small part of the southern field that remained. It was hemmed in closely on all sides by rough-hewn cabins, with narrow alleyways between them that led back to the original pods. In the center of the field was a sculpture memorializing Erna's fallen: a spiral of swirling flames with a majestic phoenix rising from its center. New life, born from the ashes of destruction. What more suitable symbol could there be for the colony's first martyrs?

Across from Angie, within the crowd of spectators, a baby cried. A baby was always crying somewhere in the camp. It was the price they paid for using as much of the Terran DNA as they could before that opportunity was lost forever. God help the colony when all those infants reached the Terrible Twos at the same time.

By then we'll have expanded, Angie thought, *and there'll be enough room for everyone.*

"Ladies and gentlemen," Chas announced. "I have the results of our election. The person who will serve as colony commander for the next twelve months is . . ." He looked down at the tally sheet in his hand. "Anton 'Sky' Rachkovsky!"

There was cheering from all corners of the field. And why not? Their first free election was a milestone, the moment at which all the plans and precautions of Earth passed into memory, and a new society— a purely Ernan society—took its place.

"Shit," Angie muttered.

Pravida looked at her. "He was part of your team, wasn't he?"

"That was the plan." She shook her head in frustration. "He's so ill-suited for a command position, with six candidates running I didn't think he'd win."

Dani and Joshua had spotted them and were coming over; Angie managed to put a smile on her face to greet them. Dani was carrying her newborn in a sling made out of parachute silk, a fabric that thus far had not been targeted by the fungus. Hopefully some chemical in its makeup would prove indigestible.

"Didn't see that one coming," Joshua said, nodding toward where Sky was receiving well-wishers.

"Why not?" Dani asked. "Out of all the people here, he's the one the fae responds to most positively. People are no doubt hoping that with him as the figurehead of the colony, that luck might extend to them."

Pravida looked at Angie. "Would it?"

"It's not outside the realm of possibility. That's why we wanted him on the team." She sighed heavily. "But that's water under the bridge now."

They had learned so much in the last year, and yet so little. The fae's response to human thoughts appeared to be random, and no one understood why it would manifest a nightmare in one case and a treasured memory in another. Since all its constructs were equally dangerous, one might argue the difference was moot. But some people seemed to invoke more benign effects, and Sky was one of them. Angie was among those who believed the deer that he had once 'willed' into range had been influenced by the fae, though exactly how that worked, she hadn't figured out yet. It would have been good to have such a charmed person in her team, but the colony had wanted him more.

"You have an extra set of camping gear now," Pravida noted. "Already packed?"

"He won't need his now, so yes. Why do you ask?"

"What if I said I'd like to go with you?"

Angie raised an eyebrow. "I asked you earlier. You turned me down. You said you had projects you had to finish."

"And then I heard rumors of a creature spotted just beyond the borders of human territory. Human-sized but with animal features, sometimes seen on all fours, sometimes standing erect. Three people have spotted it, though none saw it clearly." Her eyes were gleaming with excitement. "They all said it moved in a way that suggested intelligence, and seemed to be observing us. But it never comes closer than the edge of the forest."

"So you're hoping to see signs of it in the wild? It may not come near our party, either."

"True," Pravida agreed. "But we won't be sure till we try, will we?"

Angie laughed softly. "Well, given that I invited you before, I can hardly say no to that."

Sky was headed their way now. From the look on his face, Angie guessed he was going to apologize for abandoning her expedition. But if he didn't want to go down in the history books as one of the people who helped humanity spread out across the entire planet, so be it.

Overhead, the phoenix seemed to smile.

Say that I want to perform a magical spell to achieve a certain goal. I gather all the supplies required and perform the necessary ritual, which affects me psychologically, which causes subtle changes in my behavior, which alters the way I interact with other people, which sets in motion a chain of events that results in my goal being achieved.

Is it accurate to say "My spell was successful" if there was no magic involved?

Dr. Angela Carmelo

The Observer Effect: How Perception Impacts Our Concept of Reality

DOMINION

(YEAR 613)

Deep within the bowels of his makeshift bedchamber, Gerald Tarrant could feel the sun setting.

For a moment he lay still in the darkness, savoring the moment. Dark fae lapped at his body softly, like waves on a moonless beach. The power was weak in this place—little more than random echoes of spiritual malevolence that had been drawn to him while he slept—but it was refreshing, nonetheless.

Outside his temporary haven he could sense the hunger of creatures that crouched in the shadows, waiting for night to fall. Echoes of their impatience resonated within his own flesh. Soon the sun would set, and the balance of power in the world would shift once more. Soon all those night-born monsters that were held at bay by its blazing power would venture forth once again, ready to feed upon blood or terror or despair, or whatever else suited their natures.

I must go to the Forest, he thought.

The words rose unbidden from the depths of his mind, displacing all other thoughts. That didn't surprise him. For some days now he had been experiencing strange impulses, almost as if some outside power were placing thoughts in his head. *Cross the Serpent Straits*, a sourceless voice would whisper. *Then go east.* A lesser man might have believed that such thoughts were his own, perhaps, and obeyed without question. But he, who was more than a man, knew better.

The Forest was calling to him.

Opening his eyes, he sat up on his makeshift bed. Though the storage room surrounding him was dark to human eyes, it was anything but dark to him. Earth fae stirred in the corners of the chamber, its icy blue glow visible to an adept's sight, and tendrils of dark fae coiled like violet snakes in the room's deepest recesses. It took little effort for him to summon a wisp of the latter and bind it to his purpose, using it to clean off the dust that had gathered on him during his sleeping hours, neutralizing the faint scent of mildew that clung to him. The fact that he had taken shelter in a root cellar didn't mean he had to smell like the place.

The familiar act of Working helped him focus his mind, and for a moment the voice of the Forest was silent. But the respite would not last long, he knew. Less than a dozen miles from his resting place, the leading edge of a vast metaphysical whirlpool swept across the land, and its power would not be held at bay by a simple sorcerer's trick. A living man might ignore its influence for as long as he kept his own darker urges in check, but a creature who fed upon darkness itself had no such defense.

Currents of power tugged at Gerald Tarrant's flesh like an inexorable riptide, trying to force him toward the center of the whirlpool so it could swallow him whole. A lesser man would have given in long ago, without ever understanding what was driving him toward that hungry darkness. Only a man who knew the darkness by name understood it well enough to resist.

Come to me, the Forest whispered inside his brain.

Upstairs he could hear his hosts pacing back and forth, anxiously awaiting his emergence. While it was unlikely that they remembered the exact details of his arrival the night before, or the sorcerous commands that had driven them to cover over their windows and doors for his protection, they could sense his awakening with the same kind of animal instinct that allowed a mouse to sense the approach of a hungry cat. If he had not Bound them before he retired, knotting his power about their souls like choke-leashes, they would have fled the place long ago.

He climbed the cellar stairs and pushed open the door that led into the interior of the small house. The couple who owned the place were cowering in the corner with a young boy by their side; several feet away stood their daughter, a girl just on the edge of womanhood. They had managed to light a single lamp to fend off the shadows of evening, but it was not enough to banish the wisps of dark fae that swirled about Tarrant's feet, or the fear-wraiths that manifested briefly in his wake. But though the fae was volatile in this place, its creations had little staying power; no sooner did the wraiths come into existence than they headed off to the east, drawn toward the whirlpool of malevolence in the distance.

It is power, an inner voice whispered to him. *Raw power, without equal. You can claim it.*

Slowly, deliberately—defying the Forest's call—he entered the small kitchen. For a moment he felt a pang of regret, remembering the grand estate he had once called home, the magnificent neo-gothic castle he had designed for himself. If there was one facet of his current existence that he despised, it was that he was now itinerant. A monster without a home, mesmerizing each new host as necessity demanded, forcing families to protect him for a day—or a handful of days—until it was time to move on. What other mode of existence was possible for him now? If he stayed too long in any one place he was sure to draw notice. And he was too vulnerable during the daylight hours to risk that. The Church was sending out teams of hunters these days, to track down and destroy all faeborn monsters. They would not care that he had once been human, or that he had authored half their sacred texts back in his living days. He was a creature of darkness now, and thus beyond the pale of their mercy.

As it should be, he thought. He was perversely pleased by the thought that the Church he had once created would attempt to kill him. It showed they understood his teachings. But that success had cost him dearly, and the sense of pride that had for so long been the hallmark of his character had been sorely tested by centuries of homelessness. If the day came that he lost touch with his former identity altogether, and became nothing more than a monster in the night, might those powers which he had once so arrogantly courted take advantage of his weakness and claim the last vestiges of his soul? The possibility haunted him.

Quietly he whispered the key to a Compelling; the young girl began to move about the room in response to his will, gathering the items that he would need for his evening meal. A long knife from the nearby sideboard. A wooden tankard from one of the shelves. Her parents watched in horror as she approached Tarrant and placed the tankard on the table before him, but they were frozen by the sorcerer's power and could not voice more than a whimper of protest. As the girl bared her forearm, Tarrant could see her struggling to reclaim control of her flesh. But his Compelling was too strong for that. For a few seconds he indulged her resistance, much as a fisherman might allow his catch to struggle on the hook before pulling it out of the water: a futile display of hope. But at last her fragile will gave way. She slashed downward toward her left arm with the knife—fiercely, awkwardly—cutting deep into her own flesh. Bright red blood gushed out of the wound, splashing down into the tankard. A small moan of misery escaped the mother's lips, and Tarrant could see the father tremble as he fought to break free of the Binding, but from the girl herself there was no sound, only a delicious admixture of resignation and terror, as refreshing to him as the blood itself.

Such theatrics were not necessary, of course. He could have simply torn open her throat to get at her blood directly, with transformed teeth or claws, and drunk the hot stuff straight from her veins. He had done that kind of thing in the early years of his damnation, when his control over his transformed flesh had still been weak. But such violent feeding was crude and messy, and it threatened his self-control. He was experienced enough now to understand that if he wished to preserve his human identity and not devolve into a brainless, ravenous monster, he must hold his inner beast in check.

Do it the old way, the Forest whispered to him. *You know you want to. Tear into her flesh, as the beast inside you hungers to.*

Ignoring the urge, Tarrant shut his eyes, lifted the tankard to his lips, and drank deeply of the precious fluid. He could taste the girl's youth in her blood, along with her innocence, her femininity . . . and of course her fear. A priceless cocktail of vital energies. If only he could absorb them directly, without need for such a crude vehicle to aid in their digestion! That would be sweet sustenance indeed, if he could ever manage it.

The girl's emotional emanations were growing weaker as the last of her life poured out of her, but that was to be expected. The first drink was always the best. As for her parents . . . Tarrant whispered the key to another Working, and saw their expressions go blank as his power began to reweave their memories. By the time Tarrant was out of sight they would no longer remember that he had ever been there. Someone else had rearranged the cellar during the night. Someone else had covered over all the windows. Their daughter had taken her own life, without ever telling them why.

Eventually the Church's hunters might realize that something evil had visited this place, but they would have no way of determining its nature. And no idea how it should be hunted.

This monster left no trail.

Outside the house, the night sky was dark, nearly bereft of stars. A single crescent moon hung low on the eastern horizon, and beneath it, shimmering with power, was the place that mortal men called the Forbidden Forest. The greatest focal point of natural power on this continent . . . perhaps in all the world. A man must be willing to risk his life to explore such a place, Tarrant knew. And a creature of the night, uniquely vulnerable to such forces, might have to risk more than his life. Was it worth it?

He knew that the Forest was affecting his mind, even as he asked the question. Every thought in his head was suspect now. Every instinct in his soul would urge him to go eastward, even if certain destruction awaited him there. But he could not spend eternity as he now was. A man who had once shaped the fate of nations, who had written the sacred texts of the world's greatest religion, needed more than such a crude and limited existence.

Ambition required risk.

Drawing upon the earth-fae that swirled around his feet—how powerful it was in this region!—he worked a Summoning to call the nearest available mount to him. When an unhorse came galloping down the road a few minutes later, he used sorcery to remove the rider from its back as casually as one would swat a fly. Normally animals could sense his predatory nature and were loath to let him approach, but a minor Soothing ameliorated the situation, allowing him to mount the animal and ride.

Layering such Workings upon the animal that its spirit would remain steady as they approached the whirlpool, he kneed it into motion and let the siren song of the Forbidden Forest guide him eastward.

ⴰ ⴰ ⴰ

When Faith first awakened, she didn't know where she was. Or how she had gotten there. She didn't know very much at all, in fact, save that at some point she had set off with a dozen of her fellow knights to hunt down a particularly troublesome demon that had been plaguing communities along the border of the Forest, and . . . and . . .

Now she was here.

Which was . . . where?

Her head throbbed painfully as she sat up. Feeling her head for injuries, she discovered dried blood in her hair. Not a good sign. She started to run her hands all over her body, feeling for blood or damage. There was no open wound that she could find, but every muscle was sore, and judging from the stabbing pain she felt every time she took a breath, one or more ribs might be broken. Her armor had taken quite a beating; several of the steel scales were hanging loose, and the leather beneath them seemed to be scorched. A faint smell of sulfur clung to it, making her wonder just what sort of fire had seared it.

What had happened to her?

Overhead was a canopy of trees so dense that only a trickle of sunlight seeped through it; the ground below was in shadow, almost as deep as night. She cursed the poor visibility as she struggled to get to her feet. Her sword banged against her left leg, reassuring in its weight, but she had the uncomfortable feeling that other things weren't where they should be. A quick inventory of her weapons confirmed that fear. Everything else that she might have used to hunt the faeborn—or defend her own life—was gone. Even the smaller weapons that she'd worn close to her body, where a mere fall couldn't have dislodged them, were missing now. But she still had her sword, though the blood of the demon had dried while it was in its scabbard, making the steel stick to the leather encasement. Whoever had taken all the other things had at least left her that.

Memories were starting to seep back into her brain now, slowly, like the gray-green sunlight that was oozing through the branches overhead. She remembered the faces of her fellow hunters, grim with determination. She could hear the prayers of the One God's faithful as they were offered in preparation for battle, girding the holy warriors with sacred energy. She remembered the sound of well-oiled steel being drawn from its sheath, and the cry of a demon—

Niklause lies on the ground, badly wounded. But they can't stop to tend to him now. Their quarry has finally begun to weaken, which means they must redouble their efforts, pressing home their advantage before the demonic creature they are fighting can draw enough power from the fae to heal its wounds and recover its full strength. Unlike most faeborn creatures this one seems to be intimately bound to its flesh, which means that simple blows can dispatch it, but that doesn't mean it won't have a thousand nasty tricks up its sleeve. The less time they give it to summon one of them, the better.

Righteousness sings in Faith's blood, and sparks of sacred fury dance along the edge of her sword as she takes up position directly in front of the unholy thing, blocking its access to her fallen comrade—

"Behind you!" a companion cries.

She whirls about in response to the warning. Too late, too late! While she and her fellow knights were concentrating on the demon, a human mob had snuck up behind them. Rank upon rank of rage-maddened men, primitive weapons in hand, they are slaves to the demon's will. As they see her turn they cry out in bestial fury and fall upon her and her fellow demon-hunters like a pack of ravenous beasts. The same knight who had called out a warning to Faith cries out as he is crushed beneath their feet. She cannot reach him in time to save him. She cannot reach any of her companions in time. The knights had spread out in a circle to entrap their demonic quarry, so now they are scattered, divided. One by one they will be engulfed by this tide of angry flesh and steel, forced to choose between turning their backs on their faeborn enemy, or upon this rabid mob of demon-worshippers.

The creature is laughing at them now.

Despair is a knot in Faith's gut as she brings up her sword to protect herself from the thrust of a rusty pitchfork, barely in time; its tines scrape against the scales of her armor as she forces it aside. Who are all these people? Don't they understand what this creature really is? Or what the cost of worshipping it will be? All faeborn creatures feed upon mankind. This thing is no exception. Do these people really think that they will escape that fate just because they have agreed to worship the thing?

It's not a real god! *she wants to scream, as her blade slices through the neck of one opponent before swinging into the next.* It's not worthy of your worship! *But even if these men could hear her words, they wouldn't care. Once a faeborn creature becomes this powerful, it attracts weak-willed humans like rotting meat attracts flies. And why not? Such a creature can perform a thousand and one "miracles," and weak-willed men are easily swayed by such tricks. Why should they choose to worship a more complicated god, who might actually ask them to read a book or obey restrictive laws, when this one will indulge their vilest pleasures and ask for nothing in return? Never mind that it is a construct of the fae, not a living creature, and therefore can only have one real goal. By the time its followers come to understand what that means for them, it will be too late.*

The mob is endless. The demon's cult must have spread to all the surrounding towns. Why had the Church's scouts not reported that? On and on Faith fights, no longer able to see her fellow hunters. Whether they have gone to their deaths or merely fallen to the ground and laying below her line of sight, she doesn't know. They are not part of her universe any longer. There are only the men surrounding her and the pounding of hot blood in her veins.

But those are mere distractions, she realizes suddenly. The mob has caused her to turn her back on the faeborn creature. Even while she wastes time fighting them off, the creature is gathering the power it needs to heal its wounds. How close the holy knights had come to destroying it! One more blow might have dispatched it forever. But now, thanks to the sudden arrival of this mob, the greater battle is about to be lost. By the time she can force back the demon's worshippers—

assuming she can do that at all—the creature will be at full strength once more, and more than capable of devouring a lone knight.

She cannot allow that to happen.

A strange sense of calm comes over her, as she realizes what she must do. A pitchfork comes thrusting toward her head, but she forces it aside, stepping in toward its wielder, slamming her shield into his face. Stumbling backward, he cries out as he is impaled on another man's weapon. The moment's triumph should please her, but it does not. The next assailant should worry her, but he does not. Her mind is elsewhere, now.

This is her final moment of mortal duty.

She takes one last wild swing at her attackers, trying to force them far enough back that she can gain a moment's time. The strategy manages to clear a small space around her, but she knows that will not last for long. Men with real lances are headed her way. Once they get within striking distance, she's finished.

It's now or never.

Whipping around, she launches herself at the demon. There is no fire in her veins now, nor fury, just an eerie sense of peace as she embraces her death. It is strangely empowering. The creature is still weak from their earlier assault, she sees; apparently her sudden attack has taken it by surprise. Knowing she will have only one blow and must make it count, she swings her sword with all her strength toward that place in its neck where a thick black vein throbs. If God is willing, perhaps she can take the thing's head off before she dies. If not, if its body is similar enough to the human template, severing a major artery might bring it down. She prays that it will. Right now, that is the only hope these people have of ever being free of its influence.

But before her blade can connect with the cursed flesh something strikes her on the back of her head, hard enough to dent her half-helm. Her swing goes wild. Something else thrusts into her back, knocking her off her feet. And then the mob closes in on her, engulfs her, a tide of rabid human flesh bristling with rusty blades and twisted pikes, forcing her down to the ground, crushing her beneath its weight until she cannot breathe, she cannot breathe, darkness is closing in and air will not come—

I have failed you, my God. Forgive me.

Shuddering, Faith wrapped her arms around herself. She was grateful to be able to take a deep breath at last, though the effort sent shards of pain lancing through her chest. Where were her fellow hunters now? Almost certainly dead. She prayed they were dead. Death in battle was an honorable end, especially when one was fighting in the name of God. The possibility of being taken prisoner and sacrificed to a faeborn demon—of being devoured by the very creature one was bound by sacred oath to destroy—would be the ultimate religious defilement.

Now that she could remember the battle clearly, she knew where she was. The demon must have wanted to exact vengeance upon her for her final attack, and had ordered its followers to bring her here. Or perhaps it had done so itself. Either way, she was not to be allowed to die in battle, or even as a messy sacrifice on some pagan altar. That kind of death would be over too swiftly.

They had left her alone in the Forbidden Forest.

All around her were trees . . . or rather, what might have been called "trees" in a more wholesome setting. These were twisted, sickly structures, covered with a mottled patchwork of parasitic growths, hollowed out by colonies of nacreous insects. High in the canopy overhead, where sunlight reigned, there might be a smattering of normal life, but everything below reeked of death and disease. And power. The currents of earth fae here were so corrupt, so malevolent, that they made her skin crawl. Normally she couldn't detect such things, lacking an adept's vision, but in this place the power was so concentrated that she could feel it all around her. Its foulness made her want to vomit.

It was said that all the human nightmares of the world were drawn to this place, where they manifested on such a scale that normal faeborn horrors paled by comparison. A single despairing thought could spawn a host of wraiths, each of them hungering to devour its creator. A normal person who was abandoned here would stand no chance at all; his own fear would take on a life of its own within minutes and consume him. Doubtless that was what the demon had intended for Faith: a slow and painful demise, fleeing the claws and teeth of her own inner fears, until finally they ripped her to pieces.

With a trembling hand she drew her sword from its sheath. The blade was dull to her eyes and crusted with dried blood from her battle, but she knew that to faeborn creatures it glowed with sacred fire. Had her enemy left her this one weapon because it repelled him so much that he could not bring himself to remove it? Or had he just wanted to prolong her death-struggles? One sword might not be enough to hold every nightmare creature in this blighted realm at bay, no matter how many prayers clung to its blade, but maybe it would encourage her to fight for her life, instead of surrendering to the inevitable. And thus prolong her dying, and his amusement.

But the demon had not known about her special gift.

Kneeling in the thick loam, holding her weapon upright before her, she let her eyes fix upon the symbol etched into its guard. Two interlocked circles. Two worlds, inextricably linked. She had dedicated her life to cleansing this one of the fae's corrupt influence. And the One God had blessed her with a special gift to make that mission possible. It was not like the gift which the sorcerers enjoyed, allowing them to mold the fae to suit their will. Nor was it like the gift of the adepts, to whom all the shadowy powers of this world were visible. No, her gift was rarer than both those things, and in a world where Workings were a part of everyday life, it was something few men would envy. Most would call it a curse. But it had allowed her to become a deadly hunter in the One God's holy cause, and now it might—just might—save her life.

The fae did not respond to her. Ever. That same dread force which brought men's secret desires to life and could transform a person's fears into demons, never manifested her emotions. It did not bring her luck or misfortune, health or sickness, or any of the myriad other gifts and curses that it crafted for other men. Oh, what a precious and terrible blessing that was, and how the other knights of the Church envied her! *Earth's blessing*, they called it. A sign from the God of Earth that she had been destined to serve Him.

But just how complete was her immunity? Was she really safe from all the fae's ministrations, or had she just never been in a place where the earth-power was potent enough to test her gift to the breaking point?

Grimly she thought: *I am about to find out.*

Things were starting to stir in the shadows now, just beyond the range of her sight. Foul, unwholesome things, whose mere proximity made her stomach churn. In the distance she could hear strange chittering sounds, that seemed to be coming closer. Deathly pale insects were starting to emerge from burrows in the trees surrounding her, and were crawling along night-black branches in her direction. She needed to get out of this place, and fast. But how? The southern border of the Forest was probably closer than any other, but which way was south? The faint trickle of sunlight from overhead seemed to be coming from all directions at once; she couldn't find a clear enough shadow to judge the location of its source. In time the angle of light might change, creating shadows clear enough to be useful, but she dared not wait for that possibility. Once night fell it would be too late to make plans. She had to start moving now.

There was a clear grade to the land surrounding her, she realized. If she followed it downhill she would eventually reach running water. She recalled there was a river that flowed south through the Forest; if she could find her way there she could follow it to safety.

It was a slim chance, but it was the only one she had.

Taking up a fallen branch to use as a walking stick—shaking off the various foul insects that were clinging to it—the huntress of the One God muttered a prayer under her breath and began to move through the Forest. Promising herself that if she had to die in this foul place, at least she would go down fighting.

ᴐᴐᴐ

The currents of power surrounding the Forest were so strong that by the time Tarrant was within a mile of its border he could feel them pulling at his flesh with palpable force. Rarely was the earth-power so aggressive, so compelling. Overhead, Erna's largest moon glowed a brilliant white, nearly full in its aspect. But even that light paled in comparison to what the earth itself was emanating: a cold blue power that shimmered and shivered across the landscape, making it seem like the ground was in constant motion.

Since the day of his birth Tarrant had been gifted with the ability to see the fae directly, without need for any spell or amulet to aid him. But even he had never seen anything like this. Even the color of the earth-fae seemed different here, streaked with violet, as if streamers of dark fae had gotten caught up in it. Was that even possible? Could the two powers mingle like that? He longed to summon enough of it to craft a proper Knowing, to determine the answer to that question. But the moment he made contact with the wild currents here they would have direct access to his soul, and the power to remake him. Given how the Forest had tried to tempt him while he was feeding, that was something only a madman would risk.

This region had been normal once, he knew. Its currents of power had been unusually strong, but they'd been neutral in tenor, no more dark or dangerous than in any other place. The fae was a natural force, after all, and had no more personality of its own than air or water. But unlike air and water, the fae reflected people's fears and desires back at them, and apparently the currents here had accumulated enough human nightmares to manifest this deadly whirlpool, which in turn was now drawing even darker powers to the region.

Including himself.

Many sorcerers had come here in recent years, he knew, hoping to tap into that power, but none had ever returned. Tarrant's abilities might exceed theirs by a hundredfold, but he was also uniquely vulnerable. Mortals had living instincts to help them resist such a terrible darkness; he had no such protection.

In the distance the trees of the Forest loomed high and black, the mountain peaks of its northern border rising up like jagged islands in the distance. Wisps of earth-power played about the treetops like rippling veils, reminding him of auroras he had once seen in the far north. It was a strangely beautiful display, despite all its ominous overtones. He wondered what the place would look like when true night fell, when neither moon nor stars would be present to hold the dark fae at bay. The volatile energy would be able to rise above the treetops then, to add its eerie purple substance to the glowing display. What a glorious sight that must be!

Be careful, he warned himself. *The Forest will seduce you by any means it can. Visions of beauty can be as tempting to an adept as fresh blood is to a beast.*

He tried to urge his horse into motion again, but it whinnied anxiously and pawed at the ground in protest, struggling against his Workings. Even its dull equine brain could sense the true nature of what was
in front of them now, and a simple Soothing was not going to be enough
to reassure it. Tarrant's first instinct was to increase the power of his
Compelling, but such an act would require him to tap into the local currents, or use a portion of the fae he had Bound to his sword. That resource was limited and not to be expended lightly. Better to walk, and
save that for later.

He dismounted in a fluid gesture, the ends of his surcote rippling
down over the flanks of the horse like a silken waterfall. Then, stepping
back from the animal, he dispelled the Workings that had bound it to
his service. Last to go was the Soothing itself, and as the shackles of
unnatural calm fell away from the horse's brain it reared up in terror,
its hooves flailing as if striking out at some unseen assailant. Then it hit
the ground running, and began to gallop west as fast as its legs would
carry it. The scent of fear lingered on the breeze in its wake, sharp and
pleasing.

Tarrant watched after it for a few moments, his nostrils flaring as he
savored the sweet perfume of its terror, and then he turned his attention to the Forest once more and began to walk toward the heart of the
whirlpool.

ꝑꝑꝑ

She managed to find a stream bed at last, though it was currently empty
of water. But she could tell from the pattern of detritus it had left behind which way it had once flowed, and that was good enough. All of
the running water in the Forest emptied into the Serpent Straits sooner
or later, so even if this path didn't lead her directly to the river, it might
still guide her by some other route to the Forest's border.

Or so she told herself as she picked her way along the narrow strip
of mud and rocks, wary of the slimy black algae that seemed to be everywhere. In the dim light it sometimes seemed to her that a patch of
algae shifted its position as she approached, or that a mushroom-like
growth by the side of the stream twitched when she passed by. She just

shuddered and kept on going. Until the point when something actually reached out and grabbed her, she was not going to stop.

She had jury-rigged a small torch, binding suitable brush with a strip of fabric torn from her tabard, and as the shadows about her began to darken, she set fire to it. It gave off a foul smell as it burned, and it would not last very long, but at least for now it enabled her to see where she was going. The gloom surrounding her thickened little by little as the place began its slow descent into night, a dense soup of darkness that filled her lungs as she breathed it in, making it feel as if she were suffocating. Without the torchlight, it might well have overcome her.

As darkness came, so did the faeborn. Whispers of fear flitted in the shadows on all sides of her, shards of human emotion that had survived the deaths of their human creators long ago and taken refuge in this place. Her torch held most of them at bay, but the torch would not last all night. *She* would not last all night.

Don't think like that. Just walk.

The pain in her side was searing now, but there was nothing she could do about it save grit her teeth and keep on going. She hadn't started coughing up blood yet, which was a good sign, but she didn't have any illusion about just how bad her condition was. She could feel bone grating on bone whenever she moved too quickly, and she knew she was lucky that her lung had not been pierced. Thus far she had managed to rise above the worst of the pain, but she knew that if her mental focus wavered for so much as an instant, it would all crash down on her at once, and she might never get up again.

She'd had worse injuries than this, she told herself stubbornly. She'd survived them.

But never in a place like this.

Soon the stream bed began to widen out, and a gap appeared in the canopy overhead, a tenuous sign of hope. Now she could see the stars for the first time, and the leading edge of a full moon that cast blessed natural light down onto the stream bed. The sight of it made her heart skip a beat, and a whispered prayer crossed her lips without conscious volition. She knew in her heart that merely seeing a glimpse of the open sky didn't mean she was going to get out of the Forest alive, but the slender beams of moonlight were as refreshing to her spirit as a spring rain upon parched earth, and she turned her head upward to let them wash over her, drawing strength from them.

Suddenly a twig snapped behind her. She whipped around, seeking the source of the sound. But it had come from deep within the woods, and neither the thin stream of moonlight nor her makeshift torch had enough power to part those shadows. For a moment she held herself still as a statue, straining her sense of hearing to the utmost. But whatever had been out there was silent now. Waiting. Even the normal chitterings and rustlings of the Forest had gone silent, a deathly silence taking their place. Then she heard another twig snap, this time directly behind her. She turned to face the unseen threat, raising up her sword to the ready. But though she searched the shadows beyond the stream bed for any sign of movement, there was nothing to see. Whatever was making these noises was hidden in the inky depths of the Forest, and she was damned if she was going to plunge back into the depths of that foul brush to find it.

Maybe that's what it wants, she thought suddenly. *Maybe it's trying to tempt me to leave the moonlight behind.* The thought chilled her blood. Only a creature of the dark fae would care about something as inconsequential as moonlight. She stepped directly into a beam of light, wishing she could somehow absorb it into her flesh, so that it would become part of her.

But whatever was in the woods was clearly not going to reveal itself, so she started walking again. There was no option. She flinched as she heard a rustling on one side of the path, and then on the other, sure signs that more than one creature was now flanking her. But there was nothing she could do about it without leaving the relative safety of the stream bed, and she was determined not to do that. So she kept on moving, one hand gripping her torch so tightly that she could feel the blood pound in her knuckles, the other tight about the grip of her sword.

Then something flashed in the darkness directly ahead of her, reflecting her torchlight back at her in twin crimson sparks.

Eyes.

She could see the bulk of some large four-footed creature standing in front of her, and she thought she could hear it panting: a rasping, tortured sound. Its malevolence engulfed her like a foul wind, making the hairs on the back of her neck stand on end. Only her faith and sheer stubbornness enabled her to stand her ground, with all the primitive instincts in her brain screaming out for her to flee. Or maybe it was simply the knowledge that there was nowhere to flee to.

Suddenly there was another noise behind her. She twisted around, not wanting to turn her back on the first creature entirely—but pain shot through her torso at the motion, with such force that it left her gasping for breath. For a moment she could not see anything but black sparks swirling about her. Waving the torch to fend off attack from all directions, she moved toward the only cover visible, a cluster of close-set trunks with a wall of tangled brush between them. At least with her back to that, she'd have a bit of protection. The creatures that had revealed themselves moved closer as she took up position there, but they did not attack. She could make out their general shapes now, even pick out a few details. They looked somewhat like wolves, though with chests more massive than any wolf God had ever created, and a *wrongness* about the proportion of their limbs that made her skin crawl. She could have defended herself from both of them at once if she'd been in sound shape, but in her current condition she wasn't all that confident. Still, there were only two of them, and if they were afraid of fire, as most animals were—or afraid of the faith that was bound to her sword—she should be able to handle them.

But then another such creature moved out into the stream bed, beside the first, and her heart sank.

Another followed.

Despair welled up inside her as she watched more and more of the strange beasts come out of the forest, taking up positions in the stream bed surrounding her. Soon there were nearly two dozen of them, standing in a semi-circle just beyond the reach of her sword. Their eyes reflected the torchlight back at her in blood-red sparks, and when one of them walked into a beam of moonlight she could see just how unnatural its limbs were. The muscles in the stocky legs appeared more human than bestial, and where paws should be there were hands instead—or perhaps things that had once been hands, before the fae had deformed them.

Were the creatures fleshborn or faeborn? If they were merely animals that the fae had distorted over time, they would be relatively easy to kill. But if they were true faeborn creatures, birthed by this planet's innate power, there was no telling what it would take to dispatch them. Some faeborn manifestations took on physical forms so real that they became dependent on their flesh, and they would die like true living creatures if their bodies were destroyed. Others flitted about the night in dreamlike wisps, the nightmare energies of their creation providing the illusion of flesh without its substance. Against the latter species there was little defense but faith.

They all fed on humans. That was the one terrible constant of Erna: all the creatures that drew their life from the consciousness of man had to feed on him in order to survive. But exactly what manner of sustenance a particular manifestation required was anyone's guess. Faith had seen some gruesome things in her life, in the aftermath of faeborn feeding, but she also knew that there were creatures who sipped from the emotional exudates of a man's sleeping mind as delicately as a socialite sipped fine wine, their only spoor a shimmer of darkness at the border of his dreams.

Gazing into the crimson eyes of these beasts, she suspected they were not the delicate sort.

If they all rushed her at once, the sheer weight of their bodies would bring her down; there was no way she could defend herself against so many. A cold sweat trickled down her neck as she prepared herself for the onslaught. *At least I will go down fighting,* she thought, her hand tightening about her sword. *And I will take as many of these creatures down with me as God allows.*

Then a new one stepped forth from the shadows. It was taller than the others, but also thinner, and its proportions were disturbingly human. Its coat was not a mottled gray, but white—sickly white, crusted yellow about the edges—and its fur was stained with mud and worse. Its paws splayed out upon the ground like human hands, stunted and twisted but with recognizable fingers and even fingernails. And as she looked into the creature's eyes she saw madness in their depths. Not simple bestial madness, not the rabid insanity of an animal brain pushed to the breaking point by this terrible environment. This was something darker. More frightening.

More *human.*

Was it their pack leader, or a different sort of animal altogether? The beasts nearest Faith were beginning to edge closer now, and she swung her sword widely, trying to frighten them back. And indeed there was a spark of fear in their eyes as they backed off a bit, suddenly uncertain. But not in the eyes of the white one. The madness in its eyes was a burning ember that did not waver even when the blessed steel swept right by its face. Could it not see the blessings that clung to her blade? Or did it just not care about such things? The latter suggested that it was a fleshborn creature, despite its ghastly form. Which meant that it would be vulnerable to a simple physical assault.

If she wanted to attempt it, she would have to move quickly, before the rest of the pack managed to close in on her. With sudden determination she rushed into their ranks, sweeping her torch about her in wide, aggressive arcs, driving the nearer ones back from her, while her other hand tightened its grip about the blessed sword, preparing for a single blow. She knew that one was all she would get before the pack found its courage again and attacked her. She had to make it count.

A dark mass hurtled toward her from one side. She thrust her torch into the face of the wolf just before it hit her; it howled in pain as its jaws snapped shut about the burning brand instead of her flesh. But its body slammed into her with stunning force, driving her down to one knee; her ribs exploded in red-hot pain. As she struggled to her feet again, the powerful jaws of another wolf closed about her left calf. She thrust the torch down in its direction, heedless of the flames that flared up around her own body as she did so. But this beast was not to be frightened away so easily. It locked its teeth tightly about her leg, and although it could not bite through the polished steel of her greave, its dead weight meant she could no longer maneuver freely.

Suddenly they were all rushing toward her, and if the ones in the front ranks had second thoughts about facing either her fire or her blade, the ones in the back ranks were not allowing them to hesitate. For an instant she was overcome by the memory of the peasant mob that had engulfed her in much the same way. And she remembered the blow that had skewed her aim just as she had moved to strike at the demon; whatever happened to her in this battle, she could not allow herself to fail like that again.

Muttering a prayer to the One God under her breath, she thrust toward the white wolf with all her strength. The wolf clinging to her leg was dragged forward by the move, while the jaws of several others snapped shut on empty air where she had stood only a moment before. Startled, the white wolf began to back away from her, but the other members of the pack were crowded too closely behind it, and it was forced to stand its ground. As Faith's blade pierced its flank it was clear she had failed to strike the killing blow she'd hoped for, but the wound she made was deep, and crimson blood sprayed out of it. She put all her weight behind her sword, pushing it yet deeper, desperate to reach some vital organ. But the effort skewed her balance, and even as the white wolf struggled to free itself from her blade, she could feel herself falling. She dropped the torch and reached out to save herself, but it was too late. Powerful bodies buffeted her from both sides, and the fangs of one beast slid beneath her left bracer, piercing the cloth and flesh beneath it. The ground rushed up to meet her even as the white wolf whipped its head from side to side, trying to jerk itself free from her blade—

And then there was impact.

And blinding pain.

The sound of a wolf howling.

And darkness.

☽☽☽

If the region surrounding the Forest had seemed wild to Gerald Tarrant, its interior was chaos incarnate. Currents of creative and destructive fae collided at random intervals, setting the whole of the Forest alight with sprays of ice-blue power. Waves of raw emotional energy surged across the landscape like angry surf. No living species could possibly establish a stable presence in such a realm, Tarrant thought, but that hardly mattered. Evolution would be driven forward at such a pace here that as soon as any one life-form failed, a dozen new ones would take its place.

To his eyes it was all beautiful.

The currents of power that surged about his feet might now be chaotic in their manifestation, but they had the potential to become something else—something greater—and he could not help but wonder what kind of effort it would take to tame them, to force them to adopt a more ordered form. The creatures that hissed and howled in the darkness surrounding him might be warped and damaged in form, but a strong enough sorcerer could redesign the faeborn ones, and even fleshborn constructs could be urged toward a more reasonable evolution. Even the trees overhead, with their madly tangled branches, could be forced to serve an ordered purpose. Twist the branches even more, divide them many times over to create a fine webwork of filaments, and the canopy would trap autumn's leaves as they fell, creating a shield of vegetative detritus thick enough to cast the Forest into perpetual twilight. Would the constructs of the dark fae mature more quickly if they were thus freed from the threat of sunlight? To Tarrant it was a fascinating question, and he longed to experiment, to test various answers.

Deep within him an ancient hunger was stirring, human ambition surfacing in the black pool of his soul like a drowning man gasping for breath. He had been a scientist back in his mortal life, and his experiments in forced evolution had produced many of the Terran simulacra species that this world now took for granted. But his current condition did not allow for the luxury of a laboratory—or a scholar's library, or any kind of permanent home in which to store the specimens that scientific experimentation required. He'd had to surrender that whole side of himself when he left his home in Merentha, and since then his intellectual inquiries had been confined to a strictly internal landscape. It was one of the most frustrating facets of his undead existence.

But this place could become his laboratory now. He could mold new species to his will here and test their adaptation, using the volatile currents to accomplish in a few generations what might take centuries elsewhere. His soul hungered for that kind of intellectual stimulation as powerfully as his altered body now hungered for human blood. It was a powerful temptation.

But was it the product of his own hunger, or the Forest attempting a new kind of seduction? Would he feel the same way about the Forest if its whirlpool of dark energy were not struggling to draw him in? He was not accustomed to having to question his own thoughts like this. It was uniquely disturbing.

A scream split the night.

For a moment he thought it was a human cry. It had the emotional resonance of one, and Tarrant's fae-sight could see the ripples of frustration and rage that appeared in its wake, clearly from a human source. But the sound itself was bestial in nature, clearly not formed by a human throat. How very curious.

Loosening his sword in its scabbard, he began to head in that direction. He moved quickly and quietly, a shadow among shadows, and the local wildlife must have been moving out of his way, for he saw no other creatures. Even some vines and branches seemed to draw back as he passed, clearing a path for him. Was that possible? He knew of no plants that were sentient enough to behave thus, but that did not mean that none existed. In a place like this, anything was possible.

Soon he could hear a low keening noise coming from directly in front of him. He stopped moving and extended his senses to their utmost capacity as he strained to analyze it. Canine, he decided at last. Only one animal was vocalizing clearly, but he could hear the huffing and panting of many others. A wolf pack, perhaps? In the world outside the Forest such things were of little concern to him; animals could sense his unnatural nature and generally kept their distance. But here, where so much of the environment was itself unnatural, they might be less inhibited. Or the creatures in question might be faeborn, not fleshborn, in which case they would play by a whole different set of rules. He would take no chances.

He drew his sword from its scabbard. Blue fae-flames danced along the edge of the blade, but it was a fire bereft of heat. Frost appeared on the plants nearest to him, and the edges of a few leaves grew stiff, shattering like glass as he brushed against them.

There was a faint patch of moonlight in the distance, and he moved toward it with the steadiness and silence of a true wolf. The trees thinned out just ahead, opening into some kind of clearing. The noise seemed to be coming from there. He did not approach the clearing directly, but took up position behind the last dense stand of trees, letting the folds of his surcote fall over his sword so that its light would not betray him.

There were indeed wolves in the clearing, real flesh-and-blood animals, but they were twisted and malproportioned creatures, unlike any species he had ever seen before. There were about two dozen of them, and they paced anxiously back and forth across the clearing, snarling at one another whenever their paths crossed. In the center of the clearing, a single wolf lay motionless upon the ground. It was larger than all the others, with fur that had probably been white at one time. Now its coat was dank with filth and only a few patches of white hairs showed through. The scent of its blood came to Tarrant on the wind, and to his surprise it stirred his hunger. Since he fed exclusively on human blood, that answered one question, at least . . . but it raised a thousand others.

Sword at the ready, he stepped out from his place of concealment.

As soon as the wolves saw him they began to snarl. Several rushed at him, but they drew up just short of attack, unable to overcome their instinctive fear of an undead predator. Others froze in place, their long, matted fur rising up in clumps like surreal porcupine quills, making fearsome growling sounds as they tried to warn him away. He observed them for a moment and then, when he felt certain that none of them were likely to summon the courage to approach him, he walked over to the wounded wolf. It did not seem to notice him until he came close enough for the chill of his sword to raise frost along its flank, at which point it bared its teeth and growled a warning. But the sound lacked conviction, and its fierce expression faded quickly, subsumed into sheer exhaustion. There was a deep gash in its side, Tarrant noted, and the ground beneath it was soaked with blood. That was not good for his purposes. Whatever manner of creature this was, he did not want it to die before he had a chance to study it.

He was not able to Heal it, of course. The power which sustained him was derived from death and darkness, and he could no more work a true Healing than he could bang together two blocks of ice to start a fire. But there were other things that he could do. Lowering his sword until it almost touched the wolf, he summoned forth the earth-fae that was bound to its blade. Frigid blue fire danced along the blade's edge and a frosty mist began to rise from its surface, like human breath in winter. Then he lowered its icy tip into the wound. The wolf howled in pain and tried to pull away, but the muscles along that side had suddenly frozen in place and it was helpless to escape.

The mist turned crimson where steel touched blood, and Tarrant's nostrils flared as he drank in the scent of it. Human blood, without doubt. He licked his lips as he moved his blade along the edges of the wound, making sure that the sorcerous steel made contact with every inch of the bleeding surface. The flesh that it touched blackened and curled back upon itself, as if mummified. He continued until the whole of the wound had been treated thus, then stepped back and studied his handiwork.

It would be a long time before all the flesh he had just destroyed would slough off and be replaced, but at least for now the wound was cauterized. No more blood would be lost. The white wolf lay panting on the ground, its eyes rolled halfway up into its head, but it seemed to be calm. Now that the worst of the pain was over it seemed to understand what Tarrant was doing. A flicker of something that was almost human intelligence seemed to spark deep within its eyes . . . and then was gone again, subsumed into bestial exhaustion.

With a glance about the clearing to make sure that the other wolves were still keeping their distance—they were—Tarrant braced himself to perform a Knowing. Doing any manner of Working in this place was risky, but he needed to know what this strange creature was, and there was no other quick way to find out. The currents surrounding his feet grew agitated as he summoned forth power from his blade once more, and doubtless the Forest's fae would have been drawn into his Working if he allowed it. But he kept his mind focused and shut the local currents out, unwilling to risk any direct contact. The only power he would use was that which was stored in his sword.

Gradually his Knowing took shape, and he could sense it drawing forth information from the wounded creature at his feet. After a moment he shut his eyes and invited it into his mind, commanding it to present itself as a vision.

Pale, he is—so pale!—with milk-white skin, hair like spun moonlight, gleaming red eyes overlaid with some sort of Working. He stands proudly amidst the trees of the Forest, and its currents reflect his own essence back at him: power, ambition, vanity. So much vanity! This place is the greatest source of power on the continent—in the world— and he will become its Master.

He spreads his arms wide as if to welcome a lover, and whispers to the earth-fae: come to me, come to me, come to me . . . .

It comes. Core-bright power, life-hungry—ravenous!—pours into his soul with molten fury, filling his mind with the metaphysical echoes of a thousand human nightmares. Fear and madness churn in his brain, the final emotions of the men who had walked this path before him, who had tried to master the Forest and failed. But he will not fail. He envisions the mental patterns that will allow him to take control of the mad tide, muttering the ritual words that he prepared so long ago. He has dreamed of this day since his first Working. He is ready for it. He is strong. Soon, soon, this legendary realm that has destroyed so many will belong to him.

But he is not strong enough.

The power of the Forest engulfs him, chokes him, drowns him. It crashes into his soul with tsunami force and sweeps it clean of all human thought. Dark fae pours into his soul like wine into an empty vessel and begins to reshape his flesh, his mind, his soul. He howls in agony—a beast's agony, not a man's—and understands, in his final human moments, the full measure of his failure.

Tarrant stared down at the wolf as the vision faded, trying to reconcile the arrogant sorcerer he had just seen with the pitiful animal that now lay helpless before him. How many years had it been since the creature had last experienced a human thought? Did it have enough rational awareness to understand the magnitude of what it had lost and to mourn what it had become? The involuntary transformation it had suffered was both horrifying and fascinating to Tarrant, in that it reflected the very essence of the Forest. It was also a clear warning to him, not to lose his metaphysical footing in this deadly environment.

Kneeling down by the wolf's side, Tarrant waited until it opened its eyes and looked at him. It seemed to him there was a flicker of humanity in the back of its gaze—but if so, it was a dim and distant thing, quickly subsumed by bestial pain.

The sorcerer in Tarrant's vision had clearly made a study of the Forest. Somewhere in that man's mind there might be useful information about this place. But for as long as he was trapped in this animal form he could not communicate it directly, and Tarrant did not have enough fae stored in his sword to sustain a Knowing as long as he would need to in order to draw it out of him.

Was it possible to change him back? It was an intriguing notion, but a dangerous one. Even now he could feel the Forest's fae lapping hungrily at his flesh, waiting for a chance to consume him as it had consumed this one. It might have no real sentience of its own, but centuries of absorbing the essence of human nightmares had imprinted it with patterns of human aggression and human desperation. It might as well be sentient. If in his sorcery he forgot where he was and instinctively connected with the fae here . . . then he might well wind up like the albino, a beast in truth.

He gazed down at the wolf for several long minutes, assessing the creature's value to him. Unlike the albino he was not a reckless man, but some things were worth taking chances for. Knowledge was chief among them.

At last he said, very quietly, "I can restore your human form. Perhaps your human soul as well. But there would be a price for such service." He paused. "A high price."

The wounded wolf stared at him. It was impossible to read what was in its eyes.

"If I give you back your human life, then that life will belong to me. For so long as you remain human, you will serve me. All that you possess, all that you know, all the power you command, will be mine for the asking. That is the price of my assistance. Do you understand?"

For a long time the wolf just stared at him. Did it still comprehend human language? If not, then there would be little hope of restoring it to its former state.

But finally, in a stiff and pained motion, it nodded.

"Then you must surrender yourself to me now without reserve. Forget everything that you were, up to this moment, and permit me to reshape you as I see fit. Anything less than that, and you will not survive the process of transformation." He paused. "You were a sorcerer once. You understand why that is necessary."

There was a long pause. He could not interpret the wolf's expression, but he sensed that inside that bestial head quasi-human thoughts were struggling to take shape. Perhaps it was trying to remember the ways of sorcery, so that it might evaluate his instructions. Perhaps it was asking itself whether or not it was capable of the degree of submission he was asking for.

If not, then it would die.

"Do you agree to my terms?" Tarrant pressed.

The wolf's eyes were fixed on him. Unreadable.

Finally—weakly—it nodded again.

Stepping back from it, Tarrant braced himself for what must come next. Shapeshifting was one of the most dangerous Workings in a sorcerer's repertoire, and more than one student had died while attempting to master it. In order to adopt the form of another creature one must surrender oneself body and soul to the fae, allowing it complete dominion over one's flesh. It was a terrifying process, and a dangerous one. Failure to submit completely might result in one being trapped between forms, and such a state was rarely viable. Few were the sorcerers who dared attempt such a Working, and fewer still the ones who succeeded.

As for Working such a transformation on another human being, as Tarrant was about to attempt—that would require the same kind of absolute submission, but not only to the fae. This human-turned-wolf must be willing to place his very soul in Tarrant's control, without hesitation or resistance. Tarrant remembered the sorcerer he had seen in his vision: proud, vain, arrogant. Could someone like that manage the requisite humility? If his years in the Forest had broken his spirit—as Tarrant suspected—perhaps. If not, then Tarrant would have to conjure the information he sought from the man's ashes. Difficult, but not impossible.

Closing his eyes for a moment, he summoned forth the coldfire that was in his sword, channeling it into a fearsome Repelling. Blue flames licked outward: a heatless, unnatural fire with death at its core. Several of the wolves yelped in alarm. One of them turned and fled into the Forest, and a second one followed. Then another. Soon they were all gone, save the albino wolf, which lacked the power to flee. Tarrant let the Conjuring fade.

The clearing was silent.

Now, he thought. *Carefully*.

He could feel the Forest's power prodding at the edges of his consciousness as he began to shape his Transforming. This kind of Working called for an immense amount of power, and normally he would have used whatever was available to him, drawing upon the currents of earth-fae that coursed about his feet without even thinking about it. But even if he was willing to risk trying to control the currents here, the concentration required for that would doom his sorcerous efforts. The Transforming of living flesh left no room for distraction.

He would have to use what he had bound to his sword, and hope it was enough.

Summoning forth the death-cold power again, he directed a powerful Transforming at the wolf's body. The animal spasmed in agony as Tarrant's Working suddenly engulfed it, which was only to be expected: shapeshifting was a painful process. Tarrant persisted. Molding its body organ by organ—cell by cell—he forced it to adopt a new configuration, ever so slightly more human than the last. And then another. And another. Each intermediate stage had to be viable in its own right, Tarrant knew, a unique combination of organs and limbs that was capable of sustaining life on its own. Whether a sorcerer had enough knowledge to choose a viable biological pathway, and enough power to force human flesh to follow it, determined whether a shapeshifter lived or died.

But the albino's body had been human once, and on some metaphysical level it seemed to remember its previous form. Once Tarrant realized that, he needed to do little to guide its transformation. Slowly, the limbs of the wolf straightened and lengthened. Its ribcage contracted. Its teeth shrank. Fur fell off in sickly clumps, baring a hide that was bloody at first, then pink and raw, then white and soft. Each change was intensely painful, Tarrant knew. Normally the pain passed quickly, but a prolonged procedure like this one offered no quarter. The albino's body shook as it transformed, and once or twice a howl of agony escaped its lips, but for the most part it bore the pain in silence. Perhaps it remembered enough about sorcery to understand that pain was the price of success in such an undertaking.

And then, finally, it was done. The body that now lay before Tarrant was naked and filthy, but it was unquestionably human. The breathing was ragged, but the lungs were clearly functional. The heart was pounding hard enough that the veins under the man's skin twitched visibly, but the rhythm was within normal human bounds. The wound was gone, Tarrant noted; apparently in the process of recovering its original form the body had healed itself.

He waited.

For several long minutes the albino lay utterly still, with no sign of consciousness. Hopefully his mind had not been so badly damaged that he would be incapable of communication. If it had, then all this effort had been for nothing.

Very slowly, the thin, translucent eyelids opened. Scarlet irises were surrounded by a corona of broken vessels, making the eyes look like orbs of fresh blood.

"What is your name?" Tarrant demanded.

The albino's brow furrowed as he struggled to process the question. Tarrant gave him time. Regardless of whether the speech centers of the man's brain had survived the change intact, he had not dealt with human language for a very long time. It might take him a while to remember how to speak.

"Amoril," he whispered at last. He winced as he spoke, as if the passage of sound through his throat was painful. "My name . . . Amoril."

"Where are you from, Amoril?"

The crimson eyes squeezed shut as the man struggled to remember. He looked much more human with them closed. "I . . . not sure . . . no memory . . . maybe Sattin? Long time ago. Don't remember . . ."

Some of his long-term memory may have been damaged, Tarrant thought. *He may be easier to control if it is not restored.*

"Thirst," the albino gasped. "Water. Please."

It was a reasonable enough request, but not one that Tarrant could satisfy. "We will have to go find some. I do not carry supplies for the living."

The bloodshot eyes opened wide, and fixed on Tarrant. For a long moment Amoril just stared at him, as if trying to make sense of what he was seeing.

"What are you?" he gasped.

"A creature very much like yourself, originally." *But possessed of a much stronger will and better judgment.* "Now I am . . . something else."

The albino's eyes began to narrow—and then he flinched, and a shadow of fear crossed his countenance. He must have been about to Work, Tarrant realized. Then the touch of the fae had reminded him what happened the last time he'd tried it. Tarrant waited as the hollow-cheeked man stared at him in undisguised curiosity, trying to gather enough clues with merely human senses to answer his own question. The clues were there for the finding, Tarrant knew, if one looked in the right places. And a sorcerer should know where to look.

Consider it a test, he thought darkly.

"You are fleshborn," Amoril said at last. "But not . . . not alive."

Tarrant nodded solemnly. "That is correct."

"But not dead, either. So strange . . ."

Tarrant said nothing.

"Your clothing . . . from another time. Almost." His facility for speech seemed to be coming back to him; each word seemed less strained than the one before. "Your real time? Few last so long. The living die, the undead are destroyed by crusaders."

Tarrant said nothing. The eerie crimson eyes continued to study him intently. Assessing the paleness of his skin, perhaps, or its subtly unnatural hue.

"Blood-drinker?" he asked at last.

A faint smile flickered across Tarrant's face as he rose to his feet. "Among other things." He held out his hand, to help Amoril to his feet. "I am Gerald Tarrant, first Neocount of Merentha." He emphasized the word *first* ever so slightly. If this man knew anything about history, he would know just how long ago that title was created.

After a moment of hesitation Amoril accepted his hand, and with Tarrant's assistance he struggled to his feet. Once he was standing he seemed steady enough; his body evidently remembered how to move as a biped.

"There's a river nearby," Tarrant said. "You can satisfy your thirst there." He took in the albino's physical state, from his mud-covered legs to his blood-matted hair; a shadow of distaste crossed his face. "And bathe."

A cold wind gusted through the clearing; he saw Amoril shiver. Living flesh was sensitive to temperature changes, he remembered. It had been a long time since he'd had to worry about such things. He unhooked his cloak and offered it to him. Amoril hesitated, then accepted.

As Tarrant watched him wrap the fine wool about his filthy body, he reflected on the fact that he would probably not want it back from him. "How were you wounded?" he asked. "It didn't look like the work of an animal."

"Not an animal." The albino's words were flowing almost naturally now, though his articulation was still poor. "Human bitch. Steel armor. Don't know where she came from. All alone. Sigil of the One God, here." He struck his chest weakly with his fist. "Fought like a demon, but wounded. Won't last long here." The red eyes glittered hungrily. "Shall I kill her for you, my Master?"

Tarrant ignored the faint edge of sarcasm with which the title was voiced. It would take some time before servitude came naturally to this one. "Not necessary. I will take care of it."

Amoril cocked his head and smiled. "You are hungry?"

Tarrant did not respond.

If the sigil of the One God was emblazoned on the woman's breastplate, that meant that she was probably a knight of the Church. Perhaps even one of its sacred demon-hunters. And now she was here, abandoned by her own kind, surrounded by the very creatures she had sworn to destroy. No doubt she was afraid that she would die by their hands and thus shame her calling. It was the ultimate fear, for such a crusader.

He wondered how that fear would taste in her blood.

"Where is she?" he asked quietly.

The albino pointed southeast. "Not far. Stream bed. Some moonlight." He hesitated. "Listen to the Forest. It will tell you where to go."

"Are you saying the Forest is sentient?" he asked sharply.

"No. No. Not sentient. No." The albino wrapped the cloak tightly around himself as he struggled to recall the words that he needed. "Many dreams here," he said at last. "In the earth, in the soil, in the air. Human dreams. The fae reflects them. Like a mirror."

It was along the lines of what Tarrant himself had hypothesized.

But was it meaningful information from the time before the albino's transformation, when he had studied this place, or had his mind become so unhinged from its recent experience that he was imagining things? Only time would tell. "I will seek out this warrior," Tarrant told him. "Meanwhile, you proceed to the river. I'll catch up with you later."

He turned to leave, but the albino grabbed his arm. Tarrant was not accustomed to having other people lay hands upon him, and when he turned back his expression was so dark and fierce that Amoril backed away from him quickly, fear in his eyes.

"I can't stay here alone," the albino protested. "Not without Working. No protection. Too dangerous."

Tarrant exhaled sharply in exasperation. But Amoril was right. He was just a man now, and a weak one, with neither armor nor weaponry to protect him. The creatures that feared to come near Tarrant would not hesitate to move in on such a man once he was alone. Leaving him here was a death sentence.

Loosening his sword in its scabbard, Tarrant ran his thumb along the blade just hard enough to draw blood, then reached out toward Amoril. The red eyes glistened with fear, but he did not back away. Tarrant smeared his blood across the man's forehead, using a whisper of the sword's stored power to adhere his personal essence to it. It gleamed against his milk-white skin like a fresh wound.

"The Forest will respond to you now as it responds to me," he said. "So unless you come across something that is enamored of the undead, you should be safe enough."

Then he slipped into shadows and left the clearing, anxious to be gone before another distraction surfaced.

Ꙭ Ꙭ Ꙭ

He could smell her fear on the wind. It was carried to him by the air, by the earth, by the currents of fae that swirled about his feet. Its bouquet was as complex and enticing as that of the finest wine, and it aroused a hunger in him so powerful that it sent tremors coursing through his soul. Far more powerful than his hunger for blood.

That the fear was sacred in nature made it all the more appealing.

This was the emotional exudate of a woman who had no real fear of injury—or even death—but whose spirit quailed at the thought that she might fail her God. Sacred duty: the taste of it burned Tarrant's tongue, but like spice on a living tongue, it enhanced rather than diminished his appetite.

He was surprised at first at how acutely he could taste her emotions without partaking of her blood, but who was to say if those insights were even true? The fae might simply be reflecting his own hunger back at him, plucking choice details out of his mind and manifesting the elements he most wished to believe. Metaphysical bait. *Surrender to the Forest's power,* it whispered in its seductive tones, *and all that you hunger for will be provided for you. You can claim what you hunger for without blood, if you wish.*

Imagine if that were possible!

The woman was moving fairly quickly now; given how wounded she was, that said as much about her strength of will as it did about her bodily stamina. Tarrant had seen many men defy mortality thus, sustained by passion alone. What greater motivation was there than religious faith?

A fleeting memory surfaced in the black pool of his soul, echo of a life long forgotten. He remembered a man of faith riding to war in the name of his God, the banner of the one true Church whipping in the wind overhead. So idealistic, that man. So pure in motive. So dedicated to everything that was moral and just.

No longer.

The memory sank to the bottom of his soul and was lost again.

If I had not loved God so much, I would not have gained such power from betraying Him.

He was getting close to her now. Perhaps she could hear the occasional twig that he allowed to snap under his foot. Perhaps it made her even more afraid. Suddenly he heard a soft splash, followed by a cry of pain. Perhaps she had come to a place where there was water in the stream bed and stumbled on the wet rocks. New pain. New fear.

This one would be a rich feast, indeed.

He began to move forward quickly, ready to close the distance between them and claim his prize—when suddenly the earth-fae surged,

spraying droplets of ice-blue power high into the air. He blinked against
the brightness of it even as drops began to fall like rain all around him,
an eerie glowing shower. As they touched him, knowledge came rushing unbidden into his brain. Not the kind of ordered, rational knowledge he might have summoned with a Working. This information was
raw—unstructured—a mad chaos of data that roared down the avenues
of his consciousness, drowning out all rational thought.

He knew now exactly where his quarry was wounded and exactly
how life-threatening each wound was. He understood the nature of her
pain, her faith, her fear. A lifetime of her memories rushed into his
head, images cascading into one another with such speed and force that
his mind reeled as it struggled to absorb them. A child's nightmares—a
teen's distress—a grown woman's loss—a knight's desperation. A thousand and one battles unfolded in his mind, fought against nightmares
and bullies and despots and rivals and faeborn creatures, too much for
any sane mind to absorb. Instinctively he reached out for power, knowing that he must erect some sort of barrier to protect himself from the
mad deluge of emotion before it breached the boundaries of his own
soul. It was a sorcerer's reflex, performed without even thinking—and it
was also a deadly error, whose carelessness he cursed even as the full
power of the Forest came crashing into his brain.

Hot power, molten red, seared his soul as it engulfed him. Blazing
energy that burst up from the ground, followed by a cold so intense that
the blood in his undead veins froze, consumed him. It was a dark and
terrible power, a chaotic amalgam of earth-fae and dark fae such as Tarrant had never known before, so unstable in nature that he could not
control it. A whirlwind of fae began to take shape around him, its metaphysical force so powerful that it was reflected on the physical plane.
Physical winds began to whip about him with cyclonic force, and within
seconds he was trapped in a cocoon of flying debris, splinters of wood
and shards of stone scoring his flesh as they were driven past him.

And the Forest's hunger poured into him. It was not a human hunger, nor anything a sane man would recognize, but something far more
primal: a driving environmental need that arose from the land itself.
This was the soul of the Forest: a mad, insatiable emptiness that was
driven to absorb every human soul within its borders, hungry to drink

in every source of vital energy that came within its reach. And now Tarrant had invited it into his soul. Shards of his own memories flashed before his eyes as it ripped his soul to pieces, tearing loose bits of his past history so that they might be digested. A few shattered fragments of the woman's memories flashed by him as well, which he had absorbed, but the Forest did not care whose they were. Its hunger was mindless and indiscriminate.

Pain shot through his flesh, spears of fire and ice impaling every cell of his body. His legs lost their strength and collapsed beneath him, but the pain as his knees struck the ground was a distant thing, peripheral to the war that was taking place within his flesh. The fae was twisting each cell into a new configuration, burning away the biological codes that safeguarded his physical identity and replacing them with patterns that reflected its own warped essence. Tarrant doubled over in agony as his internal organs began to pull loose from their moorings, and he could feel his bones warp and crack as they were forced into a new and terrible template. Just as Amoril's had been.

But he was not Amoril.

In the small part of Tarrant's brain that could still think clearly, he knew what he had to do. And he also knew just how dangerous it would be, and what would happen to him if he failed. Amoril's mutation was but a pale shadow by comparison.

But he had not given over his soul to darkness centuries ago, and destroyed all that he once held dear, only to become a mindless beast now.

Opening his soul wide—dismantling all the defenses that would normally protect him—he embraced the fae.

Power rushed into his soul and he welcomed it, wrapping the force of his will around it even as he drew it deeper into himself. It complied hungrily, eager to consume him. He could sense the boundaries of his physical identity giving way, and for a moment raw panic welled up inside him. This was where Amoril had faltered, when his own panic had unmanned him. But Tarrant was not that weak, nor would he allow himself to be distracted, even by the dissolution of his own body. He had wrestled with demons in the past, waged war against jealous gods, and once—long ago—bargained with forces so dark in nature, so utterly toxic in their essence, that no living creature could stand before them.

And he had survived all that. He was still here. And he'd be damned if he'd let a simple patch of woodland defeat him now, fae or no fae.

You are mine, he thought fiercely. And he began to force his own imprint upon the fae, to mold it into a form of *his* choosing. For a moment the two powers were deadlocked against one another, as he pitted all the force of his human will against the Forest's raw strength. And then, at last, he felt it begin to yield. Only a flicker of weakness at first, but that was all he needed; he pressed forward with all the strength he could muster, struggling to impress his will upon the invading power, to make it *his.* Fresh pain shot through his flesh as his body began to reshape itself once more, returning to its original form, but that was the pain of victory, and he embraced it gladly.

And then, at last, it was all over.

He found that he was hunched over on the ground, much as Amoril had been during his own transformation. As he checked out his limbs to make sure they were all in their proper form—they were—he tried not to think about how close he had come to sharing the albino's fate.

The winds were gone now, and only a circle of fallen debris bore witness to the storm that had so recently surrounded him. His sword was on the ground nearby; he must have drawn it during his struggle. The coldfire blade flickered weakly now, its power drained. He picked it up and rose unsteadily to his feet. His legs were weak but they were functional, and all his body parts seemed to be moving properly. Good enough. He could still feel the Forest's presence in the back of his mind, a hunger simmering just below the threshold of his consciousness, but for the moment it was no longer a threat to him.

Satisfied, he resheathed his sword.

Looking around, he realized that the Forest felt different now. Less chaotic. More alive. For a moment he stood still, trying to put his finger on exactly what had changed. When he finally realized what it was, he drew in a sharp breath. The trees had not been altered, nor the beasts that lurked the shadows, nor even the currents of fae at his feet . . . but *he* had.

He could sense the heartbeat of the Forest now, an amalgam of living energies that throbbed just below the threshold of consciousness,

binding all creatures within its borders to a single purpose. He sensed
the streams of nightmare-born energy that flowed through the earth
like blood, and the vast network of metaphysical veins that channeled it.
And it seemed to him that he could sense every creature within the
Forest as well—fleshborn and faeborn, living and undead—though he
could not pick out any one entity from the chaos of data.

And he could sense the woman.

She was thirsty. So thirsty. She had found a source of water and was
cupping her hand to bring mouthfuls of it up to her lips, but the thirst
was rooted deep in her damaged flesh, and had more to do with lost
blood and exhaustion than with simple dryness. Nevertheless he could
sense her pleasure as she drank, and even the flicker of hope that she
allowed herself, having found such refreshment. A dim hope, but she
wielded it like a shield to ward off the fear that might otherwise overcome her. Such a strong soul. Delicious.

When she began to move again he was aware of her as the Forest
was aware of her, through the senses of thousands of living creatures
that were impacted by her presence. He could feel the weight of her
foot press down against insects in the earth, the warmth of her body as
it brushed against trees, the stirring of leaves in response to her breath.
And then there was her fear. Waves of it rippled through the night,
washing over him in a sweet black tide. He shut his eyes to savor the
sensation, and he could sense predators stirring in the shadows surrounding him, responding to his arousal. Then he opened his eyes and
placed his hand on a nearby tree branch, and it, too, responded to him;
the bark running down one side of it contracted, and it curled back on
itself like a snake.

Hunt with me, the Forest seemed to whisper. *Feed us both.*

He was not so drunk on the moment that he forgot the danger he
was in. What the Forest had failed to accomplish in a direct contest of
strength it might still manage by seduction. Its nature demanded that it
subsume all creatures within its boundaries, and if he gave it the right
opening it might yet succeed.

But some temptations were difficult to resist.

He stood silently for a moment, considering his options. Then, with a short nod, he began to move through the woods once more, heading toward his quarry.

The beasts of the Forest followed.

ɔ ɔ ɔ

Blood.

Hot.

Pounding in her head.

Her skull felt as though it had been split open. Maybe it had been. Maybe she had died and gone to Heaven. Or Hell. Either one would be fine by her right now. Anywhere other than where she was.

For a moment she just lay motionless on the ground, unwilling to open her eyes and resume the nightmare. But her head was on fire and her chest was growing tighter with every breath, and she knew that she had to start moving again if she was to have any hope of survival.

With a groan she lifted her face from the slime-covered ground, blinking as she tried to get her bearings. The moon was still bright overhead, so not much time had passed. That was a good thing, wasn't it? There was a throbbing pain in her arm where the wolf had managed to bite her, but the limb responded as it should, so no bones were broken. Nor was there any sign of blood trickling out from under her bracer.

Why was she still alive?

She looked around for her sword. It was lying on the ground a few yards away from her. The lead wolf must have fled when she'd wounded it, dragging the sword that far before it fell free of him. If the rest of the pack followed him, that would explain why she was still alive. All that was left of the torch was a charred stick with bits of ash clinging to it. Useless.

She crawled over to the sword, and used it to steady herself while she regained her feet. As she stood upright she swayed slightly, and for a moment her eyes refused to focus. She had lost enough blood in other battles to recognize the cause of her lightheadedness; somewhere inside her body her lifeblood must slowly be leaking out. If she did not find a healer soon to repair her internal injuries, she was not going to make it.

She forced herself to begin walking again. Her feet were numb and she stumbled often, but staying here wasn't an option. She had to keep moving. As fast as she could, as far as she could. Every minute counted now.

God of Earth and Erna, help me stay on my feet. Just for another few hours.

But she had only managed to go a short distance when suddenly her foot slipped out from under her. She hit the ground with bone-jarring force, her left knee slamming into solid rock. Ice-cold liquid splashed across her face, shocking against the feverish heat of her skin.

For a moment it was all she could do to catch her breath and make sure that no new bones were broken. Only then did the significance of what had just happened to her hit home.

Water.

As her eyes adjusted to the moonlight, she saw that she had fallen in a shallow pool, from which streamers of water stretched out like glistening tendrils along the ground. Thirst welled up inside her at the sight of it, but the thought of drinking anything from the ground here made her stomach turn. God alone knew what manner of noxious parasites it might contain. But the droplets of water trickling down her sweat-streaked face reminded her of just how long it had been since she had last tasted food or drink, and how long it might be before she had another opportunity to do so.

If you don't have the strength to make it to a healer, she told herself, *you're doomed anyway.*

Leaning down, she cupped her hand to bring some of the water to her lips. It tasted odd but not overtly foul, and after a moment's hesitation she began to drink in earnest. The chill water soothed the parched membranes of her throat, and eased the fever in her flesh. Finally, feeling the weight of the ice-cold fluid building in her stomach, she forced herself to stop.

The water had cleared her head somewhat, and she studied the pool surrounding her. Its surface had been disturbed by her motion, so it was hard to see if it had any sort of natural current. After a moment she picked up a fallen leaf from the ground nearby and placed it on the water's surface. It bobbed about randomly for a few seconds, and then slowly but surely began to move away from her. Watching it, she felt the shadow of despair lift ever so slightly from her soul. A current implied gravity and direction, therefore hope. Assuming this tiny stream did not disappear into the earth, it might eventually lead her out of here.

A wolf howled in the distance.

Panicked, she jerked her head around to look for the source of the sound, but nothing was visible behind her save moonlight and shadows. She struggled to her feet as quickly as she could, but her bruised knee was loath to support her. If the wolf wasn't aware of her presence yet she might still have a chance, but only if she moved quickly.

But then another wolf howled. And another. Their cries were eerie, ghostly sounds that made her skin crawl. Were these the same animals she had fought before? Or something worse, that the Forest had conjured? She began to move along the side of the stream as quickly as she could, but she was limping badly now, and each time her left foot hit the ground it sent red-hot knives of pain shooting through her knee. She struggled to think past it, to keep focused on her objective. *Keep your eye on the water. Don't lose sight of it! Keep moving.*

Suddenly she heard an animal moving through the Forest to her right, crashing noisily through the underbrush. A few seconds later she heard one on her left as well. Apparently they had picked up her trail, and intended to surround her. At her current pace she didn't stand a chance of escaping them.

Gritting her teeth, she started to run. A stumbling trot was the best she could manage, but it was better than walking. Once or twice her foot caught on a low-hanging branch or vine, and she had the crazy delusion that the Forest was trying to trip her up. But she managed to break free from most of them, and stumble over the rest, so she kept going.

Such an effort was not good enough, however; she could hear that the wolves were slowly but surely closing in on her. Their ghastly howls reverberated through the woods, urging her to run as an animal would run, drawing on those final reserves of strength which are stored on the threshold of death.

As prey would run.

Suddenly she realized that all the movement she was hearing was now coming from her left; to her right there was only silence. Evidently the pack had abandoned its attempt to surround her and was closing ranks. Which meant that now she had a chance—albeit a slim one—to escape them.

Channeling all her energy into one last desperate burst of speed, she turned away from her pursuers and sprinted in the direction they had abandoned—

And stopped.

Breathless, heart pounding, she knew with visceral certainty that something was wrong, but for a moment she could not give it a name. When the revelation finally came, it chilled her to the bone.

She glanced down at the water beside her, still barely more than a trickle of moisture among the rocks, and then at the empty blackness of the Forest that flanked the stream bed. The water was her lifeline; if she left it she would have no hope of finding her way out of this place. The wolves had given her a way to escape them, but it would require her leaving the stream behind.

They were herding her.

She realized that she had only two choices left: she could leave the moonlight and the water behind and flee like helpless prey through the darkness—the outcome they clearly desired—or she could make her stand here, dying as a knight of the Church was meant to die, and deny them their final triumph.

Not a real choice at all.

A strange calm came over her as she looked around for the most defensible position. The longer she could hold out, she told herself, the more of the beasts she would be able to dispatch to Hell on her way out. But the trees weren't as densely packed here as they had been at the site of her last battle, and there was no convenient cluster of them to use for cover. At last she found a place where thick black vines had established a webwork between two trunks. It wasn't a solid barrier by any means, but she knew from tripping over such vines just how strong they could be. At least they would slow down anything coming at her from that direction.

It was the best she was going to be able to do.

Facing in the direction of her pursuers, her back to the tenuous barrier of vines, she flexed her hand around the grip of her sword, drew in as deep a breath as her bruised lungs would allow, and prepared to face her final battle. *God, grant that I may serve Your holy purpose to the end.*

Then, suddenly, the howling stopped. She held her breath, listening for any other sounds of pursuit, but all was silent now. Whatever had been crashing through the Forest in pursuit of her was no longer moving.

Shifting her weight uneasily from one foot to the other, she caught her ankle on one of the vines and had to shake it loose. Or she tried to, anyway. But the thing was caught on her greave and would not come off. With a last wary glance at the shadowy tree line head of her, she reached down with her sword to cut herself loose—

But her arm would not move freely. Then something took hold of her other ankle. And her left arm. And her chest. By the time she realized what was happening there were vines all over her, gripping her body like steel bands. She knew that she could not pull free of so many at once, and that her only hope was to cut her way out, but her sword arm was so entangled that she could not get it loose. Panic flared in her gut as she felt one of the vines wrap itself around her head, but try as she might she could not shake it off. She was trapped like a fly in a web, impotent and immobile.

And then something stepped out of the Forest's shadows that was not a wolf, and it stood in the moonlight before her.

A man.

He was tall and slender, with delicate features, and skin so pale that in the moonlight he seemed to be carved from alabaster. His shoulder-length hair would probably have glowed a warm golden-brown beneath the sun, but in Domina's cold light it was an eerie, ashen hue, and the halo of moonlight that crowned it lent his entire face an unnatural luminescence. And he was clean. So clean. His midnight blue surcote did not have so much as a speck of dirt on it. Even his boots looked spotless, though the ground beneath his feet was a muddy mess, and the hilt of his sword gleamed brightly in the moonlight, looking as if it had just been polished. Suddenly she felt acutely aware of her own degraded state, mud-splattered and sweat-stained and probably reeking from all the vile slime she had been crawling through. It made his fastidiousness seem doubly unnatural.

His pale eyes fixed on her with an intensity that transfixed her, much as the gaze of a snake might transfix its prey. It was impossible for her to look away.

"Who are you?" she whispered hoarsely.

Those eyes were cold—so cold!—human in form, but without a trace of humanity in their depths. She saw him glance down at her sword, and a strange expression crossed his face. Was he a creature of fae, sensitive to the aura of faith that clung to the blessed steel? She tried to raise the weapon up so that she could protect herself with it, but the effort was hopeless. A fly in a spider's web had more freedom of movement than she did right now.

He began to walk toward her. A knot of fear twisted in her gut as she tried to draw back from him; inwardly she cursed herself for her weakness. What was it about him that unnerved her, more than all the monsters she had fought? Was it because the darkness she sensed within him had left no mark upon his physical person? With his delicately beautiful features and the halo of moonlight glowing about his head, he looked almost angelic. Was it easier to deal with monsters when they looked like monsters?

Then he was in front of her. It took all her strength of will not to flinch before the power of his gaze.

"So very brave," he said softly. There was a faint inflection to his voice that she could not identify: an echo of lost lands and forgotten times. "You would fight me if you could, wouldn't you? Even though the battle would be lost before it began."

He reached down for her sword. She tightened her hand around its grip—but then he touched her and her fingers froze, and he lifted the weapon from her hand easily as if he were taking it from a child. For a moment he just looked at it, studying the Church insignia that adorned its grip. Whatever hope she might have had that the religious symbol would repel him faded as he ran his finger slowly over the design. A hint of dark amusement flickered in his eyes.

"What are you?" she whispered.

"A servant of the One God, in ways that you will never understand." He put the sword off to one side, sliding its point into the ground so that it would stand upright just beyond her reach. Then he reached out to touch her face. She tried to pull away from him, but the vines were wrapped too tightly around her to allow for it. His pale fingers stroked her cheek gently, a mockery of a lover's caress; his touch was like ice. "Helplessness," he murmured. "That's your greatest fear, is it not? Better to suffer a thousand wounds in battle than to surrender control of your fate to another." He smiled coldly as he brushed a lock of sweat-soaked hair back from her face. The grip of the vines was so tight that she could not even turn her head away from him. "How very sad, that in the end fate betrayed you."

Anger welled up inside her, driving out all the fear and the despair; suddenly her entire soul was alight with white-hot indignation. *I will not be your plaything!* her soul screamed. She stared into his visage—so beautiful, so clean, so perfect in its vanity—and realized that she did have one weapon left. Perhaps it would not be enough to win her freedom in this life, but she could claim her freedom in the next.

I know your weakness too, she thought.

She hawked up phlegm from deep within her lungs. It wasn't hard to do; her chest was full of the stuff.

"Fuck you," she growled.

And she spat in his face.

He was clearly unprepared for such a move, and for a moment he did not react at all, as the glob of blood-flecked spittle on his cheek began to slide down his face. Then the human façade seemed to give way, and with a cry of fury he grabbed her by her hair, jerking her head to one side, baring her neck above the edge of her gorget. Her spittle shattered into a thousand frozen fragments and fell from his face, but she knew he could still feel it there, like a slow-burning brand. Imperfection. Filth. Denial of his dominion. She could sense a black rage burning inside him now, more intense than any emotion a mortal soul was meant to contain, and bloodlust stirred in its wake. Better than she could have hoped for. If he was maddened enough to kill her on the spot, she could at least go to God with a clean soul.

Shutting her eyes, she muttered a prayer under her breath as she braced herself for death. *Receive my soul, God of Earth and Erna, that I may serve you in the next world forever.*

But seconds passed, and nothing happened. She could feel his hand tremble where he held her, fingers digging deeply into her flesh, but otherwise there was no movement. His face could have been carved from marble for all the emotion it displayed. Then he shut his eyes for a moment, and she saw a tremor pass through him. So subtle a motion, but contrasted with his previous stillness, it suggested some internal struggle, powerful enough to shake him to his core.

Please, God. Let the rage overwhelm him, so that I can be freed from this place.

Finally he lowered his face to her throat, and she braced herself to have it torn open, or sliced through, or whatever other form death might take. But death did not come. She could feel his cold mouth hovering above the edge of her gorget, and then—unexpectedly—the touch of his lips upon her skin. Disarmingly gentle, perversely intimate. She felt more violated by that kiss than she had by all the rest of what had happened to her, and she shivered as his cold breath raised goosebumps along her neck. "Tell your masters that the Forest is spoken for." He whispered the words softly in her ear, like a lover's intimacy. "Tell them that trespassers will not be received well."

Then he let go of her and stepped back. The vines that had been binding her twitched, stiffened, and then shattered like glass. Frozen black crystals showered down around her as she was suddenly freed from her bondage. The unexpected absence of support left her unprepared, and she stumbled to her knees. For a moment it was all she could do to catch her breath. Then she looked up at him. The storm of emotion that had briefly possessed him was gone now; his gaze was as steady as a frozen lake, and equally unreadable.

When he saw that she was looking at him he pointed to the depths of the Forest, in the direction she had been about to run. "South is that way," he said. And he added, "Nothing that answers to me will stop you."

Then he turned and slipped into the shadows of the Forest, and a moment later was gone from sight.

She shut her eyes and trembled, struggling to absorb all that had just happened to her. Trying to decide what to do next. Her chest and her injured knee felt cold and slightly numb; had he worked some kind of spell on her? If so, it was dulling the pain enough for her to think about moving again. Perhaps even moving quickly. But in which direction?

The water might eventually lead her to the river, but its path was unlikely to be direct, and there was always the chance it would sink down into the earth and leave her stranded again. And the direction he had indicated led away from the water, into the black depths of the Forest, where she would have no landmark to guide her. Only faith.

Every survival instinct in her soul warned her that that advice of such a creature was not to be trusted. The wolves had wanted to drive her into that very same darkness, for reasons of their own. How could she be certain his motives were any different? But logic, too, had its voice. There was no point in his giving her a message for the Church if he did not expect her to deliver it, was there? If he sent her to her death, he would be defeating his own purpose.

Tell your masters the Forest is spoken for.

With a sigh she took one last look at the glimmering stream of water, then turned away from it and limped into the shadows of the deep woods, in the direction she prayed was south.

"She won't make it out."

Startled, Tarrant turned to find the albino standing only a few yards behind him. Had the man been following him? If so, he might prove more dangerous than Tarrant had anticipated. "It will be a test of her faith."

"Her Church will come here. Your warning won't stop them."

No, Tarrant thought. *My warning will do exactly what it was intended to do.*

The Church would have no choice but to come here. Not immediately—perhaps not even for a generation or two—but sooner or later it must. A religion that was dedicated to bringing the fae under control could not simply sit back and watch while a sorcerer imposed his own dark order upon the Forest. They would come. They would come in force. It was as inevitable as the sun rising in the morning. And by then, the Forest would belong to him: a weapon beyond their imagining. "It will be a test of their faith," he said quietly.

He did not expect Amoril to appreciate the irony of the situation.

The man had no way to know that in another time—another life—Tarrant had been one of the founding fathers of that Church. If its leaders came after him now, they would be waging war against their own Prophet.

If they challenge me here, in this place, then I will know my creation was worthy of me.

"You mean to stay here?" Amoril asked. Though only one question was voiced, others echoed in its wake: *Can we really leave this place? Will the Forest allow us to go? What if you are able to break free of its power and I can't?* "Is that wise?"

That Amoril still feared the Forest so much was a sign of weakness. Tarrant would have to break him of that if the man was to be a useful servant.

He remembered the moment when his own strength had been tested. When rage and bloodthirst had roared through his veins, threatening to scar his soul to ashes if he did not submit. It had taken all the force of his will to deny his hunger, and to leave the woman unharmed. But he had managed it, and in doing so had shown the Forest his true strength. All its tricks could not make him taste a single drop of blood if he did not want to, nor could it force him to kill. The Forest had tested its strength against his self-discipline, and it had failed.

Its currents lapped at his ankles now like the tongue of a beaten dog. Still violent and unpredictable—no question about that—but subservient to his will. At least for the moment. Had the Forest adapted to him, or he to it? The bloodthirst that had defined him for centuries now seemed a distant thing, bereft of power. Was he free of it at last, or was this only a brief respite? If the first, that was something to be celebrated, a freedom he had dreamed of for many years but never thought possible. To feed upon the elixir of human fear without the need for such a primitive vehicle as blood . . . that would be true transcendence.

He looked to the north, where the stark black mountains were crowned in Domina's moonlight, poised above a sea of shimmering power. Exquisite. To the south he could sense the woman slowly making her way to freedom, and though she manifested no fear-wraiths in her wake, as a normal woman might have, he could taste her fear on the wind. Also exquisite.

Nothing in the Forest would impede her progress. Not unless *he* commanded it.

So much beauty, here. So much power. It was the kind of place a creature such as himself could shape into a home that was worthy of him.

"Come," he said quietly. "We have work to do."

And he slipped into the depths of the Forest without further word, his midnight garments melding effortlessly into the shadows. The albino watched for a moment, crimson eyes gleaming with a host of unvoiced emotions. Then, lips tight, he nodded his head ever so slightly, and followed his new master into the darkness.